THE SECOND WRONG

By

JOHN T. LEONARD

ISBN: 978-1-7397224-4-9

JOHN T. LEONARD

THE SECOND WRONG

JOHN T. LEONARD

A CIP catalogue record for this title is available from the British Library.

ISBN **978-1-7397224-4-9**

SECOND EDITION

First published in 2019

Cover model: Alexander Terry
Cover photography: Amanda Adams

DEDICATION

For Amanda

Also available from JOHN T. LEONARD

SETTLING THE SCORE
PRIMUS
A LIFE'S WORK
HEART OF A LION
DEADLIER THAN THE MALE
(HEART OF A LION – part two)
CLEAN SKIN
(HEART OF A LION – part three)
WOLF'S BANE
(HEART OF A LION – part four)
ENEMY OF MY ENEMY
(HEART OF A LION – part five)
THE ARC
FALLEN VICTIM
VINDICATED
THE BLOOD ON MY HANDS
SCARRED

PROLOGUE

"Do you remember the cop I told you about?"

"Yeah, I remember."

"Well, his name is Watkins, and turns out he has a daughter. Now, I expect her name is Watkins too, so I want you to see if you can find her."

"I think I know her, and if it is?"

"Well, let's assume it's her, I want you to punish her for me, and I'm sure you know what I mean by that."

"Yes Dad."

CHAPTER ONE

"I'm off now," Ashley Watkins shouted from her upstairs bedroom. "I'll see you guys later."

This was immediately followed by excited footsteps coming down the stairs, which then thundered along the hallway towards the front door.

Her father, Mike, stood up from where he was having his dinner alone in the kitchen.

Although they had a perfectly good dining room, he had chosen to eat his dinner whilst leant over the breakfast bar.

He looked perplexed, having not expected such a farewell, not yet anyway.

"Your mum's not *even* home yet, it's just me," he said. "Is *he* here already, I didn't even hear the doorbell go?"

Whilst preparations to leave continued, so did the commentary.

"Yeah, he's outside, he sent me a text message," Ashley replied, whilst in the process of putting her coat and scarf on.

It wasn't a cold evening, but the scarf was more of a fashion statement.

"I dunno?" Mike remarked. "Is he too good to come to the front door and call for you like any normal person would, eh?

"Aren't you able to hang around for a couple of minutes, your mother will be home anytime now, and she'll most likely be in bed by the time you get back."

Although Ashley knew her father had made a valid point, she still had to take a moment to weight up her options.

"Dad, c'mon, I gotta go," Ashley said, with an ever-increasing sense of urgency. "He's waiting for me, I really don't want to keep him waiting."

She was hoping her father wasn't going to give her a hard time as she saw him walk from the kitchen and approach where she was now standing, in front of the now open front door.

Instead, Mike had a look of pride on his face as he saw his daughter ready to head out.

Ashley, his daughter, and only child looked stunning as she stood in the doorway.

You certainly take after your mother, he thought.

"What's the rush anyway?" Mike said. "I t looks like he's got plenty to keep him busy out there,"

He glanced beyond where Ashley stood, down the driveway towards the street in front of their house. Ashley turned to see for herself exactly what her father was referring to.

"C'mon, why don't you invite him in, at least until your mother gets home?" he continued. "He'll need to move his car though, as your mum won't be best pleased if she can't park in the driveway."

She could see, as her father had, that parked across their driveway was her boyfriend's car, a very sporty looking white Ford Focus ST.

Even from where they both stood, they could hear that he was listening to music as it was blaring from the car. At least there was a potential that it was music, as all that reached the two of them was an indistinguishable mess.

What with that, and the occasional unnecessary revving of the engine through a ridiculously loud exhaust, it would be difficult *not* to notice the car coming before it was ever seen.

Added to which, it could be seen that he was either messaging someone or updating his social media as his attention was firmly on his mobile phone which was illuminating his face within the car's darkened interior.

"Are you sure you don't want to take some ear plugs with you?" Mike suggested. "I have some ballistic ones from a firearms day in my kit bag."

Ashley could only look back at her father, and smile, having almost predicted such a comment from him.

"And that, dear father is exactly *why* I will *not* be bringing him in," she said, just before she placed a single kiss on her father's cheek.

"Probably for the best," he said. "As your mother won't be too impressed if she gets home and finds him *still* blocking her driveway like that, that'd certainly lose him some Brownie points from the off."

Mike then looked off up the street as an approaching vehicle caught his eye.

"Ah, and there she is now,' he continued. "Make sure you say goodbye to her before you go, okay."

Hearing that, Ashley turned back, and looked down the street as her father had, only to see her mother's hatchback coming into view up the road, just as it braked to a halt upon her mother seeing the new boyfriend's car parked, rather inconsiderately, parked across their driveway.

"You have a good time tonight," he said. "And stay safe."

Mike then watched as his little girl started to walk off down the driveway, before breaking into a brisk step, and eventually a skip.

Though he didn't know if it was from excitement at seeing her mother, or the new boyfriend.

In reality, Ashley was seventeen years old, and not far off her eighteenth birthday. But to Mike, she'll always be his *little girl.*

Once she got to the bottom of the driveway, Ashley immediately diverted her attention from her boyfriend to where her mother was patiently waiting to park.

Knowing her daughter had plans this evening, her mother, Kerry, was pleasantly surprised that she was going to get to see Ashley before she headed out for the evening.

However, it was painfully obvious that patience was not a virtue that had been bestowed on Ashley's boyfriend, as he was keen to demonstrate, even when being watched by his girlfriend's parents, as he was seen to behave like a petulant teenager.

From his front doorstep, Mike could clearly see the boyfriend thump the steering wheel of his car out of frustration, and could be heard to repeatedly rev the engine, as if the mere sound of if should somehow beckon Ashley to him.

Mike looked back along the street, towards Ashley as she talked to her mother through the open passenger window of her car, feeling that a regular father would probably enjoy, what's believed to be justifiable, satisfaction at seeing his daughter keeping such a young upstart waiting.

But Mike wasn't a regular father, and certainly not one with a blinkered, rose-coloured view of the world.

Instead, Mike was a veteran police officer, with over twenty years' service, which when added to his prior military service, meant that he was now just a couple of years away from his retirement.

In his time as a police officer, he had worked virtually every role that the job has to offer; he has been a beat officer in the beginning, then a traffic officer, and he has also served as an approved firearms officer for a few years.

Then, until very recently, Mike had been a Detective within the force's public protection unit, which dealt with incident of domestic violence, and child abuse.

During his career he had seen most of the horrors that a human being was capable of, and he knew all about the mentality of a demonstrative and destructive partner, and it was based on that knowledge, and the behaviour this boyfriend had just demonstrated as he awaited his daughter, that left Mike feeling justifiably concerned.

He looked back towards the Ford Focus ST at the end of his driveway, and where he could see the look of ever-increasing agitation on the boyfriend's face. This was to such an extent that Mike was now expecting him to start honking the horn at any moment.

The boyfriend's face then lit up again, as he had his phone in his hands again, though it didn't look like that he was making a call.

For a moment, Mike's gaze reverted towards Ashley, just in time to see her push herself away from her mother's car and stand upright. She took her phone from her pocket and glanced at it for a moment, before replacing it in the pocket, and looking towards the *ST*.

Mike couldn't hear anything of the resumed conversation between Ashley and her mother, but it must have been one of goodbye. Because the next thing that Ashley did was to again step away from the car, only this time to blow her mother a kiss, before trotting back towards the *ST*, and once there, Ashley then opened the passenger door and got in.

Once again, Mike couldn't make out anything that was being said between the occupants inside the *ST*, but from the body language and interaction between Ashley and her boyfriend, it didn't appear to be in any way affectionate. There was no embrace, and certainly no kiss, instead Ashley flung herself back in the passenger seat and folded her arms defensively.

Then with them both facing forward and apparently ignoring each other, the *ST* slowly pulled away.

That was until it was out of sight from where Mike was watching, as then he heard an almighty roar of acceleration, and screeching of tyres, which could only have been the *ST* speeding off.

Mike remained on the doorstep as he watched his wife eventually pull into their driveway and park.

She then got out of the car to see Mike approaching her. He went to the back seat and helped her with her bags, and they spoke as they walked back to the house together.

"I'm guessing this isn't the first date with this clown then?" asked Mike. "How long have they been dating?"

Kerry took a deep breath and sighed before replying.

"Too long," she said.

Mike then followed his wife through the front door, kicking it closed with a foot.

"Do we even have a name for him yet?" Mike asked.

Kerry set her bags down, so she was free to remove her coat, and when that was done, she answered the outstanding question.

"Not yet," she said.

CHAPTER TWO

The following morning, at an hour that most would only be considering getting out of bed, Mike Watkins was already at work, and on patrol with his good friend, and crewmate for the day, Ian Vale.

"Ohmigod, you should've have seen the absolute bell-end that showed up at our place last night to pick up Ash," Mike said, introducing a new topic.

However, as Ian was driving, he had to wait until his concentration on the road ahead could wane.

"Go on," replied Ian, intrigued to hear more.

Mike shifted himself in his seat, so he was turned more to face Ian.

"Oh, I tell ya, he looked like an absolute streak of piss, probably about ten stone in his clothes soaking wet," he began to explain. "Only saw him in his car though, as it would seem that he's too good to come out and ring a doorbell like a normal person. He just sat in his car and text Ash to go to him.

"He's got a mouth on him though. I didn't hear it, but it looked like he was having a right go at Ash as she kept him waiting, to say goodbye to her mum, before they took off.

"I tell ya, I was about two seconds from going up to the car and dragging him out of it."

Ian chuckled slightly, as this was not unfamiliar territory.

"Yeah, well, you don't want to start going down that road again, now do ya?" he replied.

Although this brought the conversation to a grinding halt, Mike knew that Ian was right, as the last thing he needed was another complaint against him.

He was already on a written warning for previous questionable behaviour, and that warning had formed part of the reason he was back in uniform after having spent so much of his recent career as a plain-clothed detective.

But, being immersed in public protection had taken its toll on Mike, as he had spent the last few years dealing with serious child protection investigations as well as high-risk domestic situations.

This pressure this had on him had, in turn, had led him to make a couple of dubious decisions, as well as a complaint being made against him for being heavy handed with a suspect in a case of brutal domestic violence.

Following the resulting criminal investigation, and subsequent internal disciplinary hearing, Mike was demoted, having gone from being a detective sergeant to being busted back down to a uniformed police constable.

Yet, despite the loss of rank and change of role, he cut his losses, feeling that he was fortunate to have even kept his job..

Given that he had less than three years' service left until retirement, the only major consequence that the demotion was going to have for him would be his eventual pension would take a knock.

But he felt with Kerry still working, and their only child Ashley on the verge of flying the nest, they would still be comfortable, financially speaking, after his retirement.

Despite this trip down memory lane, Mike had not finished with the topic under discussion.

"Added to which, the pillock turns up driving a Ford *Compensator*," he continued. "Revving the nuts of it too, as he pulled away."

However, this was not a model of motor vehicle that Ian was familiar with.

"He was driving a *what*? he questioned.

"A pimped-out Ford Focus ST," Mike clarified.

"Nothing like fulfilling a stereotype," Ian said, whilst laughing.

"I just hope this is a short-term thing, there's just something about him," Mike said. "I hope Ash realises what a prick this guy really is, and that he's gone in a blink of an eye like the last one was.

"I don't even know how her path would cross with someone like him. I mean, she's doing so well at college, so I really don't know what she'd see in someone like that.

"It's almost as if she's trying to spite me somehow. Y'know, go out with the baddest boy she can, just coz her old man's a copper."

As Ian was also a family man, he could draw certain comparisons, and conclusions.

"Well, you might have hit the nail on the head there mate," he replied.

The conversation was interrupted at that point at their radios crackled to life.

"Romeo-Bravo six-three, immediate grade domestic incident," the controller announced.

"A domestic?" Ian said, in surprise looking at the clock on the dashboard. "It's a quarter to fucking eight in the morning, don't these people have anything better to do?"

As Ian was driving, Mike acknowledged the transmission.

"I thought I was meant to be getting away from all this shit having been busted back?" Mike questioned.

With them having accepted the deployment, the controller continued with the address they were to attend, as well as details of the incident.

It was then down to Ian to get them there as quickly as possible.

Best speed was the correct term to be used, not just as fast as possible, just efficiently, and more importantly, safely. *Drive to arrive* was the cliché used in driving school.

Police drivers had exemptions under the Road Traffic Act that allowed for them to exceed the speed limit and certain traffic rules, but this was not at the expense of safety.

oOo

Upon their arrival at the address of the incident, they were met with one of the two extremes that police officers did not like to be faced with: silence.

The other extreme being enraged violence and an abundance of activity.

As they had pulled up outside the address, Mike called up for any updates, though the controller replied by saying that the 999 call had been lost, and that they weren't able to phone the caller back.

This wasn't necessarily proof of anything, as the call being disconnected could mean nothing more than a technical glitch.

But, given their experience, it was more likely down to one of the involved parties hanging up on the police operator and leaving the phone off the hook.

Or in more severe cases, going to the extent of ripping a landline phone from the wall or smashing the handset, which both Ian and Mike had witnessed the aftermath of on many occasions.

Mike and Ian cautiously walked up the driveway from the street to the front door and could see that there weren't any cars parked on the driveway.

But there remained a dry rectangle in amongst the damp caused by morning dew, indicating that a car, or other vehicle had recently been parked there and had since driven off.

They didn't run from the car to the house, as this was to allow themselves time to assimilate the scene and assess any risks to them or anyone else. If they were to run, they would enter the property quicker, but at the expense of not having a true idea as to what was waiting for them.

As they walked, they watched the house, the front windows, were any curtains twitching, was anyone in there expecting them?

They also listened, for any noises coming from within; screams, cries, or raised voices. As well as anything being brought to their attention from elsewhere, perhaps a neighbour who heard something who may signal to them.

As they reached the front door, they found something peculiar, the front door had been left on the latch, insecure, free for anyone to enter.

They both looked at each other with puzzled expressions. Ian then called into his radio.

"No persons apparent," he said. "Front door found insecure, we're going in."

"Roger that," acknowledged the controller.

Both Mike and Ian were TASER trained officers, and given the situation as it was unravelling before them, they both felt they had a justifiable need to enter the property with their TASERs drawn.

The brand name TASER is an acronym, which stands for, *Thomas A Swift's Electronic Rifle*, and the models carried by Mike and Ian is a pistol shaped weapon, in yellow and black plastic, which when discharged fires out two barbs on wires that when affixed to a target, delivers a current of approximately 50,000 volts travels between them.

This causes involuntarily muscular contractions and renders the target immovable. The target will then invariably just fall over as they do not have the ability to adjust their balance in their rigid state.

Ian pushed open the front door and shuffled inside, though not going any further than the immediate hallway.

He surveyed the interior of the dwelling ahead of him, before holding his gaze on the rooms beyond the front door. He was securing the hallway so that Mike could safely enter.

Once Mike was also inside, he allowed the front door to close by itself, and as he watched the door close, he noticed that there was what appeared to be blood smeared on the interior door handle. He made his discovery known to Ian.

"Pssst," and when he got Ian's attention, he said. "There's blood on the handle."

This caused Ian's eyes to open wide.

Having made entry, and secured the ground floor, the next thing to do was to announce their presence on the premises, and as Ian was in first, he did it, as anything Mike shouted would be directly into his ear.

"POLICE, IS THERE ANYBODY IN HERE?" he shouted.

They held their collective breath, hoping for anything in the way of a reply or response, then when nothing could be heard, Mike updated the controller.

"We're inside," he said. "So far no response and no-one seen, possible blood on the egress."

From there, it was then a case of searching the house, and in the absence of seeing any further blood droplets, it was a case of just adopting a systematic approach, searching room-by-room, area-by-area, floor-by-floor, which meant that the entry floor needed to be secured before they ventured upstairs.

Mike took the lead, and chose to perform what was referred to as a *left-hand search,* where essentially you could keep your left hand to the wall and then search each room in turn, before moving onto the next, and clearing each floor before changing levels.

It was only because Mike was left-handed, that he felt he favoured this search pattern.

Ian hadn't expressed any preference, so he followed on behind Mike,, his TASER aimed forward at shoulder height covering Mike.

When they reached a room, initially only Mike would enter, with Ian would keep guard at the doorway. This was for two reasons; firstly, to prevent anyone hiding within the next room from escaping, and secondly, and more importantly, it protected Mike's egress, thus preventing them both from being cornered should they both enter to then find themselves trapped, as the last thing they would want is to be barricaded into a room or attacked whilst in such a confined space.

Using this approach, they efficiently completed the search of the ground floor, finishing up in the kitchen, though it was there that things took a sinister turn, as there was a small pool of blood in the middle of the kitchen floor.

Also, they could see bloodied handprints around the counter surfaces, and Ian also noticed that the utensil drawer was partially open.

He wondered if this been snatched open in a hurry or was it simply a case of someone forgetting to shut it properly.

They took a moment to assimilate as much information from this scene as possible.

There was a knife block sitting prominently on the counter, which had two empty slots where knives had been removed.

Maybe they were just in the dishwasher below the counter, and maybe they were elsewhere in the house?

Also, as the utensil drawer was slightly open, this could indicate that something had also been recently removed, again perhaps a knife, or it could mean absolutely nothing at all.

Either way, it conjured up possibilities, and as a result, yet more contingencies had to be considered and factored into their plan of action.

This made the fact that they still hadn't heard anything from anyone, other than themselves since entering the house, even more concerning.

But with the ground floor cleared, they were now in a safe position to venture upstairs, knowing it was now unlikely that anyone could come up behind them.

As they made their way back through to the hallway from the kitchen and to the foot of the stairs, Ian whispered the update into his radio, and requested a second unit, which would bring another two officers to the incident.

He also requested the attendance of an ambulance, this was working on a worst-case scenario, given the blood found so far at the scene.

The safest way to negotiate the stairs was to have the one of them ascend, whilst having the other stay several steps behind him.

Again, this is to allow the lead officer to have space, and time to react should anything untoward happen, and the space to allow his colleague to aim and fire his TASER should the need arise.

The second officer is also in a good position to catch his colleague should he be pushed from above or fall backwards down the stairs.

However, negotiating the stairs would also be when they were at their most vulnerable.

Mike was cautious as he ascended the stairs first. He was followed by Ian who was never more than five or six steps behind him.

Upon reaching the top, Mike saw that the landing went back on itself, with doors coming off it. Having cleared the landing of any risk, he called out as Ian had done before.

"POLICE, IS THERE ANYBODY IN HERE?" he called out, before pausing to silently await any response.

Mike scanned to the right briefly before he disappeared momentarily to the left in order to clear the head of the stairs to enable Ian to follow him onto the relative safety of the landing.

When Ian made it to the landing, he turned to his left. He could see Mike aiming his TASER at the doors at the end of the hallway.

The only door now not immediately covered was the bathroom, but Mike had cleared that with his right-hand glance before turning his back to it.

"Mike," Ian said as he came up behind him, "the loft hatch is open."

Mike looked up to see that Ian was right, the loft hatch was open.

It wasn't of the type that was hinged enabling it could swing down, instead it was just a board that was pushed inwards and slid out of the way to create the opening, though no ladder could be seen through the aperture.

However, the hatch was just close enough to the upstairs banister that Mike felt it possible that an able-bodied person could climb up to the hatch, without a ladder, having used the banister as a step.

"I've got the hatch covered," Ian said, aiming his TASER upwards towards the hatch. "You go clear the rooms."

"Roger that," Mike replied, as he began to make his way towards the first door.

This first room was a box room with minimal furniture, as a result, Mike was able to clear it in its entirety from the doorway.

The second room was presumed from the layout of the house to be the main bedroom at the front of the house.

For this, Mike had to disappear completely into this room, and had to break line of sight from Ian in order to be confident that he had cleared it.

With his back to the door, he crouched down to be able to see under the bed and was able to determine that the room was all clear.

There was only one room to go now, and so far, no one had been found within the address.

The second room was deduced to be a guest room as opposed to a more frequently used room, which meant that the only room left must now be a more frequently used bedroom.

Ian had repositioned himself in order to be able to face towards this final room whilst also maintaining a firing position on the loft hatch, and from where he now stood, he could see partially into the last room, but his vision was greatly restricted by the door and furniture.

Mike made the entry into the last bedroom, and as he entered, he kept his back to the wall.

From there, he could see the entire room, with the only obstruction to his view being the bed itself. But, beyond the bed he could see the head and shoulders of a woman slumped on the floor, though the rest of her was hidden by the bed.

He looked back at Ian, he pointed two fingers at his own eyes, and then used the same fingers to point in the direction he was looking, which was to indicate that he had seen something of interest.

Mike then cautiously walked around the bed, taking as wide a path as possible, to ensure there were no unexpected surprises, whilst Ian repositioned himself within the doorway to offer cover to his colleague, whilst keeping an eye on the loft hatch.

Ian was then finally able to see what Mike had indicated towards, as he too saw the woman who was slumped on the floor behind the bed.

Realising he was covered by Ian, Mike holstered his own TASER, and looked down at the woman sat on the floor before him.

She was wearing a flowery dress which was predominantly red, but despite this, Mike could still see that it was heavily blood stained. Her head was bowed, and her long blonde hair was matted to her face.

The fact that there didn't appear to be any blood soaking into the carpet around her, and as she had colour in her face, Mike deduced that the blood wasn't her, and that she wasn't in immediate physical danger through blood loss.

He could also see that she was holding onto a kitchen knife, with her hands rested in her lap. It was a carving knife with an eight-inch blade, and the blade had congealed blood on it.

Mike looked over at Ian to ensure he had him covered, and seeing that Ian had the perfect vantage point behind the female, Mike crouched down, so that he was almost at eye level with the female, whilst keeping a relatively safe distance, beyond her reach with the knife should she swipe out at him.

"Hello, my love, it's the police," he said in a calm and reassuring tone. "Are you okay, can you tell me what's happened here?"

There was absolutely no response from the woman.

However, Mike tried again, only this time he used her name which had been given to him from the controller from a previously reported incident.

"Maggie, my name's Mike, I'm a police officer, are you okay my love?" he said before pausing, to await her response. "Maggie?"

Eventually, there was the slightest of movements from her, as Maggie lifted her head enough to cause her hair to fall away from her face. However, she refused to make eye contact, or even look in Mike's general direction.

But, from the glimpse she gave him, he was able to see her face, seeing there was evidence that she had recently been crying, as her face was puffy, and her eyes were red and drained of tears.

"Maggie, can you tell me what happened?" Mike asked of her.

Her only response was to tilt her head again, only this time to hide her face as the emotion of reliving the incident in her mind began to again consume her.

"Maggie, can you put down the knife for me please," Mike then asked.

It was then that she looked at her hands, not even realising that she was still holding the knife.

Maggie immediately threw it on to the floor immediately in front of her and began sobbing uncontrollably.

"Yeah, this is Romeo-Bravo six-three, we've got the female party here, unknown injuries at this time, can I get an *ETA* on the ambulance," Ian quietly requested of the controller.

Although Ian's message would be heard by Maggie, the response wouldn't be as both Ian and Mike were both wearing earpieces that linked directly to their radios. *ETA* referred to an estimated time of arrival of the ambulance at the incident.

Maggie looked over towards Ian, as she was expecting to hear the reply from the controller herself, but all she heard was Ian's reply.

"Thanks for that," he said into the handset.

"Maggie," Mike said, wanting to regain her attention. "Are you hurt in any way, do you have any injuries?"

Maggie took a moment to look down at her bloodied hands. She then looked back to where she had discarded the knife, only to see it wasn't there anymore.

In the time she had taken to watch Ian use his radio, Mike had moved the knife away to a safer distance, out of her grasp.

Eventually she gave an indication, by the slightest of head shakes, convinced that she wasn't wounded.

However, Mike could clearly see her face now, and he could tell that the puffiness around her eyes wasn't as a result of her crying. Instead, he could see distinct swelling and haemorrhaging, as a result of having been struck, beaten.

Mike relayed this to Ian, using hand gestures of lightly punching his right hand into his left palm, indicating punches and an assault having taken place.

"Where is he Maggie?" Mike asked.

Again, all Maggie could do was shake her head, though this time, Mike was convinced that she didn't know.

Ian then deduced that the dry rectangle in amongst the morning dew on the driveway had been underneath her partner's car, that is until he had driven off following the incident, and this led to him having another request.

"Romeo-Bravo six-three, can we have a check done on any cars registered to this address please?" he asked. "We have an outstanding adult male, possibly with knife wounds, most likely having left in a vehicle."

A moment later, there was an echoed voice calling up from downstairs.

"HELLO," it said, quickly followed by "PARAMEDICS."

Ian momentarily broke away from his position in the room, to return to the landing, as he felt that Mike was safe, and he didn't want to have to bellow down to the paramedics within earshot of Maggie.

"Yeah, come on up," he called out.

Also, this allowed Ian to brief the ambulance crew of the situation prior to them engaging with Maggie, which was done as Ian met the paramedics at the top of the stairs.

"Hey guys, yeah, we've got an adult female, very distressed, facial injuries, don't know what other injuries just yet," he began to explain. "She had a bloodied knife when we got here, which we've got that now.

"Suspect not believed to be on scene, so don't know for sure whose blood on it yet. She's not been searched, but feel free to crack on, we'll have you covered."

With that Ian led the ambulance crew into the bedroom, and as one of them approached where Mike was crouched with Maggie on the floor behind the bed, the other set down an equipment bag on the bed, and opened it and proceeded to prepare some equipment.

Mike stood up and stepped out of the way to in order to give the paramedics more space in which to work.

"This is Maggie," he said to the paramedic.

He was sure that the woman posed no risk to them, though he remained with them in the bedroom, but at a distance as such that he was able to talk to Ian without being overheard, as well as being able to hear any dialogue between Maggie and the paramedics.

"I wouldn't mind betting that she'll have to go to hospital," Ian said.

"Yep," Mike replied. "And if she goes, we'll have to go with her."

"Better that than being stuck here I s'pose," Ian confessed. "Having to guard the scene."

Given the potential severity of the offence, both Ian and Mike knew that the house would now be considered a crime scene, and with that came certain protocols and procedures that would need to be adhered to, which would include the need for forensic officers and detectives to attend.

Also, Maggie herself would need to be considered a scene. Consequently, should she need to go to hospital, so would need to be accompanied by officers until all the necessary precautions had been taken, and any forensic evidence had been obtained.

Mike looked over at the paramedics who were interacting with the woman, who were reiterating the questions that Mike had already asked.

They were asking if the blood on her clothes was hers, and if she had any injuries, but Mike couldn't hear any response, instead Maggie just shook her head.

When there appeared to be a pause in their communication, Mike then took the opportunity to gain the paramedics' attention.

"Do you think she'll need to go to hospital?" He asked. "If so, how long do you think you'll be before you need to leave?"

He wasn't asking to put any pressure on them, or to rush them in any way, instead Mike needed to know in order to work out how best to utilise the resources currently available to him.

At present, it was just him and Ian at the house, although he knew there was another couple of officers on their way.

But this meant, if the paramedics needed to leave for hospital with any urgency, he and Ian would have to split up in order to monitor both crime scenes, Maggie and the house.

But, just as Mike was about to ask Ian to decide which he'd prefer doing, another voice was heard to call up from the hallway downstairs.

"POLICE," could be heard.

"Up here guys," Ian responded.

The arrival of the back-up police unit made Mike's so far unasked question now redundant, as with the second unit there, they would be nominated to guard the house, whilst Mike and Ian attended the hospital with Maggie, with one of them travelling in the ambulance, whilst the other would follow in their police car.

Ian stepped out on the landing to greet their colleagues, whilst Mike kept his vantage point in the bedroom, just in case Maggie got upset, or became in any way aggressive towards the paramedics.

After a couple of minutes one of the paramedics stood up and approached Mike.

"We're gonna be taking her to hospital," he said.

"Hardly surprising," Mike replied. "Are you gonna need any help from us?"

"I don't think so, but thanks," the paramedic replied. "I think she'll be okay to walk down the stairs… We'll see how we get on anyway."

"Okay, that's fine," Mike replied. "Has she said anything more about what's happened yet?"

Although, having eavesdropped their conversation he was already expecting a negative reply, and he wasn't disappointed.

"When are you looking to leave?" he continued.

"Any time now," the paramedic said.

Mike nodded his understanding, as the paramedic then went back to his colleague, which left Mike alone in the doorway as he turned in order to brief Ian and the others.

"Okay guys, she's gonna be coming out shortly," he began to explain. "So, Ian and I will be going to hospital with her, care you guys able to stay here and start a scene log?"

At hearing that, one of the officers from the back-up unit turned around and disappeared back down the stairs to get a scene logbook from their car.

His colleague then followed downstairs with Ian, as Ian gave him an explanation as to what they had been faced with when they first arrived.

After a few minutes, everything was in readiness, with the paramedics all packed up, and Maggie on her feet being steadied by them as she shuffled slowly towards the door.

Mike and Ian remained on the landing as Maggie was assisted down the stairs by the paramedics, before helping her make her way slowly out of the front door of the house and towards the ambulance that was parked on the street behind the first police car.

"Before we go anywhere, I wanna check the loft," Mike said. "You able to give us a leg up?"

Ian nodded, relieved that it didn't fall to him to be so energetic so early in the morning, as he assisted Mike in climbing up onto the banister and steadying him as he reached up to the loft hatch.

"You ready?" Mike asked.

"Yep," Ian replied.

With that, Mike stepped off the banister, and onto Ian's shoulder, which gave him the height he needed to be able to peer into the loft. Then as Ian kept him aloft, he shone his torch around the periphery of the roof void.

"Nah, no one's here," he concluded. "Stand clear

With that, Ian stepped away, allowing Mike's foot to hang. Mike then lowered his body until his arms were at full extent and dropped to the floor. The two of them then made their way downstairs.

They arrived outside to see that the ambulance was still there, as the paramedics were still making Maggie comfortable for the journey.

Whilst they waited, Mike and Ian chatted outside, and it was decided that as Ian was already the designated driver for the shift, it made sense for him to follow the ambulance which meant that it fell to Mike to accompany Maggie and the paramedics in the ambulance to the hospital.

"We're ready," one of the paramedics said as he stuck his head out of the rear doors.

"See you there then," Ian said, as he started to walk off towards their car.

"The house is all yours," Mike said to his colleagues, before he climbed into the back of the ambulance.

oOo

At the hospital, both officers had to remain with Maggie within the accident and emergency department until she had been examined and the extent of her injuries had been determined.

Due to the nature of the incident, and because Mike and Ian were the first officers on scene, they were relieved soon after their arrival at the hospital by yet more colleagues, as they had a significant amount of work to do regarding the incident.

Whilst at the hospital, they had been sent a forensic strategy by email from detectives within the criminal investigation department, or *CID*.

This included seizing all of Maggie's outer clothing for forensic analysis, which was easily achieved as she had already changed out of them into a hospital gown.

The other task that had been requested, was one that they were unable to perform immediately, as they were asked to take hands swabs from Maggie, which was to allow analysis of the blood that was encrusted onto them.

However, neither Mike nor Ian had a ready supply of forensic hand swabs. So, this request was passed on to the officers that came to relieve them.

Once Mike and Ian were released from the hospital, they were required to return to the police station, so they could write up their accounts of what they had seen and had been involved in. They also had to exhibit the seized clothing, as well as liaise with CID with regards to the incident report.

This was to be a lengthy process, and although the incident was their only and only deployment of the day, having occurred early in the shift, what with the time spent at the hospital and the time it took to complete their reports, they were both well into overtime by the time they had finished.

oOo

"Well, that was a bitch of a day," Ian said, as he took his coat from his locker.

"Well, look at it this way, we've both met someone else whose had an *even* worse day," Mike replied.

Ian nodded in agreement as he shut his locker, and as he walked around behind Mike, he patted him on the shoulder.

"Best part about it is, we get to do it all again tomorrow," he said. "You have a good evening."

CHAPTER THREE

"So, what happened to *him* then?" Kerry asked, with almost bated breath between mouthfuls over dinner later that evening.

As they were eating together, they chose to make use of their dining room, unlike when Mike had chosen to eat alone, at the breakfast bar in the kitchen the previous evening.

"I don't know," Mike replied. "By the time we finished he was still outstanding."

This was somewhat frustrating to Kerry as she didn't like to be told a story that didn't come with an ending.

"Don't you wanna know how something like this ends though?" She asked quizzically.

However, Mike was not so bothered, and only told the tale as far as he did because he was asked how his day had been.

"Nah, not really," he replied. "Anyway, I know how it ends, he'll get nicked for the assault, maybe today in a hospital when he goes in for his wounds to be treated, or, out and about somewhere, or maybe in a week or so's time.

"Eventually though, he'll be found, or he'll hand himself in. Either way, one thing I can pretty much guarantee ya, and that's that she'll take him back after all that's happened, and that *we'll* be back there again at some point."

Kerry smiled and shook her head.

"Oh, you're such a bloody cynic," she replied, realising it was time to change the subject.

She'd been at this point in a conversation before, and she knew what was needed in order to prevent Mike from getting a nosebleed from standing on his soapbox.

But Mike was not one to be so easily dissuaded.

"She *will* though, despite the fact that he's done a right number on her," Mike began to explain. "But no doubt we'll get the whole '*but I love him'* routine.

"He'll probably get bail conditions pending a court date not to go back to the home address. But you can put money on it that he will, *and* that she probably won't report anything that happens the next time."

"Didn't *she* call you this time then?" Kerry enquired.

However, this question caught Mike in the middle of his last mouthful, so had to wait until he had cleared it before replying.

"Nope, came from an anonymous caller," Mike replied. "So, chances are it was a neighbour who called it in having heard shouting or something, either way, they're no good if this ever makes it to court."

Now that Mike had finished his dinner, he stood up and pushed the chair back in, before picking up his dinner plate and taking it through into the kitchen.

As he scrapped the remaining food into the waste bin, he noticed a third dinner had been prepared, which was in the process of going cold on the counter.

From the kitchen, Mike called back into living room where Kerry was still sat.

"Was Ash meant to be eating with us this evening then?" he asked.

There was a delay in any reply coming from the living room, but as Kerry had finished her meal before Mike, he could almost sense her sigh.

"She *was,"* came the eventual reply. "I was just in the process of dishing up, and she was even sat at the table doing her project, when she got a text message, and in an instant, she dropped everything.

"She grabbed her coat and was of out the front door without saying anything, not even so much as a goodbye to me."

The final words got louder as Kerry joined Mike in the kitchen, just as she mimicked his earlier actions before placing both her plate and his into the dishwasher.

She then stood up and propped herself against the counter across from her husband.

"How long has she been with *this* guy then?" Mike asked.

"To be honest, I don't even know for sure," Kerry replied. "Funny thing is, she never speaks about him, and I've only ever seen his car here a couple of times before the other night."

Mike pouted, before he rubbed his tongue across the front of his teeth.

"Well, I don't like it," Mike replied. "And I certainly don't like *him*."

However, whatever Kerry thought under the circumstances, she wasn't as keen to voice them.

"Oh, give the poor lad a chance for goodness' sake," Kerry implored of him.

"C'mon, I see guys like *him* every – single – day." Mike began to explain. "So I know a bad situation when I see one, and the fact that she stops everything at the drop of a hat, *and* is so secretive about everything when it comes to him concerns me… I mean, do we even know his name?"

Again, if Kerry knew the answer to this question, she was not letting on.

"Why?" Kerry replied. "So, you can run your checks on him?"

Mike chuckled.

"Hah, now as much as I'd like to, it's more than my job's worth," he said.

Mike was referring to the fact that officers are forbidden from accessing police databases for personal reasons.

All access and entries are logged, and any usage would need to be justified if ever it was to be scrutinised, and failure to adequately provide a justifiable reason would most likely result in disciplinary action, which could ultimately result in dismissal from the force and potentially criminal action.

"It would be nice to know a little bit more about him," Mike continued. "And just knowing his name would be a start."

"Well, I'll ask Ash in conversation when I can next pin her down for five minutes," Kerry replied. "But I expect it won't be this evening, as we'll probably both be in bed before she gets home at this rate."

Mike had already resigned himself to that fact, and as he had another early shift to go, that meant another seven o'clock briefing, consequently he would be in need of getting an equally early night.

Since his demotion, the shift pattern he had reverted to was a departure from the relatively relaxed shifts he had enjoyed whilst in the public protection team. On that team his teams had largely consisted of early and late shifts, with the occasion 'on call' night shift.

However, his current role, on a response team consisted of shifts which covered 24/7/365. As a result, he had to work many more weekends and bank holidays.

That much he could handle, but it was the early starts that he continued to have trouble with.

oOo

After an evening in front of the TV, watching a movie of limited appeal to them both, both Kerry and Mike decided at the same time that it was time for bed

But whereas Mike always settled down immediately, sometimes with the added assistance of a herbal remedy, Kerry instead chose to read for a while before finally turning the lights off.

oOo

Shortly after she had turned the lights out, Kerry heard a screech of tyres coming from somewhere along the street outside.

Normally she wouldn't think anything of it, but as Ashley was still not home, after the noise first startled her, it then raised concern.

She looked over at Mike who was already fast asleep. She then looked over at her phone, which when she picked it up, it illuminated the time, showing that it was 00:12am.

What was probably less than a minute later, she heard a key turn in the front door lock.

This was followed a few seconds later by a poor attempt of someone trying to enter the house whilst being quiet, and *not* alerting anyone in doing so.

However, Kerry could still hear footsteps walking down the hallway, which was followed by light switches being flicked, after which the fridge door could be heard to close.

Kerry breathed a sigh of relief knowing her baby was home.

But still she continued to listen intently to every sound as she visualised in her mind her daughter's every action.

In amongst all the activity Kerry could hear, she also heard her daughter sniffling, as if she had a heavy cold.

But Ashley didn't have a cold, at least not when she got in from college that day, or in the moments before her impromptu departure earlier that evening.

To Kerry, the cause of this seemed to be something more concerning.

Eventually a light switch was heard to be flicked again, presumably turning it off this time.

This was followed by muffled footsteps walking up creaking stairs.

Ashley then went straight to the bathroom before going to her room.

Kerry listened intently, though nothing specific could be heard. But the light she could see emanating from beneath closed bedroom doors was seen for some time.

Although Ashley was home, safe and sound, Kerry still pondered going to her daughter's room to address her concerns. But instead she felt that it was probably best to wait for a more opportune moment.

After the light eventually went off, Kerry took quite some time to fall asleep herself.

CHAPTER FOUR

As Mike sat in briefing at the commencement of his shift the next morning, he realised just how badly his body was coming to terms with the new shift pattern he was having to work, and with that came the conclusion that he was not a morning person.

Had the choice been his to make, he would still be in the public protection unit. But unfortunately, that choice was taken out of his hands following the outcome of the disciplinary process, with his career having come full circle, as he found himself back in the first role he had been in from training school almost twenty years earlier.

The main difference to that role in that time, was in the amalgamation of several frontline departments into a single role. This meant that the team of which Mike was now a part of, and the work it was responsible for had grown exponentially.

His first role from training school was as a beat officer. Which involved being a visible presence out and about on foot, and giving reassurance to the public, as well as dealing with neighbourhood issues.

Now the role was considered to be much more universal, or *omni-incompetent* as the rank and file considered it.

The primary role was always to respond to reported incidents, both as a result of a 999 call, and what was termed a *slow time*, in the form of a historic report, which took up most of the team's time.

Also, under the new structure, the team retained a large percentage of the investigations they were deployed to, whereas previously, after the initial investigation had taken place, when statements had been taken, arrests made, CCTV downloaded, a civilian investigator would take over the investigation, interview the suspect and reaching a charging decision before compiling the file for court.

However, as now Mike's team retained the investigation this included interviewing their own prisoners and dealing with prosecutors, which had the downside of keeping the team in the office for much longer than before. This had the resulting negative effect of being seen out and about a lot less.

At the beginning of each shift, the team would meet for a briefing, where they would be allocated their crewmate and call-sign for the shift. Briefing would also be where they were allocated any tasks assigned to the team.

It also involved a computer slide show, which showed details of recent incidents, wanted persons, and any other topics to which intelligence was required.

One such slide showed repeated incidents of drug dealing around Newton College, a sixth-form college not far from the police station.

Normally, such slides requesting information or intelligence would cascade over the team, as it was teaching them to *suck eggs*, which is a phrase used when someone or something is stating the obvious.

To any experienced officer, the need to submit intelligence reports when appropriate came as second nature to them.

But the slide about Newton College held Mike's attention, purely and simply because it was where Ashley went to college.

The slide didn't give any details as to any possible offenders, instead it was just an open plea for information to be submitted, in addition to making the team aware there was a noticeable drug problem there.

The next slide showed the modern-day version of the *Wild West* wanted poster, that related to the incident that Mike and Ian had attended the previous day.

The wanted person in question was the husband of the woman, Maggie that they had tended to at the scene before handing her over to the care of paramedics and accompanied her to hospital.

The slide showed that the husband was wanted on suspicion of causing actual bodily harm to the victim, and until his account could be determined he was considered to be the suspect.

The slide provided his details including his name and the address Mike and Ian had attended. It also included several photographs. Firstly, an extracted image from a larger family photo showing the male in question, and secondly a stock image of the Vauxhall estate he was believed to be driving, as well as the registration, or index number his vehicle was known to have.

The slide asked for officers to make regular visits to the home address in case he had chosen to return there. However, until such time that he was arrested, Maggie was safe as she had been rehoused elsewhere.

Mike and Ian were tasked by their sergeant with attending the address as it had been their job previously.

After briefing it was a case of collecting a set of car keys from the vehicle board and preparing their car for the shift.

With that complete, they each took a few minutes to log on to a computer in the office and check their emails and respective workloads for anything that needed to be done that day before they headed out.

As Mike was crewed with Ian again, and as Ian drove the previous shift it was only fair that it was now Mike's turn.

There was no hard and fast rule as to who drove, or that they even had to take turns, they just worked it out this way whenever they were crewed together.

As he pulled out of the car park, Mike said a single word which met with instant approval.

"Coffee?" he said.

However, their coffee stop of choice was nothing fancier than a service station which was just outside town.

There were other service stations, some of which were closer than this one. But this one was renowned for offering emergency service workers a discount on its hot beverages, and Mike considered this to be wholly appropriate, as he felt their coffee did not warrant the full price they were charging for it.

The service station was essentially on the same main road as the police station, but in order to kill two birds with one stone, their route from one to the other would on this occasion take them past Maggie's address to see if the her husband's Vauxhall was parked outside the address.

As they got closer, instead of just focusing on the driveway, they scoured the whole of the road, as well as the roads off it, however there was no trace of the Vauxhall.

oOo

They enjoyed their coffees within the shop of the service station, and as had become the normality, officers were now having to endure scornful looks and snide comments from members of public, in apparent disgust that they had time to laugh and joke over a coffee, when crimes were being committed.

After they finished, they chose to return to the same street and performed a second check on Maggie's address, only this time they decided to park up short of the house and approached on foot.

From the street it didn't look as if anyone was home, but despite that, still they called at the address.

There was no answer to repeated knocking at the front door, and as there were no physical barriers, such as fences or gates, they also checked around the back, having a look through all accessible windows for any signs of recent activity, suggesting that the husband had come home.

Lastly, they called at Maggie's neighbours, on both sides and directly opposite, to see if they had seen or heard any activity at the address since the incident the previous morning.

The adjoining neighbour stated that they had heard what sounded like some activity from within the address late the previous evening, which could possibly suggest that the husband had come home at some point.

This revelation wouldn't require any further actions on their part other than submitting an update to the incident log, as further frequent attendance had already been requested on the same tasking that had deployed them.

oOo

Their shift progressed towards its conclusion without anything of interest happening.

This wasn't unheard of for a weekday early shift, given the fact that most people we either at work or school.

As the time was nearing 3pm, which was when the oncoming shift would be starting and taking over from them for their late shift, Mike and Ian started to head back towards their police station.

However, on the way back, Mike mentioned to Ian about the Newton College briefing slide, and as it wasn't too far out of their way, they decided to swing by the college, hoping to gain some intelligence, and to show a police presence in the reported area of drug dealing.

Mike turned off the main road in the college grounds, and as he drove around the back of the main building towards the area reserved for student parking, he saw a group of people gathering around a parked car.

The car itself was hidden in amongst the rows of parked vehicles, and it was certainly appearing to be something of interest to those gathered around it.

Mike had to follow the marked one-way system around the car park, and in doing so, as he circled around the back, someone in the group may have seen the roof lights of the police car protruding above the height of the other cars parked there, because suddenly, the group began to disperse from around the car around, which then started to move off.

Seeing this, Mike reversed up, against the direction indicated by the painted arrows, so he could see down an aisle between two rows of parked cars. He got there just in time to see the car pass across the far end of the same aisle.

He couldn't see anything of the registration number as the car was in profile, and he wasn't able to see anything of the occupants.

But in the brief glimpse he had, he was able to determine, beyond any shadow of a doubt, that it was a sporty white Ford Focus.

A Ford Focus that had, what looked like from a distance to be, a longitudinal scrape along the offside, just in front of the rear wheel arch.

Mike then drove around the car park, towards the exit, as fast as he could. But, by the time he had reached the main road again the Ford Focus was nowhere to be seen.

"Bollocks!" Mike said, in obvious frustration.

"Oh well, never mind," Ian replied, looking at his watch. "I'm actually glad they've fucked off, it's nearly home time."

oOo

That evening, Mike was able to stay up later than he had the previous two evenings, as he didn't have an early shift with a 7am start the following morning.

As part of his new shift rotation, he would be working a late shift the following day, one that didn't need him to be at work until 3pm.

Mike was sat watching TV, when he was surprised, when Ashley shouted from the hallway that she was heading out.

Once again, it wasn't a proper goodbye, one that allowed time for any reply, and again, there was no information offered as to who she was with, where she was going, or what time she'd be back.

But as the front door closed, Mike went to the front door and peeked through the window beside it.

He got there in time to see Ashley walking down the drive towards a waiting car that was parked across the driveway.

For the first time, and much to his own surprise, he actually hoped that it was the white *ST*.

Although it was as it had hoped, it was parked with its nearside towards the house, so Mike couldn't get a view of the bodywork in front of the rear offside wheel arch without leaving the house.

Mike sighed in disappointment, as he wanted to confirm for his own peace of mind that this wasn't the vehicle he believed was associated with drug-dealing at Ashley's college.

Although Mike had the discretion as to when he could go to bed that evening, not being governed by an early alarm, he wanted to go to be early, having been up since 5:30am.

But he stayed up with the sole intention of being awake in order to see Ashley return home.

Unfortunately, he had fallen asleep in the living room, only to be woken when she eventually came in through the front door.

She froze in a moment of panic when she first saw her father sat in a chair in the living room, before realising that he was fast asleep.

This time she didn't risk going to the kitchen as she had done previously as she didn't want to take her chances and risk waking him.

Instead, she thought it best to head straight up to bed, as something had happened that evening that she couldn't face her father about.

CHAPTER FIVE

The following day, Mike was working a late shift which meant it had gone midnight by the time he finished work.

He had asked Kerry to message him if Ashley gone out again, and he received such a message at 7:15pm.

This was to be the fourth evening in a row that she had left to go out, presumably again with *Mister Focus ST*.

Mike had also asked Kerry to send a message should she be awake when Ashley got home, and so far, he had not received any such message.

So, that either meant Kerry had fallen asleep, or Ashley had yet to come home with it having gone midnight.

After he finished work, Mike drove home, during which time it had started to rain.

When he got home, having still not received a text message from Kerry, instead of parking on their driveway, or even on the street in front of the house, Mike chose to park just into the road opposite.

From there, he was able to see the full frontage of his own house, and he was hopeful that when Ashley was eventually brought home, that he would be able to see the offside of the car, and confirm if it had any damage like that seen on the Ford Focus that he had seen in the college car park what was now two days ago.

With the hypnotically soothing sound of the rain against the car windows and roof, Mike felt himself nodding off, but he found himself being kept awake, startled with every sound from passing cars.

However, it was in between passing cars that he saw what he had been waiting for, but it was far from what he was expecting.

Emerging from the left, in the direction he was hoping the *ST* would appear from, he saw Ashley appear, only to see that she was on foot.

She wasn't dressed for this weather, and from across the street, he could see she was soaked to the skin. Her arms were pinned tightly against her body to preserve warmth, but still she shivered. Her head was bowed, and her hair was matted against her face.

Mike had to fight every urge as a concerned father to resist the temptation to rush across the road and comfort her. But he knew if he did, she would most likely realise that he had parked up specially to spy on her, or on her boyfriend.

Mike had to wait until she had entered the house. He would then have to wait a short while before entering himself to avoid any conclusions being drawn and be able to look surprised when greeted with anything.

To further add to the charade, Mike chose to drive off and go around the block before parking up in front of the house as Kerry's car was already on the drive. He then went to the front door and let himself in as if blissfully aware that anything was amiss.

Part of him wanted Ashley to be downstairs, caught red-handed and having to explain why she came him half drowned, whilst the rest of him felt she probably had enough to deal with at that moment in time without his presence making her feel awkward.

When he walked inside, he could see the remnants of a bad evening.

There were wet shoeprints on the hall floor, and where Ashley had kicked off her boots, as they lay strewn at the foot of the stairs, and she had hung her coat over the bottom of the banister, which had slipped off onto the floor beside one of her boots.

This was very much out of habit, as Ashley tended to hang her coat in the cupboard under the stairs.

Mike tried to rationalise everything to make sense of it, thinking that maybe she hung her coat on the banister purely to allow it to dry out before hanging it in the cupboard with the others.

Maybe nothing is wrong after all, despite how Ashley looked as she walked home.

Whatever had happened tonight she was home safe now, and that was the main thing.

Anything else could be discussed in the morning.

CHAPTER SIX

The following morning, Mike had deliberately listened out for Ashley to leave her bedroom before getting out of bed himself.

He had waited for her to go to the bathroom and coincided his leaving his bedroom, so he was outside the bathroom door when she finally emerged.

"Good morning," he said.

In her surprised state, Ashley saw her father propped against the opposite wall, as he nonchalantly waited for the room to be vacated.

"What are you doing?" Ashley exclaimed. "Can't I even go to the toilet without you spying on me?"

Her response was certainly not matching the casual, intentionally coincidental sentiment she had been greeted with.

Consequently, she said nothing further and marched straight past her father and back into her room. Mike turned to start following her.

"Woah, whoa, woah little lady," he said. "I'd very much appreciate you *not* talking to me like th-."

However, Mike was cut off mid-sentence as Ashley shut her bedroom door on him. But he knew it would not benefit the situation to pursue the matter any further at a time like that.

Admitting defeat that his little *coincidence* hadn't gone to plan, Mike went downstairs.

He walked into the kitchen, and then silently stood watching from behind Kerry who he saw was in the process of unloading the dishwasher from the previous evening.

As she bent forward, he took a moment to admire her.

Like him, she too was in a mid-forties, and had a teenage daughter, and though she didn't make too much of a fuss about staying in shape or healthy eating, nonetheless the results were there.

Mike looked her up and down and was tantalised by every inch and every curve. He knew if she caught him staring, she would devalue the moment with some self-derogatory comment, and he didn't want that.

So, he stepped forward from the doorway as she stood up and placed his hands on her hips.

He could feel her jump under his light touch, with the plate in her grip momentarily slipped until she reclaimed it with a firmer hold, before she set it down, only to finally turn to face her husband.

"Good morning," she said softly to him.

"It is now," he replied as he pulled her closer.

"Don't go getting any funny ideas mister," she replied. "I hear a mini-Watkins coming down the stairs now."

Feeling defeated for the second time that morning already, Mike backed away from Kerry.

He turned around and walked over the table in the dining room and took a seat, not because he wanted to sit down, as he was happy to have breakfast at the breakfast bat.

But it was because the thoughts he had been having of his wife had caused him to become unintentionally aroused, and he didn't want his daughter noticing the physical effect this had caused in him.

Mike was then surprised when Ashley took the seat opposite him, as she had recently adopted the habit of collecting her meal, be it breakfast or dinner and make a hasty retreat to her room.

This habit however had extended back to long before the emergence of this guy on the scene, so it wasn't deemed to relate to him in any way.

"Good morning," he said for the second time to his daughter, having decided it best to press the reset button, and not dwell on the unfortunate outburst upstairs.

"Hey," was all Ashley said in reply.

It wasn't *War & Peace*, but it was a vast improvement on her earlier response.

Kerry set a glass of orange juice down in front of them both, which was soon to be followed by a black coffee for Mike and a glass of milk for Ashley, only for a full toast rack to emerged between them.

The resumed silence continued at the table until after Kerry had placed scrambled eggs on toast in front of them both, and a third plate for herself.

It was then that Mike felt he needed to break the silence.

"So," he began, "When are we gonna get to meet him."

"Who?" Ashley replied, without even raising her head to make eye contact.

"Who?" he continued. "The reason you've been out virtually every night this week. Tell ya, he's gotta be something special to hold your attention like that."

Mike almost choked on his own words, but he knew he needed to embellish a little bit to get Ashley's attention.

"Yeah, whatever," came her insolent reply.

"Well, if he's not all that, why you spending so much time with him?" Mike asked.

He knew this was now potentially a sore point for Ashley, and knowing her as he did, he realised this was going to be his last comment on the subject. That was unless her reply progressed the conversation.

He also knew he couldn't make any reference to what he had seen the previous evening, certainly not without in some way admitting to Ashley that he had seen her before he had come in from work.

As it turned out, the conversation didn't progress beyond that, and Ashley ate the rest of her breakfast in silence with barely so much as an upward glance from her plate.

Mike and Kerry exchanged concerned glances, but neither said a word.

They both had noticed distinct changes in their daughter since she had started seeing this guy, and none of them were for the better.

But worse than that was that they didn't like the fact that they knew so little about him.

Added to which, Ashley was also appearing to be so secretive about him. Previously, they had at the very least known her boyfriend's names, if little else, and it concerned them, that this one seemed to be treated differently.

oOo

After finishing her breakfast, Ashley was the first to leave the table, and once she had left the kitchen to return to her room, Mike and Kerry once again exchanged concerned glance. Kerry shook her head in disappointment, as she didn't like the fact that her little girl had suddenly become so secretive.

"I don't like this Mike," she began, "I don't know what's worse, this, or that's she's lying to us."

"I don't know if she's lying, but she's definitely hiding something from us," he replied. "Whoever he is, he's no good for her, if he wasn't she'd be bigging him up.

"God only knows what she sees in him, and more importantly why she suddenly feels the need to shield him from us."

Mike's words rung true, but there was something else that Kerry had taken from the limited interaction over breakfast.

"Did you notice?" Kerry asked.

"Notice what?" he replied expectantly.

Kerry sighed before continuing, as she knew where her disclosure was likely to lead.

"She's hiding something, she *never* wears that much make-up, certainly not for college anyway," Kerry began to explain. "And I'm sure I saw a bruise on her arm yesterday too.

"She had her sleeve pulled down over it, but I saw something when she was scratched at it. She's hiding something, either she's been crying coz he's upset her, or h…"

"Or he's hit her!" Mike said, finishing her sentence.

Kerry had been reluctant to share this was the reason that was sat across from her, as she could already see the rage building in Mike. His shoulders tensed and his face became contorted with anger.

"Motherfucker," Mike said under his breath.

However, Kerry lip-read him perfectly.

This only added to her upset, that Mike with all his policing experience now shared her concern.

Mike turned towards the kitchen door that led to the hallway, as he wanted to ensure that Ashley was not within earshot to what he was about to say.

When he was certain all was clear, he turned back towards Kerry.

"We're gonna have to tread carefully on how we dealt with this," he began.

What Mike was about to say drew on his previous experience as a public protection officer.

"If we challenge her now, she's likely to clam up, and we run the risk of driving her to him even more than she is now," he continued before pausing. "But, that said, the longer we leave any intervention, then the greater the time she is exposed to him.

"It's a fine balance, and we really only have *one* chance to get right."

Kerry nodded her agreement.

"What do you suggest then?" she asked.

Mike took a moment to consider their options before replying.

"It's a tricky one," he said. "But I'm thinking we just keep a close eye on things, just for the time being.

"This could just be a one-off, or it could be that this whole thing could be done and dusted, and over any time.

"But, if it isn't, then we need to be unified with what we choose to do, and when we act."

Again, Kerry nodded her agreement, though she appeared more hesitant this time.

Mike wasn't convinced she wholeheartedly agreed with him, instead that she had just nodded along merely to move things forward.

"What are you thinking?" he asked, wanting to understand her reluctance and hesitation.

"I don't know hun," she began. "I know what you're saying is right. It's just that doing nothing *now* doesn't sit right with me. I mean she's suffering, and we're just sitting back and watching."

Mike could certainly see his wife's point of view and had been intentionally lenient in his suggestion.

"Okay, how about this then?" Mike continued. "We see how things go over the next day or so, and then we'll decide how to take it forward from there.

"Now we don't want to be seen to overreact, so let's just see what happens, okay?"

He was hoping that this would strike the balance they so desperately needed.

Kerry again nodded her agreement, only this time Mike could see that she was more convinced.

They both then finished their breakfasts in an uncomfortable silence, with each of them still contemplating how best to deal with the situation before them.

Kerry was the next to leave the table. Having stood she asked Mike if he had finished as he had hardly touched a bite since Ashley had left the table. He nodded, before offering a muffled reply resembling the silent responses he would get from Ashley that had infuriated him. Kerry then took both plates through to the kitchen.

Mike brought his elbow up onto the table in the space now created.

He first had his hands in prayer with his chin resting on outstretched thumbs as he contemplated the situation before them, before interlacing his fingers and drawing the knuckles back and forth under his chin.

Having loaded the dirty plates into the empty dishwasher, Kerry looked back at him from the kitchen.

She had seen him like this on many previous occasions, and she knew that his mind was pondering over every scenario, and every possible permutation of what befell their daughter.

She then came back through and cleared the rest of the table in silence before getting ready for work herself.

CHAPTER SEVEN

As with the previous day, Mike was working a late shift again, which ran from three o'clock until midnight.

Due to his potential, though yet unproven, personal involvement with the driver of the Focus ST, Mike didn't want to get directly involved with observing its actions anymore.

However, he still wanted to know more about the driver, in case they were one and the same. As a result, Mike decided to call in a favour.

He spoke to a couple of colleagues who worked the same area as him, firstly reminding them about the briefing slide, before asking them to bare the area around the college in mind, and to keep an eye out for a white Ford Focus with damage to the offside rear panel.

Then, only if they felt they had a legitimate reason, they should they follow it, and if necessary, stop the car and determine who the driver was.

He also asked that if anything was found to identify the vehicle, or its driver, then could this be fed back to him, but when asked what his interest was in this, he only mentioned that it may involve his daughter.

oOo

As it turned out, Mike's late shift was uneventful. Given that the team had an odd number of officers, in addition the sergeant, as Ian had taken the day off, he was on patrol on his own, which although meant for a lonely shift, he didn't have to run his decision making by anyone.

When it neared 2200hrs, or 10pm, he headed back to the police station to hand his vehicle over to the officers of the night shift.

Although, there was still two hours to go until the end of the shift, this time was designed to allow an overlap between the shifts so the officers of Mike's shift had time to complete any paperwork they might have before terminating without incurring overtime, without having reduced patrols on the streets.

As Mike didn't have a great deal of work to do, he was able to take his meal break in the canteen as opposed to eating at his desk, as was all too often the case.

It was as he ate his sandwich, one that he had bought from a petrol station on his way back to the police station, the same place where he and Ian had brought their coffee earlier in the set, his friend and colleague Craig came up to where he sat, only to crouch down at the table beside him.

"You got a minute?" Craig asked.

An unexpected voice, suddenly announcing itself to Mike, startled him.

"Hey bud, yeah, of course, what's up?" Mike replied having cleared his mouth.

"I saw that Focus that you asked me to keep an eye out for," Craig said, before recounting the incident earlier in the shift.

oOo

"We were driving up the London Road, and just as we were passing the entrance to the college, so we see a white Ford Focus ST pulling out. It was three-up, with a male driver.

He obviously clocked us early on coz he was making too much of an effort to abide by the limits, and not do anything to draw attention to himself and all that.

It was only when he approached the roundabout that he gave us a reason to tug him, as when he slowed for the roundabout it was apparent that he had a brake light out.

That gave us a reason to follow him until he approached a suitable place to pull him over.

But as we followed him, someone in the car must've started to certainly feel uneasy about us being there, as on several left-hand bends, objects started to emerge from underneath the car, y'know bits of crap and stuff, probably being deliberately dropped when the driver's side was momentarily out of sight from us following.

It didn't appear to be enough to make a big deal about, not when we really wanted to just have the car pulled over for you.

Anyway, we get onto a nice straight just before the dual-carriageway, and for a moment I think he forgot all about us, coz he gunned it away from the lights.

I think maybe he thought he could make it around the next bend before we got behind him again and turn into a side road.

But, anyway, he wasn't that quick, and had given us all we needed to pull him over.

When he stopped, apart from the brake light, the car was all in order,.

The driver's name is Neil Bannister, aged 22, he's local, found to be a bit of a shit-bag when we ran him through.

OCG affiliate, known for drug dealing. It's his car, all insured and taxed.

We then did checks on the only other person who was in the car, which was a young blonde girl.

She gave her age as seventeen, which looked about right, though she had no ID on her. The name and date of birth she gave us corroborated to a known record, so we had no reason to suspect otherwise.

Bannister got arsey with us when we stopped him. We didn't turn the car over, even though we could've done, given what we saw being thrown out.

We gave him a rectification notice for the brake light and we've done an intel report for the car and occupants.

oOo

Mike pondered the details of Craig's account, realising that one very crucial point had yet to be addressed.

"Did you notice any damage to the car?" he asked.

"Yeah, we did," Craig added. "It had a big ole scrape down the driver's side."

Mike nodded, but did his utmost not to smile, as he didn't want to give the game away.

"Cheers for doing that mate," Mike replied.

"No probs," Craig said as he stood up and left Mike to his sandwich.

Blonde girl, seventeen, Mike thought.

He considered that this could quite easily have been Ashley but didn't want to ask Craig anything further.

He felt that if his daughter's now giving false details to the police, she was, most certainly, on the brink of a precipice, having gotten in with the proverbial wrong crowd.

Mike then focused on the information Craig had given him about the driver, that of Neil Bannister, OCG member.

This acronym OCG referred to intelligence being held on Bannister that he was potentially a member of an organised crime group. He also had previous charges for drug dealing.

Mike considered this fact, as it would certainly substantiate that the items that were being discarded from the car as Craig was following it, were drugs and paraphernalia.

All things considered, Craig had in fact done Mike a huge favour this evening, as the outcome could have been quite different.

Craig and his crewmate, who wasn't in on the favour, could quite easily have used their substantiated grounds to search the car, and had that revealed anything, then they would have had no choice but to everyone in the car for drug related offences.

However, Craig must've thought as Mike did, and that being that this blonde female could quite easily have been his daughter Ashley, and that her arrest would've started a ball rolling and cause a giant headache for Mike.

In arresting those in the car would have led to fingerprints, interviews and possibly search warrants being issued for home addresses, and that would no doubt have resulted in Mike becoming involved at some point, should his address turn up on a search warrant.

Anything involving Mike's daughter, or a close relative of *any* serving police officer, would most likely result in the police's professional standards department, the department that monitors, regulates and adjudicates police behavioural and disciplinary matters, becoming involved, and Mike had already felt their wrath.

His previous experiences with them was what had resulted with him losing his detective sergeant rank and role, only to find himself busted back to being a uniformed police constable.

However, Mike could feel confident that his daughter being merely stopped in a car with drugs being found in it wouldn't be a hanging offence for either of them, but it would lead to further PSD intrusion, and this was something that Mike was keen to avoid if at all possible.

Craig had exercised discretion over the vehicle stop. But he had covered his bases well, and if ever he was to be challenged about his decision making, he would be able to say it was in the interests of gaining intelligence, letting a minnow go free to catch a whale.

oOo

It was nearly one o'clock in the morning, when Mike eventually pulled up outside his home address after work, and he was used to coming home to the house in darkness after a late shift, he was surprised to see that there were lights still on.

However, the lights that Mike could see from the street weren't on downstairs, instead were on in both upstairs front bedrooms, the room he shared with Kerry, as well as Ashley's bedroom.

Given what he had witnessed the previous evening, having parked up, as Mike approached the house, he felt a sense of trepidation.

Something was clearly amiss, and given recent events, Mike felt he had a good idea what was keeping everyone awake so late.

Mike turned his key in the front door and slowly pushed it open.

He stepped into the hallway and glanced upwards, towards the first-floor landing, only to instantly see the glow of warm lights dim, as either they were extinguished, or that doors were being closed. Either way, he felt his returning home was the reason for this.

Consequently, he had to question, had he inadvertently interrupted something yet unfinished, or had he merely timed his return to coincide with its conclusion?

Having learnt from previous lessons about misinterpreting coincidences, Mike didn't feel that there was any urgency to immediately head upstairs to investigate.

Instead, he took a deep breath before taking his coat off, which he draped over others, that had been lazily placed over the bottom of the banister, as opposed to being properly hung in the cupboard under the stairs.

He then continued past this cupboard, into the kitchen, and on into the dining room, where he pulled out a chair at the dining table and sat down.

For a moment he sat motionless and silent. He looked back towards the stairs and listened for any sounds coming from above him. When nothing came, he breathed a sigh of relief.

Mike then crossed one leg over the other in order to untie and remove his work boots, only to then place them neatly, side by side, under the table, assuring himself he would put them away, in their proper place, along with his coat in the morning.

He allowed himself a brief smile whilst reminiscing about a previous occasion when Kerry had voiced her objections in finding his discarded uniform strewn about the house after a shift.

Although Mike enjoyed having some time to himself when he got in from work, he still felt pressed to go upstairs sooner rather than later, and it was this need that prevented him from being able to relax until he had addressed it.

He stood up and went back to the of the doorway of the kitchen and looked back down the hallway towards the front door, before glancing upstairs, and again, he listened, and again nothing could be heard.

Mike decided to venture upstairs, and as his eyes became level with the first-floor landing, he could see a diminished glow still coming from under the closed doors of both bedrooms.

Without going any further, Mike paused and listened, though there were no sounds emanating from either room, or even the sound of a TV playing.

Knowing he had justification to do so, Mike went to his bedroom door and depressed the handle, though he did not know what, if anything, was waiting for him on the other side.

If didn't even know if Kerry was still awake, or if she had just fallen asleep having accidentally left a bedside light on.

Having pushed the door open, allowing the invitingly warm glow flooded out onto the landing, Mike popped his head around the door before entering the room any further.

He saw Kerry sat up in bed, and she had an open paperback novel in her hands, but she didn't appearing to be giving it any attention.

However, there was one thing that was immediately apparent, and that was that she had recently been crying.

Mike stepped further forward into the room, briefly glancing back at Ashley's bedroom, before gently pushing the door closed. As he heard the latch click into place, he grimaced at the noise it had made.

He then turned to face Kerry again, hoping to get answers to the questions she probably knew he would undoubtedly have given what he had been greeted with.

"What's happened?" was the first question that occurred to him to ask.

But before he could open his mouth to utter those two simple words Kerry replied in anticipation of this question, and Mike could see the overwhelming upset in her eyes as she prepared to speak.

"He's done it *again*, Mike," she said, before being overcome with emotion. "He's hurt our baby *again*."

To avoid her upset being heard from the next room, Kerry grabbed a pillow from behind her, and buried her face in it to muffle her momentary outburst of emotion.

Mike stepped forward and sat himself down on Kerry's side of the bed. He reached out with his arms and took hold of her, only then did she lift her head to speak further.

"She came home about an hour ago," Kerry began to explain. "She tried to sneak in, and rush up straight upstairs without saying anything.

"I was in the bathroom, and she burst in on me as I was just finishing having a shower.

"She was obviously trying to make sure I didn't see anything, instead I saw *everything*."

Mike could feel an anger grow within him, but given the circumstances, he didn't want Kerry to see it in his expression, so he held her close, whispering his questions into her ear.

"What's he done," Mike asked, whilst trying his best to remain calm. "Has he hit her?"

Kerry tried to verbalise a response, but the words wouldn't come.

Mike released his embrace, retaining a hold of her hand, allowing her to she sat there momentarily, dumbfounded, until she eventually nodded to confirm Mike's fears.

However, with that confirmation, in an instant it all became too much for Mike, and he stood up, before backing away from the side of the bed, only to turn and start heading back towards the bedroom door.

"No Mike," Kerry exclaimed, in a soft yet authoritative tone, as she was trying not to draw any attention to them from the other room. "Leave her, please, not tonight.

"Let her be, let her sleep.

"She's upset enough about it as it is.

"We can talk about it in the morning."

By this time, Mike had reached the door, only to be halted in mid-action of depressing the handle and pulling it open.

He realised that Kerry was right, and that no good would come from disturbing Ashley and having her relive her ordeal yet again for his benefit alone, not at that time of night.

Everyone was already distressed enough about what had happened without unnecessary reiteration.

Mike pushed the door closed again, before slowly releasing the handle, for the latch to silently find its home.

He then turned to face Kerry, realising that he was in no fit state to get into bed, as the adrenaline that had started to surge through his system needed more time to dissipate.

"I need to have a shower," he said, almost asking permission to go out of the bedroom and onto the landing.

Kerry nodded as she rolled over to turn off her bedside lamp, just as Mike left the now darkness of the bedroom as he stepped back out onto the landing.

He could see that Ashley had also settled down, or at the very least, she too had turned her lights off. This meant that the only light was that which came through the landing window, emanating from the streetlights in front of the house.

Mike showered for much longer than he would ever do normally, as he always tended to just wash and go. But he remained until the shower until he felt relaxed enough to at least try to get some sleep.

It had gone 2AM by the time he eventually laid down next to Kerry, having looked over at the time illuminated by his watch.

Mercifully the sounds of upset were now a memory, as both bedrooms were in total silence.

CHAPTER EIGHT

The next day started off awkwardly for both Mike and Kerry, as they had both got up and started their day anxious to see Ashley, but without either of them knowing what to say to her.

Mike didn't have to be at work until that evening, but Kerry had messaged her employer, saying she was going to be late, as they both wanted the chance to see their daughter, and hopefully begin addressing the situation that befell them.

However, as it turned out, Ashley did not venture out of her bedroom until after lunchtime.

Prior to hearing the muffled sound of socked feet creeping down the stairs, Kerry and Mike heard another prolonged shower. Then it was only after a further significant delay that they finally set eyes on their daughter.

It was immediately apparent that Ashley had gone to great lengths to try and hide what she wanted to keep from her parents, but the heat, and the steam from the shower, as well as significant time in front of a mirror had achieved very little when it came to hiding her injuries from the previous evening.

Knowing she could only delay the inevitable so much, Ashley tentatively walked into the kitchen, and seeing her mother there, who she expected to be at work, she knew to expect something of an inquisition from her parents.

However, the expected interrogation didn't commence the moment they saw her. Instead, it was all smiles as, what was effectively, breakfast was served as quickly as possible, for them to sit down as a family.

Both Mike and Kerry knew Ashley hadn't eaten anything since early the previous evening, so they both had the restraint not to say anything until after Ashley had eaten her fill.

But, in the uncomfortable silence, Ashley could feel their gaze on her as she finished her breakfast.

Mike looked over at Kerry, and once again, he appeared to almost be seeking her permission upon which to act.

Despite discussions before Ashley emerged, neither Mike, nor Kerry knew how to begin what they both wanted to say.

They knew what they wanted to achieve, but equally they knew that one word out of place could cause Ashley to clam up.

"Well?" Ashley said defiantly. "Someone say something for fuck's sake."

The expletive being used solely to shock her parents out of stasis.

The shock lingered on Mike longer than it did for Kerry, so it inadvertently fell to her to break the silence.

"We never did get to talk about what happened last night sweetie," Kerry said. "Will you tell us now?"

It was evident that this was the question that Ashley had expected, as she replied without any emotion, almost as if it had been rehearsed for minimal effect.

"There's not much to tell," Ashley nonchalantly replied. "I answered back, and I got a slap for my trouble, my own fault really."

Kerry looked over to Mike, she was hoping he would save them from another uncomfortable silence.

"That's way more than just a slap, Ash," Mike added. "How did you get home last night?"

In her mind, Ashley had hoped that her first response would be seen as sufficient, consequently she hadn't planned any responses beyond that.

"He kicked me out of the car," she continued. "I mean literally kicked me out.

"Then, he reversed, trying to catch me with the car door. He then sped off, and I got left there."

Mike had been expecting an explanation that involved an assault, but he had never expected anything like that. Though he knew to keep his response to a minimum.

"For fuck's sake!" he muttered under his breath.

His volume was barely inaudible, and he shook his head at Ashley, who was now looking down at the table.

She appeared ashamed in what she had just disclosed to her parents. Though they were yet to understand if her shame came as a result of what had happened to her, or the fact that Ashley had now told them.

"So, what's happening between you two now?" Mike asked, hoping for a distinctly negative response.

Though no reply came from Ashley. Instead, all she gave a slight upwards glance, just enough to see her father angle his head down to try and catch her eye.

Her response was then to only shrug her shoulders, suggesting that the situation was yet undecided.

"You can't go back to him Ashley," Kerry interjected. "What's going to happen next time?"

This was a mother's desperate attempt to get her daughter to consider a possible worst-case scenario.

"What do you want me to do?" Ashley said softly.

"Personally, I would like you to report all of this to the police," Kerry said, looking over towards Mike, who in turn nodded his agreement.

"Uh, uh, no way," Ashley exclaimed. "I ain't talking to the *Feds* about this."

Mike shook his head in both disappointment and disgust, not only for her refusal to abide by their wishes, but he hated that expression; *The Feds,* having been called it many times.

He understood the entomology of the term, having been derived from the American Federal Bureau of Investigation, the FBI. But still, he hated being called it when out on the streets, but even more so by his daughter, in his own home.

"Well, you're not going back to him," Kerry added. "We forbid it,"

Without any acknowledgment of any kind, Ashley got up from the table.

She gave her mother a defiant glare, before leaving the kitchen, only to go back upstairs.

On each step there was what sounded to be a deliberately loud footfall, only to be followed by the sound of an upstairs door being slammed shut.

There was a momentary pause as both Mike and Kerry assimilated what had just taken place. After which Mike addressed the situation.

"You know we're not going to be able to enforce whether or not she chooses to see him anymore," Mike began. "But I'll tell you this now, if she does go back to him, and if anything like this happens again, I'll be making a report of this myself."

Kerry nodded her approval. She stood up, and stepped in close to him, wanting Mike to take hold of her.

They both knew how precarious this situation had become, and just how perilous it could be for Ashley.

They also felt that what she had disclosed to them was, most likely, just the tip of the iceberg.

Their daughter had never been so secretive before.

But how best to deal with this caused a dilemma neither of them wanted to contemplate.

CHAPTER NINE

Following his first night shift, which had Mike return home just after four o'clock in the morning, and as unlikely as the necessity was for it, given that late hour, he still breathed a sigh of relief, as he turned the corner into his road, and approached his house, he saw that there were no lights on as was the case the previous night.

However, it was only once he had pulled up and parked in front of the house that he realised that the driveway was empty.

Habitually, Mike had expected to see Kerry's car parked there, which was what necessitated him having to park in the street.

Mike immediately sensed that something was amiss, and given recent events, his mind leapt to worst case scenario.

Without even turning the engine off, Mike fumbled in his pocket to find his mobile phone.

When he found it, he saw he had already, and unbeknown to him, received a text message.

The message was from Kerry, and it simply read:

Call me

Mike tapped on the *information* icon in the corner of the phone's screen, before tapping on the icon of a telephone receiver, to return a call to the sender.

However, the call was not answered, as it didn't even connect.

Instead, it went directly to a voicemail facility, which indicated that either Kerry had switched her phone off, her battery had died, or that she was somewhere where there was no cell phone signal.

After the pre-recorded greeting, Mike was able to leave his own message.

"Call me back when you get this message," was all he said, before ending the call.

Mike was now concerned, and as his mind descended into chaos, so random ideas started running through his head.

But he knew he shouldn't entertain anything that taunted him until such time he had something more to substantiate them.

Not knowing what else to do in that moment, Mike reluctantly turned off the car's engine, before alighting from his car and approach the house.

But, before putting his key in the front door, he checked his phone again, in the vague hope that he would see a reply from Kerry, however there was nothing.

He resigned himself to reluctantly having to play the waiting game, putting his key in the lock, and entering the house.

Once inside, Mike chose to abandon his routine and any expectation he had for preparing himself for bed. Instead, he remained hopeful that he would receive an expeditious reply.

Consequently, feeling that he wouldn't be home for long, he only took off his coat, leaving it on the banister was he passed it, before walking through into the kitchen.

Mike turned the lights on, set his phone down on the counter, and went to one of the cupboards, where he took a bag of crisps from a multipack.

Closing the cupboard, he turned his back to the counter and leaned back against it.

After a few moments Mike had finished the crisps.

He went over to the kitchen bin, to put the empty bag in it, only to see that there several bloodied tissues littering the top of the rubbish.

The amount of blood wasn't significant, certainly not to suggest a life-threatening injury, but nonetheless, without a known cause, it was concerning.

However, this added to the fact that he had come home to an empty house, on top of everything else that had been happening, the gravity of the situation instantly dawned on him.

Mike snatched his phone from the counter, from where he had set it down, and viewed the screen, hopeful that it had news for him, but still there was nothing.

He redialled Kerry's number hoping that this time the call would connect.

Then pre-empting it being answered, Mike left the kitchen and re-entered the hallway, only to grab his coat as he made his way towards the front door.

However, once again, the call didn't connect, and Mike had only the option of leaving yet another voicemail message.

"I don't know where you guys are, but I'm heading to the hospital," he said, leaping to conclusions. "Call me when you get this message."

Having put his coat back on, he was out the front door.

Once Mike was back in his car, he was forced to put his phone down on the passenger seat beside him, momentarily cursing himself for not having invested in a car cradle for it.

He then sped off towards the local hospital, doing his best to remained focused on his driving whilst banishing terrible thoughts from his head.

CHAPTER TEN

The drive to the hospital was excruciating, with Mike's mind bouncing between what he perceived to be worst case scenario, and not hitting on-coming obstacles in the road.

When he eventually arrived at the hospital, he chose not to bother parking in the public pay & display car park as he should.

Instead, he parked in a row of bays that had been set aside, and especially marked as being for *EMERGENCY VEHICLES ONLY,* that ran alongside the ambulance rank outside of the accident and emergency department.

He knew he shouldn't park in one of these bays as he was off duty, and attending the hospital in a civilian capacity and knew that his actions could be seen as an abuse of his position as a police officer.

But of the three bays allocated, none were presently being used, besides given the circumstances for which he was attending the hospital, he really didn't care, and would take a reprimand at a later time, should one be deemed necessary.

Having parked, Mike entered the reception area for the accident and emergency department and approached the counter.

When it was finally his turn to be seen, he asked if an Ashley Watkins had been admitted, and whilst the receptionist checked the name given against her records of patients presently booked in, he silently prayed that the answer would be a no.

However, his heart fell when the receptionist instead asked him for further information.

"And what relation are you?" she asked.

This further questioning confirmed that Ashley was there.

"I'm… I'm her father," he replied anxiously.

"She's been booked into A&E," the receptionist explained, whilst indicating to her right. "Go through that door, then follow the corridor around to the left, and you'll see the nurses' station, I'll buzz you through."

As Mike approached the door, he heard an audible *click* as the electro-magnetic lock released granting his access.

However, Mike didn't need to rely on the directions that were given to him by the receptionist, as he knew the layout of the hospital all too well, having had many dealings there during his career.

Consequently, he knew exactly where he needed to go to find the nurses' station within the main accident and emergency department.

Having arrived at the nurses' station, as it was a hive of activity, Mike had to again patiently wait his turn to be spoken to. This was despite the growing urge within him to get answers.

However, despite the urge to do so, and having abused his position to leave his car as he had, Mike thought better of asserting his role as a police officer, albeit an off-duty one, to expedite his enquiries.

"Good evening," Mike said, as calmly as he could, when it came to his turn. "I understand you have an Ashley Watkins here…? I'm her father."

Without replying, the nurse looked away and began tapping away at her keyboard, and without even so much as an upward glance, she replied in somewhat a robotic tone.

"Bay twelve," was all she said.

"Thank you," Mike replied, as he turned and briskly walked off.

Once again, he knew exactly where he was heading, which proved useful in this instance, as the nurse wasn't as helpful as the receptionist had been.

As Mike approached the nominated bay, he saw that the curtains were drawn across the cubicle, which indicated the likelihood that medical staff were inside, and that a consultation, or treatment was in the process of taking place.

Again, Mike had drawn these conclusions based on prior experience, knowing that staff didn't like the curtains to be drawn at any other time, as they weren't able to casually monitor the condition of a patient the same as if the curtains were open.

Equally, Mike didn't want to disturb any treatment in progress, so he waited outside and listened, and tried to determine what was going on inside from what was being said.

After a few moments, the curtains were pulled back, and two staff members walked out.

One was dressed in pink coloured scrubs, the other wearing black scrubs, with the colours denoting various ranks and roles within the hospital, though Mike was not aware specifically what each colour represented. They both walked past him, without any acknowledgement, back towards the nurses' station.

With the cubicle now exposed and open to the department, Mike felt it was now appropriate for him to approach.

He was dreading what would greet him when he walked clear of the end of the preceding bay which had its curtain closed.

Mike turned the corner to see Ashley sat up on the trolley bed, he also saw Kerry standing by her side.

She was in the process of brushing Ashley's hair back with one hand, whilst resting the other on the back of Ashley's which was resting at her side. They both instinctively looked up and towards Mike as he came into view.

Mike was greeted by a welcoming smile from Kerry, and a whispered and pained greeting from Ashley

"Daddy" was all she said.

"Hey monkey," he replied.

This was a nickname he had for his little girl since the day she could set one foot in front of the other, and she had been his *little monkey* ever since.

Mike was relieved and overjoyed to see his little girl in such good spirits, despite the yet undisclosed reason for her being there.

But any degree of urgency he felt was diminished by seeing the state she was in.

Her eyes were puffy, in what was becoming an all too familiar sight, once again, at the very least, suggesting that she had been crying.

But worse still, Mike saw the tragic aftermath of a significant blow to her face, which had resulted in what was being treated as a broken nose.

Ashley also had significant swelling under both eyes, the swelling was blood red in colour signifying substantial bruising. It sickened Mike to look at it.

Kerry could sense that Mike was looking over Ashley's injuries and offered a lay interpretation of what the medical staff had said.

"She's been x-rayed, and there's no signs of any fractures," she said. "They didn't need to do anything to straighten it.

"They said the swelling will subside in time, and you've just missed them as they've literally just this minute discharged her."

"I saw them as I was coming in," Mike replied. "I *won't* ask how this happened, as I think I already know."

He looked back at Ashley, who now looked somewhat ashamed of the situation she had now once again found herself in.

"Well, we don't need to talk about any of that now," he continued. "And certainly *not* here. Let's just get you home."

Ashley cautiously leant forward to get up, and seeing her apparent discomfort, Mike stepped along the other side of the trolley bed, opposite Kerry, and between them they helped Ashley sit upright and get her coat back on.

She then swung her legs off the side of the trolley, towards her mother, and inched herself forward until her feet finally found the floor.

Then ever so gradually she added weight to them until she felt confident her legs would support her.

By this time Mike had come back around the trolley, and with a parent now on each arm, Ashley finally stood up.

Her legs were understandably shaky, despite only suffering a head injury, after having been inactive for so long.

Now confident in her abilities, Ashley sat back down, and allowed Kerry to slip her shoes back on for her.

When all was ready, Ashley again took to her feet, and cautiously whilst utilising her mother for moral, and physical support, allowed her father to lead them towards the exit.

Mike thanked the staff as they passed the nurses' station, though he got nothing in the way of a response.

After paying for Kerry's parking, at a payment machine in the A&E reception waiting area, Mike walked with Kerry and Ashley back to where Kerry had parked her car.

"Where are you parked?" Kerry asked.

"Oh, I abandoned mine in one of the emergency bays," he replied.

Kerry looked back towards the rank of bays designated for ambulances, wondering if she could see Mike's car.

"Can you get into trouble for doing that?" Kerry asked. "That's the last thing you need."

"Maybe," Mike replied. "But that's the least of my worries right now."

He looked towards where Ashley now sat, in the front passenger seat of Kerry's car, with the door still open.

His was meant as a look of concern, though given the proceeding comment, she took it as a scornful look.

"See you guys at home," he said, closing Ashley's door, whilst watching Kerry walk around to hers.

Only once they were under way, did Mike walk back to where he had left his own car.

oOo

During the journey home, Mike had easily been able to catch up with Kerry, so they all arrived home at the same time.

By the time, the convoy pulled up at the home address, Ashley was fast asleep in Kerry's passenger seat.

Not wanting to wake her, Mike chose to cradle carried her from the car, and followed Kerry into the house, and took her straight upstairs.

He laid her down in her bed, and assisted by Kerry, they removed her coat and shoes, before covering her over with the bedding.

When all was done, from the doorway, they looked back in on her, and with the shadows of the room hiding her injuries, her parents enjoyed the moment of looking in on her sleeping peacefully much as they had done countless times over the last seventeen years.

They both then went back downstairs, leaving Ashley's bedroom door open.

Back in the kitchen, Kerry made coffees for them both, as Mike propped himself against the counter next to her.

"This, stops now," he said vehemently. "We've got to do something."

Kerry turned and set a steaming hot mug of coffee in front of him, before walking past him with hers, to take a seat at the dining table.

Mike picked up his and followed on behind her, taking a seat at the table himself.

Kerry looked dismayed, knowing that Mike was right, but reminding herself of how their previous discussion had ended, she knew they had only one chance to get things right.

Knowing if they struck the wrong balance, they could inadvertently drive Ashley further into this abusive relationship. But conversely, they both knew that they couldn't just leave the situation as it was.

"Do you think we should report this to the police then?" she asked.

Mike paused, long enough to run through all available options in his mind before offering a reply. He started nodded before the words came.

"I really don't think we have *any* other option," he began to explain. "If we don't do anything this is *only* going to continue, and maybe *even* get worse.

If we do *anything*, it'll change things for sure, it's just a case of whether things initially get better or worse.

"But I'm hoping it can only get better in the long term.

"That said, there's no way of knowing anything for sure. But I do know we can't just sit back and allow this to continue *without* doing anything."

He looked over at Kerry who nodded her agreement.

"What do you suggest then?" she asked, wanting clarification. "Go to the police?"

Again, Mike paused, before committing himself to a course of action.

"I honestly think it's our *only* option," he eventually replied. "Hopefully, they'll be able to put something in place to offer Ashley some protection going forward.

"The trouble is, a lot of what needs to happen is dependent on Ash, and whether she'll co-operate with what's needed.

"Sure, we can give our accounts of what we *believe* took place, and there also medical records to show the injuries, but that can all be disputed, unless she prepared to say exactly what happened.

"I can make the report, but she'll need to be on board with it when they contact her."

"They?" Kerry asked.

"My old team," Mike continued. "This will be considered a domestic situation, as they'll assume there's been intimacy between Ash and this prick, until they're convinced otherwise, which is unlikely given their ages.

"Even if it's *not* a domestic, it's still an assault, but she considered to be at greater risk within a relationship, hence a specialist team being assigned to deal with it."

"So, when are we gonna do this?" Kerry asked.

Mike hesitated in his explanation, as he knew that once the report is made there's no going back on it, and he knew that he and Kerry needed to be united before committing to this course of action.

"Well, there's no half-arsed way to do this," Mike said, continuing his explanation. "It's not a case of making a report and asking for nothing to happen, despite what people may think. You report a crime to the police, and they have a duty to investigate it.

"So, if we start the ball rolling on this, it will most likely result in him being nicked, and interviewed, and God only knows where that's gonna lead.

"Like I say, *we* can start the ball rolling, but without Ash saying what happened, this could get messy."

"Messy how?" Kerry felt reluctantly compelled to ask, a look of concern on her face.

"Well, if we report this, and she doesn't confirm anything, then there'll be no evidence to prove anything has taken place," Mike said. "As a result, nothing will change other than him being pissed off at being nicked. Now, this needs to be something we agree upon *before* we act, as there are no guarantees here."

With every word spoken, Kerry was becoming less and less convinced that this was a good idea, despite knowing that things can't remain as they were.

"Well, nothing like having things black and white in front of you," she replied. "And this is nothing like having things black and white.

"I hate it whenever she goes out, wondering what injuries she'll come back with… And she's not going to break away from this all by herself, is she?"

Having taken a sip of his coffee, Mike shook his head before swallowing and being able to verbalise his sentiment.

"Unlikely," he said.

Mike set his mug down and stood up from the table.

He then walked around it, so he was standing directly behind where Kerry was still sat, and placed his hands on her shoulders, before leaning in, only to plant a kiss on the side of her neck. He then spoke softly into her ear.

"Only *if* we're in agreement," he said. "I'll get things started tomorrow."

Kerry then placed one hand on top of one of Mike's, before nodding, signifying her agreement.

CHAPTER ELEVEN

The next morning, Mike was good to his word when he made the call to the police and went through the proper channels to file a report of violence against his daughter.

As he was not working until that evening, he was able to make the call from home.

However, when it came to providing details of the suspect, Mike was forced to be intentionally vague.

He had to confirm that he didn't know the name of the other party involved, only that his daughter had been seen leaving in a white Ford Focus ST, and that the driver, believed to be her boyfriend, was the presumed suspect.

Although the information provided about the suspect would not be enough to identify him, Mike knew that the information he could give would be enough for the police to at least start their enquiries to identify him.

The call concluded with Mike being informed by the call-taker that enquires would be made in the hope of identifying the other party involved. But, in the meantime, an officer would need to come out and speak to Ashley to get her account, and to also document her injuries.

He was also informed that the department that ultimately would be assigned this investigation dealt with all investigations of this similar nature across the borough in which Mike lived.

Mike didn't work the area in which he lived. As a result, he would never routinely be deployed to attend an incident close to home. Instead, he worked in an adjoining borough for just that reason. That was however, unless it was ever deemed necessary due to resourcing requirements.

oOo

Later the same day, Mike received a phone call from an officer on the public protection team.

He breathed a sigh of relief when he didn't recognise either the name, or the voice of the caller, as he didn't want to get drawn into the personal side of things.

The call came to Mike as his were the only contact details on the report, added to which, it was a third-party report, meaning that the alleged victim had not made the report to police themselves. This meant that all arrangements to speak to the alleged victim had to come via him.

However, due to the ever-increasing workload of the domestic abuse team, an appointment to see Ashley couldn't be scheduled until Mike had gone back to work after his rest days, which meant they wouldn't be coming to speak to Ashley until a week after the reported assault took place.

oOo

Right or wrong, feeling how Ashley was likely to react to news of the police report, Mike and Kerry felt it best to keep her in the dark about it until the moment the officer attended.

Then having received confirmation of the appointment, on the day it was due to take place, it was then Kerry's job to keep Ashley at home for when the officer was scheduled to attend.

oOo

The evening after the scheduled visit, Mike drive home with a feeling of trepidation.

He knew from experience that police intervention in such a matter always changed things, it was just a matter of whether it was for the better, or worse.

When he got in, he was greeted by Kerry, only for those feelings to begin to be realised when he discovered that Ashley was once again nowhere to be seen.

"So, how did today go then?" he tentatively asked.

"Don't ask," replied Kerry, whilst shaking her head, and looking to the floor in disappointment.

Mike's shoulders dropped, along with his expression and spirits, however, defiant of Kerry's wish he continued.

"What happened?" he asked.

Having handed Mike a fresh coffee, she led him through to the dining room, where they both took a seat.

"I thought I was doing well by keeping her here when the officer arrived," Kerry began to explain. "I was here, Ash was here, and all appeared to be going so well.

"But before Ash agreed to answer any questions, she insisted on asking what was going to happen next, and so on.

"And, as soon as the officer said it was likely that this guy was going to have to be spoken to about this, and there was a possibility to do that, he was going to have be arrested, she clammed up.

"Her expression immediately changed, and after that she wouldn't say anything. Then shortly afterwards, she just said *I'm not doing this anymore,* and stormed off.

Afterwards the officer said that she could evidence the injuries herself having seen them, but without any testimony from Ash as to how they happened, then she doubted the investigation will go any further.

"she says they'll still need to speak to the lad because an allegation had still been made. The PC gave his name as something Banister, which Ash wouldn't even confirm… But unless he admits to anything, chances are it won't be going anywhere, and we'll have done all this for nothing."

Mike shared Kerry's disappointment, and his reaction mirrored her initial one, his head shook as it bowed.

"Well, we knew this was a possibility from the start," he said. "Where is she now?"

But mike knew the answer before even asking the question.

"I don't know for sure," Kerry replied. "She's not answering her phone, but I've got a good idea of who she's with."

"Yeah," Mike replied. "Me too."

This was exactly the position that Mike didn't want them to be in. They had started the ball rolling and had already passed the point of no return.

Even without anything in the way of co-operation from Ashley, the police had still received a report of an alleged crime, and as a result were duty bound to investigate it, with or without a victim testimony.

As the attending officer had said, without a testimony from the victim, even with the police documenting the injuries seen on Ashley, and the medical reports generated at the hospital, there was no way of categorically stating, beyond all reasonable doubt, the threshold by which blamed is determined, how they were caused, or by whom.

"We need to talk to her," Mike concluded. "Try to get her see the bigger picture here, and to reconsider."

"Oh, believe me I know," Kerry replied. "The only question is how?

"But now, with her knowing about what's likely to happen to him, she's not going to want to say anything, for whatever reason, protecting him, or protecting herself."

Everything that Kerry was saying was right, and it just make the situation they were now in all the more difficult.

"I know," Mike said. "But we at least have to try, otherwise we're buggered!"

He then looked at his watch, to see that it was coming up on five o'clock.

"If she's not home by nine," he said. "I think we should at least consider reporting her as missing."

"Given everything that's happened, do you really think we should wait *that* long?" Kerry replied.

"No," Mike replied, trying to rationalise. "But I still want to give her the chance to make good decisions by herself, but if she proves she can't, then we'll have to."

Kerry got up from the table, wandered around to Mike's side, and slipped her arms around him, before burying her face in the side of his neck.

oOo

As the evening wore on, so did Mike and Kerry's patience.

Although the had been sat in front of the television since having finished dinner, they weren't focused on the programme being shown.

Instead, they were clock watching, incessantly looking at phones and watches, unable to focus or think about anything else other than where their daughter presently was.

But as the evening drew on, they decided to push back the time limit of calling the police to midnight.

They also agreed on not stay up specially to await Ashley's return, as they didn't want to have Ashley feel any pressure from them.

As a result, they were both in bed, though awake when they finally heard Ashley come through the front door.

Kerry was out of bed like a shot. Though not to the door to see encroach on Ashley coming in, instead she went to the window to see if anyone had dropped her off.

As she parted the curtains she looked out upon a desolate scene, of a deserted street, with not a pedestrian or moving vehicle in sight.

Once again, Mike and Kerry would go to bed restless, with so much on their minds.

They knew they had to make further attempts to gain Ashley's co-operation, if not there was no way of telling where this situation would now lead.

But until then, at least they knew their daughter was home, safe and sound.

CHAPTER TWELVE

Mike's next shift at work was another early shift, his second of two, which meant that once again, he needed to be at work in time for the 7am start, and was scheduled to end at 4pm.

As always, the shift started with a briefing, and again this contained a slideshow of intelligence topics, as well as wanted individuals.

It was amongst this part of the briefing that one slide in particular caught Mike's attention.

This slide showed an individual that was wanted in connection with a *domestic abh (actual bodily harm)* assault, which was not at all unusual.

The suspect was named as Neil Bannister, and the slide also gave details of the offence he was wanted in connection with, although it didn't give any details of the alleged victim.

It was as he looked at this slide that Mike had an epiphany, for the name Bannister rang a bell for him.

It was only then that he realised that this was the very same name that Kerry had mentioned the previous evening.

Paying ever more attention to the limited information on the slide, Mike realised that as this was a restricted report. Though this could be for any one of many reasons, one of the most commonly known was a when the report involved a serving officer in one capacity or another.

He considered for a moment if this was why Ashley's name had been omitted from the slide, as it was designed to protect Mike and his family from having anyone other than the investigating team being aware of the connection.

The slide did however show a photograph of the suspect from his most recent stay in police custody, which was dated only about six months previously.

It also gave Bannister's last known address, and details of a vehicle he was known to use.

Having made the connection, based on the surname, Mike believed the address was probably out of date, as was the vehicle, as Bannister was shown as still being the owner of a black VW Golf.

Evidently, the intelligence report that Craig had submitted, following his stop of the Ford Focus, had yet to filter down to the divisional intelligence unit, as it had yet to feature on the briefings. If, in fact he had submitted the report despite the update he had given to Mike.

Now that the assault had been reported, and despite the police being aware of Ashley's lack of co-operation, the ball would most certainly roll on regardless.

It was now just a matter of time before Bannister would be located and arrested. But this was a case involving the proverbial piece of string, and how long that would eventually take was anyone's guess.

But there was one thing Mike did know for sure, and that was that he had to have faith in the system, and let the police do their job unhindered by him.

He was no longer able to influence anything that happened from the moment he had chosen to report the assault.

He wouldn't even be able to monitor, or review the investigation as it progressed, and any intrusion on his part could have a significantly detrimental effect on the outcome should it go as far as being heard in court.

If Mike's hunch was right, the investigation was probably be flagged as restricted anyway, which meant that the details of it would only be accessible by the investigating officer and his supervisor.

It wouldn't be able to be viewed by anyone else without them having first sought the necessary clearance, and any attempt to access the report would raise a flag which would identify the officer making the attempt.

This officer would then have to justify their reasoning for their attempted access, and if there wasn't a legitimate reason, then there was the potential for disciplinary action.

Access to police information was strictly monitored, and all access was audited, and in some cases, individual entries had to be justified why they were being accessed. Whilst other data bases were subjected to dip-checks, and once again a plausible explanation would be expected with consequences should one not be forthcoming.

This was certainly the case in Mike's force, and probably nationally that periodically officers had to periodically provide information of their immediate family members, associates and relationships.

The details of these associations would then be scrutinised against the officer's search audits to see if the officer in question had been using police databases to look up anyone for non-policing reasons.

Should anything be detected, this was again a disciplinary offence and carried the likelihood of dismissal as well as the possibility of criminal charges. This was why Mike dismissed Kerry's accusation about him performing checks on Ashley's boyfriend in the beginning.

The best things Mike could do now would be to distance himself from Bannister, and not be tempted to check on the progress of the investigation.

At seventeen years of age, Ashley was considered a minor, meaning she was still legally a child, and Mike was her parent. As such, as per the victim's charter, either he or Kerry would be kept informed of the progress of the investigation, so he had to rely on that and allow things to take their course.

Mike was now in two minds about having asked for Craig's involvement, not so much the traffic stop, and speaking to Bannister, but the intel report he subsequently submitted.

On the plus side, the details it would have contained would give more up to date information about Bannister, as clearly the current intel, as shown on the briefing slide, was out of date, given that the vehicle associated with him was redundant, then his home address could very well be too.

Conversely, the existence of the very same intel report would link Craig to Bannister, and however unlikely, if he was to ever be spoken to about the traffic stop, and his resulting decisions, then he may inadvertently implicate Mike.

However, Mike dismissed his paranoia at him purely being nervous, and overly cautious about Ashley's investigation becoming scuppered, or the subject of scrutiny, as so many have with police officers becoming involved as either the victim, or worse still the perpetrator, as Mike knew all too well.

Mike knew he had fallen foul of the system before, and on that previous occasion, it had cost him dearly, though not nearly as dearly as it could have done, after all, he still had his job.

oOo

Before he had been reprimanded and demoted, Mike had been a detective sergeant in the force's public protection unit.

Though it wasn't a role he particularly enjoyed, he merely saw it as a necessary move for him to get his sergeant stripes following the promotion process.

But, despite, his aversion to the role, Mike had worked hard, making his mark, as well as a positive contribution to the team.

He had led the investigative team which had prosecuted some extreme, and brutally violent domestic cases, including a few which had resulted in serious injuries being sustained by the victims.

However, anything that resulted in a fatality was dealt with by a different team, either CID, or the Serious Crimes Team.

Whilst on the team, Mike had earned himself several divisional commendations for his work. But none of this made any difference when he chose to blur the lines between what is and isn't acceptable for a police officer in the manner they choose to treat a prisoner in their care, and this compelled Mike to think back to the events that started his fall from grace.

oOo

<u>Eight Months Earlier</u>

Following a report being made to the police by a friend of an apparent victim of domestic abuse, Mike, who was at the time a detective sergeant in the PPU, along with a fellow officer had made arrangements to visit the victim at her place of work, in the hopes of gaining her confidence and co-operation.

The information that the friend had already provided them with about the victim, the suspect, their relationship, and the history of systematic abuse, was detailed, however without the support of the victim themselves, it could only help them so much.

The report made for difficult reading and provided an account that described a prolonged period of sustained domestic abuse in all its forms.

It described physical assaults, although none that had been witnesses first-hand. But the resulting injuries had been seen, and explanations offered by the victim, along with on every occasion, the victim had blamed herself for upsetting the suspect.

Psychological and emotional abuse, with the victim saying that the suspect was constantly belittling her and telling her that no one else will ever love her, and should she ever leave him he would ensure that she never got to see her child again.

It was also claimed that rape was a frequent occurrence, though the extent of the details shared with the friend was limited, and this would need to be explored as the matter of consent was undetermined.

There was also mention of taking control of the family finances, leaving the victim with the bare minimum to get by, and having to justify every penny spent.

This all added up to a very bleak situation, one where the police knew so much, but could presently prove very little, and that everything was dependent on securing the victim's cooperation.

However, having met with the victim, Mike persevered, and gained her confidence, with the victim choosing to show the officers the result of injuries from recent, as well as more historic physical abuse, which included some permanent scarring.

Mike had dealt with a significant number of domestic victims during his entire policing career. But after this meeting, he and his colleague agreed that this case was amongst the some of the worst they had seen.

After all the necessary information had been obtained, alternative arrangements had to be made to temporarily house the victim elsewhere.

This was deemed necessary as early attempts to arrest the suspect had proven unsuccessful, both at the home address and his place of work, and police didn't want the victim going back there and being exposed to a higher risk following the realisation of police involvement.

The suspect, her long-term partner Philip Mercer, turned out to be well known the police for reasons other than being a domestic abuse perpetrator, as when the initial report was being compiled, it opened what was virtually an Aladdin's cave of intelligence on him.

Mercer, however, was much like Al Capone, or at least that was how he liked to consider himself, as he believed himself to be something of a local gangster, with an army of loyal followers below him.

He was shown to have a colourful history with the police. However due to the resources at his disposal, nothing significant was able to stick.

So, in this respect was he most like Capone. Despite being investigated for numerous offences linking him to organised crime, Capone was only ever convicted and imprisoned for tax evasion, and again like Capone, Mercer was to prove equally evasive when it came to his apprehension.

Numerous enquiries were conducted, and attempts made in order to locate and arrest Mercer for the alleged abuse. However, these were to prove fruitless.

Requests had been made to his neighbours, and Mercer's employers to advise police should he either return home or attend work. Despite his criminal activities, Mercer had what appeared to be a legitimate income, and as such he had a place of employment.

Also, markers had been placed on him personally, as well as on all vehicle linked to him. This was to ensure that should anything flag up, anywhere in the country, then instructions would be provided for immediate action to be taken.

It was in response to one such vehicle alert that the Mercer was eventually stopped by police, and given the instructions on the alert, he was detained.

This happened in another police force area, when he was stopped by the local police for an unrelated traffic offence, driving a vehicle that was not linked to him, therefore did not have a marker linked to it.

However, when they ran the driver's details through, the wanted marker, for the domestic incident, flagged up. Consequently, Mercer was arrested on suspicion of the domestic assault, after which he was taken to the other force's custody centre before making Mike's force aware of the arrest.

However, at the time the notification was received, due to limited available resources of staff, it fell to Mike and a detective constable to take a police van and drive to the other police force to collect their prisoner, in order to bring him back for interviewing.

The outbound journey took almost two hours and was arduous enough. Both knew officers from experience, that the drive back would be excruciating, as they would also have to tolerate the ramblings of the prisoner the whole way back.

They wouldn't even be allowed to let him sleep, as they needed to ensure his welfare throughout the journey.

Not that him sleeping was ever an option, as the single cell in the back of the police van consisted of nothing more than a metal box, which contained two opposing metal benches. No cushions or padding in any more was allowed, as this could lead to prisoners either causing damage to it or giving them the means to self-harm.

Unfortunately for Mike, as he was the detective sergeant, and the senior officer present, his underling felt it was their responsibility to drive, which resulted in Mike having to babysit the prisoner in the back of the van.

Mike felt obligated to let the DC drive them all back as he had laid the groundwork on the outward journey by complaining how easily he gets motion sickness.

Whether this was a deliberate ploy, or he was telling the truth, Mike was kicking himself for being beaten to the punch.

The reason that motion sickness was such a relevant topic was because the officer monitoring the welfare of the prisoner, who was in the cell in the back of the van, had to sit facing the rear of the vehicle. This had been known to provoke the onset of motion sickness, and unfortunately for Mike, he had no better reason to excuse himself from the welfare role.

Once they had finally reached the other force's custody centre, they had to be escorted around the facility as they didn't have access through any of the security doors.

Upon arrival, they were taken to where the custody sergeants sat, after that, their escort left them.

"How do, Sarge," Mike said.

The sergeant was a little perplexed at seeing two suited gentleman he didn't recognise addressing him.

It took a moment longer for him to see their warrant cards hanging like ID cards from their jacket pockets indicating that they were from another police force, suggesting the reason they were there.

"Ah yes, you guys must be here for Mercer," he replied, have made his deductions.

"Yep, that's us," Mike added. "How's he been?"

The sergeant responded with the most condescending look that Mike had seen in a long time. The kind of look that a child gives when baby noises are made at them.

The look spoke volumes to both Mike and the DC, and it came with a sense of impending doom loomed over them both.

Then with an abundance sense of sarcasm the sergeant replied.

"Oh, he's been an absolute darling," he said. "Delightful. Chap."

The sergeant then stood up from his desk and leaned in towards Mike, before speaking in a volume that was only audible between the two of them, only to then withdrew far enough to then get a look of understanding from Mike.

The sergeant then turned and addressed one of his staff, who in turn got up and left the admin area behind the desks where prisoners are booked in, colloquially known as the bridge.

The sergeant then returned to where Mike was standing.

"If you pop yourself down there," he said. "James will be out with your guy in just a sec,"

"Cheers Sarge," Mike said, as he moved in the direction shown.

As promised, within couple a minutes, a dedicated detention officer, presumably the one named James came through a side door, before holding it open for an arrogant lump of a man to follow him.

James indicated that he should wait at the booking-in desk in front of where Mike and the DC now stood.

He then adopted a swagger during the last few steps before standing face to face with Mike.

"So, you're my taxi home then?" he asked. "I hope you're sorting out how I get my motor getting back too?"

Mike looked at the man and chose to disregard his opening comments, though this would prove to be Mike's first mistake when it came to Mercer, but not his greatest.

After the booking-out process had been completed, Mike and his colleague took over responsibility of their prisoner from the custody staff. Mike then chose to take the precaution of handcuffing Mercer for the walk outside to where they had left the van.

As Mercer was handcuffed, Mike had to hold on to him as they walked. This was to ensure that should Mercer fall, then Mike could cushion the impact as Mercer was unable to put his own hands out to protect himself.

However, during the short walk to the van, Mercer kept deliberately faltering in his steps causing him to stagger. This probably had its desired result, as it caused evidently further annoyance for Mike who had to keep tensing up and take Mercer's mammoth weight to prevent him from falling.

Mercer was starting to get under Mike's skin, and he knew it.

However, Mike knew things would only get worse once they were in the van and on their way back, and he wasn't wrong.

"You know this is all a stitch-up, don't ya?" Mercer said, as opening remark once the van had pulled out of the custody centre yard and back onto a public road.

"Oh really," was Mike's dismissive reply, trying not to get drawn into such a conversation.

This was because Mercer was still under caution following his arrest, and that any conversation would involve questions, and that would constitute an interview, and for that to take place he would need to be offered legal counsel, and everything said, both questions and answers would need to be documented. Yet this didn't dissuade Mercer in the slightest.

"Yeah, the bitch is probably in cahoots with her new fancy man," he continued. "I bet it was him who probably smacked her around a bit, y'know to make things look real, just to finger me."

As he felt this would continue for the next two hours, Mike chose to remind Mercer that he was still under caution, and by that warning him that anything he said could be used evidentially.

Though this could be roughly translated, that he wanted Mercer to shut up, so he wouldn't have to listen to him.

oOo

As the journey continued, so did the ramblings. Mike glanced forward to see the DC engrossed in his driving, blissfully aware, or simply choosing to ignore everything that was going on in the back of the van.

"Was it you that spoke to her then?" Mercer asked. "She likes it a bit rough, did she tell you that? I bet she didn't tell you that, did she?"

It appeared to Mike that Mercer was trying any and all means to get any snippet of information from him, but with that last comment, Mike had had enough.

"Look, you've got absolutely nothing to say," he said. "So why don't just give your mouth a rest, and give us all a break, okay?"

However, this would not get the desired response, and acted more like a red rag to a bull.

"Am I getting to you, boss?" Mercer asked. "Y'know, you're only talking tough coz you're out there and I'm stuck in here.

"You know you wouldn't be Bertie Big Bollocks if I wasn't locked in a cage!"

However, Mercer's best reply was nothing that Mike hadn't heard countless times before and chose to reply to it now as he had done then.

"I guess that's something we'll never know, now, will we?" he said.

"Fucking pussy!" Mercer exclaimed as he shuffled himself to the furthest corner of the cell from where Mike was sat, before exhaling in disgust.

Mike knew full well that the shoe was most likely on the other foot, and the only reason that Mercer was talking as tough as he was, was because he was in cuffs, in a cell, and unable to make good on any of his threats. He was protected by decorum, and they both knew it.

In Mike's experience he knew guys like Mercer liked to talk tough, but they were of an ilk could only physically assert themselves against a woman, or someone significantly weaker than them.

Mercer, like so many that had come before him, was the very definition of a bully, nothing more, and nothing less, plain and simple.

oOo

Mercer's attempts to become more despising and obnoxious. So much so, that when the police van eventually pulled into the yard of their own custody centre Mike had given up trying to interact with Mercer, and simply chose to do his absolute best to ignore him.

However, upon their arrival, Mercer tried to further test Mike's patience when he opened the rear doors to the van by refusing to climb down of his own accord.

Only when the warning was given that he would be physically extricated from the vehicle, did Mercer relent and finally climb down unassisted.

It then fell to the DC, who had been spared the abuse having been the driver, to lead the procession from the vehicle dock towards the holding cells, where they would have to wait until call through to be booked in, whilst Mike followed, escorting Mercer as he had done so before.

This route required him to access a door using his security card, he then held the door open for Mercer and Mike, before leaving the door to shut by itself, only to then scoot off ahead to repeat the process at the next door.

It was then, whilst the DC was ahead of Mike and Mercer that things went awry.

With the DC ahead of them he no longer had the other two in his vision, when Mercer decided to address Mike.

"You look like a family man, you got any kids, maybe a daughter?" her asked. "Teenager perhaps, on the verge of blossoming?

"Maybe I should just wait until she's old enough. I think she deserves to be looked after by someone like me or my b..."

In an instant, Mike turned and whilst still holding onto one of Mercer's arms, he slammed him into the corridor wall cutting him off mid-sentence.

Mercer stood with his back to the wall, with Mike's forearm now across his throat. Mike applied gradually increasing pressure as he stared into Mercer's defiant eyes.

"Don't you dare even speak about my daughter," Mike bellowed at him.

But all Mercer chose to do in return was smile.

His reaction was for reasons two-fold, firstly, at having succeeded in goading Mike into a physical outburst, one that he had every intention of monopolising later, and secondly in gaining the confirmation of the existence of a daughter.

By this time, the DC had become abundantly aware of the commotion that was taking place behind him, but unaware what had instigated it. All he saw was his colleague with a prisoner up against a wall with his arm across his throat.

Erring on the side of caution, he hit an alarm button which alerted other officers within the custody centre to their predicament. He then rushed over to where Mike still had Mercer pinioned against the corridor wall.

"What the fuck's going on?" he said to Mike. "Are you okay?"

Mike didn't reply. Instead, he continued to stare at Mercer, eye-to-eye, like at a pre-boxing match stare-off.

The door the DC was at when the commotion begun had now flung open and several detention officers, as well as the custody sergeant came rushing through into the corridor.

But by this time all was calm, though Mercer couldn't stop chuckling to himself about his petty victory.

The detention officers then took over escorting Mercer, only to walk him through the open door ahead of them, the DC followed on behind them. This eventually left the custody sergeant alone with Mike.

"I'm not gonna ask you what happened because there's AV everywhere," the sergeant said to Mike. "Just make sure you get your story straight, okay?"

AV referred to the audio-visual CCTV that was mounted around the centre, with there not being a single area where prisoners went that wasn't covered by cameras. The only exception to this being a black out area on the in-cell cameras to afford them some privacy when using the en-suite toilets.

oOo

Although Mike did get his story straight, the footage from the CCTV painted a very different picture when it was played before the disciplinary panel.

Added to which, Mercer's testimony and the account provided by the DC as to the frayed emotions during the return journey, didn't portray Mike in a particularly good light.

The ruling from the investigating disciplinary panel was that something had clearly taken place that shouldn't have.

The facts were that Mercer was handcuffed and was viewed on the CCTV to be of no significant threat towards his escorting officer. Therefore, it was deduced that if he did in fact antagonise Mike, as was alleged, then Mike shouldn't have responded as he did.

It was for that reason that it was deemed an unnecessary and excessive use of force against a prisoner, and the appropriate punishment for such was decided to reassign and demote him.

He was also given a written warning and advised that had Mercer wanted to pursue things and make a formal allegation, then Mike could have, quite easily, also been facing criminal charges for assault.

Having kept his job Mike was reassigned to a response team which would deal with a wider variety of incidents than solely domestic related reports.

Mike knew that he was lucky to keep his job, and even more so *not* to be facing criminal charges, as he had known colleagues who had to endure the full force of the criminal justice system, and for less than what he had done.

He just hoped that would be the end of it, with lessons having been learned.

CHAPTER THIRTEEN

As things turned out, given the necessity for repeated attempts to be made, the arrest of Neil Bannister took place a little after six o'clock in the morning.

The arrest was conducted by members of the force's territorial support group, which is a specialist group, made up of regular officers, who are given extra training to deal with incidents of public disorder and those subjects who have a likelihood, or propensity to be more violent or deranged.

These precautions were deemed necessary because of the warnings associated with members of the Bannister household, which in turn led to the potential level of resistance or violence that could be expected.

However, when the door was answered, it was by his mother, and the reaction officers received was as though their arrival had been expected.

Consequently, Neil Bannister was already dressed and breakfasted, and left the home address, under arrest, without incident.

"Don't worry son," his mother said. "We'll get our brief on it ASAP… What are you going to want for dinner?"

She was almost sniggering as she said it, as if to assume that her son would be home in time for dinner that very evening.

Due to the lack of resistance the officers were met with, the attending officers did not feel the need to take the precaution of handcuffing Bannister for his trip to custody.

Such a use of force and restraint had to be justified and documented as such, and without sufficient justification, the decision was made to not to handcuff him, as they had enough to deal with any unrest, should it be required.

oOo

When Bannister arrived at police custody, it was apparent to all concerned that his balls had grown somewhat during the journey.

When the back doors of the van were opened, he just sat there insolently, ignoring the first request from an officer for him to climb down and exit the vehicle.

However, it was only when two further officers appeared in view alongside the first that he eventually complied, but with an arrogant smile of victory on his face.

Bannister was then escorted from the secure vehicle dock, through a pass door and into the holding area, and it was here that Bannister stopped mid-way and appeared to give the walls a bizarre level of scrutiny.

"Something you're looking for?" one of the escorting officers eventually asked, as if Bannister would not be moved on until someone had.

"Tell ya when I find it," Bannister replied.

Then his eyes caught sight of what he was looking for, which resulted in a smile, before he started to laugh out loud. Though this was only met with puzzled looks being exchanged from those in his escorting party.

"What's so funny?" another officer asked of him, who failed to see what was so funny as to provoke such a reaction.

"My dad did that," Bannister explained. "With his head when one of you punk bitches tried to take him on."

Again, being one to have heard every tale a DP, or detained person, had to spin, the first officer took it upon himself to reply.

"Yeah, yeah," he said. "You go on thinking that."

But Bannister was one to trust the source and would not be so easily dissuaded.

"Oh, don't worry I will," he said adamantly. "I bet he handed your guy his arse to him that day!"

Normally Bannister would have been taken to a holding cell, to await such a time when he and his escorts were called through to be booked in.

But, on this occasion, before any of them could take a seat in the holding area, the intercom crackled to life, which called them immediately through into the main booking-in area.

Bannister was then led straight to one of the workstations on a raised platform, where the duty custody sergeant stood and began to address him.

But before he could get a single word out, Bannister blurted out his opening remark.

"Is my brief here yet?" he demanded to know.

Again, this behaviour was nothing previously seen, and the staff there remained unfazed by the outburst.

"Good morning to you too," the sergeant replied, giving total disregard to the comment.

The formalities of the booking-in procedure included an explanation being provided to the custody sergeant, giving the details of the original offence and the reason Bannister had been linked to it, and the necessity behind his arrest.

It was then the sergeant's decision whether to determine that ongoing detention was justified.

For an offence such as the one that Bannister had been arrested for, as well as ensuring a prompt and effective investigation, his arrest was deemed as being necessary in order to prevent any further harm being caused to the victim, or any other person, and based on this information, the custody sergeant drew the following conclusion.

"I'm happy that your arrest is lawful," he said. "So, I'm gonna authorise your detention, so we can secure and preserve evidence by means of questioning."

Once his detention had been authorised, only then was Bannister informed that his family's solicitor had already contacted the police station and had given an estimated arrival time of eight o'clock that morning.

In the interim, after being booked in, Bannister was taken through the formalities of having his photograph taken, as well as his fingerprints and DNA, after which he was taken to a cell to await his solicitor's arrival.

oOo

Once his solicitor had arrived, but before Bannister got to speak to him, the solicitor was spoken to by an officer investigating the case.

This is a normal part of the procedure, something known as disclosure, whereby the police essentially disclose what information and evidence they have gained to the solicitor, to prove the case against their client, the suspect.

Not all information acquired is given, as some is intentionally withheld as a means to prove or disprove any account given by the suspect.

It fell to Detective Constable Aiden Haynes to sit down with solicitor James Marshall to discuss the investigation thus far.

"Do you have an allegation?" Marshall asked of the officer.

His question was asked to determine if the alleged victim was supporting police action, or if it remained unsubstantiated, or had come via a third party.

"We have an account of what's happened," Haynes replied.

"Not the same thing, and you know it," Marshall persisted. "Do you have a signed statement from the victim, or anything on video?"

As the DC remained evasive in provided an answer, Marshall elaborated on his question, hoping to back Haynes into a corner.

"No, we don't," Haynes finally admitted.

"And, why's that?" Marshall asked, intentionally twisting the knife.

"Because the victim has, so far anyway, refused to co-operate in providing us with one." Haynes replied.

This was the response Marshall had been expecting, and having received it, he was able to move on.

"Or is it because nothing actually happened?" Marshall elaborated for his own satisfaction, and to unsettle the detective. "So essentially, what you're saying is, you've got nothing?

"And without any admission from my client, you'll continue to have nothing.

"Well, I can tell you right now, my client will be going *'no comment'* to any and all questions asked."

Given what he had offered by means of disclosure, this did not come as a surprise to Haynes.

"Fair enough," Haynes said conceding. "Are you ready to speak to him?"

"Yes," Marshall said without even looking up from the notes he was typing on his laptop. "Would you have him sent in."

With that Haynes got up and left the consultation room. From there he returned to the bridge and asked that Bannister be collected from his cell and taken to the consultation room.

He was then able to have a private and privileged discussion with Marshall prior to his interview, and as Bannister entered the consultation room, he was greeted by a face familiar to him.

"Good morning, Neil," Marshall said, as he stood and extended a hand to shake.

"Alright Jim," Bannister replied. "How's things?"

With hands shook, everyone took a seat, and Bannister and Marshall were left alone.

"Oh, not so bad," Marshall replied. "Now, your dad has already filled me on what's going on here, and he made me promise that I'd have you home in time for dinner.

"But given what they've got on you, I'd say I'd have you home by lunchtime."

oOo

After about half an hour of general catching up, and not actually discussing the intricacies of the investigation, Bannister and Marshall were collected from the consultation room, only to be led by DC Haynes to an interview room.

Because Neil Bannister was over the age of eighteen, he didn't need any further representation in the interview.

Had he been under the age of eighteen, or over eighteen and was it deemed necessary, then an appropriate adult would also be required.

This can normally be a family member, but only if not directly involved in the investigation. Or should that not be appropriate, or one not available, then a volunteer advocate can be brought in.

Once the interview had commenced, and after all those present, including Bannister and Marshall had introduced themselves, Haynes then explained the offence and why Bannister had been arrested.

"You were arrested today as you have been named for your involvement in an assault occasioning actual bodily harm against Ashley Watkins with whom you are believed to have been in a relationship with," Haynes explained.

Bannister was then asked to give his knowledge of the offence alleged against him.

However, given what was discussed and agreed during their private consolation, Marshall was expecting Bannister to either remain silent, or to reply only with *'no comment'* as Marshall had forewarned Haynes.

But instead, when he was given the opportunity to reply, he did so.

"I ain't in no relationship with her," he said abruptly, correcting Haynes' information. "Never have, never will."

Given what Marshall had forewarned, Haynes was surprised that he had to note down a response.

"Okay," Haynes replied, acknowledging the new line of questioning. "What *is* she to you then?"

"No comment," Bannister said.

Bannister then proceeded to adhere to the game plan as agreed with his solicitor by answering *'no comment'* to all further questions.

That was all questions, except when he was questioned regarding his ownership of a white Ford Focus ST.

When, after Haynes asked him to confirm ownership and having quoted from DVLA records, Marshall leant in and whispered advice into his client's ear. To which Bannister was seen to nod.

"Yeah," he replied. "She's mine."

"And where is this car now?" Haynes then asked.

"No comment," Bannister again replied.

When such a time came, that no further questions could be asked, and with nothing was left to be added, or clarified, the interview was concluded.

Following which Bannister and Marshall were taken back to the same consultation room as before.

There they were both sat comfortably, until after a few minutes when Haynes came back in, to address them both.

"At this moment in time, you're going to be released under investigation," he explained. "No bail, and no conditions."

But Haynes was interrupted from continuing by Bannister leaping to his feet.

"Right, get me the fuck outta here then," Bannister demanded, clapping his hands together.

"I'll finish first, if I may," Haynes continued. "And, during that time we strongly recommend you have no contact with any other party involved in this case, and we will contact you should we need to speak to you further."

"Yeah, yeah, whatever," Bannister said, already on his way towards the consultation room door.

He tried the handle, only to find the door locked, as it required a security pass to exit.

"Are you gonna fucking let me outta here, or what?" he demanded.

Marshall went from looking smug to looking somewhat embarrassed in an instant, as even he was disgusted by his client's belligerent display.

"If you're able to wait here for a couple of minutes, I'll arrange for your release," Haynes said, as he swiped the sensor with his pass card, unlocking the door for himself only, and walked out.

oOo

After a few minutes, Haynes returned to collect both Bannister and Marshall, who had waited around in order to give his client a lift home.

"Wait until I get my hands on that bitch," Bannister said to Marshall as the custody sergeant booked him out. "She'll fucking pay for this."

Marshall then gave him a look as if to say *keep your mouth shut at least until you're outside!*

Once all of Bannister's personal property had been returned to him, and all the necessary forms had his signature, the custody sergeant gave one of his detention officers the order to escort both Bannister and Marshall out of the custody centre.

"Get me the fuck outta here," Bannister said again, echoing his earlier sentiment, as he was shown the way out.

Once outside, as they both walked towards where Marshall had parked his car.

It was then that Marshall couldn't help but voice what was on his mind.

"One day, you *will* learn to keep your big mouth shut," he said.

He then slammed the passenger door shut on Bannister, before walking round to the other side.

"Gobshite little prick!" he muttered to himself, before opening the driver's door and getting in himself.

CHAPTER FOURTEEN

Whilst everything involving Bannister was taking place, Mike had been at work himself, on an early shift, one that he finished on time.

When he got home, and as he walked through the front door, he was immediately surprised, as he saw Ashley sat on the bottom of the stairs, and beyond her, he could see that Kerry was standing in the kitchen.

Kerry was on the phone, though it sounded as if she was nearing the end of the call.

"I see," Kerry said, despondently into the handset.

Mike watched in silence, feeling that the call was somehow connected to why Ashley was sat as she was. He saw Kerry nod, as if that response was sufficient, only to realise her shortcoming after a couple of seconds, when she verbalised her thoughts.

"I will," she said, before ending the call. "Thank you."

Mike stepped forward and put his hand on his daughter's shoulder as he walked past her, mouthing a greeting to her as she looked up at him.

He continued along the hallway towards the kitchen but chose to wait in the doorway until receiving some acknowledgement from Kerry.

Without even looking up, and whilst still clutching the cordless handset to her chest, she spoke, having sensed his presence.

"That was the police," she said.

The pause was too long for Mike to wait for her to continue and felt compelled to prompt her.

"And…?" he said, dreading the response.

There was another pause, only for Kerry to place the telephone handset in the charging cradle.

"They phoned me this morning to say that they'd arrested him," she began to explain. "This time it was to tell me that they've now released him.

"They also wanted to me to ask Ash again, if she was prepared to give them a statement and let herself be photographed."

Mike looked back down the hallway to where Ashley was still sat. Though now feeling the eyes of the world on her, she leapt to her feet and bolted upstairs.

"And, I'm guessing, she refused," Mike added.

"She refused," Kerry confirmed.

Mike walked to the bottom of the stairs, and glanced upwards, as he wanted to know if Ashley was still within earshot.

As he couldn't see her anywhere, he expected that she had gone to her room, bus as he had yet to hear a door slam shut, he remained unsure.

But as his daughter was nowhere to be seen, it achieved his objective, so he walked back into the kitchen.

"So, lemme guess, they've released him with *no further action*?" he said.

Once again, Kerry initially responded with a physical gesture, almost as if her words were failing her, but after a delay they came.

"No," she replied, before a pause. "He said something about him still being *under investigation*, but there's no conditions on him, nothing to prevent him from contacting Ash, except a recommendation from them not to."

Mike took a deep breath, and sighed, realising that the present situation was better than he thought it would be, though not by much.

"Sounds about right, given what they had to work with," Mike replied.

Kerry looked about the kitchen, searching for the words she needed.

"But that's not even the worst of it!" she replied.

Mike paused as his optimism was instantly dashed.

"What's worse?" he asked.

"The officer who interviewed him said that he made threats towards Ash, whilst he was still at the police station," Kerry explained. "He said that he was heard to say '*I'm gonna make her pay for this'* and '*wait till I get my hands on her'* or words to that effect."

Mike could see the upset in Kerry's eyes, and felt he needed to say something, anything to appease her, despite what he was now feeling.

"I really wouldn't worry about him, Kez, he's full of shit," he said. "I've seen his kind many times before, and he's just trying to act tough in front of the coppers.

"But I'd bet you he probably pissed himself a little bit when they slammed the cell door shut on him."

He could see that his attempt to console his wife had fallen on stony ground, so tried to change the subject somewhat.

"What did Ash have to say when you asked her earlier?" he added.

"She kept repeating that he didn't do anything wrong, and that it was *her* winding *him* up," Kerry replied. "And, that she didn't want to be paraded round like some piece of meat."

Again, his daughter's response was nothing new to him, as he had heard similar responses from victims, not just of domestic abuse, but any crime with a physical element.

But as he had no vested interest in these people, he had only ever offered a minimal amount of persuasion, to get them to change their minds, but his daughter was a different story altogether.

"Y'know, I was really hoping she was going to snap out of it by the time it had got this far," Mike said. "But, without what she'd have to add, chances always were that they'd just interview him, as that much they'd have to do.

"But without any testimony from Ash, they'd have no choice but to release him."

On so many occasions, he had been the one to make the phone call, advising of the disposal decision, he had never been on the receiving end of one, until now.

"Release him?" Kerry exclaimed. "How on Earth can they let him go after what he's done?"

Before replying, Mike listened again, for any indications as to Ashley whereabouts upstairs. When nothing could be heard, he felt it safe to continue.

"Well, they'd put all the questions to him, about everything they know," he explained. "But unless he admitted to anything, and there'd be a slim to none chance of that ever happening, then there'd be little else they could do.

"The police *know* what he's done, coz they've seen Ash, they've spoken to her, and seen her injuries, and have a good idea how they were caused. But they *can't* prove that he caused them."

Mike paused long enough to contemplate the situation.

"He was only *ever* gonna be with them for a few hours," he continued. "So, all we can do is ask Ash *again*, and hope she changes her mind."

"And if she doesn't? Kerry replied. "After what he's said, what's likely to happen?"

Mike took a moment to put himself in the shoes of the investigating officer and try to make dispassionate decisions based solely on the facts of the case.

"They *may* choose to deal with the threats he's made as a separate issue," Mike said. "But best case would only ever be that he'd get bailed with conditions not to make any contact with Ash, and should he breach those, then he might find himself getting nicked again."

What her husband was telling her echoed what was said over the phone.

"The officer did mention something about that," Kerry admitted. "But to be honest, I wasn't really paying too much attention by then."

Mike could feel that the frustration he was feeling mirrored that he could see in his wife, and he knew he had to try and take a positive step forward.

"Do you want me to speak to her?" he asked, reiterating the need for co-operation from Ashley.

"You can try if you like," Kerry relented as she felt her eyes start to well up again. "I'm all out of ideas."

Mike stepped up and took her in his arms. He held her tight and kissed the top of her head as she buried her face in his chest. He then leant back so he could see her face, and as she looked up their gazes met.

Sadly, they both knew now was not the time for intimacy. Instead, Mike smiled as he let go of her.

He walked back towards the hallway, finally taking his coat off, before draping it over the banister as he ascended the stairs.

Once on the landing he could see that Ashley's door had been closed, but not shut.

He approached the door and knocked, and awaited a suitable response before entering.

"Oh great, so you're ganging up on me now too." Ashley said, when she realised it was her father who had appeared in the open doorway.

Mike sighed again, as he stepped over the threshold, into her bedroom.

"We're not ganging up on you sweetie, we're on your side," he said, in a calm, reassuring tone. "But we just want you to understand the situation you're in, and how best to get through it."

However, despite his intentions, Mike could see that his presence was already having a detrimental reaction in Ashley, before he even explained his reason for being there.

As he had advanced, she retreated, having scooted back up the bed towards the headboard, only to hug a pillow tight to her chest, so high that it covered her to her nose.

Sensing this aversion to his mere presence, he stopped in his tracks and retreated to the doorway, propping himself against the frame.

This was evidently the right move, as Ashley lowered the pillow to eventually show her entire face.

Mike knew he wasn't the enemy, but he knew the fear of a predator in its prey when he saw it, and seeing his daughter feel she needed to behave in such a way in her own home sickened and saddened him.

"We'll support you in any decision that you choose to make," Mike said. "The only question you need to ask yourself is, do you feel that *he* was responsible for what happened to you, and how you're feeling now, and do you feel he *needs* to be punished for it?

"Now, if you can honestly answer that question for yourself, then I don't think you can't go far wrong."

Mike looked empathetically across to where Ashley was still partially hiding behind her pillow.

She made a faint, but indistinguishable verbal response, but seeing her head shake told Mike all he needed to know.

He resigned himself to the fact that things have already moved forward as far as humanly possible without the police having secured the co-operation and support of the victim.

"Okay, sweetie, it's fine," he said, as he stepped back through the doorway. "Do you want me to close your door?"

With Ashley having nodded, Mike took hold of the handle and pulled the door to but didn't close it.

He then went back downstairs, only to pause halfway to compose himself and wipe away an escaping tear, before continuing down to finally re-join Kerry in the kitchen.

As he entered the kitchen, she eagerly looked around at him, to which he responded solely with a disappointing shake of his head.

CHAPTER FIFTEEN

More than a week had passed since the police had advised the Watkins family of Bannister's release, following his arrest, and during that time nothing had been seen or heard from him.

It appeared that life was being allowed to return to some degree of normality, with Ashley becoming a regular attendee at college once more.

However, in addition to the report to the police, Mike had taken the precaution of making the college staff aware of the incident, and even they hadn't felt the need to report anything back to either him or Kerry.

The dust was being allowed to settle on the unpleasantness, and this whole sorry saga appeared to be coming to an end, with Ashley being spared any remedial suffering, and she was able to get on with her coursework as if nothing had happened.

For all intents and purposes, she was very much the former self her parents knew and loved from before this awful episode in all their lives.

oOo

It was a Saturday, and Mike was again rostered to work an early shift.

He was on patrol on his own as once again there was an odd number of officers on his team that day, when a dispatcher called up asking for an available unit to attend what was being described as a concern for safety on a borough neighbouring that which he patrolled.

Mike didn't feel he needed to listen attentively to the remainder of the transmission, after it had been determined that the location of the incident was in another borough, which just happened to be the borough where he lived.

But as that was outside of his patrol area, he wouldn't be required to call up for it, that was unless, on the off chance, no one else did, or no one else was available to.

Eventually, after a moment of radio silence, a unit covering that borough did call up on the radio requesting further details. Following which, the dispatcher responded, giving further details.

"We've had a report of a woman heard screaming from within the address," the dispatcher revealed. "We believe this is possibly a domestic incident in progress. Did you need the address again?"

The assigned unit once again responded.

"No, we got the address," came the reply. "Show us towards the incident."

Mike didn't think twice about the contents of the dispatch as the incident had now been covered, and that's all he needed to hear.

Shortly after this transmission, Mike was himself dispatched to check on an abandoned and burnt-out vehicle that had been found and called in by a member of the public.

Whilst en route to the location he was given, Mike kept an ear out for the other assigned job; the domestic incident, purely because it was the only transmissions on the radio at that time.

oOo

Mike finally booked his attendance at the abandoned vehicle having eventually located it along a track off a single lane rural road.

Had he not been looking for it, it would've been virtually impossible to find by chance, which left Mike wondering just how the member of the public had managed to stumble across it.

He then remembered that dog walkers, for instance, were responsible for coming across all sorts of things when out for walks. He had lost count of the number of dead bodies that dogs had discovered during his career.

For a moment he imagined a dog running from the undergrowth, back to its owner, tail wagging enthusiastically with a body part hanging in its mouth, and the resulting shock on the face of the owner. This image, however, drew a smile from Mike.

Due to how the burnt-out car had been abandoned, Mike didn't have to park his police vehicle to fend off and protect himself from passing traffic. This was firstly because the burnt-out shell was completely off the road, and secondly, because it was a long straight piece of road, and there was hardly any traffic that he needed to be protecting from. Regardless, Mike alighted from his car leaving the blue lights flashing for any approaching motorists to see.

The car itself was a smouldering carcass, a steaming mass of charred metal, with anything flammable having burned, or melted away.

The initial call from the member of public was to the fire service, who in turn called the police, and whilst the fire service was now long gone, and through their efforts washed the charred contents of the vehicle, along with any clues as to who had left it there down the road.

Some of the denser areas of metal, like the engine block and prop shaft were still steaming due to the significant heat still within them.

Mike stood back and tried to firstly determine the vehicle's make and model, though there was certainly no guessing its former colour.

He determined that it was a small estate car, and his first assumption was that it was possibly a Volvo V40, or a Subaru Legacy. But, without any tell-tale signs to give it away it was difficult to draw a conclusion.

Mike took out his smart phone and searched for stock images of both cars. He scrolled through various images of both showing the modifications made to each model over the years, before deciding it was most likely a 2008 Subaru Legacy.

Satisfied with his conclusion, Mike approached the still steaming vehicle, and as he leant under the raised bonnet, to try and locate a vehicle identification number panel, he heard a message coming over his radio. It was an update message from the earlier dispatched concern for safety.

"We've found the property insecure, have gained entry," the attending unit explained. "There's an unconscious and unresponsive female casualty in living room, CPR commenced.

"No other persons present. Request ambulance and additional units, and a supervisor, and can CID be made aware?"

As Mike continued looking for the VIN plate, he muttered a reply for his own benefit.

"Someone's got their hands full," he said.

Having finished examining the Subaru, Mike was unable to locate either the engine or chassis number, so the vehicle will probably remain forever unidentified.

He returned to his car to send an update to the incident log using his palm-top mobile computer as opposed to a radio transmission, and as Mike sat in his car, he heard a further update message relating to the developing situation unconscious female.

"Paramedics now on scene, taking over CPR," the unit reported. "Additional units have arrived, starting scene log, time as of now."

The dispatcher responded requesting more information.

"Is there any update on the victim's condition?" the controller asked.

"Possible foxtrot," came the reply.

The use of the term *foxtrot* refers to the letter 'f' in the phonetic alphabet, in this case describing the likelihood of a fatality, but avoids having to use obvious terminology over the air.

Although the police channel is secure, it's a practice that officers have adopted over the years as it couldn't be guaranteed who's within earshot of anyone listening to that radio channel, as news like that shouldn't be transmitted when there is potentially a family member of member of the public close by.

"Oh, bloody hell," Mike muttered to himself. "That sounds griefy, I hope they didn't have any plans this evening."

Mike was referring to the officers at the scene, and the likelihood of them having to remained there and no longer expecting to finish their shift on time due to the protracted nature of such an incident.

Mike then heard another voice coming over the radio, who opened their transmission with a CID call-sign.

"We are towards," said the detective. "Can we get the address again please?"

When the reply was given, Mike dropped his palm-top into the foot-well and went as white as a sheet, as the address that had been given for the incident was his home address.

He frantically fumbled with the car-keys as he tried to force the ignition key in the lock, and despite his response, and trembling hands, he eventually made it fit.

With the engine fired up, and Mike sped off, wheel spinning, and shooting dirt and mud high into the air behind him.

Luckily for Mike, he had already paired his smart phone with the car's Bluetooth hands-free set at the start of the shift, so he was able to utilise the in-car voice activation facility to call the landline number at home, and when the call finally connected, he could hear the phone ring.

As he was listening, praying for someone to answer the phone, he heard another radio transmission, though Mike wasn't focused on the words being said.

Instead, he focused on the sound of a phone was ringing in the background of the transmission, which was in perfect unison which the ringing phone echoing within his car.

Giving up all hope that someone would answer the call, Mike hung up, only to then try Kerry's mobile. It took a while to connect, before it finally started ringing.

"Please, please, please, answer the fucking phone!" he said rhetorically.

The call eventually went to voicemail, and after Kerry's message, Mike left his.

"Kerry, it's Mike, get yourself home *ASAP*," he said. "And call me immediately."

By this time, Mike was now back on a main road and having to deal with much more traffic than before, which significantly hindered his progress.

To combat this, Mike had activated the blues and twos, the emergency lighting and sirens, on the vehicle to help clear his path. He then called up on the car radio.

"This is Romeo-Bravo six-two," he began. "The address of the..."

Mike cut himself off mid-sentence, as he realised he couldn't bring himself to refer to the victim as *the unconscious female* or *foxtrot* knowing who they might be.

"The, um, concern for safety," he continued. "It's my home address, and I am heading there now."

There was silence on the radio, not even a response from a controller to acknowledge Mike's transmission.

Anyone who had heard Mike's words was now in varying degrees of disbelief or shock.

After a few moments became an eternity, a different controller eventually replied to Mike.

"Romeo-Bravo six-two, message received," they said. "Get yourself home, drive safe, over."

Mike didn't bother to acknowledge the response as he was already trying to call Ashley's mobile.

Yet again, it rang to voicemail, and Mike was in the process of leaving a similar message to that he had already left for Kerry when his phone started to indicate that he had an incoming call, it was Kerry.

Tentatively, Mike abandoned his message and answered the call, and although he had previously tried calling her, he didn't know what he was going to say.

Kerry spoke first, she already sounded panicked by the contents of Mike's voicemail.

"Mike, I got your message, what's wrong?" she asked.

"I don't know for sure," he replied. "Something's wrong at home, get yourself home ASAP?

"There's gonna be police there, please be careful Hun.

"I'm on my way there now, so I may get there before you."

Nothing of what Kerry had just heard made any sense, and her response suggested as much.

"How can you not know what's happening? Mike, MIKE?" Kerry asked with increasing desperation.

However, Mike was still driving at what was termed as best speed, and he was negotiating vehicles and obstacles as fast as humanly possible, and it was during their last exchange that Mike came dangerously close to sideswiping an oncoming vehicle and needed to focus solely on his driving for a moment as opposed to offering a prompt reply to Kerry.

Once the momentary predicament had resolved itself, Mike continued with his response, forgetting where he was in the conversation.

"I'm heading home now," Mike reiterated. "As soon as I get home, I'll let you know what's happening. I gotta go hun, just get yourself home."

As Mike continued to drive, he found that he was no longer listening to any radio transmissions. However, when his phone rang in the cradle, he afforded it a downward glance, but upon realising it was just a colleague calling him, he chose to ignore it. As whatever the purpose of the call was it would be an unnecessary distraction and would hinder his progress and delay his arrival at home.

As Mike turned into the street that led into his, he cancelled his emergency lights, and slowed to the posted speed limit and took a couple of deep breaths to better prepare himself for what was to come.

For it was as he turned the final corner into his street, he was met with the worst nightmare for any police officer.

As in front of his own home was a plethora of police vehicles, some still had their blue lights on, but the road was entirely blocked by police vehicles as well as an ambulance.

Mike pulled up as close as he could and made the final approach on foot.

He started at a brisk walk, giving him some time to survey the scene, and as he got closer, he looked for Kerry's car, but he couldn't see it in the time he gave himself, before finally breaking into a run.

As he approached the established outer police cordon, the area enclosed with police barrier tape, he knew he had to exercise restraint, for the sake of the investigation.

He ducked under the tape, but instead of just charging into the house as he wanted to, he approached the first officer he saw.

"I need to get in there!" Mike said.

However, the officer didn't recognise Mike, not knowing that he was the homeowner, and only saw him as being an officer, and refused him entry.

He wasn't being intentionally disruptive, but when a scene such as this is established, strict entry protocols are in place to protect the scene, and he simply needed time to ask why Mike needed to enter the protected area.

"This is my house," he said. "What the fuck is happening…? Who's in there?"

The officer scribbled some notes down on the scene logbook, before beckoned Mike to go inside. "The sergeant is in there, go see him first."

As Mike approached the front door his path was blocked by two paramedics who were in the process of exiting the premises. However, they weren't bringing out any patient with them.

"Is she alright?" Mike asked of them. "Why are you leaving?"

Both their gazes were to the ground, and they were both struggling with the amount of equipment they were trying to carry, and it didn't even register that Mike was addressing them.

Then from behind them emerged the sergeant, as he had been radioed by the first officer and told to expect Mike's imminent arrival.

The sergeant intentionally stood blocking the front doorway, to momentarily keep Mike outside.

They both knew one another as they had previously worked together.

"Mike," he whispered, as he leant in towards him to keep the conversation private. "I know you're gonna want to go in there, and I'm not going to try to stop you, I just need you to prepare yourself for what's in there."

Mike had gone from passively listening, to trying to push passed the sergeant.

"Mike, wait!" the sergeant ordered, as he struggled to keep Mike outside.

Though this was not an order given by an authority figure, but instead out of decency, as the sergeant wanted Mike to be fully prepared for what awaited him inside.

"Mike, I'm assuming it's your daughter in there," the sergeant warned. "You're going to have to prepare yourself for the worst."

At that, Mike fell his knees go beneath him, and he reached out to grab hold of the sergeant, or anything he could reach in order to steady himself.

He began sobbing, as he visualised the horrors that awaited him.

The sergeant took hold of Mike to give him reassurance and to steady him.

"Mike, you don't have to do this," he said. "Y'know, you don't have to go in there."

Finding new strength and composure, stood unassisted once more.

"Yes, I do," he said.

He exchanged a glance with the sergeant, who nodded his approval, who then turned and stepped off to one side in order to allow Mike to pass him.

Having stepped through the front door, Mike stood in the hallway. From there he could see that the concentration of activity within his own home was in the living room and having moved to the doorway, there he waited.

It became immediately apparent, that even from the doorway, a struggle had taken place, as items from the mantle were now strewn across the carpet, and a lamp from a table beside the sofa had been smashed on the floor.

However, Mike couldn't see the floor beyond a photographer wearing white forensics overall, who was busy clicking away on a camera, throwing his shadow on every wall with every subsequent flash.

The sergeant stepped into the doorway alongside Mike, and he announced their arrival to the scenes of crime forensics officers that had just begun their work.

At his command, everything ceased, and everyone turned to face the doorway, and Mike suddenly felt all eyes were on him, pitying him.

"Can you give us a minute please?" The sergeant asked of the officers.

They obliged his request without question, and immediately filed out of the living room, through the rear dining room, and into the kitchen, there to wait, as Mike presumed that they had been made aware of the uniqueness of the situation before his arrival.

Then, the once busy room was left still and quiet, and the horror that until then had been hidden from his view now fully exposed to him, and it was then that he saw her, as Ashley's lifeless body lay on the floor before him.

Her body was laid face down on the living room carpet, twisted and contorted. Her once beautiful and elegantly long hair was now matted and bloodied and covered much her face. Her arms were up, hands level with her shoulders, and it looked to Mike that she was trying to crawl somewhere, perhaps to summon help, before she collapsed, and fell into unconsciousness.

From the doorway, Mike followed her projected route across the carpet, only to see the landline phone cradle on the same table that the smashed lamp had once been. It appeared that she was trying to reach the phone to call for help for herself.

It was then that Mike realised that his daughter had taken some time to die, and after her attack she was left conscious enough to make efforts to get help before finally succumbing to her injuries.

She had died slowly, in agony, and all alone, and of the three Mike didn't know which was the worst.

It was at that moment that Mike heard a scream coming from somewhere behind him, which caused both he and the sergeant to spin around.

Mike turned just in time to catch Kerry as she ran through the front door and into the house.

She had been escorted inside the cordon by a police officer but became overwhelmed as she reached the house.

Kerry continued to try to get past them both, but Mike had a firm hold of her, for her sake she wasn't getting any further.

"Ash-ley, Ash-ley," Kerry sobbed, "my bay-be."

She reached out with a free arm out towards the lifeless body of their daughter as it laid before them on the floor. Mike turned to share her gaze, and to share in her pain.

The sergeant gave them what he believed was an appropriate amount of time before interrupting their moment of grief.

"Mike, I'm gonna have to ask that you two head outside again now," he said compassionately. "So, the SoCOs can finish off."

Without turning away from Ashley, Mike nodded his understanding.

Then after a while, he turned to face Kerry, and indicated with a tilt of his head that they needed to go outside. He then put his arm around her and started to lead her outside.

Mike led a reluctant Kerry outside, as he knew she didn't want to leave Ashley any more than he did, but he knew he had to take her outside to allow the police to do their job. He led her back out of the front door and around the side of the house, out of the gaze of anyone who came to see what was going on in their street.

They both sat down on the low wall that separated their driveway from their neighbours. Mike crouched down in front of Kerry and held her close to ensure her sobs were hidden from the world.

Their privacy was, however, short lived as their neighbour took the opportunity to come up to them and speak to them. She came baring the gift of two mugs of tea, but her ulterior motive was to find out what had gone on.

However, seeing the emotion in both Mike and Kerry's faces, she knew better than to pry. So, she just left the mugs at a safe distance along the wall to not be knocked over and left with nothing more than a grateful smile from Mike.

oOo

After what felt like an eternity, but in reality was little more than an hour, the sergeant again approached them both.

He was flanked by two other officers who weren't wearing body armour, but instead were wearing black tunics, and flat caps.

They were senior officers as denoted by the decorations on their epaulettes.

Only after the sergeant made the introductions, he left, and one of the officers then crouched down to be lower than the level at which Mike and Kerry sat, as he wasn't expecting Mike to break contact with Kerry in order to stand up in order to address him.

"How are you two doing?" he asked sympathetically.

He knew it was a redundant question given the circumstances, and he also didn't expect either of them to be in any fit state to verbalise a reply.

"Mike, you probably realise that you won't be able to go back inside your house tonight," he continued. "Not until scenes of crime have finished. So, have you got anywhere where else that you can stay tonight?"

The superintendent paused to offer an opportunity for an answer.

Then when none came, he continued.

"If not, we can make arrangements for the two of you to stay in a hotel if you need us to," he said.

Mike looked at him and nodded.

"We haven't got anywhere else," he replied.

"Don't worry," the superintendent continued. "We'll arrange one for you now."

Without saying a word, Kerry started vigorously shaking her head in disagreement.

Mike understood what she was alluding to, so felt the need to speak for her.

"We're not going anywhere just yet," he said. "We're gonna wait until our little girl comes out."

oOo

True to their word, neither Mike nor Kerry moved from their vantage point for what was almost another two hours.

That was until the sergeant again approached Mike to give him fair warning that Ashley was about to be brought out.

Mike relayed the same message to Kerry, and both stood, side by side, and hand in hand, on the driveway to await her emergence.

Kerry pulled the blanket that she had been given tight around her.

She did her best to remain composed, but the very moment that the gurney, that was carrying Ashley's body, appeared in the doorway, she broke down in tears and sobbed uncontrollably.

Mike felt her begin to collapse under her grief, so he stepped in close and held her tight.

He held Kerry's head close to his chest, firm but not tight, allowing her to turn her head to view the suited undertakers made their way down the driveway, passed where they stood, and onto the pavement, before disappearing out of sight to where their vehicle awaited.

Mike and Kerry gave themselves a while longer to recompose themselves before they agreed that it was time for them to take up the superintendent's offer.

CHAPTER SIXTEEN

As to be expected, immediately following the incident at his home address, involving his daughter Ashley, Mike was immediately put on compassionate leave, as he wasn't expected to return to work, or even attend a police station following what had happened.

As a courtesy, an officer had brought suitcases of clothes for them to the hotel, to negate the need for them to have to re-enter their house. The same officer then took Mike's body armour and protective equipment back to his station for him.

They had also arranged for Mike's car to be brought to the hotel from where he parked it for work, as well as returning the house keys to him after the policing operation had been closed.

oOo

It was four days before Mike and Kerry were allowed to return home, and in that time the police had taken all the photographs they needed, as well as undertaking a thorough forensic examination of the entire house.

As they approached the front door for the first time since the incident, Kerry faltered.

"I can't do this," she said. "Can you go in, then come out and tell me exactly what it's like in there, so I know exactly what to expect?"

"Of course," Mike said, having to let go of Kerry's hand to facilitate her request.

Leaving Kerry on the driveway, in almost the exact same spot she had been standing on when Ashley was taken from the address, Mike approached the front door on his own.

He had the key ready in his hand, and unlocked the door, pushing it open, before tentatively stepping inside, leaving Kerry alone on the driveway.

After a short while he re-emerged, and approached where Kerry had since moved to. He took her hand again and gave her reassurance before he led her inside.

"It's gonna be fine," he said.

Mike's intention was to lead her straight through to the kitchen, but having got her as far as the hallway, Kerry broke away from him, only to enter the living room.

She again stood on the exact same spot as she had reached the last time she was in the house.

Mike returned to similarly stand next to her. He placed his hands on her shoulders, he felt her jump under his touch, before they both surveyed the living room.

Apart from their memories of that night, there was nothing else to suggest that anything dreadful had taken place.

After the crime scene had been closed, a specialist clean-up company had been sent in, again as a courtesy as this wasn't common practice, to sanitise everything and return it to some sense of normality.

Despite having seen what she wanted to see, Kerry didn't walk back out into the hallway.

Instead, she walked further into the living room, but she was very careful not to step on the spot where Ashley had been found lying.

It was almost as if the exact spot was shielded, preventing Kerry from walking across it.

She continued into the dining room, and from there into the kitchen, and when Mike caught up with her, she had already reached for some kitchen towelling, and was wiping her face.

As Mike approached her, she turned around to face him.

It was then that he saw a look he had never seen on her face before, a look of rage.

He could understand her anger, but at the situation, but he couldn't fathom why her rage appeared to be aimed at him.

"*You* did this," she erupted. "*You* brought this on us.

"It was *you* going to the police that caused this to happen.

"If *you* hadn't done that then *this* would *never* have happened.

"*You* killed my little girl. I hate you, *you* robbed me of my baby."

This outburst left Mike completely dumbfounded.

He could understand her upset, but he knew he wasn't responsible for what happened.

Nothing he had done hadn't been done without prior discussion and agreement with Kerry, and he had even given her a learned opinion as to the situation at every step.

He had explained to both Kerry and Ashley all possible eventualities. All except the one they were enduring now, as neither of them could have ever foreseen this.

Kerry ran out of the kitchen into the hallway in tears and headed straight up the stairs.

Mike was suddenly torn. Should he follow her or give her time to herself? After all they had spent the last four nights in a small hotel room together, with absolutely no privacy whatsoever.

Maybe now was the first opportunity Kerry had to allow her feelings to surface, and this was her reaction to the situation.

Mike felt it appropriate to allow her time to herself. He made himself a coffee and sat down at the dining table to drink it.

Instead of taking even a single sip, Mike just sat there staring at it, staring into nothing, as he relived the horrors, and imagined the pain and suffering that Ashley had endured.

He tortured himself with thoughts of how long she had held on to life before finally succumbing to her injuries.

Mike never got to see beyond where she was found, the carnage that had been left around her, and now it was impossible to determine the extent of any altercation following the thorough clean-up.

Mike's thoughts were brought abruptly back to the present moment by the sound of banging coming from the stairs.

He got up from the dining table and went back into the kitchen, and it was from there, as he peered around the doorframe into the hallway, that he saw Kerry struggling down the final few stairs dragging a suitcase behind her.

"What's going on?" he asked.

Hearing his voice, Kerry stopped before she made it as far as the front door.

"I'm sorry Mike, I just bear to even look at you at the moment," she said, in a pained voice. "Every time I do, I just see you as the reason all this happened."

Kerry paused to wipe a tear from her face.

"I need to be on my own for a while," she continued. "I need to do this, so please don't try and stop me."

Kerry felt the need to add the comment at the end, as she saw Mike begin to inch forward into the hallway.

But, as ordered, Mike froze, and he didn't know what to say.

So, he just stood there and watched Kerry struggle with the suitcase as she dragged it the rest of the way towards the front door.

Kerry had to release her grip on the case in order to open the door, she then held the door open with a foot.

As she reclaimed the suitcase, she accidentally glanced back at Mike. This caused a moment of hesitation, before realisation of the moment compelled her to defiantly continue.

Having stepped outside, Kerry didn't shut the door, instead leaving it ajar.

Through the a small gap Mike heard a car door slam shut, before an engine was started, signifying that his wife had left him.

He remained dumbfounded in the kitchen doorway for some time, before eventually approaching the front door.

But, instead of simply closing it, he opened it fully, only to step out onto the doorstep.

He sat down on the step, in order to allow himself time to contemplate what had just happened.

CHAPTER SEVENTEEN

Almost a week later Mike received a letter. As per usual, the postman made his delivery mid-morning, typically between ten and eleven am.

Mike was in the kitchen when he heard the letter drop onto the doormat.

Although it was mid-morning, he was drinking a whisky, and it wasn't his first of the day.

Mike set his glass down and went to retrieve the letter. Having picked it up, and turned it over, he instantly knew it was from Kerry from her handwriting on the envelope.

However, he chose to return to the kitchen to finish his whisky before opening the letter.

The letter stated that Kerry said that she would be taking care of all the arrangements for Ashley's funeral.

However, the letter didn't confirm any specific details, though it did suggest a venue, and that a provisional date and time had been booked. The date was eight days away, at midday.

Kerry also confirmed that Ashley was to be cremated, and that she was to be interred in the local cemetery where both of Mike's parents and Kerry's father had been laid to rest.

The reason the date could not be confirmed for the funeral was because Ashley was still under the control of the County Coroner, and this meant that until she had been released back to the family, no specific arrangements could be made. But in lieu of that, a provisional date had been agreed in anticipation of the release being granted.

Kerry didn't make any mention about what had happened the last time they were together, including the outburst in which she blamed Mike for everything that had taken place since he had reported Ashley's abuse to the police.

As it turned out, Mike had to read the letter several times before all the details sunk in through the alcohol fuelled haze that was increasingly consuming him.

When the letter finally made sufficient sense to him, he set it down on the counter and went back to his drink, only to realise that the glass was empty, so he took the liberty of pouring himself yet another.

One thing Mike did notice about the letter, was that it didn't have a return address. But, from the franking impression, Mike knew Kerry to be staying with her mother.

All things considered, this letter couldn't have come at a better time for Mike, as he was on the verge of drinking himself into oblivion, and this letter, and the notification of the funeral, was the kick start he needed in order to start taking some pride in himself again.

After a sensible lunch, the first decent meal he had in several days, he went to his wardrobe in order to choose suitable attire for the funeral.

He went through an array of suits, but he discounted all but one immediately based on colour.

He had only one black suit, though it was one that hadn't seen the light of day for quite some time.

He took it from the wardrobe, removed it from its dust cover and laid it out on the bed.

Mike shook his head, as he was not expecting it to fit. He wasn't sure if he was disappointed to find that the jacket was now too small across the back of the shoulders. It was so small in fact, that the buttons didn't even come close to being able to be done up.

"Bollocks," he exclaimed.

Mike knew that this would now compel him to have to go into town to look for a new suit, which couldn't be seen as a bad thing, as he hadn't left the house since returning home with Kerry.

Although he felt compelled to go out straight away, he conversely felt that given the amount he already had to drink that morning that it was probably best to wait until the next day.

CHAPTER EIGHTEEN

When the next day arrived, it was almost lunchtime by the time Mike had parked up at the local shopping mall.

Given what now laid ahead of him in the short term, he was already trying to get back into something that resembled a respectable routine. He had showered, and for once decided to wear something other than sportswear.

As there was an overall negative aspect to this excursion, shopping for his daughter's funeral, Mike tried to not feel guilty in enjoying being outside again, after having been a drunken hermit for the last week, and was hoping he'd allow himself to enjoy himself further.

However, as the priority, and sole purpose for the trip was to purchase a new suit, Mike's first stop was at a well-known department store.

It was there that he saw exactly what he was looking for, with the added bonus being it was discounted in a sale, which was even better.

Having found a suit in his size amongst those on display, Mike took off his own jacket and draped it over a rail of clothes before removing the suit jacket from the hanger.

He slipped it on, to find that it fitted him perfectly. He felt that a bespoke suit wouldn't have fitted any better, not that he would ever get to make such a comparison, not on his salary.

But Mike was not a person to be content in buying the first suit that ticked all the boxes, so he took the jacket off and replaced it on the hanger, before taking his phone from his pocket, and taking a photo of the label showing the size and price.

He then checked to see if they had more than one in this size, before deftly placing this one at the back of the rail, content in the feeling that it would probably be there should he have the need to return.

Conversely, Mike wasn't going to spend all day trying on suits. He felt he would try one more place, a shop equally known for rentals as well as sales, and then make a choice between the two.

When he got there, he was somewhat relieved to discover that the only suits that matched his requirements were significantly more expensive than the first suit and didn't fit anywhere near as well, as Mike had taken a real liking to the first suit.

oOo

Having returned to the department store, Mike purchased the first suit, which was exactly where he had left it, secreted at the back of the rail.

After which, given it was such a pleasant afternoon, he made excuses not to expeditiously return home, deciding to stop for a coffee, which he chose to enjoy outside.

He hadn't been there all that long, and hardly any time to start enjoying his flat white coffee, that he had ordered with a side-order of a slice a salted caramel cake, when he heard the distinct sound of emergency sirens in the distance.

Instantly, Mike became transfixed on the sound, and his first thought was to try and determine from where the sirens were coming from, and the direction they were travelling in, to determine if they were getting closer.

He listened intently, deducing that they were in fact getting closer and heading in his general direction.

It was then that Mike suddenly had a flashback, to that fateful day almost two weeks earlier.

oOo

Mike imagined himself back in his patrol car, when he heard the fateful radio messages, before he made his way through heavy traffic, struggling to get home as quickly as possible, not knowing what terrible sights awaiting him.

Only this time, as Mike played out the sequence of events in his mind, when he eventually pulled up outside his home there was not another emergency vehicle in sight, no police cars, and certainly no ambulances.

However, despite this change to history, Mike ran from the car, up the driveway, to the front door, only to find it already ajar.

Mike went to push the door open, and as he did, he heard voices arguing from somewhere inside his house.

The female voice he instantly recognised to be Ashley, whilst the male's voice was one he had never heard before, and as Mike pushed the door further open, so the voices got louder.

Mike cautiously stepped into the hallway, his TASER was now drawn.

"POLICE OFFICER WITH TASER, COME OUT NOW!" he wanted to shout, but although his mouth opened, no audible sounds came from him.

From the hallway, Mike could see flailing shadows on the living room walls, so he rushed into the living room, hoping to catch those involved in the act.

But when he got there, the room was exactly how he found it when he was led in by the sergeant on that day.

He again saw Ashley lying face down on the floor, with no one else in sight, and in that same instant, the shadows had vanished, and the voices silenced.

oOo

The voices in Mike's mind were replaced by two police cars, driving in tandem, down the High Street in front of where he sat, it was this that brought him back to the present.

Suddenly Mike stood up, almost disgusted at himself for allowing himself to enjoy a moment when his daughter had been recently murdered.

He picked up his suit that had been draped over the chair next to him, and left, having hardly touched his coffee.

This flashback had been something of a setback for Mike, and as a result, he made a pit-stop on the way back to the car, to restock his dwindled whisky supply.

It would appear that the course of the last two days had now come full circle for Mike.

CHAPTER NINETEEN

Having been contacted by the coroner's office, Ashley's body had been released back to her family, in this case to Kerry, and as such the provisional plans for the funeral had now become set in stone.

Having been advised of the same in a second letter from his wife, Mike woke early on the day of Ashley's funeral, as he wanted to make sure everything that he was involved with, however minimal, went to plan. As he didn't want to cause anyone any distress or embarrassment.

The initial bout of alcohol abuse, following his trip to buy his suit, and once again subsided, as he knew he had to have a clear head for what lay ahead.

Mike had also chosen to adopt some of the practices as he had on the day before his wedding, having chosen to shave the night before with a fresh blade, as opposed to that morning to negate any risk of shaving cuts, and should any occur, to give them time to heal.

After eating a proper breakfast, he laid out his suit, shirt and tie on his bed. He then gave his shoes yet another fresh coat of polish.

Mike chose not to rely on the layman's technique of using two brushes. Instead, Mike used the age-old practice, as adopted by military and the emergency services, of using a duster, or polishing cloth and working the polish into the shoe leather before shining it to a high gloss finish using either spit or water.

After everything was ready, Mike checked the time for the umpteenth time that morning, only to realise that he had woken and had made all necessary preparations far too soon.

So, with little else to do ahead of the allotted time to leave, he went for a walk around the block to clear his mind. But as Mike walked, he found his emotions began to get the better of him.

He was out in public on a bright sunny morning, but he was not afraid to allow his emotions to manifest themselves into tears that absolutely anyone passing him could see.

On a day like today, he knew they would come out sooner or later, and regardless of when, Mike was going to let it run its course.

When Mike got back home, he again checked the time, only to find that it was still too early to start getting ready. So, he made himself a coffee and took some time to sit down.

Sat alone in the living room, Mike thought about what Kerry would be doing at that exact same moment.

He imagined her at her mother's house, surrounded by her family; her mother, her sisters, and possibly even cousins would be descending on her mother's house, so they could travel to the chapel for the service en masse.

Mike then thought of where Ashley was. He pictured her lying in a coffin, as beautiful as always, awaiting her final journey.

Because Kerry had taken care of all the arrangements, Mike didn't even know where she was at that exact moment.

He considered the options, as she was either at the funeral director's offices, or already at the chapel, or the unlikely option was that she was at Kerry's mother's home ready to lead the cortege.

It was then that Mike realised that his face was now buried in his hands.

He was alone, and felt as much, which was the only thing he now had in common with his daughter.

There was no one around him to console him, to take away any of the responsibility or blame for what had brought them all to this day, as Kerry's word still bore deeply into his heart.

Having also realised that his coffee had gone cold, before he had given himself a chance to finish it, Mike returned to the kitchen and tipped what was left down the sink.

Once again, he checked the time by the clock on the wall. It was as close to the time to get ready as he was prepared to wait for.

oOo

Mike was immaculately turned out as he got out of his car after parking it behind the crematorium chapel, in good time ahead of his daughter's funeral.

He was a world away from the dishevelled shell of a man that had only existed and appeared to have given up living for the previous few weeks.

He stood tall as he slipped into his suit jacket which had spent the journey laid across the back seat, adjusting the collar, before taking a deep breath, only to hold it and let it out slowly. He then headed towards the chapel for the service and to say his goodbyes to Ashley.

The second letter to arrive had only confirmed the funeral arrangements, and there was nothing in the way of anything personal being said or implied within it, and no arrangements had been requested to attend with Kerry, or even to meet at any point during the day.

Consequently, Mike had made his own way to the crematorium, choosing to drive, so as not to be tempted to have a drink at the wake, as he felt that would be a slippery slope, especially on a day like today.

As he drove towards the crematorium, he wasn't even sure if he would attend the wake, but chose to leave it until nearer the time before deciding, as a lot had to, and could, happen before then.

Mike entered the chapel with plenty of time to spare.

So much, that he was the first one there and could easily have taken any seat of his choosing. But instead, he chose to wait at the back, and leant against the wall. From there, he watched as others entered before deciding where to sit himself.

As the congregation filed in, Mike felt more and more comfortable with the idea of hiding in the shadows at the back and decided to remain there.

This had the added benefit of giving him an elevated view of the proceedings, which he used to convince himself that it was acceptable to stay where he was.

The chapel filled in good time before the service began, and from where Mike stood, he could hear the hearse and the cortege pull up outside.

Another advantage that staying at the back gave Mike, was that he was free to move about as his desire, or mood took him. So, at this moment, it took Mike outside, and as he hadn't taken a seat, there was not one to be stolen.

The unexpected brightness of the sun at the lunchtime service caused him to squint as he stepped outside.

Even before the cortege stopped, he could feel himself start to well up inside, much like he had during his morning walk.

He didn't want Kerry or her family to see him like this, so he retreated inside, and hid himself up against the back wall of the chapel before anyone was able to alight from either of the limousines.

The procession itself then began to enter the chapel.

First to enter was Ashley, carried solely by employees of the funeral directors, as Mike hadn't even been given the opportunity to act as a pall bearer himself.

He didn't know what his decision would have been had the offer been made to him, but he felt as if he should, at the very least, had been asked.

After all, Ashley was his daughter too, and this would be the only aisle he would ever get to accompany her down.

The procession then continued towards the front of the chapel with Kerry and her mother, and the rest of the entourage, of which Mike was again not invited to be a part of.

When Kerry had entered the chapel, accompanied by her mother, her gaze was to her daughter in front of her, so she failed to see Mike, as he was stood in the shadows against the back wall to one side.

It was only when she had taken her seat in the front row, that her mother, who was only generally having a look round at all the faces there, caught sight of him.

She then relayed this discovery to Kerry, who in turn turned around herself to see Mike.

When he sensed she was struggling to pick him out, he stepped clear of the wall to make himself more prominent.

They exchanged glances, but for all intents and purposes, they looked upon each other as strangers. There was nothing intimate, or even familiar that existed between them at that moment.

When the service itself began, Mike's gaze was transfixed on the coffin mounted on a raised plinth at the front of the chapel. He was so focused on it, that he was oblivious to the sermon being given, or the readings being read, or even the hymns as there were being sung.

In Mike's mind, he was again conjuring images of what had happened on that dreadful day.

In his deductions, he began to agree with Kerry, that it was he who was responsible for what had happened, and that it should fall to him to strive to make things right.

Mike was only brought round from his trance by a well-wisher, who had recognised him, and wanted to shake his hand and offer his condolences.

But Mike didn't want to be wished well, he was in his own personal hell, and from his agreed opinion of perceived blame, that was exactly where he deserved to be, with no salvation due to him.

Nevertheless, he offered a pained smile, shook the offered hand, and politely thanked them for coming.

Mike knew this would be the first of many, with more still, should he attend the wake after the service.

His mind had fortunately come back to the present in time to say his last goodbye to Ashley, as her coffin was taken, by conveyor belt, through a now open hatch to the inevitable that lay beyond.

Which, in his mind, didn't bear thinking about, as it was commonly seen as one of the biggest tragedies in life, for a parent to outlive their child.

Even more so when the death occurred in such tragic circumstances.

As the service had now concluded, the congregation started to file out of a side entrance, as opposed to the way they had initially entered, as the next congregation was already amassing outside.

However, Mike continued to stand fast, as he watched and waited for Kerry to also pay her respects at the front of the chapel, and to offer her thanks their priest who had delivered the service. She then took a firm hold of her mother's arm to be led out of the side door.

Mike watched her from afar and saw as Kerry faltered in her steps. He pushed himself from the wall, as if leaping into action, wanting to catch her from falling. After recovering herself, Kerry turned back towards the front of the chapel, and blew a kiss towards the hatch that Ashley had passed through, before facing forward once more and continued outside.

As she drew level with the doorframe, she threw the briefest of glances in Mike's direction. He was sure it came with the welcoming smile that he knew and loved, but it was over all too briefly for him to be sure.

Then, just as Mike was the first to arrive, then he was also the last to leave the chapel as staff prepared the interior for the next service.

Once outside, he kept himself to himself. But, despite this, he still had to contend with more well-wishers offering thoughts and prayers, and condolences. Mike was as gracious as always but remained distracted.

He was just grateful that no one from the police had chosen to attend, either as support for him, or to represent the force itself.

He felt truly alone, and with no one there to have to tend to, he could be alone.

The service had proved to Mike everything that he felt he needed to know, and as a result, he chose not to attend the wake.

His rationale was, that as Ashley wasn't there, so he didn't need to be. But he still couldn't bear to bring the day to an end.

So, after everyone else left to attend the wake, Mike instead chose to spend the remainder of the afternoon wandering around the memorials in the grounds of the chapel, until such time that the sun disappeared below the treetops, and a distinct chill filled the air.

It was only then that he realised the time, and decided it was time to go home.

On the way home, Mike realised that he was in no mood to prepare himself anything for dinner. So, along the way, he took a slight detour and grabbed himself a fish & chip supper.

As he stood in the queue, he must have looked as though he had just come from a funeral, as his mere presence appeared to command looks of sympathy from other patrons and staff.

But he didn't want their sympathy, he didn't want anyone's sympathy, because he felt he didn't deserve it.

When Mike got home, he set down his dinner in the kitchen before stripping off his suit jacket which he hung on the back of a dining room chair, before undoing his tie, and draping it over the jacket.

Habit had unfortunately taught him that the first thing he now needed was a drink, and he poured himself a large whisky, which drained the bottle, and left him shaking the dregs into the glass.

It was the realisation of him holding yet another empty bottle, and one that had only been purchased a few days earlier, that the extent of his recent self-abuse had dawned on him.

He set the empty bottle down next to the glass and didn't touch either again.

Instead, he returned to the kitchen and made a start on his supper.

Although he had gone since breakfast without eating anything, Mike could hardly bring himself to eat any of it.

As a result, most of it ended up in the bin before Mike eventually went to bed.

His head hit the pillow with mixed emotions, as part of him didn't want this day to end, whilst the remainder couldn't wait for it to be over.

CHAPTER TWENTY

At the beginning of the week following Ashley's funeral, Mike unexpectedly received a phone call from his sergeant.

The purpose of the call was two-fold; firstly, it was a welfare call.

Better late than never Mike thought, as his sergeant went through a spiel of asking how he was and offering employee support programmes.

The second reason was a less than diplomatic, and completely tactless request for information, asking if Mike has yet considered a date for returning to work.

His sergeant also chose to kindly remind him that he had already been on compassionate leave for four weeks.

"To be quite honest with ya sarge, I don't have a clue when I'll be back," Mike replied. "Some days, I feel up to coming back, others, whilst others aren't so good. I wouldn't have thought it'd be too much longer though."

Mike knew full well that, personally speaking, his sergeant didn't give a hoot about his welfare.

He knew the call had been a diarised task based on a request from either senior management, human resources, or occupational health. Either way, it wasn't going to lead to Mike walking back through the doors of a police station until such a time that it suited him.

The sergeant suggested that the two of them get together for what was described as a *keep in touch* meeting.

However, Mike was damned if he was going to have his sergeant, a man he didn't have any respect for as a human being, let alone a police officer in his house.

So, instead, he agreed to a time, suitable to him, to go into the police station and have their meeting there.

Mike felt that he could also use this opportunity to pop into the CID office and get an update on Ashley's investigation as he hadn't heard anything thus far, possibly because any updates were most likely going solely to Kerry.

"How about I pop in this afternoon?" Mike said, and with his sergeant having agreed, the call was ended.

oOo

That afternoon, Mike attended his office and spoke to his sergeant as they had arranged.

The sergeant proceeded to ask Mike, yet again, when he felt he would be able to return to work, apparently oblivious to having him the very same question that very morning, though Mike went through the motions of being polite.

"I really don't know yet sarge," he said. "Things are still very difficult for me."

Their meeting concluded, having proven to Mike exactly what a pointless exercise it was always going to be, having achieved absolutely nothing beyond what the phone call had that morning.

Admittedly, Mike couldn't wait to get out of the sergeant's office, as after all, seeing his sergeant wasn't the real reason he was there.

"Stay in touch," were his sergeant's parting words.

"Of course," Mike replied, as he exited the office.

oOo

The CID office was in the same building as his department, but on a higher floor, and having left the response office, Mike took the stairs, as the lift in the building was notoriously unreliable.

But he found that he was out of breath having ascended the four floors, and had to wait for a moment on the landing in the stairwell to catch his breath, before entering the CID office.

"This is what all that boozing has done to ya," Mike said to himself.

As Mike entered the office, heads instinctively turned to face towards the door, and once again Mike felt the pressure of being the centre of attention, something he despised.

Amongst those gawping were some familiar faces, as Mike himself used to work in a branch of this department, public protection, before his fall from grace. He recognised them, and they recognised him.

Mike walked down the main aisle through the office, as he heading towards the section partitioned off for the *Serious Crimes Team*.

Along the way, given his notoriety, Mike had to again put up with yet more well-wishers offering evermore thoughts and prayers for him and his family.

"Thanks," he said, over and over.

Fat lot of good they've done for us, he thought.

Though Mike felt content not to correct any of them, to inform them that Kerry had left him.

When Mike found the team he needed to speak to, he leaned over the back of an unused chair and, almost apologetically, addressed a couple of officers who were sat with their backs to him, their attention at computers terminals.

"Hey guys," Mike began. "Am I able to get an update on my daughter's investigation?"

One of the officers then spun around expecting to see a member of the public standing there at having been ask such a question.

His immediate reaction was to challenge them as to why they were in a secure area, but instead, he spun around only to see Mike.

"Ohmigod, Mike," the detective replied. "I didn't know it was you, I hardly recognised you with a beard... Why didn't you tell me that you were coming in today?"

The reply compelled Mike to smile, albeit a slight one, though the first seen on his face in some time.

"Hi Nat, at least you bloody noticed, my skipper sure as hell didn't," Mike said. "I *didn't* know I was gonna be popping in until this morning.

"I had to come in for a keep in touch meeting, so I thought I'd kill two birds whilst I'm here."

There was a silence, as the other officer turned around to acknowledge what a poor choice of words Mike had just used give the nature of their investigations, and his enquiry.

The Nat to which Mike had address was Nathaniel Alexander, a detective sergeant, and former colleague of Mike's from when he was on the response team first time around.

They were always more colleagues than friends, but they always got on well enough to exchange pleasantries in the office, though never associated outside of work apart from at work events.

"I was hoping I could get an update on how things are going," Mike asked. "As I haven't heard anything from you guys since day one."

A perplexed look came over Alexander's face, as in the time since the incident, he felt that Mike should've had at least some contact.

The department wasn't working many investigations at the moment, so Ashley's case was prominent in his mind, so he didn't need to ask Mike for any details in order to open the report on his computer.

"Well, on one hand, it looks like there *haven't* been many updates," Alexander began to explain. "But it looks like they've all been going to Kerry Watkins… Is that your wife?"

Mike had been expecting this to be the case, and his expression reflected as much.

"Well, *ex-wife*, or at least *will* be," Mike said, "She moved out shortly after all this happened."

Although nothing had been said, or alluded to in any of the letters, Mike was merely resigning himself to what he believed to be inevitable.

"Oh dear, sorry to hear that." Alexander replied.

"Well, maybe I'm getting ahead of myself," Mike explained. "She's only moved back to her mother's for the time being, though I'm ever hopeful she'll come back home, now we've had the funeral. So where are we then?"

By this time, DS Alexander had opened the report in the Ashley's murder, as was perusing the information on the screen.

"Let me see," Alexander said.

He had a two-screen computer set-up on his desk, and using the mouse to navigate, he clicked on a hyperlink which opened another report. Which he then dragged onto the other screen so he could continue scrolling through the progress log.

"Okay, we've got a Neil Bannister down as a suspect," Alexander revealed. "Though it looks like that's *only* because you mentioned him in your account."

This wasn't the update Mike was expecting, given the time that had passed since Ashley's death.

"Is that it?" he exclaimed. "Haven't you got anything to link him to the scene, surely there's some forensics?"

Given Mike's response, DS Alexander knew he had to do better if he were to appease the grieving father.

"Hang on a sec," he replied. "He's linked to the victim for a previous domestic assault. He was arrested for that but released under investigation.

"Okay, here we are, house to house enquiries mentioned seeing a white car in the street, but no make, model or index given.

"The neighbour that called nine-nine-nine mentioned hearing a male's voice from within your address, but she couldn't be any more specific than that, and she didn't actually see anything either."

Alexander continued to scroll down. He paused, then scrolled back up to a section he had missed.

He then clicked on another hyperlink, which opened yet another sub-report.

He scanned down it, and as it was a sizeable report, it took him a good few seconds to scan through it.

"There does appear to be forensics linking the suspect to the scene," Alexander revealed. "But by the looks of things, they're considering their existence to be nothing more than circumstantial."

"Circumstantial?" Mike said, with a sense of shock. "How the *fuck* can they be considered *circumstantial?"*

This outburst not only caught Alexander off guard, causing him to physically jump in his chair, it also served to once again cause all eyes in the office to descend upon Mike.

"Well, it's stating that because Bannister was in a relationship with the victi..," Alexander paused, having realised his faux pas. "I mean, with your daughter, then he had a legitimate reason to be the house.

"So, the forensic hits they came back with, identifying his presence there, aren't in themselves evidence of anything, *other* than him being *there*."

"And, precisely, what hits were they?" Mike asked.

There was another moment of silence as Alexander returned to the top of the forensics report and began scrolling down again.

"Okay, so they found Bannister's fingerprints in the living room, kitchen and in the hallway," he paused. "Um, also on the banister, no pun intended."

None taken, Mike thought. *Prick!*

Alexander continued, realising his attempt at humour had fallen on stony ground.

"Also, there was seminal DNA found on a bathroom towel and her bed sheets," he concluded. "Which suggests intercourse in the recent past."

Having finished the report Alexander remained silent, as he had nothing more to say without risking further questions being asked. But there was nothing forthcoming from Mike, who just sat there in silence.

Alexander looked up from his computer and started watching Mike.

He could see that Mike's lips were moving, almost as if he were talking to himself, and his head went from bobbing to shaking as if gesticulating in reaction to his conversation with himself.

"Mike, are you okay?" Alexander eventually asked.

"He was *never* in my house before *that* day," Mike replied. "Not, once, Ash never brought him home, *ever*."

"But how can you be so sure Mike?" Alexander began. "I mean, don't get me wrong, I'm just playing devil's advocate here.

"You'll *never* be able to convince a jury that he *never* visited your house prior to the attack, either with or without your knowledge, during the whole time they've known each other."

Mike knew that Alexander was right, and that everything hinged on what a jury would be likely to believe.

"I don't know," Mike resigned himself to reply.

"Exactly," Alexander explained. "And because *you* don't know, and *can't* prove, is what makes the DNA evidence inadmissible.

"*Yes*, it puts him at the scene, but when, the day before all this happened, the week before that?

"Even his DNA on her body doesn't conclusively prove that's he's the one who did this, and that's where the problem lies."

Knowing what he knew, and all that he believed, Mike tried to come up with a plausible explanation, a version of events that considered everything that was provable, and what he believed could have occurred.

"Okay, I mean, yeah, the spunk on the bedding could've come from them having sex, but I doubt it," Mike said, beginning his contrived version of events. "Who's to say that this guy Bannister didn't attack Ash just to abandon her to die in the living room, go upstairs and mess up the bedding in her room, only to then throw one out over the sheets.

"For all we know, he could've had all the time he needed to make it look like they were in an intimate relationship, knowing that any defence will want to rule out all the forensics found in the w*hole* house, as being nothing more than circumstantial."

Alexander could see the increasing agitation in Mike, and knew he had to do something to appease him.

"C'mon Mike, you know how this works," he replied. "If there's an alternative plausible explanation, however unlikely, then, chances are the evidence will count for nothing, or even the case will get thrown out."

Alexander had tried to rationalise, relying largely on Mike's own experience, and Mike hated to admit it, but he knew that Alexander was right.

He had previously sat precisely where Alexander was now and has had to make the same justification to victims sat before him.

It was an awful truth, to accept such a disappointment. But Mike knew that with a smart barrister, the defendant, Bannister could get away with murder if this came to court.

"But we both *know* he did it!" Mike pleaded.

Mike could see Alexander sigh, as his chest rose and fell.

"Mike, it doesn't matter what we *know*," he said. "All that matters it what we can *prove*, you *know* that."

However, all that was being discussed was future events, skipping over the here and now, which Mike now wanted addressed.

"Proving stuff can happen later," Mike said "What's being done to find him now?"

"The usual, I'm afraid, nothing more at this time," Alexander replied apologetically. "He's shown as being *wanted* on the national computer system, and the feelers have gone out amongst all those who have got associations with him."

Alexander ceased with his commentary whilst he opened a new screen on his computer, which listed the names of other offenders, all of whom had links to Bannister.

The link was either from having previously offended with him, or from intelligence associating them with him in whatever other capacity, which could include merely being seen in the company of, in the same car as, or offering a family relationship, such as a parent or sibling.

Once the screen was open, Mike repositioned his chair to get a better look at the information on it, and began to scan down what was an extensive list of names.

Some of the names he immediately recognised, others he didn't.

Some he was surprised to see listed, while others not so much, and there were even quite a few names of those that Mike himself had previously arrested.

Of the names he recognised, some held Mike's interest more than others, as he looked to determine just how or why they were linked to Neil Bannister.

Which, in turn, dispelled the notion that, before now, Mike had never had any dealings with either Neil Bannister, or anyone in his family, as this information certainly appeared to prove otherwise.

It was only then that Alexander saw Mike perusing the list, and realised that as Mike was on compassionate leave, he shouldn't be viewing restricted information, so thought he'd better close the report on the screen.

Once the information displayed no longer held any interest for Mike, he sat back upright, and pushed his wheeled office chair back away from the desk.

Mike paused, as he was waiting for Alexander to suggest other lines of enquiry that were being followed, though the only thing to follow was a continued silence.

Mike felt embarrassed for Alexander, and that he needed to save him from it.

"What about the car?" Mike asked, with a tone of hope in his voice.

"What car?" Alexander replied.

"Bannister's car!" Mike again exclaimed. "He's got a Ford Focus ST, a white one, and it's probably the same white car that was seen in the street."

"Yeah, I saw something about that, gimme a sec." Alexander asked.

Mike watched as Alexander scrolled through yet more reports. He minimised some and dragged another to the other screen until he found what he was looking for.

"Here it is," Alexander finally said. "We went to put a locate trace marker on his car, only to find out it had already been reported as stolen."

"Hah!" Responded Mike. "What a crock of shit."

"Yep, my thoughts exactly," Alexander replied. "Chances are, it'll turn up as a burnt-out shell, *if* it turns up at all!"

They were both was referring the unlikelihood of Bannister's car actually being stolen, and that it was more likely the case, that to absolve himself, and eliminate any further forensics, that the Ford Focus ST was driven to the middle of nowhere and set on fire or dumped in a flooded quarry somewhere.

"He's gonna get away with this, isn't he?" Mike concluded.

However, Alexander didn't reply, as he didn't know what he could honestly say.

He would've had a spiel prepared for a member of the public, but he knew he couldn't convince Mike of anything beyond the obvious truth.

This left Mike was left feeling sickened and disheartened.

oOo

After leaving the CID office, Mike took a moment in the stairwell again to compose himself and come to terms with the disappointment he was just dealt.

As he descended the stairs, he realised that it would be useful for him to go to his locker, as he felt he would be a good opportunity to check to see if there was anything that he should take home.

Whilst he was there, he sorted through his uniform, and selected a couple of shirts that could do with freshening up. He also took a couple of other items that he felt would be more useful to him at home.

With that done, he left the police station, but as he passed through the front door, he paused, as a strange sensation came over him, a feeling he had never felt before.

As for the first time ever, before leaving the police station, Mike felt the need to have a look around before heading outside, almost as if it was to be his last chance to look, as if he were to never get to see it ever again.

CHAPTER TWENTY-ONE

Mike sat slouched in an aged leather chair, in his counsellor, Maureen's home office.

"So, Mike, how are you feeling about things now?" she asked of him.

He had the fingers of his right hand resting against his temple and feeling that such a question felt wasted on him, he raised them away from his head momentarily so to physically illustrate a non-verbalised response.

To delay his verbal reply, he repeated the question to himself.

"How do I *feel* about this?" he said. "How do *I* feel that the guy who destroyed my family is still walking about? How would *you* feel about this?"

His counsellor nonchalantly redirected the question.

"Mike, this isn't about me," Maureen replied. "This is about you, and more importantly, how you're coping with the situation you find yourself in."

To this question, the answer was much simpler.

"Oh, I'm totally fucked off, if I'm to be completely honest with you," Mike replied. "Fucked off that he's still out there, and that the police don't appear to give a shit anymore."

As per her remit, every answer conjured another question to ask.

"Why don't you feel the police don't *give a shit* anymore Mike?" Maureen asked. "You're in the privileged position to know the inner workings of the police, surely this gives you some comfort?"

"Hah!" Mike exclaimed, as he repositioned himself to be sat more upright in his chair.

He sat tall momentarily, before leaning forward, only to rest his elbows on his thighs, just above his knees.

He then gave Maureen, a glance as if to say, *'if only you knew.'*

"You don't have much faith in the police investigation, do you Mike?" she asked.

"Nope," Mike said as he shook his head.

"And why is that?" Maureen asked.

There was a pause as Mike deciphered a polite response from his usual trail of expletives that would have followed such a question.

Mike wanted to make his response constructive as opposed to a political rant, so he again sat back in his chair, and took a deep breath, as he took the pressure of his chest.

"It's become pretty much a case of, unless you have someone standing over a body with a smoking gun, or a bloody knife in their hands screaming *'I did it, I did it'* then it's not gonna get solved," he cynically concluded. "That's the long and short of it. So, if they haven't caught him already, and if he's not stupid enough to do something else that'll get himself caught, then we won't find him."

"We?" Maureen tentatively enquired. "So, you still consider yourself to be a police officer then Mike?"

There was an even longer pause than before, though this time Mike didn't even bother to verbalise his reply, instead he merely shrugged his shoulders to illustrate his sentiment.

"And, whilst on the subject of work, do you have any idea when you plan to go back yet?" Maureen said, before pausing to allow time for a response.

Then when none came, she felt compelled to continue.

"How long have you been off now?" she asked.

Mike again responded with a non-verbalised reply, looking more like a petulant teenager than a grown adult.

"I dunno, maybe a couple of months now," he replied.

"Not far off it Mike, after all you've been seeing me for the last five weeks," Maureen revealed. "I think it's probably nearer three months. So, do you have any plans for going back to work?"

Again, Mike shrugged before replying.

"I know I should," he replied. "But to be honest, I can't be arsed right now."

"That's understandable Mike," Maureen said. "But it may do you no end of good to have a focus for your efforts again."

"I know, and maybe you're right," Mike answered. "It's just that I can't stand people tiptoeing around me."

"I can certainly appreciate that," Maureen said. "But I think it's something you should at least consider. Would they have a phased return for you?"

"I would have to talk to *Occ Health* about that," Mike replied.

Occ Health, or Occupational Health Services is a department designed to keep employees healthy and safe whilst at work and manage any risks in the workplace that are likely to give rise to work-related ill health.

It would fall to them to decide on a return-to-work strategy for Mike, to ease him back into his role, as progressing too fast could have a detrimental effect on both Mike as an individual, and any member of the of the public that he would have to come into contact with through the course of his work.

"I really think it would benefit you to at the very least discuss your options about getting back into work," Maureen reiterated.

"Okay, I'll give them a call when I get home," Mike relented. "At least it will give us something to discuss next week."

CHAPTER TWENTY-TWO

As always, Mike kept his word, and following his counselling session, when he got home, he phoned up his force's occupational health services department and discussed his options for a return to work.

Since his absence had started, he had exhausted the compassionate leave afforded to him, as well as his self-certification period.

So, now he had to make regular visits to see his doctor in order to have his certificated absence extended, and this he now saw as something of an inconvenience, and something that he would be glad to see the back of.

The strategy that Mike and the advisor from occupational health had initially discussed and agreed, involved Mike returning to work on restricted duties.

This would involve him being in his department's office, but this would restrict him to only having limited interaction with members of the public, and only on the telephone.

Mike wouldn't be able to deal with anyone face-to-face and would not be required to have any dealings with suspects or offenders. This was deemed necessary in order to minimise any stress and aggression he would potentially be faced with.

It was also agreed that Mike would initially only work four hours each day for the first couple of weeks following his return. This would then increase over a period of a couple of months until he was back up to his full hours.

Mike also had the option to work his hours at the same time each day, or to align his time at work to that of his team. Mike chose the latter, in the hope that being with his colleagues would make his integration less unbearable.

oOo

With the date agreed, and as the days counted down towards it, so did Mike's level of anxiety rise.

So much so, that the night before his first shift back, he hardly slept a wink. Instead, he laid there, in his bed, staring at the ceiling, and clock-watching until he decided he could bear it no longer, and got out of bed.

It was just before four o'clock. He didn't have to be at work until seven o'clock.

oOo

Mike walked into his department's office within the police station.

It was the first time he had been back there since having the keep-in-touch day with his sergeant, which was the same day as his meeting with CID and getting the less than pleasing update from DS Nathaniel Alexander.

Mike could feel his heart start to race within his chest, although he knew exactly what he was doing here, and what was expected of him, what he didn't know was the human element and how were his colleagues going to react to him?

As he crossed the office, he ran through the options as to his involvement in what was about to happen, should he announce his arrival, or just keep it low-key, and wait to be noticed?

As it turned out, it wasn't long before his choice was made for him.

"Ah, there you are Mike," his sergeant said.

This was said untactfully loud, as if intentionally wanting to announce his return to the entire department.

Instantly, Mike felt uncomfortable, and instinctively checked his watch as he felt that kind of greeting should be reserved for those sauntering in late.

He despised being the centre of attention and given the sergeant's announcement all heads had turned to face him. Although they had smiles on them, to him it made very little difference.

The discomfort was thankfully short lived, as Ian Vale walked up behind him with a mug of tea in each hand. Both had been previously allocated, but Ian took delight in handing his one to Mike.

"So, you decided to keep the beard then?" he asked.

After taking the mug, and relieved in the distraction, Mike responded.

"Yeah, I felt I needed to look at someone different in the mirror each day," he said. "How'd you know about that?"

Ian knew the comment was meant as a joke but realised that the truth probably ran far deeper.

"I saw it when you popped in a few weeks back," Ian confirmed. "Hardly recognised you at first."

With his now free hand, Ian placed it on Mike's shoulder and led him towards his desk.

Along the way he placed the remaining tea on a desk for another colleague with a smile. It was only then that Mike realised that the tea he had been given was not in fact meant for him, and felt guilty that Ian had given his up, which reflected in his hesitation to drink from it.

"Oh, don't worry," Ian said, seeing his reaction. "I'll sort myself one in a mo."

As the office was usually *hot-desked*, where an officer sat at any available computer, as opposed to having a designated workspace, Mike had to wait for Ian to continue leading the way after delivering the tea as he didn't know where he was sitting.

Mike was relieved when Ian led him to a bank of desks away from the bustle of the office, where they both sat down.

Realising there was more to Mike's earlier comment about the beard than what had already been said, Ian picked up where he left off.

"So," he began. "Beyond the obvious, how have things been?"

"I needed a change, that's all," Mike began, taking a deep breath and sighing before continuing. "I wasn't lying when I said I couldn't bear to see myself in the mirror, I'm starting to understand why Kerry left me."

Ian felt as if his friend was only pausing and chose to jump in before he could continue.

"C'mon mate," Ian interrupted. "She hasn't left you, she just needs some time to herself, y'know, to come to terms with all that's happened.

"You just need to give her a bit of time and space to allow the dust to settle on all this, and when that's done, then she'll be ready to come home."

However, the expression on Mike's face led Ian to believe he remained unconvinced.

"She blames me for all this though," Mike tried to rationalise. "Even though we discussed it all and agreed on what we were gonna do *before* doing anything."

"It's just a gut reaction," Ian continued. "We all look for someone or something to blame in a time of crisis, it's human nature.

"If we can find someone to blame, it exonerates us of any guilt. It's what she needs to be able to put some distance between you two, just so she can deal with it."

Mike pondered Ian's advice, wanting to be able to believe him.

"I dunno, maybe you're right," Mike said. "It's coz I'm home alone that partly prompted me to come back.

"Being there, where it happened all day everyday wasn't doing me any good at all."

Ian paused as his tried to understand what Mike was going through.

"Well, I'll certainly agree with that," he replied. "Tell you what, how about we stop off for a quick pint on the way home? Y'know, have a proper catch-up, without the walls having ears like round here."

"Sounds good to me," Mike agreed. "But I'm on reduced hours for the foreseeable."

"Don't worry 'bout it," Ian answered. "We'll sort something."

oOo

As Mike was working reduced hours he had finished around lunchtime, after which he chose to simply go home.

There he waited for Ian to message him to let him know he was on his way to the pub having finished work himself.

The nearest pub to where Mike lived was only a few streets away, it was named *The Game Cock,* and was a family run pub, and although Mike chose to walk there, he still managed to arrive first.

As he walked across the sparsely populated car park, he realised that the last time he walked this route he was in uniform, and on that occasion, he was on duty. Following which he ended up walking out with a bloodied patron in handcuffs after a rather nasty scuffle.

It was one of those rare occasions when Mike had to respond to an incident in the borough where he lived, and consequently led to him avoiding the pub in case he was recognised. But that seemed like eons ago now, given all that had happened since then.

But, as so much had happened since then, added to which Mike felt he had changed beyond recognition, that he felt safe that no one would, put two and two together, and identify him as a police officer.

However, as Mike entered the bar, a moment of doubt descended upon him.

Maybe this isn't such a good idea after all, he thought.

fortunately for him, the population of the bar was indicative to that of the car park, and to say it was sparse would be an overstatement.

Like Mike, the pub itself had changed beyond recognition, perhaps having changed owners. Added to which as he approached the bar, he didn't recognise any of the bar staff, and so began to feel more comfortable in his surroundings.

However, he wasn't there long to order a drink before Ian joined him.

"What you having then?" Ian asked, as he stood next to his friend and colleague.

"Pint of bitter please," he said, directing his reply to the barmaid. "Something local if you got it?"

The young brunette behind the bar smiled and moved along the bar towards the array of brass taps.

Mike mirrored her movements and stopped opposite her, just as she indicated towards a tap for a bitter, which was produced by a brewery within the county, to which Mike concurred.

When the glass had settled, and received a top up, it was placed in front of Mike with a smile.

Mike took out his wallet, opened it and took out a ten-pound note which he attempted to hand over.

"No, no, no, I've got these," Ian said, thrusting his hand across the bar with a twenty pound note he had already to pay.

When Ian was given his change, the brunette apologised for handing him a fistful of pound coins, explaining that they were out of five-pound notes. Ian rolled his eyes as he took the change, before stuffing it into his trouser pocket before putting his wallet back in his jacket.

He then picked up his glass and indicated to Mike that there was a suitable table towards the back. He followed on behind Mike, and they both took a seat.

Mike sat first, claiming the seat with its back against the wall. He chose it instinctively, to having a vantage point for the front door and most of the bar area, as he never did like having his back towards the populous, not here, and not anywhere, if he could help it.

It was then that the conversation continued, as predicted, from where they left it that morning.

"So, when was the last time you spoke to Kerry then?" Ian asked.

"Not since *before* Ash's funeral," Mike replied.

This forced a realisation upon him that he hadn't spoken to his wife for well over a month.

"Well, isn't it about bloody time you pulled your finger out of your arse and spoke to her?" Ian paused to allow his point to sink in, as well as to take a mouthful from his pint. "You're as bloody stubborn as each other. It doesn't matter who calls who, just bloody well do it, tonight."

"If you come in tomorrow, and you haven't done it, there'll be all bloody hell to pay... You get me?"

Mike nodded along, as he knew Ian was right, on all points, including that he *was* just as stubborn as Kerry.

The call did need to be made, and it didn't matter by whom, just as long as someone did it.

oOo

They were both still on his first pint when the bar area started to fill up, with an eclectic mix of patrons, ranging from those who had probably just finished their homework in the previous hour, through professionals having a quick one on their way home, right up to the more senior members of society.

But despite this, the levels of noise and frivolity didn't increase all that much, and for this reason alone, Mike was grateful, as he was wanting to allow himself to enjoy the time he was spending there.

After their first pint, a second soon followed, though this time Mike took a turn to pay.

It was as he placed a fresh glass in front of Ian, before retaking his own seat, with his glass still in his hand, that he noticed a familiar face entering through the front door.

The face was instantly familiar, but it was certainly someone that Mike had absolutely no intention of approaching, or even alerting them to his presence, as they were certainly someone that Mike would not consider a friend, or even friendly.

It was upon seeing this man, that a large penny dropped for Mike.

It was like the proverbial bus, waiting for what seemed like ages for one, only for two to then come along together, and it was the same here.

Mike hadn't had anything to do with Dean Carter, since he had arrested him for the supply of cannabis, well over a year ago.

Yet in addition to seeing him now, Carter's name was also seen listed amongst Neil Bannister's associates, which was before Nat Alexander had realised his oversight and cleared it from his computer screen, when Mike had visited the CID office.

In the time since Mike had arrested Carter, two things had distinctively changed in Carter's appearance.

Firstly, he had put on a significant amount of weight, and secondly, as he stood at the bar, Mike could see that he had acquired a sizable scar around his right eye.

As Mike continued to sit watching Carter from a distance, he realised he was neglecting his company, though nonetheless remained transfixed on Carter.

Carter also appeared to move with laboured movements, which suggested to Mike that maybe he was nursing an injury of some sort.

As Mike watched him, he imagined who Carter must've pissed off in order to sustain such injuries.

The scar to his temple looked like he had been hit with a blunt weapon, a knuckle duster or something similar. The wound was well healed but had scarred badly.

Mike concluded that the original injury must've damn near taken his head off.

An occupational hazard, Mike thought. *Some things never change, and some lessons must be learned the hard way.*

He didn't have an ounce of sympathy for Carter, as there was no doubt in his mind that Carter's injuries came as a result of the same reason that Mike had previously arrested him, for drug dealing.

The young brunette behind the bar hadn't served Carter in the time he had been at the bar, but she certainly appeared interested in whatever it was he had to say to her.

From where Mike was sat, he was unable to hear anything of the conversation between them. But he could deduce from their body language that they were on very familiar terms with one another.

During Carter's conversation with the brunette, Mike could see him repeatedly looking around the bar.

He may well have been looking for someone, but Mike was certain that Carter was ensuring that no one was within earshot of what he had to say to her.

At one point, Mike could see that Carter was about to check in his direction, so he immediately averted his gaze, and picked up his glass before taking a mouthful.

As he lowered the glass, he could see Carter withdraw his hand back from across the bar, and in that instant, Mike was certain that had missed something crucial.

Again, he had no doubt in his mind what it was, it was just a case of in which direction the item had been passed.

Either Carter had passed something to the brunette, or that she had passed something to him. Either way, an exchange had just taken place, and it was apparent that Carter was still up to his old tricks.

With the exchange having taken place, Carter made a parting comment to the brunette, before leaving through the front door.

Mike checked the time, to see that it was just before eight o'clock.

Without Carter being a distraction, Mike was now able to give Ian his full attention again, with their conversation moving onto the topic of office politics.

This was a subject that grinded Mike's gears at the best of times and was the reason he had excluded himself from many a work function in the past, as they invariably only ever involved bitching about work, or the powers that be.

The brunette barmaid then came around the bar to clear three empty pint glasses from the table that Mike and Ian had left.

Ian was still there, but by this time, Mike was nowhere to be seen.

Mike had made an excuse to leave the table to use the toilet. But instead, he had gone out of the back door of the pub, into the beer garden, and had hopped over the low side fence into the street that ran alongside the pub.

He made his way round to the front of the pub just in time to see Carter drive out of the car park, seeing that he still had the same black SAAB 9^3 that he was driving when Mike last had dealings with him.

Mike continued to casually walk along the pavement as Carter drove passed him. Mike's gaze was to the floor, so he didn't know if Carter had looked over at him at all.

Mike then allowed himself a brief glance behind him for a few seconds after the SAAB had passed him.

He turned to see it turn left at the end of the road, though where it was heading was irrelevant, as all Mike was concerned about was that it hadn't stopped with Carter showing an interest in him.

Mike walked back into the pub through the front door and retook his seat next to Ian.

"I thought you'd fallen in," Ian said, joking about the toilet. "I was about to send out a search party."

As Ian was now sat there with an empty glass. Mike felt obligated to make the offer of another round.

"Best not," Ian said. "I'd best get home."

"Fair enough," Mike replied, as he remained standing.

Ian groaned as he eased himself to his feet. He had also reached the age where any movement was impossible without being accompanied with a sound effect. They both then headed back outside.

"Thank you very much," Mike said to the brunette as he passed by where she stood.

Once back out in the car park, Mike and Ian said their farewells and offer thanks.

"See you tomorrow bud," Mike said. "And thanks for this, I really needed this,"

"My pleasure," Ian replied, as he got into his car.

Mike then walked home, and unbeknown to him he was smiling, given this newly acquired knowledge.

CHAPTER TWENTY-THREE

With history repeating itself, honouring his promise to Ian, much like he had promised his counsellor, Mike swallowed as much pride as he could as he picked up the landline phone, before pressing the pre-set button that would automatically dial the number stored for Kerry's mother.

The phone rang for an extended period, which for Mike it seemed like an eternity, an eternity during which doubt started to cloud his mind.

During this doubt, the handset lowered from his ear, as his finger inched ever closer towards the end call button with the intention of terminating the call.

But, before he could reach it, the call was answered.

"Hi, it's Mike," he tentatively announced. "Is Kerry there please?"

There was a delay in response, possibly due to the surprise of the caller's identity.

"Hold on Mike," came a reply from the other end. "I'll just get her for you,"

Mike didn't instantly recognise the voice, but by a process of elimination, he felt it had to be Kerry's mother.

Given her abrupt reply, Mike was filled with even more trepidation than before.

After a few moments, Mike could hear clutter as the handset was picked up and Kerry responded.

"Hello Mike," she began. "I hoped to have heard from you before now… How have you been?"

Given the two possible responses, this was the one that Mike had hoped for, but not expected.

"I'm okay, I guess," he said. "I'm back at work now, Occ Health feel it's the best thing for me right now, y'know keep me busy, and out of trouble."

Mike heard the slightest chuckle before Kerry continued.

"Well, it's good to hear from you," she said. "I wanted to call you, but for some reason every time I tried, I just couldn't pick up the phone.

"I just can't have *anything* to do with *that* house at the moment. But believe me, it's just the house, and *not* you.

"I just needed some time away… Still do."

This explanation took a great deal of the load that Mike was carrying away.

"I can appreciate that," he replied. "I kinda wish I had somewhere else to be myself."

The only alternative accommodation available to him would have been a hotel, as both of his parents had passed on, and he was an only child.

"How have you been keeping?" Kerry asked.

"I've been okay," Mike explained. "Jack's been keeping me company, though a little too much for my liking."

Though Jack wasn't to be considered a friend, instead referring to his abundant consumption of whisky both before and since Ashley's funeral.

"Oh Mike," Kerry interrupted. "You can't do that to yourself!"

Normally Mike's spontaneous reaction would have been to respond with some quip remark about making the best of the situation after having been abandoned at home.

But even as his mouth was opening to form such a reply, he thought better of it.

"Granted, it did get a bit silly at one point, but the worst is behind me now," he said. "It's good to be back at work, if at least as a distraction.

"Any idea when you're coming back?"

He was conscious to avoid using the word *home* to avoid unduly putting pressure on his wife.

"I really don't know just yet," Kerry replied.

Mike could accept that, but given the progress he had already made, he was keen to push his luck.

"How's about I come up to see you sometime soon?" Mike asked. "Or we meet somewhere else?"

He remained desperate to make some progress in their reconciliation.

"I dunno Mike," Kerry said. "It *still* seems all too early, I think I need some more time to myself."

It was fortunate that Mike was speaking to Kerry on the telephone, as his body language did not match his words.

"Take all the time you need," he said. "I'm not going anywhere."

"Thanks Hun," Kerry replied. "Listen, I've got to go now, but I'll speak to you soon, bye."

Kerry then ended the call. Mike put the handset down on the counter, and took a couple of deep breaths to settle himself, though he wasn't angry or upset, he was just drained.

Those few minutes on the phone to his wife were crucial to everything that was happening to them both.

It hadn't gone as well as he had hoped, maybe what he had hoped for was unrealistic. But equally, it could have gone a lot worse.

All in all, Mike's first day back had been a good one.

Thanks Ian, he thought.

CHAPTER TWENTY-FOUR

The next day found Mike on his second early shift, having intentionally timed his return to work to coincide with the start of his team's shift rotation.

Following this second early shift, he would work two late shifts, and then two-night shifts. But, given his reduced hours, due to his phased return to work, although he intended to start his shifts at the same time as his colleagues, he would be finishing much sooner than they would be.

Between the events at the pub the previous evening, and speaking to Kerry, Mike felt a burning urge to seek an update on Ashley's investigation, and found himself distracted from his work by accessing the crime report.

Mike was fully aware that this was essentially a breach of protocol, as he had no legitimate reason to be accessing the report.

Although he was the father of the victim, he was not the investigating officer, and it was for those two reasons that he would be prohibited from viewing the report.

However, Mike didn't care, and had already weighed up the options, concluding that it was simply a case of cause and effect, and he had decided it was worth the bollocking, should one ever come.

But, given the circumstances, that's all it would be, a bollocking, and nothing more.

Mike felt that given what he was presently going through, they wouldn't dare impose anything greater upon him, after all, he was a grieving father.

Should any reprimand take place, it would most likely be in the form of an informal discussion, one designed to highlight Mike's lack of sound judgement and oversight, and to remind him of proper protocol, and that would be the end of it.

Officially, should he ever need to obtain an update into this, or any other investigation that he wasn't actively a part of, then Mike should approach the relevant investigating officer, give his rationale, and seek any update directly from them.

However, what Mike was looking to achieve was not something any investigating officer would grant him.

Mike was intrigued by the chance sighting of Dean Carter the previous evening, and he was keen to find out if there was a still a credible link between him and Neil Bannister.

The *associate* link between them on the police database could have been forged for any one of several reasons, including merely having a mutual third party.

Mike accessed the report into Ashley's murder investigation only to in turn access the profiles of both Bannister and Carter to establish the nature of this link.

It didn't take a lot of digging to find out that they had both been linked to several intelligence reports relating to the supply of class *A* and *B* drugs, specifically heroin, cocaine, and amphetamines.

It looks like our boy Carter's going up in the world, Mike thought.

This was based on the escalation from dealing cannabis from when Mike last had dealings with him.

Some of the linked reports were dated several years earlier, but the most recent only being dated in the last few months before Ashley's murder.

To Mike, this confirmed a long-lasting, and well-establish relationship between the two criminals, which was what Mike was hoping to find.

He was also hoping one would ultimately lead him to the other, as he made a quick note of Carter's address, and the vehicles he was currently linked to, in addition to the SAAB 9^3 before closing his report.

oOo

For the remainder of the time Mike had to spend in the office that day, he attempted to make a dent in the sizeable number of emails that had clogged up his inbox during his absence.

As there were so many, he decided to filter down the number by immediately deleting anything that wasn't solely address to him. Being of the opinion, that if something was important enough after his extended period of absence, it would be addressed to him personally, and even if it was important, then they'd send him another one.

oOo

Having got home, after working only four hours, Mike spent some considerable time thinking about the substantiated link between Dean Carter and Neil Bannister.

He felt with the way the police investigation was going, that Bannister may evade capture for quite some time, and this thought, combined with his imposed guilt, led him to reach some drastic and extreme conclusions.

As a result of these deranged thoughts, this led Mike to go into the dining room and pour himself a large whisky from his replenished supply.

He didn't sit down to drink it immediately, but instead nursed it as he paced around the ground floor of the house.

He went from the dining room into the kitchen, and from there into the hallway. He wasn't conscious of his actions, only of his thoughts, and his thoughts were all consuming.

So, consuming they were, that Mike hadn't even realised what he had done whilst in his focused trance.

He had walked from the hallway into the living room and had sat down as if he were getting ready to watch television.

There was nothing remarkable in this feat, except for the fact that this was the first time that Mike had sat down in the living room since before seeing Ashley lying there, face down on the carpet.

When he realised what had happened, he leapt from his chair, sending the contents of the whisky glass cascading across the carpet, forming a damp patch on the carpet.

The contrasting darkened area was immediately reminiscent of the blood stains on the same carpet, that had since been removed given specialist cleaning that had taken place during the time that Mike and Kerry had stayed at the hotel. When he still had some remnants of a family.

Once on his feet, Mike was pleading forgiveness aloud, though there was no one to hear him.

He wanted forgiveness not only for causing the spillage, but also for the lapse in his concentration that he felt could be misinterpreted as his getting over the tragedy.

"Oh God, I'm sorry, I'm sorry, I'm sorry," he pleaded, almost as if he was expecting a reply.

Mike went back through the dining room, and into the kitchen, there to collect a tea towel to mop up the spillage.

He was back in the moment, whilst exercising extreme care and consideration not to step on the living room carpet anywhere that Ashley's lifeless body had once occupied.

When he returned, he knelt off to one side and overextended himself to mop of the mess, and once done, he eased himself back to his feet, finally collecting the glass on the way up.

Mike again went back into the dining room, and there he again picked up the whisky bottle and loosened the cap.

He was midway through tilting the bottle to pour himself yet another glass when he paused.

Mike looked at the bottle, only to rotate it in his grasp to view the label. He then looked down at the empty glass on the table, and shook his head, disgusted at himself.

Though this chastisement was not for drinking, or even wanting another drink, but that his mind has wandered sufficiently enough to be oblivious of his own actions.

It was in that moment, that Mike knew his thoughts would become an obsession if he let them.

He resealed the cap and replaced the bottle in the cabinet, and as he closed the glazed door, he saw his own reflection in the glass, and he didn't like what he saw looking back at him.

But still he smiled, though it was a menacing smile, with Mike no longer recognising himself, and that went far beyond his physical appearance.

CHAPTER TWENTY-FIVE

The following morning, Mike was afforded the luxury of a lay-in, as his shift that day wouldn't start until 3 o'clock in the afternoon.

He woke with a clearer head than he had for some time, due to the absence of having consumed anything alcoholic the previous evening.

As he continued to lay in bed, staring up at the ceiling, this clarity allowed him a new perspective on a few things, and consequently he was more focused and energised.

One was that concerned him was his alcohol consumption, and he made a vow to stop it.

Another was Mike continually putting off something that was in dire need of taking place, and given these delays, he now felt disgusted and knew this hiatus must end, and that he finally needed to visit his daughter's grave.

This would be the first time he had been back there since Ashley's ashes were interred after the cremation, and his drive to the cemetery was a slow and painful one.

Once again, Mike continued to beat himself up about his delayed attendance, but at least he knew this pain would end very soon.

He stopped off along the way to buy some flowers to place on her grave. Though, he knew that nothing offered for sale at a supermarket or service station would do for such an occasion, instead, choosing a florist, knowing they would have something more suitable.

oOo

Having arrived at Ashley's grave, Mike took a moment to look upon the headstone which now stood in place of the temporary wooden memorial that had been erected at the time of the interment.

He looked upon the white marble, with black inlay engraving, and seeing his daughter's name, along with dates, that showed she was only seventeen years old, brought tears to his eyes.

Mike placed a bouquet of lilies in front of the head stone, before sitting down on the wet grass alongside it, only to lean against it, propping himself against the side of the stone. The wetness of the ground soaking into the seat of his trousers.

He rested his head against the stone, as if leaning in to a loved one sat next to him and began speaking to Ashley as if she were there to hear him.

"Y'know, your mother blames me for what happened to you," Mike began to explain.

However, before he could continue, he had to pause as he felt himself begin to well up, which needed to be address first.

"Please don't blame me baby," he continued. "We spoke about everything, and before *anything* was done, we agreed what we all felt was best. No one could ever have predicted this."

Mike then rotated himself around so that he was on his knees, and manoeuvred round so that he faced the inscription on the front of the stone once more. He reached out and traced the engraving of his daughter's name with his fingertips.

"I can't go on like this Ash," he said. "I can't go on with your mother, and God knows who else believing that I caused this, that this is somehow *all* my fault.

"I can't go on like this, not without doing something to make it right."

Mike then flopped back only to sit down again, only this time in full view of the inscription. He brought his knees up, and his arms folded on top of them.

Mike then glanced across the cemetery towards the chapel. His gaze then panned around, as far as he could see, only to determine that he was the only person there at that time.

As is typical to many cemeteries and churchyards, there was an abundance of yew trees, and one of these trees in particular grabbed Mike's attention, situated directly beyond Ashley's headstone from where Mike sat.

It had a long low, almost perfectly horizontal bough, that protruded from the main trunk, and below the bough, enjoying the shade the tree provided was a wooden bench.

As Mike continued to look at this tree, he estimated the horizontal bough to be about eight, maybe ten feet, approximately three metres, off the ground.

Then given the height of the bench, approximately three feet, or one metre, he visualised throwing a rope, with a noose in one end, over the bough, before standing on the back of the bench.

He thought, in this instance, he would only need to maintain his balance on the back of the bench momentarily, just long enough to slip a noose around his neck, as after that his balance would no longer matter.

Mike also visualised looking back towards Ashley's headstone as he took that single step necessary to be reunited with her.

He lingered on that thought. Before he reimagined it from where Ashley rested, and imagined her seeing his lifeless torso swinging beneath the bough like a timeless pendulum, and he wondered just how long he would be there, and who would be the first to discover him, and most importantly, if he would be missed?

These thoughts consumed Mike's mind for all too long, and it was only an alarm on his mobile phone that brought him back to the here and now, reminding him that it was time to get ready for work.

Because Mike was so out of step with his new work routine, he felt the need to set reminders for when he was expected to be at work, with the alarm giving him sufficient notice to prepare, as well as get there, should he have forgotten.

It was fortunate that Mike had taken this precaution as the thoughts that were, until that moment, consuming him were becoming all too tempting.

oOo

The four hours that Mike was required to work of his shift were spent in the office and were productive only in as far as they proved to be a useful distraction from the thoughts that had clouded his mind in the hours before getting there.

However,, once his shift was over, he wasn't in any hurry to leave the building and return to the solitude of his home.

Having finished his work, Mike popped his head around the door of the station gym, and saw that no-one was in there. Though this came as no surprise, as it was midway through a shift.

Given that it was empty, he decided to enter, though he wasn't dressed for a gym session, and didn't even have any suitable gym attire with him, feeling that what he had on would suffice, at least on this occasion.

The gym was sparsely equipped, but for its intended purpose was deemed adequate, being seen a token effort, on the part of his employer, to encourage staff to maintain a reasonably high standard of fitness, as the job role required it.

The equipment consisted of a poly-gym, a multi-stationed piece of fixed weight equipment, as well as some free weights, some kettlebells, and several aerobic machines including a treadmill, a rower and a recumbent cycle.

There was also a punch-bag that was hanging from a wall bracket in the corner, and this was the first thing to attract Mike's attention having entered.

It was an old canvas bag, and wasn't likely to be an item that had been financed by the police. Instead, most likely, it was brought in by a colleague after finding no further use for it at home.

Mike approached the hanging bag and took a stance, before throwing a few punches at it. He felt the impacts surge through him, and his heart began to race and pump adrenaline into his system.

He felt good, he felt empowered, and he felt that for the first time in a long time, he was doing himself some good.

As he continued to strike the bag the repetitive monotony of his actions allowed his mind to again wander, in search of its own stimulus.

With every strike, Mike imagined that it was Neil Bannister in front of him and not just a canvas target.

His blows continued to punish the bag as Mike's mind continued to torment him, as he imagined himself *mano a mano* with the man who single-handedly was responsible for destroying his entire family.

Mike hadn't realised that he had skinned the knuckles of his right hand through repeated strikes of the bag, and that blood was being left behind on the canvas with each successive blow.

Even when the dull thud of each impact was gradually being replaced with a sound like stamping in a puddle, Mike still failed to react.

It was only when the accumulated blood splashed across Mike's face as he withdrew his fist that he realised to what extent he had injured himself.

He stopped, heavily into oxygen debt, his lungs fighting to recover, his heart relieved at the timeout.

Mike looked down at his hands to see that they were trembling with fatigue as adrenaline still coursed through his veins. His knuckles were heavily bloodied, with spatter across the backs of his hands.

He then glanced up at the bag as it still swung gently in front of him, to see that within the recess he had created was now stained, the sandy coloured canvas now red, such a deep red it was almost black.

Mike was still fighting to control his breath, as his finally dropped his hands to his sides. He glanced around to room, hoping that no one had been there to see him.

To his relief, there was still no one else in the gym, and to his knowledge no one had entered in all the time he had been there.

As he glanced around the gym, Mike noticed the kettlebells that were on the floor beneath a rack of dumbbells.

He remembered having a couple of them at home, though he couldn't immediately recall where they would be.

But an educated guess, to narrow the search parameters, was that they were most likely in the garage, as that was where everything else seemed to end up, and upon his return home, finding them would be at the top of his to-do list.

oOo

When Mike got home, having opened the front door, he found a delivery card from a courier on the doormat.

It stated that a delivery had been made, but as the package was too large to fit through the letterbox it had been left somewhere, moderately secure, and concealed from passers-by.

The card instructed Mike to look behind the wheelie bin at the top of the drive.

Mike went to the wheelie bin as instructed, and lo and behold, there was a small brown parcel tucked behind it. Mike bent down to retrieve it.

As he walked back towards the still open front door, he began to examine the packaging, only to see that it was in fact addressed to *Miss Ashley Watkins*.

Mike immediately stopped in his tracks, froze for a moment in quiet contemplation, undecided what he should do with this package that was addressed to his daughter, who would never be there to open it herself, not knowing for sure if he should open it himself.

He however came to a decision based on the rationale that should the non-descript package contain any demands for payment, or an invoice of any kind for money owed as a result of the delivery then it would be ideal to know that and be able to settle any outstanding payment.

Rather that, than leave the package unopened and have the risk of debtors, or worse still bailiffs attending unexpectedly at any time in the future.

In all essence, the decision was a simple and rational one to make and having made it Mike continued into the house.

Once inside, Mike went into the kitchen, and placed the package down on the counter. He stared at the package, and again contemplated his decision, finally agreeing with his own rationale.

Picking up the package, he flipped it over, and pulled on the rip-strip that opened the package.

Without venturing any further, Mike could already see that it contained a Blu-ray or DVD box set of some kind, as it was thicker than a single movie.

He reached inside and slid the box out of the outer packaging, to reveal that it was the latest series of a medieval fantasy TV series that was amongst Mike's favourites.

However, unbeknown to him though, as he slid the box set from the packaging another item, a much smaller item, fell from the packaging only to land silently on the floor and bounce behind his feet.

As Mike looked at the boxset, he wondered who the intended recipient of the box set would be. This question occurred to him because Ashley never showed any interest in the show, and although it was one of his favourites, it was something that he used to enjoy on a regular basis with Kerry.

Mike then looked inside the packaging, to see that all that was remained was an invoice, which when scrutinised gave no further clues to the intended recipient.

All the invoice confirmed was that the box set had been a pre-order, which explained why it had only just been received, and Mike could see that the date of the order was several months ago.

The invoice also stated that in order to ensure free delivery all the items ordered were to be sent together.

"Items?" Mike queried.

He then looked at the listed items on the invoice, to see that there were two items enclosed.

The first was the TV box set, and the second was only described as a *keyring/pendant*, though this was nowhere to be seen.

Mike investigated the packaging again, only to confirm, beyond any shadow of a doubt, that it was empty.

He then stepped back away from the kitchen counter, to be able to examine the area beneath where he had stood.

In doing so he kicked the fallen item across the floor. However, Mike didn't notice the impact of the kick as the item was so small and light and he still had his heavy work boots on.

Having checked the area of the floor without any success, Mike resigned himself to the fact that the item was lost.

As the packaging wasn't in the best condition, he concluded that maybe it fell out during transit, and realising it was just a keyring, he wasn't too concerned.

At least having opened the package he had confirmed that no monies were owed as a result of the delivery.

Leaving everything as it was, Mike left the kitchen, walking into the hallway, and as he walked, he took off his coat, only to hang it up.

It was as he returned to the kitchen that a beam of sunlight through the kitchen window caught the fallen item in such a way as to reflect the beam directly into Mike's face. He stopped midway along the hallway and focused on the glinting item.

As he got closer to it, Mike was able to determine that this was the outstanding item, that it was a keyring of some sort.

It consisted of a small metal disc, not much bigger than a fifty pence piece, on a split-ring. It was sealed in a cellophane bag and was face down, with a plain side uppermost, as Mike picked it up.

Still crouching, Mike turned it over to see the other side, and read the words engraved on it:

Mike's legs instantly went from beneath him and he collapsed against the range of kitchen counters, dropping everything he was holding.

Once on the kitchen floor, and having taken a moment to compose himself, Mike retrieved the keyring from the floor as he slumped against the lower-level cupboards.

He began to sob uncontrollably, having realised that the package's contents were originally destined for him, as a present as his birthday was little over a month away.

He concluded that Ashley had pre-ordered the TV box set as she knew it was one of her father's favourites, and because it would be released in plenty of time to arrive before the big day.

Time passed, yet Mike didn't move. Instead, he just sat there, clutching the trinket, a trinket that had a material value of very little, but something that now meant the whole world to him.

CHAPTER TWENTY-SIX

For the next few days Mike continued to abstain from drinking anything intoxicating.

However, this proved to have an equally detrimental effect, as his body went through the process of purging itself. He felt rough, but he knew it was necessary.

During this time, Mike gave a lot of thought to recent events, and as he did so random pieces of a jigsaw began to fall into place before him.

Due to Mike continuing to work reduced hours, he wasn't going to be working the night shifts alongside his team. Instead, he worked another two late shifts, though these would have him working alongside a different team.

Given the limited time he had to spend in the workplace, each day had become more or less identical to any other, and Mike now chose to begin them with a hearty breakfast, in the hope of satisfying his renewed alcohol-free appetite.

Then each morning, after he had given his breakfast a chance to settle, Mike had eased himself back into something of a physical workout routine, having found his kettlebells, under a thick layer of dust, in the back of the garage, as first thought.

His workout was basic but given the time that had lapsed since he last paid any attention to his fitness it proved to be more of a challenge than expected.

However, as the days passed, so the workouts became more structured and designed to improve his mind as well as anything else.

oOo

After arriving home after working the required four hours of each of his late shifts, Mike had felt had compelled to go out for a walk.

This purpose of these walks was mainly for exercise, but also to allow time for his thoughts to wander.

Today it was still early, about half past seven, but it was only just after sunset.

But, before heading out on this occasion, Mike had chosen to revert from using his police warrant card holder as his wallet to using a normal folding leather wallet, to contain both his bank cards and cash.

The reason for this was very specific, as he didn't want every Tom, Dick and Harry getting an eyeful of his warrant card every time he wanted to pay for something.

This was because this evening at least, Mike didn't consider himself to be a cop and had no intention of drawing any attention to the fact that he was.

For the preceding three evenings, he had walked the same route, a route that, at about eight o'clock, was intended to have Mike pass by *The Game Cock* public house.

On the first occasion, his walk had the desired result of seeing the black SAAB 9^3 that belonged to Dean Carter parked in the car park, which was then confirmed on every subsequent occasion.

This led Mike to believe that Dean Carter was a creature of habit, or at the very least routine, and with three sightings out of three, he could now potentially be relied upon to be at the pub, more often than not, at about the same time. With this assurance, Mike's plan could evolve.

As a progression, unlike the previous evenings, Mike had decided to enter the pub on this occasion.

He was more confident than ever that Carter hadn't recognised him from their previous encounter, and wouldn't recognise him now, even if one of them was to spill their drink over the other. Though Mike wasn't planning to put that theory to the test.

oOo

Instead of entering through the front door as he did on the previous occasion when he met with Ian, Mike went along the side of the building only to enter through the back door, accessed via the rear beer garden.

As Mike entered, he had a feeling of déjà vu, because as he entered the main bar area, he saw Carter propping up the bar in exactly the same manner as he had on the previous occasion.

The brunette barmaid was also there, and she still appeared to only be pretending to look interested in anything he was saying to her.

The two of them equaled about half of the total population of the pub, though this was now upset by Mike having added to the number.

Mike approached where they stood, and as he reached them, he placed both hands, palms down, on the bar.

He felt he was close enough to Carter to get his attention, though not close enough to be invasive, or perceived as threatening his personal space.

Nonetheless, once Mike had arrived, Carter gave him a scornful look, though this was wasted as Mike's casual gaze was towards the taps in front of him, and the range of bottles behind the bar.

However, he could see, in his peripheral vision, that Carter's eyes were on him, and Mike could feel his gaze burning into his cheek, before it scorched down his left arm and focus on his hands.

Mike looked down at his own hands, and it was then he saw what must have been the focus of Carter's interest.

Both of Mike's hands were still heavily scabbed across the knuckles, as a result of taking his anger out on the punch bag in the station gym a few of days earlier.

Mike's intention was to look over to the brunette barmaid, but as he did so he couldn't help himself making the briefest of eye contact with Carter. Just long enough to see Carter give him an approving nod.

Mike deduced that this was Carter acknowledging his battle scars as being as the result of a fight or brawl.

Carter was a waster, a thug, and consequently it appeared he only had respect for those of a similar disposition.

"Yes, my love, what can I get ya?" the brunette said.

“Um, pint of bitter please,” Mike replied, taking out his wallet.

Again, Mike could feel Carter’s gaze on him. But on this occasion, Mike wanted to have his full attention, for Mike wanted Carter to see his wallet, as it was full of cash, far more than he ever normally would.

Habitually, Mike hardly ever carried cash, as he would pay for even the smallest purchase on his debit card.

But now, Mike was hoping to get some attention, and potentially make an unspoken statement, as he had a wedge of bank notes, about a quarter inch thick, in his wallet. He took one out, not knowing if it was a ten, or a twenty and handed it across.

In reality, there was now just under eight hundred pounds in the wallet, as Mike had visited a cash machine on each of his walks, including today’s, and had withdrawn the maximum daily allowance on each occasion.

Then once his drink had been poured, the brunette rang up the sale, and gave Mike his change which he stuffed into his pocket without even checking it.

Having picked up his pint glass, Mike deliberately turned in a counterclockwise direction so not to turn his back on Carter, and as before as their glances passed each other, so he saw that approving nod again.

Although Carter was a punk, there were things he would still have some respect for, and two of those were undoubtedly violence and money, and this evening, Mike had inadvertently indicated he had a penchant for both.

Another thing that Mike had also proven, was that it appeared that Carter didn't have the slightest clue who he was.
Mike took a seat, towards the back of the pub, at the same table that he had sat at with Ian, and as he sipped his pint, he feigned interest in what was being shown on the television. Though his smile had nothing to do with what was being shown. Instead, it was in having already achieved everything he had set out to do.

Whilst Mike enjoyed his pint, he saw Carter leave, and recognised the sound of his SAAB as he drove out of the car park.

Once his glass was empty, Mike courteously placed it on the bar, to save the brunette from having to retrieve it from his table, before leaving and walking home.

CHAPTER TWENTY-SEVEN

As Mike had finished his rotation of shifts, he was now into his four rest days off work.

However, now having more time on his hands, with no distractions, so his mind chose to revert to the disturbing thoughts that he had begun to entertain during his compassionate leave.

Only now his thoughts had manifested themselves beyond a notion, even beyond an idea, as he now had a plan, to which he had already added the information he had gained over the previous few days.

As Mike contemplated his plan, he decided it was workable, but knew that links between certain aspects of it were tenuous at best.

He felt there was too much down to luck or chance, but Mike wasn't a firm believer in relying on either.

For what he was considering, and the price it was likely to cost him, Mike knew he had to either be committed to this one hundred percent, having a virtual guarantee of success, or not at all.

So, before committing on this course of action, Mike needed to substantiate certain details, and he already had a good idea how to go about this.

oOo

So far, whenever Mike had visited *The Game Cock* it had been to see if Carter's SAAB was in the car park.

However, now he needed to go there when he could be sure it wasn't.

Mike deliberately went outside of the times he had been going there previously, to improve the odds of still seeing the brunette barmaid there, but without any chance of Carter being there himself.

Mike didn't know the hours she worked beyond the times he had seen her there in the evening, and he knew he didn't want to make any enquiries to the same. All he knew was that he didn't want to be there at any time Carter would most likely pop in.

So initially Mike went to the pub at lunchtime on the first day, and when that was unsuccessful, revealing she wasn't there, he went gradually later and later on each of the successive days.

oOo

It was on the third day, that all the elements fell neatly into place, as firstly there was still no sign of a black SAAB 9^3 in the car park, and when Mike entered the bar, he saw that there were only a few scattered patrons, and the brunette was now the solitary figure behind the bar.

"What can I get you, my love?" she asked in her customary tones as Mike approached the bar.

"Pint of bitter please," Mike replied. "And, er, I don't s'pose you know where a guy can score a little something else in the way of entertainment?"

A puzzled look fell across her face as she took a glass from the rack and moved along the bar to the bitter taps.

"I'm not sure I know what you mean," she said innocently.

"Yeah right, of course you do," Mike interjected. "C'mon, a little bird has told me that your fella, y'know, the guy's who's in here most evenings can help me out in that department.

"Look, I ain't the filth, if I was, well that'd be considered entrapment, and that's something that ain't allowed."

By this time the brunette had finished pouring Mike's pint and had placed it on the bar between them.

Mike had now taken out his wallet and was already holding it in such a way that she could see the amount of cash he had in it, having added to it from his previous visit.

Mike took out a twenty-pound note and handed it over, which the brunette cautiously took before she turned her back on Mike to go to the till.

The process of ringing up the sale appeared to take longer on this occasion than on any previous occasion, and Mike didn't know if she was just pondering the decision before her, or whether she was awaiting someone's approval. But, either way, when she returned with Mike's change, she also returned with instructions.

"Give me your number," she said. "And he'll give you a call."

She then took out her mobile phone out and got ready to type Mike's number into a text message.

"Who's gonna call me?" Mike asked.

"Who you asked for," she replied.

"Do I get a name?" Mike asked. "Y'know, so I know who it is when they call me?"

Mike was only making a casual attempt to fish for more information, though the brunette realised the legitimacy of the question, and realised she was out of excuses.

"It'll be Dean or Neil," she replied, though in a much fainter voice than before.

Mike was about to ask her to repeat herself, just as he felt the need to metaphorically kick himself and thought better of it.

"And when can I expect one of these fine gentlemen to call me?" Mike instead asked.

"Most likely later on this evening, I'd say at a guess," she replied.

As Mike was satisfied with this response, he gave his mobile number to the brunette, along with giving his name as *Mark*, for no other reason than it sounded like his, so if ever it was called, he would subconsciously be alerted by it.

Mike then picked up his pint of bitter and raised it in a gesture of thanks, before retreating to his usual table towards the back of the pub.

Mike casually watched the brunette from his table, but no more than he watched the rest of the bar area. He watched her use her mobile phone, to probably write and send the remainder of the text message that had begun with Mike's number. She then busied herself behind the bar until she was interrupted by a message being received.

With her attention back to her phone, Mike felt her gaze upon him as she read the reply.

He felt as if he was being sized up, and wondered if it was for the legitimacy of his enquiry, or whether Mike was seen to be the sort of person who could handle himself should the situation go bad.

Although it was too early to tell, but Mike was sure that eventually he'd find out.

Having finished his pint, again partially out of courtesy, but mainly to have an excuse to have a further interaction with the brunette, Mike took his glass back to the bar.

He made sure he made eye contact with her, and offered a smile, before leaving out the front door.

oOo

Within the hour after leaving the pub, Mike's phone rang, and when he retrieved it, he discovered that it showed the caller was withholding their phone number.

As Mike wasn't expecting any other calls, he had a good idea as to who the caller was.

"Hello," Mike said nonchalantly as he answered the call.

"Is that Mark? the caller asked. "Are you the police?"

"Yes, no," Mike replied.

"What?" the caller questioned, confused by the reply.

Given this confusion, Mike felt that he needed to over clarify, and simplify his response.

"*Yes*, I'm Mark," he said. "And *no*, I'm *not* the police."

He could then hear muffled profanities at the other end of the call.

"What is it you want then Mark?" the caller eventually asked.

"Just a few ten bags," Mike asked. "Bit of weed, and maybe a bit of white, if you've got it."

He was asking for some cannabis and cocaine, with a ten bag being a small, individually wrapped portion, which costs ten pounds for ease of distribution.

"Yeah, I can do that," the caller replied. "Where are you?"

"Walking distance of *The Game Cock*," Mike replied.

There was a pause as the caller contemplated his reply.

"Okay," he said, eventually breaking the silence. "How's about I meet you in the car park for the boating lake… It's just around the corner from the pub… Shall we say nine-ish?"

It all sounded good, except for one small detail.

"*Ish?* What's all this *ish* shit?" Mike replied. "I don't wanna be waiting around all bloody evening, y'know?"

Mike knew he needed to come across keen to do a deal, but he didn't want to seem too eager, as those who use recreational drugs aren't renowned for their patience and tolerance, so he needed to come across as a little bit edgy.

"Okay, I'll see you at nine then, on the dot, that any better?" the caller said, just as the line went dead.

Mike looked at the clock on his phone as he lowered it from his head. He still had a few hours to pass until nine o'clock.

Given how the call had so abruptly ended, Mike was now left feeling unsure of things, had he struck the right balance between urgency and understanding, or had he just blown the deal.

Once again, only time would tell.

CHAPTER TWENTY-EIGHT

Mike spent the few hours he had until the rendezvous, contemplating his next step.

His actions, should the intended transaction go to plan, would intentionally involve him crossing the line into criminality, for he would be buying a controlled substance, and should he ever be caught in the act, or details of it come to light at any later time, then he would not have a leg to stand on, and there would be no way of justifying his actions as part of any criminal or disciplinary hearing.

However, there were so many variables apparent at this moment in time, as Mike was unsure even who would be turning up at the meeting.

He could potentially expect to see the same black SAAB 9^{3} that he had seen in the car park of *The Game Cock* on numerous occasions, with the lumbering lump that he knows to be Dean Carter offering to sell him illegal drugs, or it could be an unknown vehicle, with an unknown occupant, or occupants that attend.

What if it's Bannister? Mike thought. *Then what do I do?*

However, these were all eventualities that Mike needed to consider and decide upon a course of action before even attending the meeting.

oOo

Mike had got to the car park that served the boating lake well ahead of the agreed time.

He knew the area well, as it was in his locality, and had visited the park that encompassed the boating club on many occasions.

But he hadn't been there recently, so wanted to use the time he had to determine just how busy the car park was prior to making himself known to anyone.

In addition to his decision to walk to the location, Mike had also dressed down for the meeting, having gone from habitually wearing jeans, shoes and a jacket when he would leave the house, to wearing tracksuit trousers, trainers and a fleece.

This was because he felt he needed to wear something loose and light, should things become physical, or should the need arise for him to make a quick getaway on foot.

On first arrival, Mike chose not to enter the car park, instead he kept to the woodland that surrounded it and completed a reconnoitre of the area.

The car park itself was an area that was unmade, covered with loose gravel, and in very bad condition. This tended to mean that only patrons of the boating club used it, as the dog walkers in the area favoured another car park. Despite the club itself being closed, there were still a couple of cars parked up.

As Mike continued to walk around the periphery, he saw a sign on the gate that led from the road, that the club had put up.

It stated, amongst other things, that the gates closed at 6pm daily, and advised against getting locked in, though it did go on to offer a means of contacting club staff should that happen.

Despite this impartment of information, Mike smiled, he had never known the gates to ever be shut., and as it had most definitely past six o'clock in the evening, they were still wide open.

The car park was also unlit, so all-in-all it did make an ideal place to meet for something like this to take place, and was probably somewhere that Dean, or whoever, had nominated on numerous previous occasions.

Though for Mike, it was even more suitable, as the location gave him virtually three hundred and sixty degrees of egress should the need arise. With the only exception being the lake itself, as the rest lent itself to fields and parkland in the immediate vicinity.

Mike kept to the shadows as he checked his watch, revealing that he still had another ten minutes until show time.

Whilst he waited, he kept a close eye on the entrance to the car park., though he didn't have to wait long before the glow of headlights lit up the entrance.

From solely being able to see the front of the vehicle, and given the low light conditions, added to which its beams were projected towards him, Mike wasn't able to determine what make or model the car was, and he couldn't even to determine its colour yet.

The car performed a manoeuvre, much like that Mike had done on foot, slowly driving around the entire car park before parking up facing towards the exit.

Mike concluded that it was most likely being positioned for a quick getaway, should the need arise.

Mike continued to watch the vehicle as the headlights went out, and the engine was turned off.

He could now clearly see the car in profile and was able to determine that it was Carter's black SAAB 9^3.

Mike assumed that he was the driver, but he had no way of telling who else, if anyone, was in the car, not yet anyway.

Mike moved around the periphery of the car park, remaining in the shadows, only to emerge and approach the SAAB from the direction of another car that was already parked in the car park, as he didn't want them to think he'd just emerged from the undergrowth, instead giving the impression that he too had driven there.

Having walked clear of the parked car, Mike continued in a circular path, and like so much else, the reasons for this were two-fold.

Firstly, this was so the occupants of the SAAB would see him approach sooner rather than later and be less startled when he finally reached the vehicle, and secondly, and most importantly, Mike would hopefully be able to determine just how many people were inside the car, and if he would recognise any of them to be either Carter or Bannister, or possibly both.

Mike approached confidently, yet cautiously. He made sure he had his hands out of his pockets, and that his head was up so he could be recognised, in case the brunette had introduced him as being the guy from the pub the other night.

As Mike got closer, he could see two people in the car, the driver and a front seat passenger. He recognised the driver to be Dean Carter, but the passenger was someone unknown to him, only being able to rule out it being Neil Bannister.

Carter opened his door, which caused the interior light to come on, which offered further confirmation of the anonymity of the passenger. This also confirmed that there was no-one sat in the back seat.

Having got out of the car, Carter shut the door before taking a step towards Mike.

"You here for me?" Mike asked. "Was it you I spoke to on the phone?"

Carter nodded and extended a hand to be shaken. Mike looked down at the hand for a moment and thought how inappropriate it would be to shake it.

But to Carter this was a nothing more than a business transaction, and any deal would be off if Mike failed to engage in such a simple gesture of civility.

So, despite it paining him, he reached out and shook the hand, turning his hand so his palm face uppermost, which can be seen as a subliminal sign of submission, giving Carter the upper hand, allowing him to assert dominance, as well as a subconscious sense of superiority and confidence.

"Nah, weren't me, do I look like a fucking secretary?" Carter replied, releasing Mike's hand. "I don't do that side of things."

He then started to walk around to the back of the SAAB, and indicated to Mike that he should follow on behind him.

At the rear of the car, Carter lifted the tailgate, which caused lights on either side of the interior to illuminate. This revealed, in amongst, the usual items found in an aging car's boot, there were three boxes that had once contained sports shoes. Carter hinted towards the boxes, and once Mike's gaze was upon them, he continued.

"So, what do you want?" Carter asked.

"I'll take fifty of each," Mike said. "And if it's any good I'll be after a whole lot more next time."

Mike reached a hand into his trouser pocket and pulled out of handful of twenty-pound notes.

Upon seeing the wad of cash, Carter smiled, and proceeded to lean into the boot and knock the lids off the shoe boxes.

From within one box, he rummaged around and selected a single bag containing a white powder, and from within another he took three bags containing something similar in appearance to chopped up mint.

Carter held up the bags in one hand and extended his open other.

"That's fifty of one, and sixty of the other, three times twenty, yeah?" Carter explained. "Let's call that a nice round hundred for a new customer."

Mike counted out the cash before handing it over, as Carter offered him the bags to take, and with that, the deal was done. Mike scrutinised the bags and looked approvingly at the contents.

"So, how do I get hold of you next time?" Mike began. "I don't really wanna have to go via your missus every time I want some gear."

"Are you on *chat*?" Carter asked.

"I don't even know what that is," Mike replied.

This made Carter smile, as he and Mike were clearly from different generations.

"It's a app, call *chat,*" he explained. "Go to your app store and download it. Then search for the username *dudes t,* all lowercase, all one word.

"Then message it, whenever you want something and we'll get back to you, okay?"

Mike nodded, his agreement, if not his understanding, as he didn't have a clue what Carter had just told him.

All he remembered was to look for an app called *Ch@t* and a username of *dudest*, as he was sure that he would figure out the rest later.

With his reason for being there at an end, Carter walked around behind Mike, back towards the driver's door of his car.

"Enjoy," he said, as a parting gesture.

Mike was still stood at the back of the car when he heard a door slam, and the engine start.

The lights then came on, illuminating Mike in an ominous red glow, who instinctively stepped to one side, so not to be directly behind a car with the engine running.

Mike watched as the SAAB pulled away, shooting up some loose gravel against his legs.

Once the car had left the car park, Mike started to walk home, though this time his route took him around the lake, and as he passed it, he pierced the bags he had just purchased before throwing them into the lake.

Mike was now one hundred pounds out of pocket over the deal, and now had nothing to show for it, except the means to make further contact, which to him was far more valuable.

CHAPTER TWENTY-NINE

It was late the following morning when Mike eventually woke, and after having a coffee, he retraced the events of the previous evening in his mind.

He had downloaded the *Ch@t* app to his phone on his way home the previous evening, so he wouldn't forget it, and now all he had to do was to set up an account of his own.

It was as he did this that it dawned on him why this medium had been adopted for making contact.

This was because it required nothing more than an email address to set up an account, and none of the account holder's details were shared beyond his username, and he knew that anyone can create an email account out of nothing, which would leave nothing to trace any incriminating conversations back to them.

Having set up his account, and verified his email address, that Mike also realised that maybe the username might not be *dudes-t* as Carter had stated, and that just maybe it was *dude-st,* referring to what was likely to be Neil Bannister's pride and joy, his Ford Focus ST, and he was the dude in question.

Things were now falling into place as far Mike's plans and desire for retribution were going, as he had now established a credible link between himself and Bannister. However, and for what he had in mind, Mike now needed to find a suitable location, before he could entertain aspects of his ideas any further. But from his time working the area as a police officer, so many possibilities as to a suitable location readily leapt to mind.

What he needed was a suitable building in a remote location. It didn't even have to be secure, it just needed to be large enough to shelter a car and have sufficient space for the task at hand.

Initially, Mike considered any one of several disused industrial complexes that existed in the locality.

Near to where he lived there was a disused sand quarry that comprised several buildings, of which any one of them would be suitable, as well as there being a largely derelict industrial estate nearby.

However, Mike was aware of numerous reports over the years of youths using these sites for recreational activities including drug use, raves, and various types of street-racing.

Consequently, Mike felt he needed to rule such places out, as the last thing he wanted was any interruptions, or for any preparations he had made being discovered before he could put them into effect.

This compelled Mike to consider other types of sites that were privately owned, as well as disused farm buildings, and though he needed somewhere that was conveniently located, but still relatively isolated, yet again several locations occurred to him.

oOo

Mike spent the rest of the morning driving between three possible locations, all of which were within a twenty-minute drive of the boating lake.

He had considered other sites, which were perhaps more suitable once he was there, but Mike chose to dismiss anywhere that required a longer drive. This was because, when the time came to make the journey, he may very well have an unwilling passenger.

Of the three locations that he visited, two were more suitable than the third, purely and simply because they had a concrete and tarmacked approach road from the highway.

Mike felt that anything less could prove problematic should, when the pieces fall into place, it be on a day with adverse weather conditions, and he certainly didn't want to get bogged down or stuck in any mud.

Mike was a stickler for preparation, and so wanted to be able to rule that out as an aggravating variable from the outset.

He also considered that should the police become aware of his actions earlier than anticipated, and helicopters potentially being overhead, then any fresh tyre tracks to any perceived disused buildings may set alarm bells ringing, and cause Mike to have unwanted company.

Of the two locations that remained, each had elements that made it more suitable than the other.

One had a more a suitable building, remote to anything else on the site. But this outbuilding, if anything, was in too good condition, which suggested that it was being maintained, and therefore didn't really qualify as derelict.

It gave Mike the impression that there was a responsible owner somewhere off site, who visited the location on a semi-regular basis. This again made it unsuitable to Mike's needs. Also, the outbuilding was found to be virtually empty, which meant that Mike would need to source, and transport everything he required to the location himself.

However, the last site, ticked all the boxes, as it had the remoteness that the second site had, as well as the desirable hard standing approach. But overall, it appeared to be in an overall state of abandonment and disrepair.

The site itself consisted of several buildings, which spoiled Mike for choice, and as some of the buildings were completely hidden from the narrow approach road, only increased their suitability.

Mike had entered the site and parked out of the sight of the highway behind a building.

Having got out of his car, he just stood motionless, and listened, and all he could hear, in the distance was a faint hum of a motorway which he knew to be some distance away.

It was then a passenger jet flew over, only for Mike to realise that he was under the flight path of the nearby airport.

He knew this would prove useful in keeping any unwanted air traffic at bay, as permission would need to be sought from air traffic control before conducting any airborne searches, as any takeoffs or landings from the entire airport would need to be suspended for the duration of any search, which had always proved problematic for the police.

With the first couple of boxes ticked, Mike then began to explore the site.

He knew he needed a building that he was ideally able to drive into, so this ruled out a few instantly, at least for that purpose. Mike then approached a single storey brick-built building, which appeared, from the outside, to be some sort of workshop.

Before he entered the building, Mike slipped on a pair of black leather gloves.

They weren't just normal gloves, as they had a Kevlar lining, which meant that they were moderately effective against a knife attack.

These were one of the items he had taken from his locker on the day he visited the CID office, and they had previously served Mike well. To such an extent that they were now battered, and had small cuts all over them, though they still proved serviceable.

Mike found that he could only gain access to the building through a pedestrian side door, as the double doors to the front were secure.

Once inside, he could see that the building was divided into several smaller rooms, none of which were spacious enough to serve his intended purpose. Though, one room, however, did intrigue him.

He could see that it had once been a workshop, as it had a waist height wooden workbench that ran the full length of the wall under the window, and it still had a table vice affixed to it.

Also, there was a shelving unit which still had a couple of hand tools on it that had, for some reason, been left behind, and having stepped in for a closer examination of the tools, Mike could see why.

Amongst them, there was a bow saw, which had less teeth than an old crone, also a cracked and split wooden mallet, and finally there was a wood smoothing plane.

Mike picked up the plane and ran a gloved finger across the blade. The blade was dull, rendering it just this side of useless.

Granted it was useless for its intended purpose, but as he handled it, it gave Mike and idea, an idea which he would allow to flourish, before placing it back on the shelf and stepping outside once more.

The last building on the site was a derelict looking timber framed, and cladded barn, and Mike could see from the outside that he would have absolutely no problem gaining access to it as there was a distinct gap between the hinged main doors.

Once inside the barn, Mike realised that this building would prove to be ideal, as not only was there sufficient space, but there was also clutter.

Just from looking around, Mike was coming up with ideas as to how to utilise some of the disused equipment that had been left there.

Given its suitability, only one thing remainder, and that was to enable him to be able to bring a car inside, and for that he went back to the doors, and with a little persuasion, eventually they both opened fully.

Mike stood in the open doorway and concluded that the vehicular route to the barn was simple enough, and that there was ample space inside the barn to accommodate a large vehicle, so fitting a car inside wouldn't be a problem at all.

Turning to face inside once more, Mike saw there was a huge pile of baled hay off to one side, as well as a few pieces of farming machinery which he was unfamiliar with.

But what had caught Mike's eye was an old and battered red pick-up truck, a Datsun, which had the rear end elevated, and was being supported on axle stands.

Mike approached the vehicle and peered into the cab, and as both door windows were down, he was able to have a good look inside.

From the cab, Mike walked around to rear of the flat bed, and released the latch on the tailgate to see if it would lower, which it did.

In the back of the truck, he saw a trolley jack, which had most likely been used to elevate the truck in the first place.

Again, having a fledgling idea come to mind, Mike reached into the back of the truck, and grabbed one of the wheels of the trolley jack, pulling it towards hi, and as he did, he felt the truck groan on the axle stands beneath him as it took his added weight, which unnerved him.

Mike picked up the jack and was taken off guard by just how heavy it was, which caused him to have to half drop, half lower it to the ground as soon as it cleared the tailgate.

He then retrieved the jack handle from the back of the truck, and inserted it into the socket on the rear of the jack and pumped the handle, but even after a few strokes, nothing happened.

"Bollocks," Mike said aloud.

His experience of such a piece of equipment was limited, but he was mechanically minded, and he knew that if the plate failed to lift, then it had to be due to a lack of pressure, that was most likely caused by either a lack of hydraulic fluid, or a faulty seal.

Mike then realised that the release valve was open, and tutted to himself, as he rotated the turnkey, closing the valve. Then once sealed, the piston rose evenly with every handle stroke.

Satisfied that the jack worked, Mike moved on, although he remained unsure just how such a piece of equipment would feature into his plans.

As it turned out, the rest of the contents of the barn didn't require anywhere near as much scrutiny or examination.

On a pallet in one corner, were stacked several bags of cement, probably surplus to when the concrete base and driveway were laid.

Also, there were a few hand tools hanging from the various posts and beams, which included hand saws, sickles, and scythes. Though again, their presence interested and intrigued Mike, he had no specific plans for them.

Having achieved all he felt he could at that moment, Mike left the barn, and the site as a whole as he had found it.

He then drove in the direction of the boating lake to get an idea of the route, as well as the approximate time it would take to drive from one to the other.

CHAPTER THIRTY

Having chosen a location, based on its merits, and taking into consideration all the equipment that was readily available to him at the barn, Mike was now able to begin to formulate his plans into actions.

He now felt confident that when the time came, he could get hold of Bannister. However, the main variable there would be whether he needed to go via an intermediary, but there he would allow circumstances to dictate.

Though once he was finally able to get his hands-on Bannister, Mike was much more certain about his actions.

With the pieces of his plan coming together in his mind, all that remained was the need for contemplation, whether to move forward and go beyond the point of no return, and for contemplation, there was only one place for Mike to go.

oOo

"Everyone knows who did this to you Ash," Mike said, addressing Ashley's headstone. "And, without you even having told me I now know his name, I just can't bring myself to say it here.

"He's wronged us, all of us, though none more than you.

"Your mother is suffering, so much so that she can't stand the thought of even being at home right now, and she can't bear to be around me either. Our family has been destroyed over this."

Mike sat himself down on the grass beside his daughter's grave, pulling his knees up, only to wrap his arms around them.

"If I don't do something now, this will never end for us," he continued. "You may not agree with what I'm going to do. It's contrary to everything we have brought you up to believe.

"But right now, I feel that two wrongs *can* make things right."

Mike averted his gaze away from the headstone to the ground in front of him as he could almost feel Ashley's disapproval at what he had just implied.

"I *need* to do this, for *all* of us," Mike went on to say. "He can't be allowed to get away with this, and with the way things are going, he just might do."

Mike interrupted himself before getting to his feet.

"But I can't be a police officer and still do this," he said, as he straightened up. "Back, before you were born, I took an oath to uphold the law and protect people."

As he spoke, Mike took a small black leather folding wallet from his pocket, and opened it.

What it contained was a metal crest, the emblem of Mike's police force, and opposite it was an identification card which included a photograph of Mike, along with his name, rank, and warrant number.

He looked at the crest, and then at the photograph, and smirked as he bore little resemblance to the person in the photograph, and in ways that went far deeper than merely his appearance, as not only was the image now grossly out of date, having been taken during Mike's initial training over two decades earlier, but greater changes had taken place inside the man.

Long gone was the desire to seek out and bring criminals to justice, and to strive and help the vulnerable members of society.

It now appeared that twenty years of systematic abuse by society, the institute of modern policing as a while, not to mention the government of the day, had taken its toll, and had broken this once noble man to the point where he was now readily contemplating the uncontemplatable.

All his training, experience and knowledge that had been focused on removing criminals from the streets would be for nothing if he became lawless himself to pursue justice.

It was then that Mike recalled, having once read, though not remembering the source, *if you kill a killer, the number of killers in the world remains the same.* Mike accepted that there were some obvious flaws with that quote, but he certainly took the meaning as it was intended.

He then took one last look at his ID card and force crest before kneeling again, only to tuck it behind the bouquet of fresh flowers he had laid in front of Ashley's headstone.

But this was not before having taken out his security pass card, as he still had use for that.

"Look after this for me will ya?" he said to Ashley. "I promise I *will* be back for it... afterwards."

Mike remained kneeling momentarily, with his eyes closed, as it in prayer, before finally standing again.

He then took a step backwards, kissed the tips of the finger on his right hand, only to them on the top of the headstone, allowing them to linger there, before eventually turning and walking away.

CHAPTER THIRTY-ONE

As Mike walked back across the garden of remembrance to his car, he took out his mobile phone.

He opened the new Ch@t app, and messaged the account with the username *dudest,* the message read:

> I need some gear, more than before. I've got the cash, when can we meet?

Then in the time it took him to reach his car, Mike had notification of a reply.

> Same time, same place, ok?

Mike replied to this message, confirming the meeting, before driving away.

With this confirmation it appeared to him that everything appeared to be in readiness, and it looked like that night would be the night that his plan would be put into action.

oOo

Mike drove from the cemetery back towards town, and parked up in a side road, just off the main road.

However, before alighting from the car, he allowed himself another moment of quiet contemplation.

Having finally alighted from his car, Mike walked back towards the main road, before heading towards a service station, just along from the junction with the road where he had just parked.

Once passed it, he continued to walk down the road, as he wasn't there to visit the service station. Instead, he only wanted to have a look across the forecourt.

It was a service station that was familiar to him, as it was the same service station that he and Ian had used as a coffee stop on many occasions. The last time being the same morning when they had gone looking for the perpetrator of the domestic assault.

As he walked past the forecourt, he had seen that there was only one vehicle at a pump, which was a black crew-cab 4x4 pick-up.

Mike continued walking on the same side as the service station until he was level with a public telephone kiosk, only then did he cross the road.

Before opening the door to the kiosk, Mike put his Kevlar lined gloves on. He then entered and lifted the receiver, intentionally coughing to clear his throat before dialling the number, 9-9-9.

After less than two completed rings, the call was answered.

"Emergency operator," came the answer. "Which service do you require?"

"Police please," Mike replied.

The line then went quiet as the call was connected to the contact centre for the local police force, which was the one whom Mike worked for.

"Police, what's the emergency?" The police call handler asked.

"It's the petrol station along the High Street," Mike replied. "There's a group of lads who look like they're trying to break into the cash machine."

Mike could hear frantic typing coming down the phone.

"I see you're calling from a telephone box, is this near to the location?" the call handler asked.

"Yeah, that's the one," Mike replied. "I'm opposite it now."

"I see, I've got your location from the phone number," the call handler said. "Can you describe any of them?"

Mike paused, to glance back towards the forecourt.

"I can't see them now," Mike replied. "But they did get out of a black 4x4."

Again, more frantic typing could be heard.

"Are you able to stay on the li…" the call handler asked.

But before she could even finish her question, Mike hung up on her, having already achieved all that he needed to, and he couldn't need to stay on the line any longer, as he now had places to be.

Having exited the kiosk, Mike crossed back over the road and headed back to his car, and from there he drove towards the police station.

Along the way, between the service station and the police station, Mike saw exactly what he was hoping to see.

For as he drove casually in one direction, he was passed by three police cars driving hastily in the other. They were all driving using their sirens and blue emergency lights, evidently having somewhere to be, and as they passed Mike he kept his gaze straight ahead, but he did allow himself a smile.

oOo

Within a couple of minutes Mike had parked just up the road from the police station.

Although he was off duty, his security pass card, that he had taken from his warrant card wallet, still worked, and he entered the police station through a side door and went up the back staircase.

Mike exited the staircase onto the floor that his department's office was on, knowing that it was only preferable, and not essential that he wasn't seen, at least not until the final aspect of this visit.

His department's office ran the entire length of the floor in an 'L' shape. It had exits at both ends, and a mid-way door that led to toilets and a locker room next to the station gym.

From one end, Mike looked through the Georgian wire pane in the fire door to see an office devoid of any human activity.

But before he was prepared to stroll into the office, he needed to be sure that there wasn't anyone lurking around the corner, out of sight from where he was.

Mike went back into the corridor, then he entered the locker room from the other side. He then glimpsed through the door that led into the office, and confirmed that still, no one could be seen.

He then went back into the corridor once more, and around to the last door to the office, and again before entering, he surveyed what he could see through the fire door, with still no sign of any one there.

Mike had achieved exactly what he had hoped, with his 999 call from the telephone box getting a deployed response that would clear the department.

He knew that an incident, such a robbery or burglary in progress, with an identified vehicle would get as many police units to the scene as possible, whilst others would conduct a search of the surrounding area for the black 4x4 in case it had fled before police arrival.

For a moment, Mike pictured the black 4x4 being followed, only to be stopped by officers, maybe even firearms officers.

Though he didn't think too badly about it, as they'd no doubt be allowed on their way after a short delay, after probably having their wits scared out of them.

With his mind back on the task at hand, Mike still cautiously entered the office, knowing that the place he needed to get to be a cupboard that was just inside the office on the left.

He knew that the cupboard itself would be locked, but that the key was kept inside a combination key safe affixed to the wall beside the door.

It was in accessing this key safe that Mike knew he would be at his most vulnerable. Should he be seen engaged in that activity, he would have no excuses as to why he was trying to access a secure part of the police whilst he was off duty.

Mike approached the cupboard door, and went to the key safe. He already knew the combination because he had prior reason for legitimate access to this area whilst on duty, but not now.

As Mike began to rotate the combination tumblers, he heard a toilet flush.

"Fuck, fuck, fuck," he whispered to himself as he finished the combination and opened the safe to get the key inside.

The question, and indeed the dilemma now presented itself, as did Mike now enough time to unlock and open the cupboard and gain access before whoever was in the toilets came back out?

He had no excuses if he were to be discovered, and as such he wasn't prepared to take any chances.

Mike chose to close the key safe and secure it by rotating one tumbler by one number only, before exiting the office taking the key with him.

From there, Mike then went back to the locker room in which the toilets were situated as he anticipated that whoever it was would be going back to the office, and that he would now be positioned behind them.

For that much he was right, because just as Mike entered the locker room, so he saw the opposite door, the one that led back into the office close.

Mike then slowly approached that door, and through the window, he could see an officer returning to their seat.

it appeared that a single officer had remained in the officer when all his colleagues had gone to the service station incident. Mike considered that he was probably in the middle of another job and couldn't be redeployed.

Mike analysed the officer's potential view of the cupboard from where he was sitting, and felt confident that if he could keep noise to a minimum, then he could access the cupboard without being seen.

Mike went back into the corridor, and back around to the door nearest the cupboard and entered the office once more.

From where he now stood, Mike couldn't see the officer. He advanced until he stood facing the cupboard door.

Keeping his back to the wall, he glanced to his right, and still couldn't see the officer, feeling that conversely, he was sure that he couldn't be seen.

Mike inserted the key, slowly and silently into the cupboard door lock, before turning the key, slowly and silently.

With the door unlocked, Mike depressed the handle and stepped inside, shutting the door gently behind him, whilst keeping the handle depressed before slowly releasing it.

Mike now stood in a large storage cupboard, with the only thing in it with him being a large floor safe.

This safe was accessed by the same security pass that got Mike into the building along with a six-digit code which he already knew for legitimate access.

Mike swiped his pass card, and grimaced as he input the code, as each keystroke was acknowledged with a beep.

In the silence of the cupboard, each sound echoed and was amplified, and probably sounded louder than it was.

With the safe now unlocked, and Mike turned the handles to withdraw the bolts and opened the door.

The safe contained the station's supply of TASERs, along with battery packs and spare cartridges. It was this that Mike needed, and the reason why he had come to the police station.

Mike took a TASER from a drawer, though he knew he couldn't risk the noise it would make if he tested it there, so he switched out the battery pack for a fresh one just in case, as well as grabbing a spare. He then took two single-shot cartridges from another drawer, before finally easing the safe door shut, leaving everything as he had found it. Concealing everything he had taken in his pockets.

Now, he had most certainly crossed the line, having left the point of no return in the distance behind him.

He was also at the time he was at his most vulnerable, as he now had to exit the cupboard without knowing what was on the other side of the door.

In the time he had been in the cupboard he hadn't heard any activity, but his attention had been so focused on other things, so he hadn't been attentively listening.

Before doing anything else, Mike checked that he had left the safe as he had found it. He then listened intently.

He couldn't hear anything on the other side of the cupboard door, and it certainly didn't sound like anyone had returned from the service station deployment just yet.

But there was no way of knowing what was on the other side of the door without opening it and opening it would indicate to anyone nearby that Mike was in there, an off duty officer, one who was now unlawfully in possession of a firearm.

What he had already done was enough to have him face disciplinary enquiry, which would potentially result in him being sacked from his job. There were no longer any excuses for what he had done.

Mike couldn't hear anything on the other side of the door, and he said a silent prayer to himself, hoping the officer, the only person he knew to be in the whole office was still sat at his desk. If he was, great, if he wasn't, Mike was potentially fucked.

Mike took hold of the door handle and eased it downwards, before pushing the door open only, but only about an inch.

He held the door firmly as he put an eye to the gap, looking in the only direction available, which was thankfully towards the office.

Though there was no sign of any activity, he knew the longer he procrastinated, the greater the chance of him being discovered.

With that, Mike was out of the door like a shot, closing it gently behind him. However, he chose not to waste time, and risk being seen by locking it, or by replacing it in the combination safe, instead leaving the office taking the key with him..

Mike then walked briskly back down the corridor to the back staircase, before descending it and exiting the building just as he had entered it.

As Mike walked back towards where he had parked his car, he nonchalantly dropped the cupboard key down a convenient sewer drain.

Once back at his car, Mike drove to a quiet side street. There he took out the components he had just stolen from his pockets and began to assemble them.

First, he inserted the new battery pack, or power magazine into the base of the TASER handle, much like a bullet clip, or magazine for a pistol.

Then he tested the device by depressing the trigger, which caused a brilliant arc of electricity to jump between the electrodes, that lit up Mike and the interior of the car. Once the cycle was complete, Mike then attached a blast cartridge to the front of the TASER, and with that, it was now ready for use.

Mike knew he only had two cartridges for the TASER, because at the time of taking them, he didn't want to take more, as in doing so would make his intrusion obvious at the next change of shift. Which could have led to an access audit which would have showed his unauthorised entry.

However, given the issue with the key, when it was found to be missing, he felt that such audit was now likely to determine who could've lost it, when no one would be admitting to it, but those were the breaks.

This meant, he should only fire the TASER it if the situation absolutely warranted it.

Though less than completely satisfied, Mike headed off.

Although he had already passed the point of no return, his evening had barely started.

CHAPTER THIRTY-TWO

Like his previous meeting, Mike chose to be at the boating lake car park rendezvous with plenty of time to spare ahead of the scheduled time.

His attire was much like the previous meeting too, with the only difference being that this time, he also had a rucksack with him.

Whilst on his way to the car park, Mike again pondered the variables, so he was as well prepared for every eventuality as he felt there could possibly be.

He was hoping that, at the very least, he could rely on Carter being there again, ideally on his own this time. Or better yet, for Bannister to be there.

If not, then Mike had the fall-back option of just doing the deal as before and postponing anything further until such a time that circumstances allowed.

If either of them should not be there alone, then hopefully it would only be just with a plus one as it was before.

Should that be the case, Mike would consider his options and deal with things at each stage. However, should there be more than two people, in addition to Bannister or Carter, then again, he would just consider doing the deal, and postponing the main event.

But he kept his fingers crossed that one of the primaries would be there on their own, as that was his best-case scenario for progressing this tonight.

oOo

Having arrived in good time, Mike again performed a quick reconnoitre of the car park.

He determined that there was roughly the same number of cars as before, parked up as near to the boating clubhouse as possible, suggesting that's where the occupants were.

Remaining in the shadows of a leafed canopy, Mike didn't have to wait long to see the Carter's black SAAB pull into the car park.

Unfortunately, as before, Mike couldn't determine the occupancy, or identity of anyone in the vehicle from where he was hiding.

It was only once the SAAB was parked, that Mike stepped out of the shadows and approached the car from a forty-five-degree angle from the front offside again, so not to be dazzled by the headlights, and lose his night vision.

As he got closer, he saw that it was just Carter in the car. Though it was not quite his *Plan A*, it came as a close second.

Mike concluded that maybe this time Carter had come alone because Mike was now considered a repeat customer, and that consequently he was no longer considered an unknown factor and perceived as a threat.

Or maybe it was nothing like that, and something as simple as they just couldn't find someone to hold Carter's hand on this occasion, and they're just greedy, focusing on that wedge of cash known to be in Mike's wallet ahead of Carter's welfare. Either way, it was a positive turn of events for Mike.

As Mike got closer to the parked car, Carter turned off the headlights, much to Mike's relief.

Mike had to blink a few times in quick succession, hoping to lose the haze caused in the middle of his vision.

Carter then turned off the engine and alighted from the car.

"Didn't expect to see you again so soon," he said. "Certainly not after buying all that shit only last night, what d'you do with it all, have a party or something?"

Mike had expected a handshake, like before, but this time round, no hands were extended.

Perhaps now the pleasantries were over, having already suckered in a new customer.

Again, Carter led the way round to the back of the car. Once there, he tried to lift the tailgate but found it to be locked.

"Fucking hell," he said cursing himself.

Before fumbling with the remote on his keys to unlock it. Finally, he lifted the tailgate.

They stood side by side, both looking into the boot.

"What you after this time then?" Carter asked.

Only this time Mike was more focused on the dimensions of the storage space as opposed to the specifics of the items contained therein.

"Hmmm, what – do – I – want?" Mike repeated to himself.

However, Carter was clearly becoming agitated, possibly because he didn't like to be parked up with a few thousand pounds worth of illegal drugs in his car.

"C'mon, will ya," Carter reiterated. "I don't have the time to stand around here all day, waiting for you to decide what you want, y'know."

Carter then lifted the lids off the shoe boxes, as before, to show off is wares.

But Mike was not one to be rushed, and this comment provoked nothing more, by way of a physical reaction, than a smile from him.

"No, no you don't," Mike said. "In fact you've got less time than you know."

A puzzled looked descended upon Carter's face, as these words were spoken behind him, making him look even more boorish than ever.

"What did you say?" Carter replied in an equally puzzled tone.

However, unbeknown to Carter, as he was lifting shoebox lids to show off his wares, Mike had taken a knife from his pocket, and had opened the folding locking blade behind his back.

As held the knife, concealed in his right hand, with his left hand he grabbed Carter by the hair, only to then kick him across his back of his knees, causing him to collapse onto his knees behind the car.

He had to use both hands to prevent his face from crashing against the lip of the boot.

Mike then pulled Carter's head back, exposing his neck. It was then that was when he finally brought the knife into Carter's view, which glinted in the moonlight with the reflection dashing across Carter's now terrified eyes.

Mike brought the tip of the blade to rest against Carter's cheek, just below an eye, which meant any movement of his head would result in impalement.

"Give me your car keys," Mike said releasing his grip on Carter's hair.

This was only to free up a hand to receive the keys, and when handed them, Mike stepped back and away from where Carter was still kneeling.

"On your feet," Mike said.

Then only once Carter had obeyed him, he continued.

"Now, get in the car," Mike continued. "You're driving."

Mike followed the now limping Carter to the driver's door opening it for him, and holding it open as Carter tentatively lowered himself into the driver's seat.

Mike then walked around the front of the car and opened the passenger door. He slipped off his rucksack before getting into the passenger seat and shutting the door.

"What do you want man?" Carter asked. "You want money, drugs? I got it, take it, take it all."

Carter sounded pathetic as he tried to bargain his way out of the predicament he suddenly, and unexpectedly found himself in.

"Give me your phone!" Mike said.

"My phone?" questioned Carter

"YOUR PHONE!" Mike shouted, reaffirming his request.

Carter rapidly rifled through his pockets, before handing over his smart phone to Mike.

"Put it in flight mode." Mike instructed before taking it from him.

Once this was done, Mike took the phone, and without taking his eyes off Carter, he dropped it into the door pocket next to him.

"I don't want your money, *or* your drugs, and I don't want *you*," Mike confirmed. "But you *do* have what I *do* want.

"I want your pal Bannister, and I want you to arrange for us to meet, and if you don't, well, then I guess you'll just have to do."

This declaration caused a look of confusion to replace the panicked expression on Carter's face, which in no small part was fuelled by a sense of relief.

"Neil?" Carter asked. "What do you want with Neil?"

Only then realising that he'd given up his only bargaining chip, no longer being able to deny any knowledge of Bannister. Instantly choosing to change his stance.

"Don't you know who he is?" he said. "Don't you know who his father is?"

However, Carter's attempts to scare Mike into submission were wasted.

"Yes, I do," he replied. "And do you know what else he is?"

Mike intentionally paused, though not to allow time for Carter to offer anything by way of a reply.

"He's dead," Mike continued. "He just doesn't know it yet, he died the moment he touched her."

Mike then held up Carter's car keys between them.

"Now drive." he instructed.

However, Carter vehemently refused, shaking his head vigorously

"You can fuck right off," he replied. "I ain't driving you anywhere."

There was a moment of quiet contemplation from Mike as he considered his next move carefully.

Though this delay was wrongly interpreted by Carter as being doubt on Mike's part, as he felt Mike was less prepared for this than he actually was.

Mike glanced down between the two of them, at the centre console, and saw that the SAAB was an automatic and with that, knowing that his actions wouldn't impede his chauffeur in any way, he proceeded to stab down on Carter 's left thigh, to the outside of the femur.

But it wasn't with the blade of the knife, it was with the butt of the handle, and even though it didn't cause a piercing injury, the blunt force trauma, to such a localised area, caused excruciating pain for Carter.

He yelped and grabbed at his thigh, expecting to feel blood seeping between his fingers.

But he was surprised to find that he was enduring such significant pain from such an insignificant injury, and didn't know whether to be shocked or relieved?

"Now, drive," Mike said. "Whilst you still can."

He withdrew his hand so that Carter could see the still clean blade pointing uppermost, before jiggling the keys in his other hand to reaffirm his request.

"Fucker," Carter muttered under his breath, as he snatched the keys from Mike.

Carter fumbled with the keys as the pain coursed through him, finally managing to get the ignition key in the barrel.

He started the engine and turned on the headlights, before selecting drive, and slowly and agonisingly pulled out of the car park, stopping where the car park met the road.

"Which way?" he asked, wanting to avoid making a wrong turn, which he felt would be met by punishment.

"Left here," Mike replied. "Don't worry, I'll give you plenty of notice when I need you to turn.

"Just don't go thinking that you're over the worst of it, okay, as I still have use for you."

CHAPTER THIRTY-THREE

After what was a short journey, where the only things spoken were directions from Mike, and expletives from Carter, Mike lastly directed Carter to make a turn off the main road into a driveway.

"Pull up just there," he said, pointing to where he was indicating. "Switch her off and give me the keys."

Carter did as he was instructed, without the need for any reiteration this time.

"Now," Mike said. "Get out!"

He then opened his car door and reclaimed Carter's phone from the door pocket, and was quickly out of the car.

Mike was already on his way around to Carter's side, slipping his rucksack back on, by the time Carter had eventually got out of the driver's side.

He was clearly unsteady on his feet now as his bruised leg was having to take his bodyweight for the first time.

"Hold your hands out," Mike said as he reached Carter.

Carter felt he had no choice but to oblige him, and having done so, Mike efficiently handcuffed Carter, using his police issued handcuffs, which was another item that he had taken from his locker.

It was then that the penny dropped for Carter, as until that moment, he only had a niggling thought in the back of his mind, one that he couldn't quite put his finger on.

But now, with Mike standing in front of him, handcuffing him, Carter suddenly had a feeling of déjà vu. Everything had a vague familiarity to it, and now he realised that there had been a previous encounter with the bearded man stood before him.

But now, as he was securely cuffed, it was too late to do anything about it. Being restrained, Carter was essentially helpless, plus he was in no fit shape to try and make a run for it.

"I know you, don't I?" he said. "Yeah, I knew I knew you."

With his notoriety suspected, all Mike could do was smile, confirming Carter's belief.

"Yeah, that's right, you *do* know me," Mike replied. "And that's why you're gonna help me. Coz if you *don't* deliver Bannister to me, what I was gonna do to *him*, I'm gonna do to *you*, makes no difference to me."

Mike could see Carter turning visibly paler. However, what he couldn't be sure of if it was due to trauma he had sustained to his leg, or if he on the verge of losing bodily function through fear.

Either way, Mike didn't want Carter collapsing anywhere that would require him to be carried to where Mike needed him to be.

With that, Mike took hold of Carter under his left arm. He grabbed hold of Carter's tricep muscle and squeezed, essentially pinching him.

As with the trauma to his leg, the pain was again instantaneous and excruciating, as Mike knew that the back of the upper arm to be one of the most painful places a person can be pinched, and Carter was no exception.

In experiencing the pain, Carter was instantly up on his toes, trying to lift his body up and away from the cause of his discomfort. But it had little effect, as Mike rose his grip with him.

Mike then used this persuasion to best effect and began to lead Carter, who was still on his tiptoes into the single storey, brick-built workshops that had previously proved unsuitable for other intended purposes.

Once inside, Mike led Carter into a small room. There was no artificial light inside, and although there was a single light bulb hanging from the ceiling, the power had long since been disconnected. So, the only light came through the broken panes in the otherwise filthy window.

Carter had been led to the room with the workbench, that had the vice mounted on top of it. The same workshop that Mike had visited previously, when the contents he had found caused him to come up with some ideas.

He instructed Carter to sit on the floor with his back to the workbench directly below the vice.

"What hand do you normally text with?" Mike asked.

The question didn't immediately appear to have any logical relevance with the situation that Carter now found himself in, so a response didn't compute, and a reply wasn't readily forthcoming.

"What hand?" Mike asked again, though much more assertive than before.

However, having understood the question, instead of verbalising a response, Carter tried to raise his right hand to indicate it as his predominant hand.

Mike then crouched down to release Carter's right wrist from its handcuff, and whilst holding, and maintaining control of the still cuffed left wrist, Mike dragged the cuffs down towards a supporting leg of the bench. There he closed the now spare cuff around the bench leg, securing Carter to where he sat against the workbench.

Mike then used the bench to help himself stand up, before stepping back, away from the bench to see Carter squirming on the floor in front of him. He then took off his rucksack on placed it on the bench beyond Carter's view.

"Now," Mike said.

Before pausing to catch his breath from the exertion of having to virtually carry the injured Carter into the workshop.

"What I need from you is to contact Bannister and arrange for the two of you to meet," he continued.

"Now *why* would I do that?" Carter replied defiantly. "Do you know what him and his family would do to me if I set him up for you?"

Mike knew exactly the type of person Bannister was, as well as his family, and their reputation to intimidate, so he had a fair idea of the consequences that would befall Carter should he give him up.

"I see where you're coming from," he replied. "But look at it this way, I'm gonna find him either way, and if you get out of here unscathed, they're not gonna look upon that too fondly, now, are they?"

Mike paused, as he started to pace back on forth in front of Carter.

"So, what I'm gonna do is," he continued. "I'm gonna start hurting you, y'know, to make it look like you've at *least* tried to refuse me.

"And tell ya what, feel free to interrupt me, at any time, if you decide to *actually* help me out, how's that sound?"

With that said, Mike stopped pacing and lurched forward, grabbing hold of Carter's free hand, that was, until that moment, draped by his side.

Mike then yanked the limb upwards, pulling up his sleeve and wedging the forearm between the already open jaws on the vice fixed to the bench immediately above Carter's head.

Mike held the forearm in place with his body weight and one hand, whilst with his other hand, he tightened the sliding jaw, trapping the limb.

Carter was now well and truly at Mike's mercy. He was immobilised, now having had both arms pinioned, and he was extremely vulnerable.

"Still not gonna help me?" Mike casually asked.

"Fuck you!" Carter replied, though sounding significantly less defiant than before.

A wry smile came over Mike's face, after all he really didn't want Carter to give up too easily.

Also, and Mike was being honest with him when he said it wouldn't look good for him to walk away from this situation without any injury beyond superficial bruising.

But, even in the frame of mind that he was in, Mike didn't want to inflict injury for the sake of it. Ideally, he had to have a reason, an objective, or at the very least as a response to provocation.

In order to prove to Carter that he wasn't full of empty threats, Mike began emptying his pockets, and the rucksack of all manner of implements that he had amassed for just such an occasion.

Firstly, Mike took out the folding pocketknife that Carter had already become acquainted with. Mike opened the blade, locking it into place, before setting it down on the work bench.

Next, Mike took out a pair of pliers, followed by a cutthroat razor, and finally a vegetable peeler.

All were handled with exaggerated movements, so that Carter could see them clearly before they were placed on the bench.

However, the last item got a snigger of laughter from Carter.

"You gonna peel some spuds, are ya?" he asked.

Disregarding the comment, Mike was amazed that Carter was even familiar with such an item.

Mike then approached Carter and started to pull the sleeve back even further along his arm that was extended above him.

"So, what's it gonna be then?" he said. "Easy way, or hard way?"

Carter refused to offer anything by way of a response, instead he sucked in his bottom lip and stared defiantly at the wall opposite where Mike stood.

Seeing the continued defiance, Mike felt he needed to ensure Carter's understanding of his predicament.

"Now, just to clarify before I begin," he said. "*All* I'm asking is for you to contact Bannister and to ask him to meet you, simple as that."

However, this appeared to have little impact on the situation, as Carter remained unwavering.

"Very well," Mike said, resigning himself to what was to come.

He picked up the folding knife, and again squatted down, so he was practically eye-to-eye with Carter.

Mike held the knife, much like a paint brush, so that the blade was prominently between them, and that Carter was under no illusion as to what was to come.

In this realisation, he took a deep breath, as did Mike.

As the knife dropped out of Carter's view, Mike changed his grip, so that the blade extended below his fist. He then jammed the base of the handle, which now protruded between his thumb and fore-finger, into Carter again, only this time, it was into his exposed armpit under his right arm.

In this area, the axillary, or circumflex nerve passes from the spinal column into the arm, and pressure to this nerve can cause excruciating pain, as Mike knew all too well, having been taught such techniques during officer safety trainings sessions he'd had throughout his career.

Carter again yelped in pain, as Mike continued to drive the butt of the knife into his armpit, twisting it as he did, to keep the nerve endings firing.

As a result, Carter continued to squeal and squirm and to try to pull away, which only resulted in further pain elsewhere, as he pulled on his wrist that was still trapped in the vice on the workbench.

Mike released the pressure in the armpit and allowing Carter a moment to catch his breath.

"You see," Mike said. "I am *more* than capable of causing you a great deal of pain... Now, shall we try again?"

However, this little demonstration did nothing to convince Carter beyond his earlier stance.

"They'll do far worse to me than that," he replied, in between sharp breaths as he winced in the lingering pain.

"Oh, of that I have no doubt," Mike said, as he again stood up.

Carter looked up at him, to see Mike looking over the bench, as of pondering which implement to use next, before seeing a hand disappear out of view, only to return to view now holding the vegetable peeler.

Though This time, Carter had a less than cocky look on his face.

Again, Mike crouched down, and held the implement for Carter to see, whilst with his other hand, Mike traced a finger along the underside of the Ulna bone in Carter's elevated and exposed right forearm.

It was then that it occurred to Carter what Mike was planning to the do with the peeler, he was going to peel him, he was going to flay him.

Mike then stood back up, before looking down upon Carter, again wanting to give him every possible opportunity to co-operate.

When there was no response, Mike grasped hold of Carter's forearm, above the inverted elbow to steady the limb, before placing the blade of the peeler against the forearm, just below the wrist bones, and began to apply ever-increasing pressure.

Mike maintained this position, only to stare down towards Carter, on to see his gaze now transfixed on the wall opposite. He was visibly gritting his teeth, either tolerating the pain, or preparing himself for pain yet to come.

With the apparent lack of response, Mike only had one course of action, and began to assert even more pressure through the handle of the peeler.

This caused the plastic handle to flex. But, before it had even started to break the skin or draw any blood, the handle snapped, just below the head.

The detached head fell to the floor, before cartwheeling away from the workbench, only to eventually come to rest in such a way that the end of the broken handle was obscured from Carter's sight.

Consequently, this meant that there was one thing that Carter couldn't see, and was that the shaft of the peeler had been intentionally weakened, having been sawn half-way through.

Mike had deliberately weakened it, as his intention was for it to snap, but sooner than it did.

After all, he was not looking to cause Carter any significant injury, as he wasn't his target, and Mike didn't bear him any ill-will.

Carter was merely the errand boy, a go between, a link to Bannister, and involving him was seen to be nothing more than a necessary evil, a means to an end.

Mike didn't consider himself to be a mad man on a bloody rampage, or someone with psychopathic or sociopathic tendencies.

Instead, he was a grieving father, one who had set on exacting a meticulous, and terrible revenge, whilst wanting to keep collateral damage to a minimum.

However, Mike didn't feel that he needed to share his motives, and his reaction to the snapped peeler reflected as much, as if taken by surprise by what had just happened

"Fuck it!" he exclaimed.

He then stepped back from Carter, and threw what remained of the handle, that was still in his hand, to the floor in apparent disgust.

He then began to examine the tools left on the bench, and looked as if none would serve his purpose, which resulted in him shaking his head, and although they were out of sight, Carter knew full well what was there, pliers and a cutthroat razor.

Still with a look of disappointment on his face, Mike turned, and walked towards the shelving unit that stood against the opposite wall, and having reached it, he then turned back to face where Carter sat on the floor.

"*One* text, or *one* call," he said, reiterating is earlier request. "That's all I'm asking you for, that'll be the end of it, and then you can just sit here and wait for help to come, I'll even call them myself."

When there was no discernable reaction from Carter, Mike again turned to face the shelves, and with his back to Carter he picked up an item from a shelf.

He turned to face Carter again, only this time he held up the wood smoothing plane, the one he had examined during his previous visit, the one with the dull blade.

Mike walked back towards Carter and placed the plane against his forearm, just below the wrist, in the same place as before.

Though this time, the mere weight of the plane caused the blade to make a small cut, which released a trickle of blood from the wound.

Blood trickled down Carter's forearm eventually dripping onto his face.

It dribbled the length of his face, across his mouth before dripping off his chin into his lap, and it was when he tasted his own blood that he finally relented.

"Okay, okay, I'll do it," he said between sniffles of self-pity and pain. "You gotta understand, I *only* ever text him, I can't promise he'll reply."

Mike removed the plane from Carter's forearm, and wiped it down using a rag that was found on the workbench.

He was hopeful that he had no further need for it, and that the act of cleaning of it, despite using a dirty rag, would be somewhat symbolic for his disregard of Carter's welfare.

"That's good enough," Mike said, as he backed away from Carter, and replaced the plane on the shelf.

Mike released Carter's trapped arm from the vice, and with gravity assisting, Carter brought the arm into his lap, and began examining his injuries.

He saw that although there was a significant amount of blood, though the wound itself was superficial. Also, apart from the injuries that Mike intentionally caused, Carter had extensive abrasion injuries caused by the jaws of the vice itself.

Mike looked down on Carter who was well into the process of feeling sorry for himself. He kicked out at one of carter's extended legs, and the shock of which caused Carter to look up in panic.

"Don't go getting comfy," he said. "Time to live up to your end of the deal."

Mike then held up Carter's mobile phone, before he dropped it into his lap.

Carter looked up at him, and pulled against the cuffs that were keeping his left hand restrained to the workbench.

"Aren't you gonna let me out of these?" he asked.

"Nah," Mike replied. "I'm pretty sure you kids are able to send a message with one hand."

Carter picked up his mobile phone from his lap.

"What do you want it to say?" he asked.

"Just tell him you need to meet him, as soon as possible," Mike said. "No code words, no warnings, okay…? Or you may *just* live to regret it... Remember, you going free is conditional on him turning up."

Carter tried to unlock his phone using a fingerprint, but the print bed on his forefinger was so inlaid with grease, dirt and blood that the sensor failed to recognise it.

Finally, Carter had to resort to inputting his PIN, which Mike was conscious to observe.

This proved to be a lot easier as the phone rested in Carter's lap, balanced between his thighs as he input the code with one finger.

"Can I take it off flight mode?" he asked.

Mike merely nodded. Carter then went into the messaging screen, and opened a previously received message from Bannister, before pressing the option to send a reply, to which he typed:

Need to meet up ASAP,
say where/when

Carter then showed the phone to Mike for his approval before sending the message.

"And now we wait," Mike said.

Mike took the phone from Carter, and reclaimed his rucksack from the workbench, before sitting down on the workshop floor opposite Carter, only to place the phone down beside him.

From his rucksack, he pulled two Cornish pasties, he chucked one to Carter, and tucked into the other himself.

He watched Carter struggle to open the cellophane wrapping with only one hand and his teeth, and Mike had absolutely no intention of offering him any assistance.

Midway through their impromptu meal, Carter's phone alerted them both to a received message. The alert startled Carter but came with an equal sense of relief.

Mike casually rested his pasty down in his lap and retrieved the phone from the floor beside him.

Carter was expecting Mike to ask him to unlock the phone with either a repeated attempt at using a fingerprint or with the PIN, but instead, he was shocked to see Mike re-input the PIN that he had earlier seen Carter use.

Mike then accessed the received message, which read:

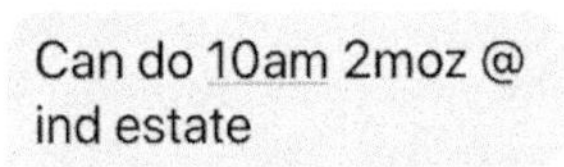

Mike read the message aloud for Carter's benefit.

"You're in luck, your boy's talking," he said. "Now what does he mean by *ind estate?*"

Carter cleared his mouth of pasty before replying.

"That's the industrial estate, y'know the one off Holmeswood Road," he began to explain. "There's an alleyway under the railway tracks at the end of the road, and that's where we usually meet."

Mike was familiar with the industrial estate, and he was familiar with the footpath that ran under the railways.

"And which way will he most likely come in from?" Mike asked.

"He usually comes up the alleyway from the north side," Carter replied. "I usually come in from the south, from the estate, we meet somewhere in the middle. He then tends to go back the way he came. I think he must park up on that side and walk up."

Mike nodded his understanding of this tactic and considered to be quite a smart plan in all honesty.

This way the encounter on foot would appear random as their cars would never been seen driving the same route.

Having prior knowledge of the industrial estate, and the alleyway, Mike instantly had an idea as to how best to approach and ambush Bannister.

Mike looked at his watch, to see that it wasn't even ten o'clock.

But it was getting dark outside, and Mike didn't want to illuminate the workshops and risk drawing any attention to him or his activities into the night with torchlight.

"I'm gonna need to take your car in the morning, I hope you don't mind," he said rhetorically. "I'm just gonna move it for now though, gonna stick it in the barn, if that's okay? Do you have any blankets or anything in the car?"

The mere mention of blankets caused Carter to react to the temperature that until then had been far from his mind.

"Yeah, there's some in the boot," Carter said as he nodded.

Mike used the wall to assist him back on his feet.

"I'll be right back," Mike said. "Don't go anywhere."

Mike left Carter alone in the workshop, and as soon as he was out of sight, Carter discarded what was left of his pasty, and tried desperately to pull on the leg of the workbench, to free himself. But the pain caused to his wrist, that was still cuffed, soon became too much.

After a few minutes, Mike came back into the workshop, to find everything just as he had left it, though the room was now in darkness. He was now carrying a blanket as Carter has described.

But as the skies were clear, this meant Mike could still see relatively clearly, and he could see that Carter was now on laying on his right side, using his arm to support his head.

As Mike had no intention of sleeping under a blanket that was probably used by Carter for God only knows what, so the retrieval of the blanket was solely for Carter's benefit.

Mike laid the blanket over him, before he again retreated to prop himself against the opposite wall.

From the text message they had received, it was now predicted that tomorrow would be the day.

CHAPTER THIRTY-FOUR

When Carter awoke, he was startled, in the realisation that the elements of his nightmare were in fact real.

He was also surprised that his captor had the grace to make his ordeal as comfortable as possible, having fed him and gone some way to ensure his comfort.

Carter looked across the workshop to see that Mike was still asleep. He had wedged himself into a corner, so he remained relatively upright, his head tilted back, and to one side, his mouth hung open.

As if feeling Carter's gaze burning hatred into him, Mike stirred, finally opening is eyes, and taking in the room around him.

Having taken a moment to gathering his thoughts and his whereabouts, Mike rolled himself onto his knees and pushed against the wall to stand up, and once on is feet, he checked the time, realising that there was no need to rush.

"Good morning," he said sarcastically to Carter, who was now sat up before him.

"Now," Mike began. "I'm gonna need your top, and you jacket for today's little charade, so, we're gonna play it like this."

Mike paused, as he walked over to the workbench, and much like the previous evening, Carter craned his neck to see what Mike was doing, and again failing to do so.

Though it wasn't long before Mike's hands came back into view, seen to be holding yet another set of police issue handcuffs.

"Right, take off what you can of your jacket from your right arm," he instructed. "Then, I'm gonna handcuff *that* arm to the bench, I'll then release your left arm for you to finish off, okay?"

It sounded convoluted, and somewhat unnecessary, but Carter still nodded his understanding and began to try to withdraw his arm through the sleeve.

Mike could see this was a near impossible task for Carter to execute with only one arm, so he felt it was required that he render some assistance, certainly if he didn't want this to take all day.

Once the task was complete, he saw that Carter also had a hooded fleece top on, and demanded that be removed too, as he felt a hood may prove useful.

Mike then took off his own jacket, which he replaced with Carter's fleece and jacket, which confirmed his expectation, that anything of Carter's was going to be too big for him, but for what he needed it for, it wouldn't matter.

Mike now stood wearing Carter's hooded fleece, and jacket, and Carter sat on the ground before him, with wearing only a t-shirt on his top half with the blanket now wrapped around him for warmth.

He was now again cuffed as before, with his left hand to the workbench, as Mike had reverted to that considering the injuries, with all be them, although minor, being to his other arm.

"Right, I'm heading out now," Mike said. "I'll check in on you when I get back.... You gonna wish me luck?"

He wasn't disappointment, as he wasn't expecting a response.

Mike then left the workshop again, this time taking his rucksack and Carter's car keys with him.

Having been left on his own once more, Carter tried to get up, as far as his restraints allowed him, to see out of the window, but the cuffs kept him low enough that he couldn't see anything.

However, in the distance he could hear his car being started up, before being slowly driven off.

He was now convinced he was all alone and wondered how long he would be left here.

CHAPTER THIRTY-FIVE

Mike drove to the Holmeswood Industrial estate, which he knew to be a largely derelict estate, with many disused and dilapidated units.

Before being an industrial estate, it was part of a sand quarry, which had its own rail depot, as a consequence, many of the roads around the estate had remnants of the old rail tracks, and even the level crossing gates remained.

The alleyway to which Carter referred was at the far end of the estate.

It consisted of a long tunnel that passed under the elevated railway tracks, designed initially to link the sides of the industrial estate.

But as the north side of the railway now consisted of new housing, and the south was largely disused, potentially under planning and development itself, the foot traffic in this area was virtually non-existent, which again, made this location ideal for Bannister's and Carter's illicit purposes.

oOo

Mike parked Carter's SAAB across the south side of the tunnel. He did this intentionally so anyone entering from the north side, including Bannister couldn't help but see it.

He checked his watch to see that it had just ticked over 9:30am.

Before alighted from the SAAB, Mike rifled through his rucksack, which was on the passenger seat beside him, and removed a couple of things from it that he felt he would need. Only then did he leave the car and enter the tunnel.

As Mike walked the length of the tunnel, he examined the walls, on both sides, along the entire length. He was looking to see if there were any alcoves large enough in which he could conceal himself, only to find that there were none.

He also scrutinised the integrity of the path along the tunnel, checking for any trip hazards.

At one point, Mike got down on one knee and brushed away some debris, leaves and dirt around that had collected, in order to expose the asphalt beneath.

He wasn't someone to leave anything to chance, least of all today.

Whilst he was on one knee, a dog walker approached from the far end, he was a senior looking gentleman, someone of such character that he didn't think twice about addressing a stranger.

"Lost something have we?" he asked without breaking his stride.

The comment startled Mike, which was apparent to the stranger having seen his body convulse.

Having composed himself, Mike looked up at the gentleman, and realised the comment was addressed to him.

"Yeah, my little girl lost something down here," Mike replied, not intending to sound vague.

"Well, I hope you find what you're looking for," the gentlemen replied.

"I hope so too," Mike replied.

The old man then continued on his way, and Mike turned in time to see him leave the tunnel, passing the SAAB.

Satisfied that nothing could literally trip him up, Mike continued along the tunnel, only to emerge from the other end, onto a three-way junction in the path, just as a young lady walking a black Labrador walked past him.

He carried on walking to avoid suspicion, only to look behind after she passed him, as he wanted to see if she would enter the tunnel also. But instead, she continued along the footpath that ran parallel to the rail tracks.

Having conducted a brief reconnoitre of the area, Mike's intention was to hide in the bushes on the north end in order to await Bannister arrival. But as the dog walker remained in sight, he chose to continue along the path until she had completely disappeared.

Once she was gone, Mike doubled-back on himself and took up his position.

There he waited for Bannister, and from where he had positioned himself, he had a good view along the entire length of the tunnel, back towards Carter's SAAB, but also along the footpath in both directions, one that led to the housing development, the other where the lady with the Labrador had headed.

From there, Mike felt he would have ample time to prepare for Bannister once he came into sight.

During the time Mike waited, still hidden, the lady with the Labrador returned.

As her dog kept falling behind to have a sniff, this appeared to infuriate the lady, as she kept calling her dog in an ever-increasingly agitated tone.

"Toby," she called. "TOBY",

Once the dog had come to heel, she continued back in the direction that Mike had first seen her emerge.

It was as Mike's gaze followed her, looking back towards the housing development, that a male came into view.

Mike checked his watch, to see that it was now just before ten o'clock.

He took Carter's phone from his pocket, checking for any calls or messages, only to confirm that he hadn't received anything to contradict the previous arrangements.

He concluded that this could, very well, be Bannister. Mike felt his heart begin to quicken in his chest, as his breaths started to match them.

As the figure got closer, Mike became more adamant that this was Bannister.

Mike allowed him to pass in front of where he was hidden, blissfully unaware of his presence, and as he turned into the tunnel, Mike could clearly see that there was nothing physically remarkable about him.

What could Ashley have possibly seen in this streak of piss? he thought.

Mike waited until Bannister had fully entered the tunnel before he emerged from the undergrowth, before entering the tunnel himself.

Mike was about ten yards behind Bannister upon first entering the tunnel but gaining with every step. He had pulled the hood of the fleece up over his head to disguise his profile and silhouette.

As the gap continued to close between them, Mike took the loaded and readied TASER from his jacket pocket, and trained the weapon on his target as he got ever closer. In the darkness of the tunnel the red targeting dot shone brightly in the centre of Bannister's back.

Mike was now only a matter of feet behind Bannister, as they approached the midway point of the tunnel.

Beyond Bannister, Mike could see the tunnel was clear, and a brief glance behind him confirmed the same. Now was the time.

"Neil," Mike said in a soft voice, hoping to somewhat mimic Carter.

Bannister stopped and turned, surprised that his name was being called from somewhere behind him, especially when he could clearly see Carter's SAAB parked up ahead of him.

As he turned, two things happened in an instant. Firstly, Mike shone the torch from a TASER directly into Bannister's face.

The reason for this was two-fold, firstly, to positively identify this person to be the same male from the briefing picture, and secondly, to obliterate Bannister's night vision, and to distract and disorientate him.

This was followed immediately by a slight lowering of the weapon, so the red targeting dot was aimed at the centre of his chest.

When Mike fired the TASER two probes were fired from the front of the device which struck Bannister simultaneously in the upper and middle chest.

In the instant they made contact, a circuit was completed and the shock was deployed. This resulted in Bannister's body going into an involuntary muscular contraction. His body was seen to go rigid, before he toppled to the ground, still convulsing.

Again, Mike checked both beyond him, and behind him, to conform that there was still no one to be seen.

Seeing the coast was still all clear, Mike was down on his knees in a flash. He rolled Bannister onto his front before dragging one arm, then the other behind his back, only to handcuff him with his hands behind his back.

Mike then rolled Bannister onto his side, so he could easily rip the barbed probes from his chest, before gathering up the debris that came from firing the TASER and stuffed what he could easily retrieve into his pockets along with the TASER itself.

With both hands now free, and whilst he's still prone, Mike gave Bannister a quick pat down search, finding only a bunch keys, with one to a Ford vehicle, and a mobile phone on him, of which he relieves him of both.

Then having lifted Bannister into a seated position and crouching as low as possible, Mike pulls Bannister up and across his shoulder, then pushing hard with his legs, he lifts Bannister from the ground, and into a fireman's carrying position.

After another quick glance all-round, confirming the coast was still all clear, Mike hurried south along the tunnel, back towards the SAAB.

But before he emerged from the tunnel, he peeked around the corner, still all clear.

Mike rushed around to the rear of the SAAB, and once there he used his free hand to lift the unlocked tailgate, and with the boot was open, Mike deposited the unconscious Bannister into the luggage space.

Mike had to rearrange Bannister slightly, so he would fit into the available space. He then tore of a strip from a readily placed roll of duct tape, only to place it over Bannister's mouth to prevent him from screaming in the car, should he come to along the way.

Then after one last look around, Mike shut the tailgate, before joining Bannister in the car and casually driving off.

oOo

The drive from the industrial estate was uneventful, with hardly a peep from the boot.

Mike pulled back into the farm, and drove up to the barn. He was able to drive straight inside as he had left the doors open after retrieving the SAAB earlier.

Before doing anything else, he went back to the workshops to check on Carter.

Mike peered around the doorframe, and watched him sleep for a few seconds to ensure he was breathing. When he was sure that he was all in order, and just asleep, having not succumbed to his injuries, or any mishap had befallen him during his absence, Mike went back to the barn.

Once the barn door was closed on him, Bannister from the outside world, Mike took a moment to rearrange a few bits and pieces within the barn, before finally opening the tailgate and retrieving the still unconscious Neil Bannister.

CHAPTER THIRTY-SIX

Mike kicked flippantly at the prone figure laying restrained on the ground before him.

"Wake up," he said.

When no response came, he felt he needed to be more assertive.

"WAKE UP," he now bellowed.

However, this still led to nothing in the way of any reaction from Bannister.

No matter Mike thought, as he didn't need Neil to be conscious during this phase anyway.

Mike took a deep breath and crouched down, taking hold of a string of a ladder in each hand, and proceeded to lift one end of a ladder.

What he was lifting was a single section that had been taken from a triple extension ladder, the widest section, whilst the remaining two sections remained propped back up against the wall, where he had found them.

Although the section was made of lightweight aluminium, Mike was unable to lift it outright. Instead, he lifted one end to about knee height, and dragged the other end through the dirt, cutting troughs as he did.

The reason he couldn't lift it was because Neil Bannister had already been dragged from the boot of Carter's SAAB, before being laid on the section of ladder, only to be handcuffed and strapped to it.

His arms were now outstretched above him, with each wrist handcuffed to a different string. He was also securely fastened to the ladder using the same Velcro straps that Paramedics used to secure their patients to a spinal board or stretcher.

Neil Bannister had a strap wound, in a figure-eight, around his ankles, with another just above his knees, and a final strap around his waist.

The duct tape had also been removed from across his mouth, and the SAAB had been moved outside of the barn to create more space.

Once Mike had moved the ladder to roughly where he needed it to be, he dropped the elevated end to the ground.

It landed heavily, which finally roused Bannister. However, Mike didn't immediately notice this as he was pacing back and forth, with his hands to the small of his back, stretching off, and rubbing the pain from his muscles after his exertion.

As much as he hadn't noticed Bannister, so Bannister hadn't noticed him, as Mike was out of view when Bannister first opened his eyes., and as it turned out, it was Mike who first lay eyes on the other.

He could see Bannister trying to make sense of his predicament and his surroundings, trying to figure out where he was, and if it hadn't already occurred to him, why he was there, and if that hadn't already occurred to him, everything would soon become very clear.

Mike took a moment of pleasure in seeing the look of confused panic on Bannister's face.

Bannister tried his best to look all around him, and above him to figure how and why his hands were restrained above his head. He squirmed on the ladder, only to be held fast by the brightly coloured straps at his waist and below.

Bannister's scope then extended beyond his immediate predicament, as his vision extended above the ground level where he found himself. His eyes started to search for any clues in the distance that could help him figure out where he may be.

He could readily determine that he was inside a barn, and a derelict one at that, and that it was daytime, given the amount of natural light that shone through the gaps between the slats that made up the walls.

This provided ample light to see around the barn, but his vision was limited due to his position on the ground.

All Bannister could determine was that he had been left on the ground next to a red pick-up truck that was partially suspended on axle stands.

This left him with only about one hundred degrees of vision, and within what he couldn't see was that he was himself being observed.

"So," a voice boomed from somewhere above him. "Have you had time to figure it out yet?"

This unexpected input instantly made Bannister physically jump and inadvertently pull against his restraints, proving beyond any doubt that he was securely fastened to the section of ladder. This reaction raised a look of glee on the face of his captor.

"Figured out what?" Bannister responded, trying to sound defiant.

He craned his neck trying to locate the source of the voice that was addressing him. However, he still couldn't see anyone amongst the shadows which were bisected with fingers of light.

It was then he heard a metallic tap, tap, taping sound, before a scrapping sound of metal on metal, which served to give Bannister a direction in which to focus.

It believed was coming from somewhere beyond the red pick-up truck that was beside him, somewhere he couldn't see.

The scrapping noise sounded like it was moving along the far side of the truck, towards the front., yet Bannister still couldn't see who or what was making the noise.

Then, finally, a figure came into view from around the front of the truck, a figure silhouetted by a brilliant beam of sunlight emanating from between the woodwork of the barn wall behind him.

All Bannister could make out was that it was a man, a man apparently relishing this moment of dominance he had over him.

He could also see what had been used to scrap along the metalwork of the truck. The man held a long metal pole in one hand.

After a few seconds, the man took a couple of steps towards where Bannister lay. He stumbled on the unevenness of the ground beneath him and had to steady himself by placing an outstretched hand on the bodywork of the truck.

This raised a snigger from Bannister, consequently, the man froze in his actions.

"Unbelievable," Mike said. "You have absolutely no idea what situation you've found yourself in, yet still you attempt to taunt your captor... Are you really that *fucking* arrogant?"

This led to a momentary act of defiance from Bannister, as aggression descended upon his face, as he tried to assert some dominance on the situation.

"Y'know, if I wasn't tied up down here," Bannister began. "I'd be splitting your head in two about now!"

However, it was anything that Mike, in all his years of service, hadn't already heard many times before.

"Yeah, yeah, whatever," Mike said, as he came into full view.

He walked alongside the ladder and stopped about level with Bannister's waist.

There Mike crouched down, using a metal pole to support, and steady himself.

He was now within Bannister's natural path of vision.

"Do you recognise me?" Mike asked. "If you don't, you should."

He paused long enough to allow Bannister to make a response. However, instead he merely offered an insolent smirk as he shook his head.

Mike clearly wasn't comfortable in the posture he has settled in, as his knees were stressed, which caused him discomfort, and this was proving to be an unnecessary distraction for him.

He used the pole to bring himself back to a standing position before glancing behind himself.

Seeing a hay bale behind him, and in front of the pick-up truck, Mike took a couple of steps towards it, only to ease himself down on it. He set the pole down at his side, placing it easily within reach for when it would next be needed, but, in the meantime, freeing up both hands, which he cupped over his knees only to attempt to rub some life back into them.

Still looking down at his knees, as he rubbed them, Mike continued to address Bannister.

"C'mon, think about it, as if your life depended on it," he said. "How do you know me?"

Bannister's gaze was anywhere but on Mike, with his thoughts anywhere but on the question at hand.

He didn't even appear scared, or even phased by his predicament.

His supreme arrogance ranked himself above this situation, and although his arrogance infuriated Mike, it would serve him well in what was yet to come.

"I was the one who had you arrested," Mike announced cryptically.

"Oh, come on bruv, you're gonna have to be more specific than that," Bannister replied, having unwittingly given Mike his attention.

"It was for one of the ones you beat up," Mike began to explain. "I'm sure you remember, you slapped a young blonde around, who refused to talk to the police.

"So her old man called it in instead and got you yourself a night in the cells... Ringing any bells yet?"

In an instant Mike could see a look of genuine fear was seen to descend upon Bannister's face as the final pieces of the jigsaw began to fall into place.

Suddenly for him there was a causal link between the young blonde he knew as Ashley and his current predicament.

"But you're a cop?" Bannister said, though less of a question, and more of a statement of fact.

"Yes, I am," replied Mike. "But don't think for one second that's gonna save your sorry arse.

"You're gonna pay for what you did to my little girl, and no amount of grovelling or squirming is gonna make the slightest fucking difference, you understand me?"

Mike took a deep breath as he pressed down on his knees to help him stand up once more.

It appeared that the exertion of the last couple of days had clearly taken its toll on him, and once on his feet he walked back around the pick-up truck, and out of sight from where Bannister lay.

Though he tried craned his neck, to locate Mike in the shadows, but without success.

After a few seconds, Mike re-emerged with a bag of cement over one shoulder. The bag was leaking, leaving a thin trail of cement dust along the route he had walked.

As Mike reached the rear of the pick-up truck, he stooped slightly before launching upwards, giving him the added momentum to lift the bag from his shoulder, tossing it into onto the truck's cargo flat bed.

It landed heavily causing the whole truck to momentarily rock, and groan on the axle stands.

"Be right back," Mike said, in amongst catching his breath. "Only a couple more to go."

He again disappeared to retrieve more bags of cement from where they had been stored.

Mike knew he could quite easily have loaded the cement the previous evening, but this was as much about building suspense as it was in spreading the workload, and with the truck now loaded, Mike eased himself down onto the hay bale again to give himself ample time to catch his breath.

"So, where were we?" Mike asked rhetorically.

However, in the time that Mike had taken to load the truck, the same look of insolent defiance had replaced to temporary look of fear on Bannister's face.

Mike then took hold of the metal pole that he had originally entered with and had since propped up against the hay bale where he again sat.

He stood up and stepped over where Bannister lay on the ground before him, deliberately letting the pole drag along the ground and allowing it to impact Bannister in the side of his rib cage.

"You fucker," Bannister called out.

A surprised Mike looked down on him in utter disbelief.

Here lay Bannister, in an obviously precarious situation, unaware of which way it could possibly unfold, yet here he was, insulting and disrespectful to the only person who had any influence over the possible outcome.

"Y'know, you really haven't considered your role in all this, have you?" Mike asked. "Or even concluded what's required to get you out of this shit situation in one piece?"

Bannister looked at Mike, and their eyes met, with Mike seeing the most mocking of smiles on Bannister's face.

It was then that curiosity got the better of him, as Bannister glanced down to see what Mike was doing with the pole, only to quickly found his answer.

Mike had inserted the pole into a trolley jack that was now situated beneath the suspended pick-up truck and having turned the pole clockwise to close the release valve, he was now ready to pump the handle to raise the jack.

The first few strokes were only to build up the pressure within the casing, after which the lifting arm began to raise the saddle up under the chassis of the truck.

There was a groan from both the trolley jack and Mike as the jack started to take the added load imposed by the truck.

Mike continued to pump the handle and raised the truck until the axle stand fell away.

He then paused in his actions to reach underneath the truck and completely remove the axle stand on the side which he was jacking.

In the time it took to remove the stand the truck had dropped a couple of inches, as the seals on the jack were failing and were unable to maintain hydraulic pressure.

Mike had already discovered this when he had previously tested the device but was unfazed by it.

As it would soon be realised this defect would be something of a necessity, as opposed to a hindrance.

Mike found himself having to sit down and take another break on another hay bale, away from the rear of the truck. Though this wasn't so much from the exertion of what he had undertaking, it was the notion of the work yet to come that required a brief respite.

"You still think this is some sort of game, don't you?" Mike asked looking over at Bannister.

He was sat with his hands now clasped, forearms resting on his parted knees, thumbs tapping together.

“You’ve still got that arrogant look on your face," he continued. "As if all this is being done simply to scare you, and that you *won’t* be scared by it.

“You feel that somehow, you’re calling my bluff, and that somehow there’s still a way out of all this for you.

“That’s the only reason I’ve been taking my time about things.

“Y’see, I’m waiting for the penny to drop, for it to sink into that thick skull of yours that you’re deep in the shit, that *all* this is real, *none* of it is for comic effect, or designed *just* to scare you.

“But either it’s because you’re too fucking arrogant, or maybe you’re just too stupid to realise that either way, it doesn’t really matter.”

The now despondent look on Bannister’s face told Mike everything he needed to know.

Bannister now knew exactly why he was there, yet his supreme arrogance had thus far defied any realisation of the gravity of the situation and had allowed him to feel that he was beyond any blame or responsibility.

Mike stood up, once again having to push down on his knees to assist, though this time it was accompanied with an audible groan.

A *tut* could be heard coming from his physical superior who looked up at him from where he was manacled on the ground.

“I guess there’s always time for one last laugh, Mike said softly. “I’ll give you that.”

Though he did not expect, nor intend Bannister to hear him.

Mike held on to the rear of the truck as he used one foot to push the foot of the ladder under the suspended chassis, being crude and imprecise in his actions.

He then walked around to the head of the ladder, where Bannister's hands were outstretched and cuffed above his head. He then crouched down and picked up the ladder holding a string in each hand as he had done so before, and rotated the ladder, pivoting it around the grounded foot until it was perpendicular to the truck, but with the rear axle now suspended over where Bannister lay.

The nearside rear wheel was suspended directly over his sternum, with about six inches clearance. However, the jack seemed to have found its level, as it had sunk no further since its last usage.

With the task at hand complete, and Mike once again breathless, he again wanted to sit down. However, in order to be able to maintain eye contact with Bannister, Mike had to reposition one of the hay bales.

"I understand that when you came into my home you didn't kill Ashley outright," Mike began. "According to the police reports she managed to crawl a short distance after you left her, perhaps she was trying to summon help.

"But one thing's for sure, she died alone, terrified, and in agony because of what *you* did to her."

Mike paused to allow himself time to relive the emotions of that day.

He sniffed a couple of times and wiped away tears with his back of one sleeve before finally looking out towards Bannister again.

"And now," he said. "It's your turn."

As Mike had earlier alluded, the penny had finally dropped, and Bannister now realised just how grave the situation he found himself in.

Gone was the look of arrogance from his face, only to be replaced with a look of sheer terror.

Now it was Mike who was defiant, as he stood up before taking hold of the jack handle, twisting it clockwise to ensure the seal was tight.

He then began to pump the handle once more, with each stroke lifting the rear of the truck higher and higher, as the distance between Bannister's chest and the wheel got greater and greater.

Suddenly Mike couldn't pump it anymore as the jack had reached its full travel.

Mike then let go of the handle and leant against the side of the truck.

He looked down at Bannister, though only his upper torso and extended arms were now visible from underneath the truck.

"There must've been a moment when you consciously chose to leave Ashley," Mike said. "Knowing she was going to die where you left her on the living room floor, knowing she couldn't possibly get help for herself, and you weren't going to be there to get it for her.

"You knew your decision to abandon her would condemn her to death.

"Well, now you must have at least some understanding of what she must've felt when you left her on her own to die."

Mike extended his hands towards the jack handle, with no doubt in Bannister's mind what was to follow.

"Wait, wait… WAIT!" Bannister pleaded.

However, Mike ignored him and continued in his actions, turning the handle just a fraction of a rotation.

A faint hiss could be heard as hydraulic fluid began to drain from the piston back into the reservoir.

"Wait, please wait," Bannister begged. "I didn't do this. It was my dad who wanted me to find your daughter and date her.

"He told me he wanted her punished for what *you* did to *him*."

Mike's curiosity got the better of him, and he closed the bleed valve to stop the jack's descent. Once tightened, he pumped the jack back up to its original position.

"You've got one chance!" Mike said, without ever removing his hand from the jack handle.

"My dad made me do it," Bannister pleaded, now sounding even more pathetic. "Please, this *isn't* my fault."

Mike maintained his posture, now toying with Bannister, as he knew nothing, he could possibly say would make any difference to the outcome.

"Your dad, who's you dad then?" Mike asked, entertaining Bannister's pleas.

"Phil Mercer!" Bannister replied with a renewed sense of hope that he was making progress in staying his execution.

"I'd already put two and two together genius," Mike revealed "I know you're your father's son, a right chip off the old block.

"He may very well have asked you to abuse my daughter, but *he* didn't bring us to where we are today, you did that part all by yourself. More's the question, why did your dad want it?"

"He wanted me to punish your daughter for what you did to him," Bannister tried to rationalise. "My mum left him because of what *you* did."

This, however, was an accusation that Mike was not expecting

"Because of what *I* did?" Mike questioned. "If only you knew, you stupid little bastard.

"Your shining example of a father beat the shit out of your mum, that's why she left him, yet you think he's still some great guy.

"Did he tell you to kill my little girl?

"Did he?

"He *actually* told you to do that, of course he is fucking didn't.

"That was all *your* doing.

"Well, I'll tell you something for nothing, he's gonna know just how you made me feel when he finds out about all this.

"He's gonna know what it's like to discover the body of your child."

With everything said that needed to be said, Mike turned the handle the same fraction as before, and he watched as the truck began to collapse the jack, only to let go of the handle and stand back.

Mike looked down upon Bannister, to see his attention darting between the wheel above him and his restraints him, as he didn't know which one to solely focus on.

"Please don't leave me like this," Bannister pleaded. "SOMEBODY HELP ME."

He squirmed frantically as he tried to shuffle his entire body out from beneath the path of the descending truck with no avail, as he had neither the mobility nor the momentum to shift the ladder in any way.

By this time, Mike had walked off to view this spectacle from the distant shadows.

He had opened the barn door to cast light across the barn, only to let the door slam closed.

He wanted to give the illusion of abandoning Bannister to die alone, but he wasn't going to leave, he had no intention of doing so, as he knew he had to see this through.

Although Bannister thought he had been abandoned, he continued to scream for help.

"Help m…, I'm in here, will somebody help me, please…" he cried out over and over.

Mike couldn't see him given his line of sight and the lighting, but he knew exactly what was happening from the sounds that Bannister was making.

He could tell precisely when the weight of the wheel finally reached his chest, as his cries for help suddenly became more constricted. Eventually to be replaced with groans and moans of terror, and finally pain.

Then as the suspension compressed and the weight of the truck itself settled, there eventually followed a deathly silence.

oOo

It was in the silence that Mike finally left the barn, letting the door slam closed behind him for the final time.

He walked to the SAAB, and got in, only to sit in the driver's seat in a moment of quiet contemplation.

After a few moments he took Bannister's mobile phone from his pocket and powered it back on.

The reason he had powered his phone off was so that the phone couldn't be used to triangulate his location.

Though this wasn't an exact science as the movies and TV would have us believe, but it was a good indicator, using signal strength and directionality to determine proximity to a mobile phone mast.

Mike felt that given his proximity to a mast may lead to his location being determined by a topographical study of likely locations on a map.

Once the phone had powered up Mike dialled a number.

"999 operator, what's the emergency?" The voice said when the call was answered.

"There's a dead boy in a barn off Manor Green Lane," Mike said. "Send police and ambulance, and don't forget to check the workshops too."

Mike then ended the call, before any further details could be requested, and turned off the phone to prevent any calls being returned.

CHAPTER THIRTY-SEVEN

Later that same day, sometime after Mike had driven away from the barn in Carter's SAAB, having left behind both Bannister and Carter, DS Nathaniel Alexander was in the CID office, as he continued to receive updates from the crime scene to which police officers and paramedics had been called that morning.

There were separate scenes consisting of the barn and the separate workshop on a disused farm, and the updates provided him with the status of those that had been found there.

Also, these updates suggested the involvement of a police officer, and given one of DS Alexander's current investigations, which also involved a named suspect who was now one of the victims at the scene, he felt confident in reaching certain conclusions.

Having explained these conclusions to his inspector, Alexander decided to phone Mike Watkins, to establish his status and whereabouts, and knowledge of the events that that morning, not knowing how the call would pan out, or even if it would be answered.

However, the call was to be answered, though initially there was no response heard.

"Hi Mike," Alexander said, assuming that it was he who answered the call. "I dunno if you know but there's been a development in your daughter's case... Neil Bannister has been found dead."

However, despite certain expectations on Alexander's part having disclosed this update, Mike still chose not to respond.

"Mike, you didn't have anything to do with this, did you?" Alexander asked. "Look, we've got officers there now, where we've found Bannister dead.

"We also found a second kid, who's gonna be fine, who gave us your description, and saying you've got his car. C'mon mate, what the hell happened there?

Alexander paused, hoping that Mike would at the very least give some indication he had heard what had just been said.

"Mike, you need to listen to me," he continued. "Right now, the finger of suspicion is pointing at you, so the best thing you can do is to hand yourself in, just tell me where you are, and I'll come get you myself?"

It was this suggestion, that Nat Alexander come after Mike himself, that prompted him to enter the conversation

"I've done *your* job for you, and now you want to come after *me*?" Mike replied. "Well, if you want me, I'll be with my family."

With that, the line then went dead.

"With his family?" Alexander muttered, as he replaced the handset in the phone's cradle.

From their time working together, when they were on the same team, Alexander had made the acquaintance of Mike's wife, Kerry, which made the call he now had to make easier, yet difficult in equal measure, though for the same reason.

As Kerry was listed as Ashley's next of kin following her initial investigation, he already had her phone number, and with the call having connected, it rang a few times before being answered.

"Is that Kerry Watkins?" Alexander asked as the call was answered.

When he got the response he required, he continued.

"Kerry, it's DS Alexander, do you know the current whereabouts of your husband?" he asked. "It's important that we need to speak to him urgently with regards to your daughter's investigation.

"I've just briefly spoken to him on the phone, but he was very cryptic with me, and refused to say where he was, other than being *with his family,* so my first thought was to call you, is he with you, or do you know where he might be?"

On the other end of the call, there was a pause before Kerry replied.

"No, I don't know where he is," she said. "Truth is, I haven't seen him since our daughter's funeral, if he's not at home, then I don't have a clue where he might be."

Kerry paused again as she reflected on the conversation and the specific details that Nat Alexander had thus far disclosed.

"Wait a minute," she paused. "What did you say he said that he was *with his family*?

"I'm guessing he's gone to be with Ashley, at her grave, ohmigod, what's he done?"

Only after having scribbled down Kerry's response, was Alexander able to continue.

"Kerry, at this moment we don't know what Mike's done or not done," he said. "Like I say, he's being very vague with us, but I do need to speak to him.

"So, the best thing you can do for him right now is to help us find him as quickly, and safely as possible. Where is your daughter's grave?"

Kerry took a deep breath as she tried to assimilate all that she had been told, before providing an answer to the outstanding question

"She's at Lakeview Cemetery," Kerry finally answered.

Once again, Alexander scribbled down the information.

"Something tells me we're gonna need you there," Alexander concluded. "Can I have a car pick you up, or are you able to meet us there?"

"I'm not at home at the moment," Kerry replied. "I'll have to meet you there. Can you tell me what he's done?"

This time Alexander paused, as he contemplated disclosing his thoughts with Kerry, but though better of it.

"I can't right now, as nothing's known with any certainty," he said. "Just keep yourself safe and call me should you see him."

With that, DS Alexander ended the call, only to immediately stand up and grab his coat from the back of his chair as he made a hasty exit from the CID office.

oOo

Elsewhere, as the same call was ended, Kerry Watkin's face erupted with a sense of panic.

The information the police had just given her was no less cryptic that what they had just complained about as having allegedly received from Mike.

Though given what was discussed, she too put on her coat, before grabbing her keys and disappearing out of the front door.

Having got into her car she hesitated, as she didn't know what she was going to find when she arrived at her destination.

CHAPTER THIRTY-EIGHT

Mike was woken by the distant wail of emergency sirens, and the low tone whirling of a helicopter.

Although he had arrived at the cemetery before speaking to DS Alexander, in the time since the call, he had fallen asleep at his daughter's graveside.

He rolled himself into a seated position, before brushing dirt and leaves from his face, there to await the inevitable.

Mike knew it was only ever a matter of time before they found him here, and he wasn't planning on going anywhere.

After all, he had told them exactly where he was, with it simply being process of elimination, as since Kerry had left him, Ashley was the only family he had.

The recurring dull thud of the helicopter was getting louder, getting closer, and Mike knew it to be the distinctive sound of the police's Eurocopter EC 135 T2.

It was immediately distinguishable from other helicopters because of its loud engine noise, which was often considered ironic, considering its stealth requirements.

As it turned to face the origin of the sound, he saw the blue and yellow livery come into view above the tree line, and with a clear line of sight, he knew that the pilot and observer would also have a clear view of himself below them.

Even if Mike was so inclined, running now would be a futile option, as being tracked in the open by the helicopter was not a good situation to find oneself in.

However, running, was the last thing Mike was intending to do.

Why would he tell them where he was, if he was planning to run?

Although sirens could no longer be heard, the over revving of engines, along with the occasional screech of tyres suggested to Mike that the arrival of police cars was imminent.

He concluded that the sirens were probably turned off due to his reported sighting from the helicopter and were no longer deemed necessary and turned away from the helicopter to face towards the cemetery's entrance.

However, as the cemetery was old, and well established, with Ashley having been interred in a new phase towards the back, which was some distance from the main entrance, Mike couldn't actually see the entrance from where he was sat.

He just knew it was now only a matter of time before he had company, which meant that that time he had to make any decisions where he could influence the outcome had now long since passed.

He stood up, and finished brushing himself down, before looking at his daughter's grave, and in that moment, nothing else mattered.

Mike crouched down again, and rearranged a couple of flowers, as well as deadheading a couple more, and only when all was perfect, he smiled.

It was then that his mind reverted to the primacy of the moment.

"Just like I promised, Daddy's made things right sweetheart," he began. "Now, I'm gonna have to go away for a while, so I won't be around to visit you.

"But you look out for you mother, okay, we both love you very much."

By the time Mike had stood up and straightened himself out for a second time, he could see the police entourage coming through the cemetery.

He could see three marked police cars that had their blue lights extinguished either out of a diminished sense of urgency, or maybe just out of respect for where they were.

Mike knew full well what was about to happen, and he was adamant that this was not going to take place in front of his daughter's grave.

As before, he took his right hand from his pocket and kissed his fingers tips before resting them momentarily on the top of Ashley's gravestone.

"Goodbye," he said, as he turned and started to walk away.

As Mike walked, he could also imagine the radio messages being exchanged between the helicopter crew and the ground officers as he walked towards where the police cars had come to a halt.

As he got closer to them, he could see that the first vehicle was an armed response vehicle, a firearms unit, which had been followed by two divisional patrol units.

As officers alighted from the front vehicle Mike could see that they had their weapons drawn. This meant that he had been perceived to be such a risk that an authority had been given for the overt carry of firearms, which went far beyond a TASER authority, having been assessed by a tactical advisor and authorised accordingly.

Seeing the firearms officers move into a flanking position, Mike knew he needed to minimise any perceived threat he posed, and stopped where he stood, whilst raising his hands into the air.

The two firearms officers approached Mike from a *ten and two o'clock* position, shouting orders as they got closer.

"Hands on your head, do it now," one said.

Mike immediately complied, as he had no intention of being shot.

"On your knees," the orders continued.

This brought Mike down below the level of some of the gravestones that surrounded him.

Once down on his knees, and still with his hands on his head, Mike turned as best he could, to look back in the direction of Ashley's grave, and was grateful that he could no longer see it, so he couldn't be seen from it.

As the armed officers closed in Mike faced forward again, his gaze now to the ground in front of him to avoid any eye contact being deemed as an act of aggression.

"Don't move!" one of the officers said as he closed in on Mike from his right side.

He let his Heckler & Koch G36 fall to his side, its weight taken by the shoulder strap, whilst his colleague kept Mike in his sights, and any perceived aggression from Mike would result in a fatal shot at such close range.

"Just relax now buddy," the first officer said.

He then took hold of Mike's right hand with his left and handcuffed it, before bringing the cuffed hand behind Mike's back. Once there, he took hold of his left hand, and brought it behind him to complete the handcuffing.

Once secured, he nodded to his colleague who also lowered his G36, though kept a watchful eye on Mike as the first officer helped him to his feet. They then began to lead Mike back towards where they had left their vehicle.

As he was being led, with on officer holding each arm, Mike's gaze remained towards the ground. Though he did try to turn to look behind him once more, to again see Ashley's grave for one last time in what would mostly likely be a very long time.

However, the officers felt his resistance, as he slowed and tried to turn, and they pulled against his efforts to keep him facing forward, unaware of his reasons for wanting to look back.

Mike then heard a commotion coming from somewhere ahead of him. He looked up but couldn't see anything other than yet more officers walking towards him, some were in uniform, others not, and amongst them he saw DS Alexander, and concluded that this wasn't the cause of the commotion, then he saw it.

From behind the advancing officers, Mike could now see Kerry rushing up behind them.

Upon hearing her approach, DS Alexander turned to face her and being unaware of her intentions, he took hold of her and stopped her in her tracks.

Mike instinctively hastened his pace towards his wife, only to he held back by his escort.

Kerry's delay was brief as Alexander allowed her through, though still cautious of her participation.

She ran to where Mike was and threw her arms around him, and buried her face in his neck, whilst he was incapable of reciprocating.

The firearms officers looked to the Alexander, as he was the one who had allowed Kerry through, and having received an acknowledgement from him, and despite their apparent disapproval of such a decision, they both released their hold of Mike and took a couple of steps back, and although they both kept a watchful eye on the couple, they afforded them one final private moment.

Kerry lifted her face from her husband's neck, and their eyes met. They hadn't looked upon each other like this since before Ashley's funeral. Kerry held Mike's face in her hands and looked lovingly at him, before glancing over at one of the firearms officers, only to wonder what her husband had been accused of to demand such a response.

As she could also now hear footsteps closing in behind her, Kerry knew they didn't have much time, and pulled Mike's head down towards her, and as his head lowered, she turned it to be able to press her lips to his ear.

"Thank you," she whispered, expressing her gratitude for having avenged their daughter.

Their joint well-intentioned intervention had resulted in their family being destroyed, but solely he had found justice for Ashley, and for this Kerry realised her renewed love for him.

As Kerry released her tender hold of her husband's face, they saw tears in each other's eyes, and this would be a look neither of them would forget of the other.

Kerry then knew their moment together was over when she felt a hand on her shoulder.

"Okay, that's long enough," DS Alexander said. "we need to go now,"

She turned to see him now looking empathetically down on her.

Kerry nodded her understanding despite her reluctance to allow this moment to be brought to an end.

Upon hearing the same comment, the firearms officers closed in to resume their roles in escorting Mike to the vehicles.

They had to take a wide path around where Kerry remained stood, and she turned to see them walking away, before finally disappearing out of sight behind the first vehicle.

DS Alexander then left, following on behind them, and leaving Kerry all on her own.

She remained where she was as she continued to watch the activity around the police vehicles, and after a few minutes, the armed officers led the procession of police vehicles out of the cemetery.

Beyond where their cars were, Kerry could now see where she had left her own, and with the helicopter had also long since left, a sense of peace returned.

Kerry walked on, further into the cemetery, as she wanted to visit Ashley whilst she was there.

As she reached Ashley's grave, as the eerie silence of the cemetery began to engulf her, so did her emotions.

It was as Kerry looked towards Ashley's headstone that she fell to her knees and started to weep.

Only then did she see a glint of low afternoon sunlight, reflect off something metallic that had been placed on top of the headstone.

Kerry stood up and stepped forward, before reaching out for the item that now commanded her attention.

She picked it up to find it was the same keyring that Ashley had bought for her father for his birthday, it was something that she knew Ashley was getting him as their daughter had shown it to her when it was ordered.

Mike had chosen to leave it on the grave to show that he had received it safely, and for her to look after in his absence.

As Kerry held it in her hand she began to read the inscription it bore, silently at first, before saying the last two words aloud.

"My hero," she said.

As she wiped away a tear, she allowed herself a smile, as she had to agree.

EPILOGUE

As Mike Watkins was still a serving police officer, following his arrest in the cemetery, he was taken to a police station in a neighbouring county, so no one who would know his status.

There he was further arrested for the suspected kidnap and assault of Dean Carter, and when interviewed regarding that in addition to the death of Neil Bannister, Mike made a full admission, and was subsequently charged with both offences.

In court, Mike Watkins again pleaded guilty to all charges against him, with his counsel adding on his behalf that he merely acted on the grounds of diminished responsibility following his daughter's brutal murder.

However, this defence was dismissed by the Jury and Mike was subsequently found guilty on all charges, and is currently serving a life sentence for the murder of Neil Bannister.

oOo

Kerry Watkins remains married to Mike and visits him regularly. She continues to refuse to make any comment on the events surrounding her daughter's death or her husband's actions.

oOo

Having become aware that Neil Bannister was in fact Philip Mercer's son, after DS Alexander had inadvertently allowed Mike to view the list of Bannister's known associates, and given Bannister's confession, Mike realised that it was Mercer who had orchestrated the scheme for his son to approach Ashley.

However, Mike didn't feel the need to punish Mercer beyond causing him to know the suffering, he had himself endured, at experiencing the loss of a child.

As far as Mike was concerned, this second wrong at least went some way to make things right, and if Mercer had any sense, he would leave things as they are.

THE END

ABOUT THE AUTHOR

I first published *The Second Wrong* in 2019, however since losing my publishing representation in 2022, I released my catalogue again under a rebranding. This enabled me to revisit certain works and offer, shall we say, an extra layer off polish, and that's where the *special edition* banner comes in as my aim was to bring the quality of writing up to my present standard from where it was left when I was a fledgling author.

In 2023, at the time this rebranded, I am still a serving UK police officer, with over twenty-five years working for the emergency services in various roles.

I first dabbled in writing a novel in 2004, when I was still a firefighter. This was a contemporary horror story based on the Burke & Hare tale. This project progressed to a mid-point of some two-hundred pages. However, due a career change, and with fatherhood beckoning, this project was never finished.

Then in October 2016, whilst I was recovering from having, rather ironically, carpal tunnel syndrome release surgery, to both wrists, I met up with a friend in London, and during the normal progression of the conversation, it was discussed what each was watching on television.

When it became to my turn, I stated that I was watching *Californication* with David Duchovny of *The X-Files* fame., and for those who haven't seen it, or don't know it, first it's highly recommended, and secondly, it tells of a writer whose first novel was hugely successful, and turned into a movie, with the series depicting his exploits, issues and successes.

Anyway, the point looking to be made is that this brought up the topic of the unfinished project, and the disappointment at having not finishing it.

The friend suggested '*well, why not finish it?*' to which I explained that the project was on a 3½" floppy disk, somewhere within the ex-wife's domain, and now possibly lost forever.

So, the friend then suggested, '*why not start another one then?*' and this got me thinking.

I went home, and within a day he had a story arc, and ten days later he had 300+ pages, a completed first draft which would become *Settling the Score.*

This went through a couple of months of re-writes before being released on 24th January 2017, which was deliberately coincided with my mother's birthday.

When *Settling the Score* was released, I initially didn't have any plans to continue writing. After all, *Settling the Score* was a semi-autobiographical tale written for generally therapeutic reasons, with some of the story elements having happened to me, whilst some were purely fictitious.

Though the names chosen for many of the characters are of friends and acquaintances. Also, locations described are real, yet the names used are not.

Having decided to continue writing, the idea for my second project *PRIMUS* came about by chance.

Whilst I was juggled with ideas for the next story I came up with the idea of a police officer with split personalities, one being the cop, the other being the criminal, and he is essentially investigating himself. I admit that this was a bold project to undertake as a second project, but I am proud of the result.

It was during the writing of *PRIMUS,* that several ideas occurred to me for upcoming projects.

Some have been given structure, though remain on a pending list, whilst others remain completely unrealised, beyond merely having a title and a basic plot.

Many of these ideas have been mapped in *post-It* note form on the internal doors of my home, as this method allows me to map out the story arc, and add specific plot elements, and to be able to rearrange, and add to at will.

Since this project was originally released, I have continued to write, and the rebranding of *The Second Wrong* will coincide with the release of my fourteenth title which is the fifth instalment in my *Heart of a Lion* saga, titled *Enemy of my Enemy.*

What defines a successful author? Is it sitting in a mansion, surrounded by many shelves containing all of your published works, never actually having to write again?

Or it is producing a finished work that you're truly proud of and is something that brings pleasure and enjoyment to others.

Wherever you consider yourself to be on that scale, consider yourself a success…

As always, I can be contacted via my website at www.JohnTLeonard.com or by scanning the QR code on the next page, or directly at jtlnovels@gmail.com, and I seek to reply to every correspondence.

www.JohnTLeonard.com

Printed in Great Britain
by Amazon

29138780R00199

ALSO PUBLISHED IN ENGLISH BY IRINA PAPANCHEVA
SHE, THE ISLAND (2021) AND *PELICAN FEATHER* (2016)

BRUSSELS, NAKED

This book was originally written in English.
First published in Bulgarian language in 2022 by Znatsi publishing house.

ISBN 9786199057094

Brussels, Naked

Irina Papancheva

A novel

"Irina Papancheva opens up the city very smartly, through its districts and diverse narratives. The construction was cleverly managed, the shifting roles of the characters. The story is open to Europe and the wider world, the interconnected pains of migration and settlement. It gives me the flavour of lives lived; meals, drinks, exchanges, solitude."

Iain Sinclair, Author

"A city may have boundaries, but a city is never contained. There is always more to a city. An undiscovered corner, an incubated wonder. Brussels, Naked is an unflinching homage to this. Irina Papancheva sees Brussels with a clear-eyed, deceptively simple romanticism. She asks you to think about the lives it describes. It is very specific in place. It is universal in its heart. There is always another story"

Phil Madden, Author

"I have really enjoyed working on 'Brussels, Naked', I admire Irina Papancheva's writing and its evocative quality. I particularly liked how the stories intertwined and built a picture of Brussels and its social issues of the day through the characters."

Rachel Robson, 100% Proof: Proofreading and Editorial

"*Brussels, Naked* is an extraordinary multicultural novel that explores human relationships in a unique setting and passes a Bulgarian literary milestone in conveying the emigrant experience."

Christopher Buxton, Author

"I am especially glad because Irina Papancheva has been able to write a novel which shows Brussels as it is, sometimes raw, sometimes bright and always full of people that meet – over and over again, intertwining relations and I have indeed sensed that she loves this city. Brussels really lacks this sort of literature, unfortunately."

Jan Dorpmans, Passa Porta Literary guide

"In *Brussels, Naked,* Irina Papancheva skilfully and fascinatingly undresses Brussels, Europe and the world, by exposing people, feelings, faith, religiosity, passions and destinies; united in a novel construction.

The novel covers existential and social themes and asks important questions such as whether we are truly united in diversity, without demagoguery and offering unequivocal answers."

Emil Andreev, Author

"*Brussels, Naked* is a novel written with deep intimate knowledge of the multinational context in the capital of united Europe. Irina Papancheva's elegant, composed style harkens back to the best examples of contemporary European prose, and the original structure of the novel adds to its impact.

As a narrator, Irina Papancheva demonstrates an enviable inner self-confidence and balance that help her bear the paradoxes of Europe's cultural puzzle, but also the complexity of interpersonal relationships. Without being overtly emotional, the novel 'Brussels, Naked' is imbued with a subtle eroticism and sensitivity that touches and fascinates the reader."

Alek Popov, Author

"Going back to Italo Calvino's 'one should never confuse the city with the word that describes it', *Brussels, Naked* does just that. 'But if you give it time, if you free your mind from labels and preconceptions, and instead become curious, following your intuition without a google map, you'll really start to see it,' promises Irina Papancheva in this her most mature, complex and extended novel – a European-level novel."

Antonia Apostolova, Author

"Irina Papancheva's style is impressive not only in terms of language, syntax, measure of descriptiveness and dialogues. She is distinguished by a penetrating intellect, deep emotionality, excellent knowledge of modern European history, hypersensitivity to the culture and problems of the Other and Otherness. Every character in the book is built without any cracks in their psychological completeness. Everyone reminds us of someone, something, and — all together — the world in which we live. If I had to sum it up in one sentence, for me this is a novel about the path we walk and the lasting trace we leave in each other and in the world. A novel about the hope that whatever we choose it is always the best for us."

Viktoria Beshlijska, Author

"I was strongly impressed by the psychologism with which each character was constructed – a very difficult task, considering how different they are. So many stories have been told, and they are all complete and connected – woven into the body and history of Brussels, which, like its inhabitants, breathes and evolves. *Brussels, Naked* is a modern European novel – European both in subject matter and quality, which I sincerely recommend."

Nevena Mitropolitska, Author

"I liked the authentic atmosphere of the city, it seems that the novel was written with love, that the author lived in Brussels cafés and streets, that she was truly interested in getting to know it. The main character Iris evolves, from a naïve Eastern European girl she turns into an independent, slightly bitter, but emotionally mature woman. The human destinies are wonderfully woven together, and the pace of the novel is truly engrossing."

Ina Ivanova, Author

Contents

We

make

many journeys,

not all of them ours.

We do not appear

in all the scenes

of our lives.

Phil Madden, 'Paths'

"No one, wise Kublai, knows better than you that the city must never be confused with the words that describe it."

Italo Calvino, "Invisible cities"

There are cities which lure you with their prominent beauty. Cities which shine in colours and look as magnificent as a fairy tale. Cities whose elegance leaves you breathless and makes you feel privileged to be admitted to their realm. Cities which are unworldly and leave you in awe in front of their perfection. Cities which enchant you, make you fall in love with them, make you yearn constantly for the illusion of the life you could have in them. Cities which cannot be described but must be seen. Cities which come with their own myth or legend, which are themselves the stuff of myth and legend, which compel you to contemplate their great past and wander in their ruins. I have felt lost, lonely and desperate in some of these cities.

Then there are cities which seem plain, casual, closed; which would not care how you perceive them; which make no effort to seduce you nor to convince you of their worth. Cities with a certain structure in their chaos which builds excitement in you, which make you want to absorb them, become part of them yourself. These are the cities which have interested me.

And then there are these other cities, the "invisible cities," who exist in both the former and the latter and which are known only by the insiders and by the patient and careful searchers; those which want you to see through what they appear to be. These are the cities I seek. And I believe that in these cities the contrast between the visible and the inner invisible makes this discovery even more special, like a secret which has been revealed to you only because of your attention, curiosity and patience in exploring. You feel like a guardian of a treasure.

This, of course, is a self-deception.

In reality, we are all puppets, parts, expressions, qualities of a city. Our unique role is to give it life.

1050 Ixelles – Elsene

2003

Iris, Bulgarian

La evidente decadencia de las naciones europeas, ¿no era a priori necesaria si algún día habían de ser posibles los Estados Unidos de Europa, la pluralidad europea sustituida por su formal unidad ?[1]

Ortega y Gasset, La rebelión de las masas, *1930*

I had never wanted to go to Brussels. There was nothing about it that appealed to me or seduced me into adding it to the long list of cities I wanted to visit. As a child I loved receiving letters. I imagined I lived somewhere else, and I wrote my imaginary addresses on white envelopes. The cities and states on these envelopes differed but Brussels, Belgium was not among them. In fact, I didn't know anything about Brussels, other than it was the capital of a union, to which my country didn't belong. What I had heard of it was not flattering at all — boring and institutional — but still it possessed

[1] "The evident decadence of the nations of Europe was not a priori necessary, if one day the United States of Europe would come into being, the European plurality substituted by its formal unity" (Ortega y Gasset, *The revolt of the masses*, 1930).

something of interest. That very thing which gave it its reputation, the institutions.

After I graduated from university, I worked as a reporter on a daily newspaper for almost three years. My day usually started on a crammed bus. In order to alight, any method was allowed, elbows, weight, high heels… whatever it took to get you on there. Once on board, the adventure wasn't over, on the contrary, it became more and more intense. Squeezed between other human bodies, mine fought to preserve its dignity, to keep my balance and to avoid being pushed. I inched forward or sideways as much as I could, as men used the jostling and lurching to press and rub themselves against me. By the time I arrived, I felt contaminated and full of frustration.

The initial excitement of securing a contract and of learning the craft had long gone. The range of the events I covered — from sports press conferences to political ones — didn't allow me to specialise in a particular area and to progress as a journalist. Of course, this was only the tip of the iceberg. Underneath I was losing perspective and yearning for something better. Bulgaria's transition after the collapse of its totalitarian system had been shambling along for thirteen years; governments changed one after another, but living standards stayed the same, and on my journalist's salary I was not able to afford to rent a flat on my own; even a weekend trip to the country had to be carefully budgeted for, to ensure it didn't capsize the household finances. Luckily, I was married and did not have to be able to afford a place to live on my own. But my aspirations and dreams went beyond our means, and I could not come to terms with the idea that this would be my life – travelling to work on cramped buses, with a boss who said 'no way' to a pay rise and with one week's holiday in the summer by the sea and another in the mountains. I wanted more. I wanted a taste of the emblematic West and for the names of those dreamt-of cities of my childhood to become my reality. I wanted multiculturalism and multilingualism. The European institutions offered paid traineeships and one of them, in Parliament, was even advertised to journalists. My husband, tired of my endless restlessness and discontent, supported my decision to apply, we had never been apart for so long, but we reassured ourselves that the months would pass quickly. I had to enclose a couple of articles with my application and the only ones I had in English were about culture.

The letter of acceptance which arrived was surely a joke, a mistake, or perhaps it was a sign that culture truly mattered in those European institutions. Perhaps it did, but Ann, the English head of the Visits and Seminars Unit, had her own reasons for selecting me, I was fluent in Czech, and she needed someone to guide groups of Czech visitors around the Parliament. It happened that there weren't enough Czech applicants that term, and so the stars aligned for me.

I reminded Ann that I had been selected to do a journalistic traineeship during our introductory meeting. 'You might like to join the Association of Trainees at the European Parliament,' she replied, 'They have a monthly newsletter. Perhaps you could write some articles for that.' And so I found myself working at the European Parliament in Brussels.

My new life started in a basement. I was to share a studio on *Chaussée d'Ixelles* with Brigitte, a French-speaking Belgian for 250 euros a month. It consisted of a living room with another level above it, which served as her bedroom, and another room in the basement. When I saw that the window faced a wall, my instinct was to make my excuses and leave. But it was evening, and I had nowhere to go. So I said nothing and, with Brigitte's help, one hour later my bedroom was pleasant and liveable enough for me to be able to see myself sleeping there. Lying on my single bed I thought of my husband, sleeping alone in our one-bedroom apartment in Sofia, which we had furnished together, and of my family and friends, and asked myself whether I hadn't made a mistake by coming to Brussels. It was Sunday. On Monday morning my traineeship started.

My love,

The days are going by so fast that I can hardly manage to keep up with them. The first week is almost at its end. The coming weeks will pass just as quickly, and before we know it, my traineeship will be over.

The Parliament dazzles me with its vastness, light and self-sufficiency. As well as the canteen, there is another restaurant for the MEPs, several cafés, banks, a hairdresser, a flower shop, kiosks and what have you.

I am sharing an office with Vassiliki, a Greek secretary, who is constantly on the phone. Her 'Ne. Ne. Ne.*' drums on my brain like the rain on the pavement but she is very kind and sweet and has introduced me to our colleagues from the neighbouring offices.*

I already told you that I will be in charge of guided tours for the Czech visitors at the Parliament and at the moment I'm translating the presentation that I will be delivering.

Last night, Bridget and I went for a walk in the old city. Grand Place *is truly marvellous, surrounded by charming streets with fish restaurants which create a lovely seaside atmosphere.* Manneken Pis, *the symbol of Brussels, is hilarious. It's pretty ridiculous how much attention this little boy peeing gets! There's always a crowd of tourists around it, taking photos. They have dedicated an entire museum to him which contains his wardrobe of hundreds of suits and they regularly organise dressing ceremonies for him.*

All the streets have plates with two names on them, in French and in Flemish. Often, they are completely different, my street is Chaussée d'Ixelles *in French and* Elsense Steenweg *in Flemish, imagine what a conversation about directions between a Francophone and a Flemish-speaking citizen would be like!*

Another thing which impresses me is how cars stop at pedestrian crossings the moment the drivers see you approaching and patiently wait for you to cross. I think it will take a while for me to get used to exercising my rights with confidence!

For now, I like Brussels very much. It's unbelievable really, as it's a dirty city with chaotic architecture and it's not outstandingly beautiful. But it's alive, present, real and — you may laugh — reminds me of Sofia.

But there are moments when sadness washes over me like a wave. Mostly, when I go to bed in the evening. I miss your embrace.

How are you doing? Have you found a handyman for the bathroom?

I will call you tonight from the Internet shop, so I can hear your voice.

Kisses,

Iris

*

In the second week at the Parliament, two significant things happened. A couple of days after my training, I guided my first group. There were some twelve people of different ages. They listened to me carefully and bombarded me with questions to which I didn't have sufficient answers. Why do MEPs have to travel to Strasbourg for their plenary sessions? Why are the MEPs' salaries different depending on the country they are elected from? What would be the benefits of Czechia joining the EU?

Ann gave me another task too – to cover the session of the Convention on the future of Europe and to prepare a briefing for her. From the Parliament's website I learnt that the Convention was formed in order to tackle four themes, a new delimitation of competences in the EU, a simplification of the political instruments of the Union, increased democracy through legitimate institutions, and the route to a European constitution. Having seen the end of the ‘bright communist future’, I was to witness the forging of a bright European future.

In my basement bedroom I listened to people passing above me, the lingering echo of their steps. I heard the buses running in opposite directions. Midnight laughter. Words fallen out of conversations. Brigitte’s returning home, her hasty movements in the living room, her hesitant steps descending the stairs to my bedroom to check whether I was still awake and offer me a cup of tea.

‘In the sixteenth century, it was the clatter of the carriage of Margueritte de Parme passing on her way to *La Cambre* to make her devotions to the relics of Saint Boniface. And as there was no pavement, the Duchess's coach overturned, and it took many *Ixellois* to rescue her out of this embarrassing situation. In 1815 the soldiers marched against Napoleon here.’ Sat on my bed, holding her cup of tea, Brigitte was giving me a guided walk on our street through the centuries.

From *Porte de Namur* to *Place Fernand Cocq* with its bars, restaurants and the exquisite theatre-like district city hall, *Chaussée d’Ixelles* was a commercial area. After the district hall, the street narrowed, became cozier, and descended precipitously towards the *Place Flagey*, revealing a magnificent view of the Church of St. Croix. Walking back home on those evenings, when the sun bathed the roofs and the church tower in its dying light, I always slowed down and marvelled at the view with humbleness and quiet gratitude that this was happening; that I was there; I had a room, even though it was underground, on this universe of a street; that at that moment I belonged to the street and the street belonged to me.

'You know the district hall; it was once the pavilion of the opera diva *La Malibran.* And before that it was a popular cabaret, the *Villa Tulipant.* Malibran's husband had the pavilion built for her, but they had lived in it for just a few months. During a stay in London, she fell from a horse and died from the injuries she sustained when she was on tour in Manchester. Bériot, her husband, never allowed another woman at the villa. Later, the commune bought the pavilion and turned it into a prison. At number 79 was the famous cabaret *Au Chasseur Vert* in which in 1840 the painter Paul Lauters and his friends founded the *Cercle des Arts*. The Belgian writer Camille Lemonnier was born at number 50 in 1844. In 1857, at number 45, the future founder of the *Theatre Molière*, Gil Naza, opened a hall called *Theatre Malibran*. The meetings of the Shooting Society and the Crossbow Society also took place there and their golden books were signed by Leopold I in 1858 and Leopold II in 1869,' Brigitte told me, and I listened to her and imagined all that she described. She was a final-year student at ULB majoring in history and supported her studies by giving guided tours in Brussels for tourists over the weekend. It was one of my first evenings in Brussels, but having tea on my bed and midnight conversations would become a ritual.

'How did you end up in this studio?' I asked her.

'You know, I lived in the neighbourhood with my boyfriend. On the evening when we decided to separate, I walked towards

Flagey. I wanted to go to the ponds and be by myself for a while. I passed by this place and saw the notice on the door. I immediately called and came to see it on the following day. And I loved it. Over the weekend, I moved in.'

'Was it painful – the separation?'

'You know, there is always sadness involved when something is ending. But it is less sad when it has reached its natural ending. That is what happened with us and to me this studio was a symbol of a new beginning.' She had furnished it alone with IKEA and excellent taste. The living room was very charming and even my bedroom was pleasant to live in after her skilful intervention.

'The first name of *Chaussée d'Ixelles* was *Montagne Pénible. Zwaerenberg* in Dutch. "The Cumbersome Mountain" in English.'

I smiled to myself. From Sofia, a capital at the foot of a mountain I had landed on the cumbersome mountain in the European capital.

In the Convention, a hundred wise women and men discussed the role of God in the Constitution. Some believed He should be mentioned, others referred to the different religions of the EU citizens. The weight of the votes in the decision making when ten new member states joined the Union was a hot topic too. I listened and wrote and sent Ann briefing after briefing. We met once a fortnight for fifteen minutes to catch up on how I was managing my time at the Parliament. Other trainees sometimes had breakfast or lunch with their supervisor, but Ann hadn't offered this. Our brief contact, however, gave me a certain autonomy and, other than sticking to the schedule of Czech visitors, I could attend events or committee discussions that interested me and socialise with colleagues and other trainees.

Every day I met new people. Usually, on Fridays an email from a fellow trainee arrived, announcing an outing and that 'everyone is welcome to join'. We went to different bars downtown. As we were drinking beer and chatting, someone would start dancing, another would follow and, elated to be here, in Brussels, to be young, educated, speaking different languages and together, we danced until late in the night, and all the bars in the centre became discotheques, loud music wafted from everywhere and other young people like us set off another night of the EU capital dancing. Once we were in a gay bar, a few metres away from *Manneken Pis*, where there was a drag queen performance. On another night, we were at the opening of a new *@seven* concept party where we danced on a revolving stage, balloons fluttered in the air, champagne was poured, and the mood exploded like a cork.

'The DJ kicked off at 9pm so by 11pm I had taken my share of dancing and could be in bed before midnight and fresh in the office this morning. Isn't this a great concept – an early party for working people on a Thursday night? Not by chance on Thursday, as on Friday many Bruxellois return to their countries for the weekend or just go on trips. I am looking forward to travelling too. I'm waiting for you, so we can share all this,' I write to my husband in the morning.

*

In the Parliament, I had most contact with Karel and Marketa, a Czech and a Slovak, interns like me. Every so often, Karel and I had lunch together in the canteen. One of our first conversations was about the Constitution and how, through it, its authors have tried to create a common identity among the Union citizens by introducing the flag, the anthem, the emblem, the currency and Europe Day. But Karel was sceptical.

'Will I start to feel like a European in a few months just because we have joined the Union? It's out of the question. And if those of us who benefit from internships, Erasmus, projects, well-paid jobs and cheap flights don't have that identity, what is left for the majority who don't travel and have no contact with other nations, or access to this wonderful world of the EU? Then add that national governments blame the Union for every unpopular measure they take, but they're quick to take sole credit for the good initiatives introduced thanks to that same Union. Of course, most people believe them, so it's clear that the problem is very deep and can't be solved artificially with a constitution. But anyway, we're not going to solve it at this table either, so tell me, are you coming to the cocktail party tonight?'

Karel, Marketa and I had made attending receptions at the Parliament a hobby. This was not at all difficult, as there were at least two every day. Vernissages, tourist presentations, traditional dances. Day after day, we tasted wines, beers, cheeses, breads, sausages, olives and other products from different European regions.

Whatever the occasion, we were there, glasses in hand, sharing stories of our day in a mix of Czech and Slovak, and laughing at our newly acquired habits.

'What's so funny, Karel?' A dandified man had approached us.

'Oh, Iris was telling us a story…'

There was a twinkle in his blue eyes when they stared at me.

'Will you tell it to me too, Iris?' His face and voice were somewhat familiar.

'Let me introduce Mr Felix Treu, a German MEP,' Karel said.

'I think Iris and I know each other,' Felix replied, his eyes still fixed on me. 'Do you remember me?'

'I have a feeling I've met you before but I've no idea where.'

'Let me give you a clue, bubbles.'

'Bubbles like champagne?'

'No. Try again.'

And then it came – a flashback like in a film. Ten days or so earlier, in the evening, when I was rather exhausted having guided two tours that day, Brigitte spontaneously invited me to join her in going to a sauna with a friend, and as she also mentioned swimming pools, I took her up on the offer. Alice picked us up by car twenty minutes later and in half an hour we parked in front of a large building, in the middle of nowhere. I had taken off my sweater, top and bra, when a couple appeared, stopped next to me and removed their bathrobes. They were both naked. My eyes darted away from the man's penis, and I whispered to Brigitte,

‘They’re *naked*?’

‘Oh, yes, sure. It’s a sauna.’

I wasn’t prepared for that, but there was nothing I could do but put my swimming suit back into my rucksack.

‘Is that a problem?’ Brigitte asked.

‘No, it’s ok. It’s just that I didn’t know.’

‘You don’t have saunas in Bulgaria?’

‘Not like that, no. Not nude ones.’

It wasn’t only about being publicly naked. It was publicly undressing which I found a greater intimacy, the act of stripping of layer after layer until there is nothing but a naked body, exposed and vulnerable. After the changes in my country, all things erotic became very trendy. Eroticism was on show everywhere, perceived as one of the early attributes of freedom. The first striptease and topless competitions took place. But here, in a Belgian sauna complex, this mutual undressing was no striptease. It was nothing more than a means to an end, stripped of any erotic or sexual connotations. Or at least that’s what I thought while undoing the zipper of my jeans and pulling down my underpants. I covered my nakedness with a white towel and entered the Belgian Eden.

In the outdoor swimming pool, thick steam formed a mist over the water in which bodies blurred into ghosts. Candle holders, placed at the corners of the swimming pool, threw out pale light, which only increased the ghostly effect. Couples had taken refuge in the anonymity offered by the mist and shared moments of intimacy, proving my assumptions of innocence to be premature. A big tree stretched its bare branches towards the tiny stars and the fragile moon. I swam slowly back and forth, cherishing the movement, the freedom, the sensuality of my naked body.

'Iris, will you join us in the jacuzzi?' Brigitte and Alice had been resting on the periphery, their quiet voices reaching me every so often as I swam by.

The coolness of the air, the prickling of my skin, the rush to get the towel, the comfort of it wrapping around me. A moment later, the intense bubbles in the jacuzzi brought the warmth back. A man approached, removed his towel and stepped in. For an instant, his penis was at eye level; then it sank under the bubbles. He looked at me, smiled and said something in Flemish.

'Pardon?'

'Oh, I was saying it's quite nice here,' he switched to English. 'Where are you from? Bulgaria? Sooo far away!'

'Less than a three-hour flight.'

'For us that's like another world. You need a visa for here, don't you?'

'Yes. I needed a visa.'

'It must have been easy for a girl like you to get one,' a cunning smile on his face.

'What do you mean "a girl like me"?'

'Well, I can see that you are very nice.' The smile becoming even wider.

'Shall we try the saunas, ladies?' I turned to my companions.

'Oh, did I scare you?' the man defiantly narrowed his blue eyes.

'Not at all. I've just had enough bubbles,' I smiled at him with my coldest smile, got up and tried not to notice his eyes creeping up my naked body.

'I just had enough bubbles!' Alice laughed in the car on the way back. 'I love that! I like you.'

Back to the present, at the Parliament reception, I blushed.

'Remarkable memory,' Felix stared at me. Karel and Marketa looked at us, puzzled.

'I will leave it to Iris to tell you that story.' He walked away with a thin smile.

'How do you know him?'

'Oh… well, another reception.'

'He could be a useful contact for you,' said Karel, 'he sits on the Convention.'

*

Alice asked me out on a date, as she put it, and we went to the Museum of Ixelles to see an exhibition of Delvaux. His paintings were lucid dreams. Mystical naked or half-naked women with enchanting eyes and slender bodies in public places and outdoors at night-time. In some of them only one woman was nude while the rest wore elegant dresses, but the nude woman didn't seem to be bothered; on the contrary, she held herself with poise and calm.

'You know, I have been having this dream for years, it's night-time and I am at a ball or reception, where everyone is dressed up. I walk around and talk to people until I realise that I am the only one naked. It's a shocking revelation, and I don't know what to do. Should I run away or continue acting normal? I always wake up before I make up my mind. Perhaps the women in Delvaux's paintings were also dreaming and what he captured was that last moment of deep calm and poise before they realised they were naked and woke up,' I told Alice later, as we were having a drink at *Café Belga*.

'As far as I am aware, he had a powerful mother and was scared of women,' Alice said. 'Hence the women in his paintings being such unearthly creatures, you see.'

An only child in a wealthy Flemish family, Alice had got all the love and attention one could wish for without the devastating impact of excess. Her dream had been to study linguistics, but as her parents were lawyers and had a law firm in Leuven, it made sense that she would follow the family tradition. So she did, but still managed to find a compromise between her passion for words and her academic choice, a paid traineeship in the law department of a popular Flemish magazine. The money was just enough to cover the rent for her one-bedroom flat downtown; her parents took care of the rest. In her red dress, shoes with high heels and face relying only on its natural beauty, she radiated confidence.

'Do you remember that man in the jacuzzi?' I asked her.

'Your bubbles line? How could I forget!'

'Imagine, I met him at the Parliament. He happens to be an influential MEP!'

‘Hmm, not a very good advertisement for the Parliament.’

‘Besides, he sits on the Convention which I am now covering for my Head of Unit. I had a drink with him at the Parliament yesterday.’

‘You did?’

‘Yes. He’s not that bad. He invited me to join him at a dinner, hosted by another MEP from the Convention.’

‘Was he very disappointed when you refused?’

‘I didn’t, actually.’

‘Are you serious? You’re married.’

‘He’s married too. But it doesn’t matter. There is nothing else there other than me wanting to have a glimpse into his world.’

Alice’s eyes radiated scepticism when she said, ‘I hope you know what you are doing.’

Felix had contacted me the day after the reception.

‘What a lovely surprise last night. I must say you also look stunning in clothes. Shall we have a drink?’ he wrote.

His boldness left me speechless. After a couple of hours, I replied, ‘It was nice to meet you Mr. Treu. I am following the Convention’s discussions and would be interested in getting your views on it.’

An immediate answer, ‘Of course. I will meet you tomorrow at 6pm in the MEPs’ restaurant.’

When I entered the restaurant, he was already there. He stood up to meet me, hugged me and lightly touched my face with his lips as if we were old friends, his spicy aftershave filled my nostrils.

‘What will you have, Iris? Beer, wine, bubbles?’

'Still water, please, with a slice of lemon.'

He ordered red wine for himself.

'So how is life in Brussels, Iris?'

'Very good. I really like it.'

'Yeah, it's ok. I can show you places your trainee buddies wouldn't know.'

'Thank you, that's very kind. And how about the Convention? There is quite a big discussion about God and Christianity.'

'Indeed. You see, Iris, deep in our hearts we Germans are believers, we value the family, love… Is someone waiting for you in Bulgaria?'

'Yes.'

'Hmm, it wasn't very smart of your partner to let you come here alone.'

'He trusts me.'

'Well, there is trust and there is distance. Here you are, so young and beautiful, meeting new people...'

'How about you, Mr Treu? Aren't you married?'

'As a matter of fact, I am.'

'So we are in a similar situation. Shall we focus on the Constitution now?'

'You sound like a journalist.'

'I happen to be one. But don't worry, this conversation is off the record.'

He stared into my eyes; the thin smile was back.

‘Very good. The Constitution… Yes. I am confident that we will get there – with or without Christianity and God. Always in our hearts, of course. But there is no need to always publicly declare what’s in our hearts, is there?’

‘Well, I suppose public declarations bring a certain level of official commitment.’

‘You’re smart. Listen, a French MEP from the Convention is hosting a dinner on Saturday. Why don’t you come with me? There will be quite a few people there you might be interested in meeting.’

I thought for a moment, then heard myself saying,

‘Alright, Mr Treu.’

‘But there is one condition.’

‘Which is?’

‘Stop mistering me. I am Felix to you.’

‘Fine, Felix.’

‘That’s much better,’ he smiled.

*

On Saturday morning I went to Zara and bought a blue dress. Felix picked me up in his shiny Mercedes.

‘You look stunning,’ he said. We were silent for a while.

‘Etienne is a nice guy, a socialist. He and his wife organise such dinners once or twice a year for forty to fifty people. It’s the EU crowd – MEPs, Commission officials, diplomats. I believe you’ll get enough to satisfy your curiosity’, his blue eyes were laughing when he turned to me.

We had entered a neighbourhood with beautiful houses with gardens. As if we were no longer in Brussels but in a posh village.

'Where are we?' I asked.

'Uccle. The district of wealth.'

He stopped in front of a high gate and fence, hiding the world beyond it from prying eyes. A metallic sound accompanied the door slowly opening. We were in a garden with rose bushes and green grass. In front of us stood, lit up, a pale-yellow house. As we took the path leading to it, a tall woman opened the door. She had naturally orange hair, styled in different layers, the longest ones touching her shoulders, indigo eyes, a myriad of freckles and a well-built body. She wore a green dress and high heels.

'Good to see you again, Felix!'

And to me, 'I am Helena, pleasure to meet you. So where are you from? Bulgaria? Ah, I am Danish.'

We entered a living room which looked like a dance hall. It was long, with windows on both sides, art deco furniture and lamps, red carpets with some figures on them and tobacco-coloured curtains with a golden sheen. It was already full of people in expensive suits and glamorous dresses, holding slender glasses. Different languages and accents filled the room. There was food on a long heavy table in the middle. Food is too indelicate a word to use for the exhibits there, each plate was a piece of art. We took a couple of appetizers and joined a group standing next to a small circular table. Felix introduced me to a tall man whose chestnut hair was turning silver and went to get us drinks. Etienne, the host. His brown eyes narrowed when they looked into mine, as if there was something in them which he was trying to decipher. He said something.

'Sorry, but I don't speak French.'

'You don't speak French? What are you doing in this institution then?'

A fleeting thought that his house was the institution, and I was the intruder who not only imposes her presence but isn't able to be civil and communicate. But then it was clear, it wasn't his house he was referring to. 'I speak other languages. Besides, my language will be an official one in the not-too-distant future.'

He laughed. 'You don't lack confidence and sense of humour.'

Felix came back with two glasses of champagne.

'*Salut*!'

They spoke French. I sipped my champagne and looked around.

'Iris is interested in the Constitution', Felix switched into English.

'*Mais oui*! It's a great project. We are almost there now. Aren't we?'

'Almost. But we still have to agree on a couple of minor things… Would your group be willing to reach a compromise?'

'It depends. We could figure out something, especially if we reach a compromise on that other package…'

'Let's have lunch tomorrow and discuss,' Felix said.

At that moment, Helena came and stood next to me.

'Are they boring you with their politics?'

‘Not at all, it’s very interesting…’

‘Oh, you are so sweet but not a great liar. Come with me, let me show you around.’

We crossed the room and went into a corridor with stairs leading up to a spacious room, with a blue, plush sofa in the middle and a small circular table, a carpet with geometric figures in blue, orange, grey and white. It looked too modern for the furniture, yet they went together like an eccentric couple.

‘We’ve got five bedrooms, can you imagine? It’s just the two of us with five bedrooms. Etienne has got teenage children who stay with us every second weekend. But even so five bedrooms… I feel as if I am living in a guest house.’

I had the feeling she was talking to herself, not to me. She walked around and opened the three doors, one by one.

‘There are two more on the top floor. Look, this is ours. It’s huge, isn’t it? As if, when the architect designed it, he imagined Nero’s orgies…’ Her indigo eyes on my face. ‘You sleep with Felix, don’t you?’

‘No.’

‘Ah, not yet.’

‘What makes you so sure?’

‘Well, you know, I’ve been around…You think you’re the first one he’s brought?’

‘I don’t think anything.’

‘You’re a smart girl. He’s married, you know. His wife is a very nice woman, beautiful, fine but she’s got three huge disadvantages, she's not in her twenties anymore, she's too busy with the children, and she's his wife.'

'Why are you telling me this?'

'I don't know. Perhaps I am jealous of your youth and beauty. Perhaps I see in you the girls whom Etienne is certainly fucking. All of you, young, beautiful users of someone else's husband.'

'What you have got, these girls don't have.'

'I know. So what? Anyway, it all comes at a price. And that's usually the package which comes with a wealthy, attractive, influential man, remember that.'

'I'm not out there searching. I'm married myself.'

'You're certainly out there searching, my dear. What are you doing here if you aren't?' Those eyes again. I heard steps and Felix appeared.

'Ah, here you are. I've been looking for you, milady. Come and let me introduce you to some more people.'

The rest of the evening was all introductions, small talk, more food, more champagne, desserts, tea. Once in a while, Felix nonchalantly touched my hand or shoulder, the blue of his eyes becoming more intense when they rested on mine. He smiled gently and checked whether I was alright, made sure my glass was full, I was taken care of. The arrogant bastard from the MEP restaurant was gone. Or well hidden.

He drove me home around midnight, kissed my cheek, keeping his face close to mine a little bit longer than necessary, and wished me good night.

'How was your evening?' asked Brigitte.

'Great! One day I will live in Uccle.'

Of course, Helena was right in assuming that I wasn't there just for the politics and the networking. The intensity in Felix's eyes that night hit me like a wave, breaking on the deserted shores of my desire. The anonymous desire, conceived in the dark bars as dancing salsa or kizomba with the Latino guys, their smooth movements and warm embrace, the fire in their eyes, and the drops of sweat, perfect like morning dew, on their hands; or by the warmth in Karel's smile at times; or by the longer glance of an attractive stranger… It was now taking shape in me and had a destination. Felix. He messaged me in the morning to thank me for the lovely evening and to ask when he could see me again.

'You shouldn't be doing this,' said Brigitte.

Alice nodded with a serious expression. 'You're married.'

They had a point. I felt a little bit ashamed, shivering naked in front of the white wall of their morality.

'On Friday,' I replied to Felix.

My love,

I'm sorry I haven't written to you in the past few days. There are too many things going on and I need time to process them.

I was at a reception organised by an MEP from the Convention. It was very interesting but sobering to see how politics and agreements happen beyond the plenary hall, at receptions, over a glass of champagne and salmon bites. I tried truffles, mmmm!

You ask me about the bad weather here. Well, I hardly notice it. And often the sun appears unexpectedly at the end of a dark and gloomy day. One of the most striking views I have ever seen, the triangular roofs and the upper floors of houses bathed in soft golden light, in stark contrast to the rest of the building, sunk in the shadow. That special light, I call it.

I still go to listen to the Convention. They have been debating for weeks about whether or not to include God and Christianity in the Constitution. I decided to write an article about it for the trainees' newsletter.

I was sad when you didn't respond to the text I sent you on Saturday morning. I know the decision to come here was mine and I do not regret it. But it is only natural that there are times when I feel lonely and sad, in a foreign city and a foreign country, far from you. In such moments I need your words, your assurance that you are there for me...

Kisses,

Iris

God is on the agenda of the Convention. A hundred wise women and men are trying to decide whether or not God and Christianity have a place in the Constitution.

'Europe as a whole is based on a Christian heritage', said a German MEP. 'The inclusion of God will only strengthen our European identity'. A British MEP took the floor, 'A specific mention of Christianity would offend those many millions of people of different faiths or no faith at all'

The debate has been running for months now and has spilled out of this hall. A Polish cardinal has said that he supported his country's entry to the EU entry but only with God. A Hungarian Catholic cardinal has stated that without Christianity, the heart of Europe would be missing. The Polish Pope has insisted on a clear reference to God and the Christian faith being included in the European Constitution. The European Christian-Democrats suggested that the EU treaty's preamble contains a reference to a European collective cultural heritage "based on the Greek-Roman philosophy, the Christian message and Jewish-Christian values." The Swedish Aftonbladet stated, in response, that referring to Christian values in the Constitution and placing them above other values would be a 'huge mistake' because it would 'exclude groups and raise new walls.' A French socialist made the point that specific mention of Christianity and God is 'absurd' because it would exclude Muslims and others of non-Christian faiths, as well as citizens who do not believe in God.

A hundred wise women and men talk about God and His presence in the future of Europe. Their voices reverberating with passion, conviction, enthusiasm, concern, anger. One thing unites them all though, the faith in a united future... with or without God. But can there be a future without God?

I come from a country where God was forbidden for forty-five years. Christianity was not on the agenda at all. There were a few moments when God sneaked into my ordered socialist childhood, my grandmother and I sitting on the grass in front of a chapel near our house in a small village in Strandja mountain, her telling me the story of Christ. I clearly remember the Last Supper, the twelve men in white, the long table, the candles, the silence before the betrayal – God is a legend; that same grandmother baptizing me, a secret from my parents, in the church of that same village with a neighbour becoming my godmother, the darkness, the water, my new cotton underwear – God is a magical secret; my best friend and I dare to enter the church on Good Friday and pass under the altar, representing Christ's grave – God is a ritual – but then a teacher on guard outside, to make sure that no pupils enter, sees us and takes us to the Director's office the following day resulting in a warning about our behaviour marks being decreased by one degree. During the regime, each pupil had a behavioural mark which could be decreased for bad conduct; a very severe measure; this mark could be decreased twice only. On the third time, the pupil would be expelled – God is punishment; in biology class that same friend writes in an essay about the origin of man, that we all descended from God via Adam and Eve; the teacher gives her the lowest mark and asks her to correct her statement by saying that we all descended from apes, in front of the entire class, to which she replies that she, personally, did not come from an ape but from God, however if the teacher felt she had come from a monkey, she would respect that; off again to the Director's office and this time her behaviour mark is indeed decreased by one grade which is among the most horrible things to happen in the life of a socialist pupil – God is a danger; I wear a crucifix earring, imitating Madonna, my father makes a huge scene and forces me to take it off, as this would have a devastating impact on my bright socialist future – God is a threat; the bright future is cancelled, Christmas and Easter are back with all the surrounding rituals – God is a tradition; crowds of young people go drinking on Easter night and then stand in front of the church waiting for midnight, when, after the priest's announcement that Jesus has risen, they will circle it three times with candles in hands, laughing and swaying, followed by the egg knocking and joining the party in a night club – God is a trend; icons with the Virgin Mary and the Child, Christ and popular saints appear in our flat – God is decoration; books about spirituality, reincarnation, yoga, kundalini energy and meditation flood the book market – God is bigger than religion. And now, in the House of the People, God is an item on both the plenary agenda and the political one. And I am wondering why the reference to God should be linked to religion. Why not have just God, and all the religions as long as they respect the European values and human rights. Diversity, diversity, diversity...But will diversity work without God?

Spring came and the weather stayed good for days. After the first few months of intense socialising, I had started reconnecting to myself and appreciating my own company. I had got a bit tired of meeting new people all the time and answering all the same questions, Where are you from? How long have you been in Brussels? What are you doing? Etc., etc. Conversations usually stayed shallow which, after the initial euphoria of being in an international environment, bored me. Over the weekend, I often had a cup of tea and a croissant for breakfast in *l'Amour Fou*. I glanced at the district administration building, imagining how the diva Malibran lived in it, and wrote in my diary. Sitting on the grass by the two nearby lakes, *Étangs d'Ixelles*, I read *L'œuvre au Noir* by Marguerite Yourcenar, whose labyrinth monument had just been opened on *Avenue Louis*, next to the place where she had been born a hundred years earlier. I drank beer and wrote at a small table in front of *Café Belga*, which was always full of people, but their presence did not disturb my privacy. On the contrary, the multilingualism surrounding me made me feel like an anonymous part of this community. I walked in the gardens of the Abbey, where I always felt deeply calm.

At least once a week I would see Brigitte and Alice for drinks or dinner at an Italian, Thai, Chinese, Mexican or Brazilian restaurant. The food was always a feast for the senses, even at the cheaper places. As the evening progressed, we went dancing – mostly at Havana and the Brazilian Bar. The time with Brigitte and Alice was dense, rich and joyful. I also had outings with each of them separately. One evening, I was with Alice and her friends at *Roskam*, a Flemish bar downtown. Among them was a guy who looked at me intensely and then said,

‘You are the first Bulgarian I’ve ever met. Bulgaria sounds very exotic to us.’

Then he continued pressing my buttons, asking me how things were in Bulgaria, if it wasn’t a poor country and if it was so great over there, what was I doing here. Three or four Alice’s friends who sat close to us listened. Initially, I was in defence mode and talked about the riches Bulgaria offers. But as he wouldn’t stop, I fired,

‘Why don’t you leave my country alone and tell me some interesting facts from your country’s history? For example, how Leopold II treated the Africans. You must be very proud of that.’

Suddenly it was very quiet. This continued few seconds which felt like minutes. Then someone asked,

‘Does anyone need a drink?’

I left soon after. Alice tried to soften things by telling me he was drunk, but this didn’t diminish the chill inside me. I walked across *Grand Place*, full of tourists taking photos, sitting in the restaurants or on its cobblestones, cherishing its breathtaking beauty, and for the first time I felt like a foreigner in this city, a capital of a union of which I was not a citizen.

*

'I like you very much, Iris.'

Felix's voice stopped my train of thought and pulled me back into the long dark space of *Goupil Le Fol*, lit with candles on each table, whose pale light revealed walls covered with paintings, and the ceiling adorned with old vinyl records, verging on kitsch, yet artistic and romantic. A few weeks had passed since the French MEP's dinner, during which we had seen each other twice – for a glass of champagne in the MEPs' restaurant and for dinner in some snobbish restaurant. Then he left for Strasbourg, where he wrote to me every day. This was our first meeting since his return. After dinner I wanted to go home, but he insisted on showing me one of the "hidden treasures of Brussels". I enjoyed the time with him. He shared behind-the-scenes stories of the Convention, peppered with episodes from his countless travels around the world. With persistent naivety, I tried to deceive myself that there was nothing in these outings that would harm the relationship with my husband. I told myself that it was natural to get to know people from different backgrounds, that this was my first contact with an MEP, and it could be useful. To reinforce my self-delusion, I even wrote to Stefan about my new acquaintance. But with his confession, Felix shattered all my exculpatory thoughts. As if this was not enough, Felix stretched his hand across the table and held mine. His face, bathed in candlelight, had softened. I felt I could become dependent on the wrinkles which appeared at the corners of his lips when he smiled, on the hair falling over his forehead, on the tenderness that his eyes radiated when he looked at me. I drank the sweet raspberry wine, pulled my hand away and said,

'I'm tired. Let's go.'

He finished his wine in one go.

'I wish I could take you somewhere for the weekend, but my family is coming back tomorrow,' he said in the car.

'I've got plans too,' I replied.

I turned towards him to give him a goodbye kiss on the cheek, but he moved his head and kissed my lips. We froze for a moment, our lips just a millimetre apart. Then I withdrew and got out of the car. I felt dizzy as I took the two steps to my door and entered quietly; it was past midnight. There was light coming from my underground room. Next to the open latticed window, cigarette in hand, stood Stefan.

Stefan and I lay on the grass in *Bois de la Cambre*, a vast forest-park with a busy road running through it. He took out a cigarette and lit it.

'When did you start smoking again?'

'I haven't started smoking.'

'Really? Then what are you holding?'

'Iris is there anything you are not telling me?'

Around us, the lawn looked like a promotional video on EU multiculturalism. Two guys of African origin were having a beer. Next to them, a family comprised of a white mother and a black father, and two children with light brown skin sat on a blanket. Further on, a group of young men and women played with a ball. They jumped, trying to hit the ball, and screamed with satisfaction or disappointment, depending on the outcome. The large blanket next to them was covered with the remains of their picnic and many empty glasses.

'How do you like it here?' I asked.

'You didn't answer my question.'

'I didn't get it.'

'Is there anything going on between you and the MEP you wrote to me about?'

'Of course not. Our relations are entirely professional.'

'Entirely professional? And you go to receptions together?'

'Since when do you not trust me?'

'I do trust you. I am sorry.'

'You didn't answer my question either.'

'It's nice. But then can you compare this pond to the Seven Rila Lakes or any other lake in Bulgaria? This park to Vitosha? I don't understand your fascination with Brussels.'

A six-or-seven-year-old girl in a pink t-shirt threw a red ball towards her father. Another girl of around four sat on the grass with crossed legs, watching a boy playing with a Pomeranian dog.

'It's a nice city and that's about it. It's rather plain, compared to Paris or London,' Stefan continued.

A teenage girl with long dark hair gathered in a ponytail on the top of her head, wearing headphones looked at her mobile, a melancholy expression on her face. In front of us, groups and couples, engrossed in conversations, were flirting, caressing, laughing.

‘I want to stay in Brussels.’

Shade fell over my husband’s face, but there was no shadow.

‘How do you imagine that happening?’

‘I’ve started sending my CV around to various media and organisations.’

‘Have you had any response?’

‘No. But there is still time. I have only just started.’

‘You won’t be able to find a job. Perhaps as a waitress. But not as a journalist. Is that what you want? To throw away your diplomas and lead an immigrant life? To replace the home we have built together in Sofia for a basement? And what about us? I would never move to Belgium!’

More frisbees, balls, dogs, children. The pond sparkled and a few boats moved slowly by.

‘I don’t know. I never felt so independent and free in my life before. So complete and authentic. Do you understand that?’

Words in French, Arabic, Spanish, English, Polish drifted across to us.

‘No matter how hard I try, I don’t. I don’t want to believe that you are ready to give up on our marriage and all that we have built together for this student’s existence.’

‘It’s not the student’s existence that appeals to me. As I said, here I feel independent, free, respected and happy.’

‘Respected? I wasn’t left with that impression from your emails.’

‘Why do you have to be so mean? I had one accident and I didn’t share it with you so that you could hold it against me! One accident in three months! I like the international environment; I like accessibility of travel and culture. Like going to Paris for the day just to see an exhibition. I feel connected to the multiculturalism, I feel like I belong here.’

‘Don’t fool yourself. They will never take you as one of them. You will always be the poor relative from Eastern Europe in their Western world.’

‘Or maybe they will. Maybe I will prove you wrong.’

‘Maybe you will. But this will come at a price and both of us will have to pay it.’

Deep down I knew he was right, but I was not prepared to accept it. After the initial shock, joy and guilt of seeing him, after quickly crafting an explanation for my late return (drinks with other trainees and my mobile’s battery had indeed been flat); after hiding my liar’s face in his embrace and letting myself slip into the gentle flow of our love making; after the breakfast in *l’Amour Fou*, followed by showing him my neighbourhood and walking downtown, after all the sightseeing and brief updates of what we had been up to, as the days passed, I increasingly felt the growing distance between us.

When he left, a few days later, having given me a strong hug and a kiss, while trying to hide the dampness in his eyes, I cried my heart and soul out and refused to see Felix. One part of me was gone and I didn't know whether it would ever return.

Brigitte took me to lunch with her mother. She lived in a street with pretty houses in Schaerbeek, a district of Brussels with an area known as the Turkish quarter. Pauline was a beautiful woman in her fifties. She had short dark wavy hair and large hazel eyes. She wore a loose purple dress and slippers with heels. The table was set when we arrived. Flowers, some olives, some pâté, a cheese platter. All was very proper, somewhat bourgeois.

'So Iris, tell me how things were during communism?' Pauline didn't waste any time with pleasantries. She got straight to the point with the bubbles which she had offered us as soon as we entered.

'We were building communism, but we never got there. What we lived in was called 'the socialist order.''

'Pardon?'

'In the bright future, called communism, we were supposed to be all equal, there wouldn't be money, all goods would be free and sufficient for everyone.'

'I see… And what was it like… to live in this *order*?'

'There is no simple way to describe what we went through. On the one hand, friendships, support and closeness were there. On the other hand, however, some of the biggest damage caused by the system was undermining trust, planting the seeds of insecurity in each and every one, as anyone could be an agent of the state security service, even husbands and wives would spy on and betray each other. Self-censorship was the common denominator. But, again, this is something I found out later and, perhaps, it wasn't as present in the last years of the regime, certainly not in my parents' circle. What I recall is how once in a while, there would be whispering and secrecy. That there were forbidden and dangerous things. It made me curious, yes, but also afraid.'

'Very interesting…'

'The most interesting of all, to me, was the intellectual potential, a bubbling, potent energy. There was so little by way of entertainment, that people were hungry for books and art. Everyone had a huge library of world classics and actually read them. People were very imaginative in getting access to forbidden books, music or films and cherished them tremendously. They were hungry for knowledge, had ideas, searched for meaning. Ironically, our best films were created then, showing a horizon which spread much beyond the Iron Curtain. The July Morning tradition started then too. You know the song, right?'

'Of course. What tradition?'

'Inspired by the hippie movement. Thousands of people from across the country gather on the beach, some bring guitars, they build fires or just contemplate the sea waiting for the sunrise on 1st July. The tradition only exists in Bulgaria, which I think is fascinating.'

'How interesting…'

'The energy faded during the transition out of socialism. And now I think so much has been lost to consumerism. Not forever, I hope. Anyway, I don't believe in black and white. If someone took a forensic eye to Western Europe, what would they find?'

'But you had a revolution?'

'We didn't have one. But the Romanians did. In Bulgaria, it happened abruptly, from one day to the next. Overnight, the regime was over, and life went on as if it had never been. With no explanation from my parents or teachers, the only thing I knew was that we were suddenly living in a democracy. At first, democracy was exhilarating, it brought people onto the streets searching for their inner selves, drunk with their newly acquired freedom. Then there were food coupons, empty shops and long lines just to buy basics. Democracy was also porn and erotic magazines, beauty and striptease competitions. It was all my parents' savings, enough to buy flats for me and my brother, disappearing in an instant. Democracy was the end of friendships because some supported the changes and others supported the past. It was two million Bulgarians leaving the country. The long-dreamt-of democracy brought poverty and disillusionment to my grandparents, resulting in my grandmother's depression and suicide. Democracy meant an end for my parent's generation and the ones before them and an (almost) fresh start for their children.'

'I see…' Pauline said and served the soup.

I didn't know how to convey that no matter how happy I was that the regime was over, the change and the transition were not easy. That my parents weren't socialist party members or supporters of the regime, but their life felt more secure before the changes. Their generation got the freedom of speech to be able to curse one government after another; got the free market but also the impossibility of maintaining a business without being involved in shady dealings; got the liberty to vote for different political parties but no trustworthy candidates within them; freedom of movement but not the financial means to exercise it, even within their own country; abundance in the shops but an inability to afford it. Access to art came at a price so instead of cherishing it they found themselves stuck at home in front of the TV screen spilling out dark news, reality shows and all sorts of brainwashing. The main thing taken away from them was their bright future. Any future at all, for that matter. So that we, their children, have a future. A future in which Bulgaria will be part of the European Union and, one day, of the free labour market, and, with a bit of luck, we can leave to find our fortune elsewhere.

Pauline was looking at me and I wondered if I matched her image of an Eastern European, of someone who came from a poor, traumatized country. I remembered a picnic with five or six other trainees, of whom I was the only Eastern European. In the course of the conversation, something, which I had already noticed earlier, struck me again. On the surface we were all very similar – we spoke a few languages, most of us already had some professional experience at home etc. But when we started talking about our backgrounds, a huge gap revealed itself. All my colleagues had lived in other countries – for Erasmus, language classes, jobs. I was the only one who didn't have access to such opportunities. When I told them I put all my savings into private English lessons with a British teacher, their jaws dropped. They had travelled Europe and beyond. Nothing could erase these differences, defined by our divided historical past which was embedded in each of us. We had simply had profoundly different starts in life, impacting our world view, our perception of abundance and our future options. Perhaps, one day, these differences might be erased, who knew, but it would take years for me to catch up. Was Pauline aware of that?

'I suppose it is weird to see your own capital flooded and taken over by foreigners, to experience prices rising because of the standard of living imposed by the well-heeled European institutions, rents going up for the same reason…' I said.

'Brussels is many cities,' Pauline said. 'There is the Brussels of the expats and the migrants and their tribes and then there is our Brussels.'

But what did "ours" mean in a country where its citizens identified themselves as two main communities and might not even have a common language? Where was this Brussels? While the city was broadly French-speaking, there were concentrated areas where Flemish people lived. One of these areas was downtown, in the vicinity of *Place St. Catherine*, where Alice rented a flat. All her friends were Flemish except Brigitte. I was the only other foreigner admitted to her world.

'So when are you leaving Belgium?' asked Pauline, as we were finishing the main dish.

My second column was about diversity.

The European Convention: Diversity Seeks Unity

Power is another item on the Convention's agenda, which has created a lot of discussion. More precisely, ensuring its equal distribution among all the member states, including the newcomers. The main preoccupation of the smaller states is to not find themselves in a union where other countries decide for them and where they have no say. A fair concern. United in diversity? There is diversity. But there is not much unity from what I can see. I have been in Brussels for three months now and I have noticed the ironic smile of the Germans when it comes to the working habits of the Spanish (siesta, siesta...); the indignation of the Italians when they talk about the arrogance of the Germans; the scorn of the Brits talking about the Easterners flooding their country and stealing jobs; the bewilderment of the Swedes commenting on public toilets in some of the Central-European countries; the Central-European citizens being offended each time someone calls them Eastern Europeans and implying a superior vs inferior difference; the Western and Northern Europeans nevertheless making no such distinction – each territory behind the former Iron Curtain is, for them, Eastern Europe; the prejudices of the Dutch towards the Flemish; the look of superiority when more than one French administrator has asked me how come I don't speak French; and the scepticism on the face of almost any citizen of the current member states when I mention Bulgaria joining in 2007. Where is the unity then? The countries seem more concerned with keeping their sovereignty and being able to defend their national interests than with the solidarity and the moulding of a European identity.

If even the regions in some of the countries are not in agreement and want to split, what is left for unity among the countries? Take Belgium with its three main communities and regions that couldn't be more different.

'Belgium is like a marriage', said my Belgian flat mate once. 'A marriage between a poor woman, Wallonia, and a rich man, Flanders. They don't love each other. But they are married and forever united by their child, Brussels. It is impossible to get an agreement on Brussels since although it is mostly French-speaking it belongs to both the Walloon and Flemish communities. So should the couple file for divorce? No one would be willing to give up the child. They are condemned to stay together, bound by obligations.'

What is the Union then? A club where everyone comes together with different agendas, pursuing the sole objective of preserving it instead of focusing on joint interests? A group of individualists not willing to commit and expand themselves to a more potent "we"?

Perhaps I am exaggerating. Who am I to judge, at the end of the day? An Eastern European novice looking at the privileged club members from behind a glass wall.

*

I had two months left till the end of my traineeship and wanted to visit as many places as I possibly could. In the preceding months, I had made day trips with other trainees to the main Belgian cities. Now the time had come to explore other territories. If Eurolines had a VIP client category, I would have certainly been entitled to it. Weekend after weekend I headed for Paris, Amsterdam, Maastricht, The Hague, Cologne, Luxembourg, Berlin… I walked the European cities, spent hours in their museums and galleries and fed my burgeoning European-ness.

During the week, I sent indiscriminate applications, dozens of them.

'A thousand euros? Will that be enough?'

The dark Flemish eyes of the man sitting across from me fixed on my face, studying it with curious coolness. He was the Director of the European Association of Journalism to whom I had sent a spontaneous application. I had just told him that I would be willing and happy and strongly motivated to work for them for a thousand-euro salary – that was my trainee allowance at the Parliament, and it was enough to cover my basic costs and trips.

'Net or gross?' he wanted to know.

I had no clue about Belgian taxes but to be on the safe side said, net.

'Do you speak French? Or Flemish?'

I didn't speak either. But I spoke English, Czech, Spanish and Bulgarian and was eager to learn and motivated to put all my energy into achieving his organisation's objectives.

He stared at me and then said,

'I will let you know if something comes up.'

The end of my traineeship approached but the idea of leaving Brussels was incomprehensible. I didn't want to go. I spoke four languages, I had a master's degree, I had experience in qualified jobs. Why should I leave? I am like you. I belong here. Please let me stay. Let me contribute to the diversity, the unity, the multiculturalism and multilingualism. I will do my best. I will use all my past socialist discipline, commitment and loyalty. I will be a dignified member of your lovely society. Like you. Or even better, because for you all this is granted. And things you are used to, things you've always possessed, things you did not dream nor fight for, you don't appreciate. While I, I lived totalitarianism. I lived the Iron Curtain. I lived the transition. I lived the fantasy of your normality. I will be grateful. I already am. Please! I have never in my life begged like that…

'You have a letter,' Brigitte said. It was on the table and had the commune's stamp on it. My residence card was ready, and I had to go to collect it, two months before the end of my stay.

*

Ann asked me to go to Strasbourg with the Czech observers. Members of the parliaments in the ten accession countries were appointed to come to the European Parliament and observe proceedings by joining the parliamentary sessions and committee meetings as silent guests. In the glass building, surrounded by a lake like an island, we put together information packs and arranged them on stands, then sat behind them for hours. Every so often, an observer would show up, grab a pack in his or her language and leave.

On the following day, the MEPs voted against God and Christianity being included in the Constitution. In the evening, a reception was thrown for the accession of the ten candidate countries, during which the observers were officially welcomed as MEPs. The ceremony took place at the Contemporary Art Museum. All the trainees were invited. I walked around with a glass of wine and contemplated the paintings to the sounds of a piano coming from the ground floor. On my way back to the main hall, I saw a familiar figure in an impeccable suit. I had been avoiding him ever since the night my husband arrived. On the phone, I was distant and elusive. I was busy, travelling, had other plans. I had seen him at the Convention but always made sure to disappear quickly once the session was over. Somehow, we hadn't met. The Parliament is a big village. One could easily live in it without seeing everyone all the time.

'The phantom lady. Let me touch you to check whether you are real,' Felix said.

I smiled. He asked me how I was doing and when he heard I was looking for a job, showed an interest in whether my husband would be inclined to move to Belgium. At the end he said, that in autumn he would have an assistant position available in his office and suggested that we discuss it over dinner. I replied something vague and returned to the main hall, where everyone was leaving. A bus took us to a restaurant outside the city, in the middle of nowhere. It was a traditional place with live music. The President of the Parliament gave a speech on the future of a larger, more united and stronger union. He warmly welcomed the newcomers. Then he led a Greek sirtaki and quite a few MEPs joined in. He waved towards our trainees' table and three or four of us dared to follow. When the dance was over, the President came to our table and asked about our names and nationalities. Having heard 'Bulgaria', he exclaimed, 'Oh, you are joining in 2007!' Finally, someone had confirmed the beginning of the bright future.

The party continued with more music, food and wine. On my way back from the bathroom, I found myself face to face with Felix again. He was talking to an older man. I attempted to pass by them, but he stopped me.

'Iris, let me introduce you to Dietrich. He is a former Commissioner, now a MEP. And Iris is a very talented Bulgarian journalist, now a trainee at the Parliament.'

Dietrich looked at me and said,

'Meeting someone young and fresh like you makes me feel like a dinosaur.'

'Meeting someone with your experience makes me feel like a complete novice.'

He laughed and turned to Felix, 'I already like her.'

Another MEP joined and started talking to Felix.

'How was it being a Commissioner Mr…?' I turned to the man he had just introduced me to.

'Dietrich. You know, there is a joke, that countries send politicians they need to get rid of to be Commissioners.' He laughed again and I figured he was at least tipsy. 'It was good, yes, very busy and a lot of travelling. So not so great for my personal life… I was lucky to have the support of our government.'

'But isn't the Commissioner's role supra-national?'

'It is supposed to be. But in reality, things are different. For one to be a strong Commissioner, you need to be supported by your government, have erudition, a strong personality and be favoured by the President of the Commission. I suppose I was lucky to have all that, so my term was very successful.'

'Are you also sitting on the Convention?'

'No, there was no way for me to do that. I don't like wasting my time.'

'What do you mean?'

'The European Constitution. It won't work out. It's not in the interest of the governments to let go of more of their powers.'

'How can you be so sure? Besides, the governments represent the people…'

'In theory. But the majority of people believe what their governments tell them, right? You're still innocent my dear, which could be an advantage somewhere else. Not here. If you are planning an EU career, the sooner you get rid of your illusions, the better. The Constitution won't pass the member states' test, trust the old dog on that.'

He smiled widely, showing all his teeth, which were way too perfect to be real. The issue of power again. Fuelling passionate debates in the Convention… and elsewhere.

'That would be very unfortunate. Especially if we think of Ozymandias.'

'Of whom?'

'"Nothing beside remains. (…) The lone and level sands stretch far away." Shelley. An older dog.'

It was my turn to smile now. He was nonplussed. I felt I had skewered his somewhat patronizing glibness.

'Nice meeting you, Dietrich. See you around,' I said and walked away.

*

A reception again but this time a really special one, the European Constitution had been adopted. The hundred wise women and men were celebrating the fruits of their lengthy efforts. Now the only thing left was for the member states to sign it and adjust their national legislation. Bottles of champagne were opened. Marketa, Karel and I chin-chinned and took in the sparkling taste of the bright European future. Inevitably, I thought of Dietrich's words at the party in Strasbourg. Perhaps he was just drunk, perhaps he was just a cynic. Felix nodded to me from a distance. Since the night in Strasbourg and my refusal to join him at his hotel, his enthusiasm had cooled. He didn't contact me again. I didn't contact him either, despite the prospect of a job at the Parliament.

*

My third column didn't work out. I had a couple of ideas but there was too much going on in the preceding weeks and no time to really focus. But my last group of Czech visitors got a special treat. I made sure to finish the obligatory programme early and then I took them to the ground floor where the banks, the post office, the supermarket, the canteen, the cafés, the newspaper kiosks and the hairdresser are. Parliament's perfect, self-enclosed world; its self-sufficiency. The city within the city. Finally, we entered the Mickey Mouse bar on the third floor - the playground of the Parliament's world. It happened to be almost empty as the MEPs were in Strasbourg for their last session before the summer break, so we could have a relaxed coffee, sitting on the garish Mickey Mouse shaped chairs. The visitors seemed to be enjoying this additional programme even more than the official one. Then I walked them to the exit and wished them well. This frivolous act was rather spontaneous. Perhaps I did it more for myself than for them – sharing this world I was now so used to before leaving it for good.

Vasiliki was jealous of me returning to Bulgaria. 'I do miss Greece,' she said, 'despite all these years. You might laugh at me, but I have a dream of going back to Athens once without telling anyone. To spend a long weekend incommunicado from all my family and friends, just enjoying my city the way I used to when I lived there alone. Maybe call a friend, one, not ten, spend some slow hours, even go to the movies. That's my dream.'

I didn't laugh. But I didn't relate to it either. As far as I was concerned, I just wanted to stay and continue this international, independent, carefree life. To make it mine.

*

I am saying goodbye to Brussels as if it were my lover, I wrote in my notebook, sitting in *l'Amour Fou* as I had done on so many other mornings. Looking at the district hall building, I, once again, felt loss and life's injustice.

I had had a dream the previous night. I was back in Sofia, my husband and I were driving among the ugly grey blocks and my heart was cold, cold, cold... With awakening, came the realisation that I no longer knew where my home was. Would Stefan, who had been eagerly awaiting my return, understand this? Would our life together and the years we had spent together take over my longing for this world I had to leave? At that moment, I had no answer to these questions. And that was the saddest thing of all.

'I am sorry, I haven't read anything from you, so I can't give you a reference regarding your journalistic skills,' Ann said during our last catch up. 'But I can give you a general one, listing your tasks during your traineeship.'

'Why didn't you use the time to learn some French?' Brigitte asked. 'That could have helped.'

'Or at least some Flemish,' Alice added.

Well, I did other things.

We had this conversation in the same jacuzzi we had gone to in those early days. This was their farewell gift to me. I smiled at the irony of this, recalling the entry in my diary. Indeed, I was separating from Brussels as if from a lover. Naked.

1000 Brussel Stad

2006

Herman, Dutch

If there was one place away from home where I felt at home, it was *Métropole* on the bustling *de Brouckèreplein.* They recognised me now and offered me smiles which were different from the professional ones. A bit more personal like between accomplices. When you travelled for work as much as I did, any personal touch made a real difference. But not too personal. This is professionalism. The fine distinction between respectful politeness and being over-friendly. The way they say, 'Good evening, Mr.' — followed by my surname — 'It is a pleasure to welcome you again.' It is a big hotel. But they remembered me. And the place itself – elegance, comfort, class. The bed and the pillow were exactly as I liked them – the mattress of medium firmness and the big pillow embracing my head. I've had some of my most relaxing deep sleep there.

I would usually arrive in the early evening after a day of meetings, take a shower, read my notes, and go out. I knew my way around and had grown to like the city. Its subtle friendliness. Easy and accommodating. That's how I would describe it. Unlike the crazy speed of London, the overwhelming vastness of Paris and the somewhat vulgar prettiness of Amsterdam. Yet cosmopolitan, diverse, lively, with delicious cuisine. Before I started going there for work, for me, like for everyone around me, it was a place to cross on the way to France. I never looked at it as a possible tourist destination, not even for a weekend city trip. Other Belgian cities, perhaps. In the early days with my wife, when we were still fresh and new, we did a lot of that stuff. City trips. Being romantic in many places. But Brussels isn't exactly known as a romantic get-away.

We did lots of travelling with my parents, too. We'd been to Brussels, of course, but there was nothing that tempted us to revisit it. We did the tourist stuff, *Grand Place*, *Manneken Pis*, *Place St. Catherine*, a fish restaurant, tasty mussels and *au revoir*. It was only when I started coming for work and staying over for a couple of days, that I could really make a mental construction of the city beyond the vague outline of those memories. In fact, a city uninhabited by memories. The visit with my parents didn't count; it was just passing through, a snapshot of experience. If I am, let's say, in Paris, of which, by the way, I'm very fond, no matter how much I like it, there would always be the past, interfering. In an instant, I would see Heather and I walking by the Seine holding hands. Heather and I having dinner in Montmartre. Me proposing to Heather on the top terrace of the Eiffel tower… The past is always there, imposing on the present and not allowing it to breathe freely. Whereas a city, any city, without memories has the air of freedom, of potential discovery, of adventure. Not that I'm looking for adventures, don't get me wrong. A married man with three kids, adventure is certainly the last thing on my mind. It's the possibility I cherish, not the happening. A sweet reminder of youth. Here I am, in a city without a past, going out, no engagements, no responsibilities, just me and a city to be discovered and tamed.

Funnily enough, and I hope I don't sound cheesy, my favourite scene in 'The Little Prince' is where the fox tells the Prince that he must tame her. I read it in my late teens, and it was somewhat an eye-opener for me, the gradual approaching, the persistence and patience of building closeness. All that… And now I am thinking, isn't it the same with cities? You arrive at a new place, and it's alien to you. A complete stranger. But if you give it time, if you free your mind of labels and prejudices, and take a good dose of curiosity instead, following your intuition without a map, you will really start seeing it, a deserted street, a building, a moment of shared privacy like those two Asian girls who just passed by and one of them, holding a green balloon, smiling at me… Moments like that make me feel happy. And young. And connected to the city. As if we are partners without a crime. I know what you will think. I've heard it before. 'Too sentimental for a man.' Perhaps I am. So what? What's wrong with that? My idea is that the more you allow yourself to see the true heart of the city, the less it is a stranger. You will inevitably make your own discoveries. Ordinary places sometimes, but still special for you for inexplicable reasons. Then you return to these places and experience something close to the joy and excitement of having a date. And the more you return, the more you can call them, and the city, home. It's like what the fox said, isn't it? That ridiculous song '*Ring-ding-ding-ding-dingeringeding! What does the fox say? Wa-pa-pa-pa-pa-pa-pow*!' Grrrr, so irritating. Anyway, it's actually better with cities. People can disappoint you. People can change with time and turn out not to be the way they were. On an unexpected day, the fox might show its teeth and bite you. While cities... well, they change too, but not in such an intimately overwhelming way. With cities, this could more often be a discovery than a disappointment. Besides, it's easier. You enter the place where you have been so many times, but it's suddenly different. The music, the sound (too loud, too quiet), the crowd. Oh well, you finish your drink in one go and leave, only to find a new place a few metres down. It's not as simple as that with people. You cannot just get up and leave this person because they don't suit you anymore... How did I get here? Yes. Brussels has tamed me. And I feel I have tamed it too.

Something else which enhances this connection is the shared history with Belgium and the element of familiarity. I wander around, and places talk to me. Everyone marvels at the *Grand Place* but how many are aware that it used to be a sandy mound between the tributaries Spiegelbeek and Smaelbeek of the river Senne which after the year 1000 became the scene of a market, *Nedermerckt*, where merchants and artisans offered their goods; that in the 13th century three indoor markets were built on its northern edge, a meat market, a bread market and a cloth market, side by side with buildings of wood and stone which enclosed the square; that it was a place of executions; that it was completely destroyed by the French bombardment on August 15, 1695 with the town hall ironically being the only survivor, despite the fact that it was the main target. But they probably don't care either.

I walk on *Anspachlaan*, where cars drive bumper on bumper, reach the stock exchange building, *Beurs*, cross the street, follow the nondescript *Paul Devauxstraat* and take *Sint-Katelijnestraat*. I like this street with its Chinese and rib restaurants. *Monk* is full, mostly with young people. The discreet lighting; the caramel taste of the beer; the careless air around the young crowd. So liberating.

Half an hour later, I meet Jan in a fish restaurant at Sint-Katelijne. Jan is Flemish. We used to work together and now he often saves me from solitary dining. We are both foodies and like checking new places out while eating our favourites. We would enjoy a good meal with some fine wine and discuss the two subjects we are both passionate about, politics and history. Seated at an outside table, next to the first pool at the so-called *Vismet*, after ordering, we instantly tackle the news of the day, the Dutch referendum on the European Constitution.

'So how does it feel to be a national of the country which put a knife in the body of the European Constitution, thus killing the idea of a united Europe?' he is smiling slyly at me.

'Well, well, well, we both know, the executor of this deed was not the Netherlands but your Southern neighbours. One 'no' was enough to dig a hole for the grave of the Constitution. To nevertheless proceed with our referendum was more a sign of stubbornness than anything else.'

'I know, I know. However, technicalities and game playing notwithstanding, it is a loud 'No' to the future of Europe, isn't it?'

'The future of Europe as shaped under the skilful guidance of the very French who then rejected it.'

'Let's go back to the Dutch "tegen". What's your take on it?'

'It's very similar to what happened in France. People aren't happy with Balkenende's government. Nor with the accession of Bulgaria and Rumania and potentially Turkey. General unhappiness with the increased cost of living after the introduction of the euro… So it was a sort of revenge. But also the "yes" campaign was way too aggressive for the tastes of the average Dutch. Warning of increased chances of war in the case of a "no," mentioning the Holocaust, the genocide in Srebrenica and the terrorist attacks in Madrid came across as way over the top. Which is very unfortunate. The Union does need more structure and representation in order to be strong and functioning.'

The meals arrive – seabass with vegetables and chips for me, *gambas* for Jan, accompanied with a bottle of Riesling. Delicious. It's a warm evening and it feels good to sit outside and see the crowded restaurants and bars around, the people enjoying their food and drinks, the life which continues to flow beyond the complex politics.

*

A month later we have a beer in *Café Orts*. In the past it was a brothel, now it is a well-respected hybrid of bar and brasserie.

‘The history of this place reminds me of a joke I was told recently. Four Flemish are driving in Amsterdam in the red-light district. They ask a hooker, how much? She says, fifty from the front, 100 from the back. One of the Belgians sitting in the back row asks, why do I have to pay more?’

Jan laughs.

‘That’s a good one.’

We have a couple of beers and walk to *Table de Muss*. It’s raining so we sit inside. I like this place, the meals always look like works of art, exquisitely arranged. In all senses a celebration of good taste.

‘So how does it feel to come from the country blamed for the biggest genocide of our times after WWII?’ Jan would never give me a pass.

On the previous day, Kofi Annan, on the tenth anniversary of Srebrenica had announced that the UN had made serious errors of judgment, rooted in the absurd philosophy of impartiality.

‘What happened in Srebrenica was horrible. But it is too simplistic to blame it on the Dutch.’

The smell of the Sauvignon Blanc fills my nostrils. I breathe it in, my eyes closed, and I see hands collecting the amber grapes in a life of a beautiful simplicity…

‘Are you saying that the Dutch have no responsibility to bear at all?’

‘No, that’s not what I’m saying. The government was responsible for sending troops on a mission impossible. It was the UN who was in charge, though, and declared Srebrenica a safe zone, which it clearly wasn’t. Tension had been building, the war had already been on for a while, so what happened seems inevitable. That the Dutch were there was bad luck. It could have been any other nation. Could have been the Austrians or the Germans with the same success, or failure in this case.’

‘True. But they also didn’t do anything to prevent the massacre or save lives. Heroism wasn’t exactly on display there.’

‘It was an impossible situation. Imagine them, a bunch of young men. Many had never used weapons in real circumstances. Coming from the safety of their reality, thrown into the cruel wilderness of the Balkan conflict. They weren’t psychologically and emotionally equipped for that. Also they weren’t even appropriately armed for what surrounded them. On the one hand, they were doing their job sticking to the rules. And that included impartiality. Being professional meant not being involved, not taking sides. On the other hand, even if they wanted to interfere, it wouldn’t have changed the balance. The Serbs were heavily armed, they had tanks. So the narrative of saving lives is fabricated and implausible. They might have saved a couple of lives in one situation just to postpone the inevitable, till the next time when their own lives would have surely been taken as well.’

'Voilà. We finally got there. Heroism doesn't come across as being among Dutch qualities,' Jan smiled.

We were done with the starter and our mains arrived.

'How are Heather and the kids doing?'

'Good. Pauleen just finished first grade, and the twins are also growing. And how about Martha and Roel?'

'We are divorcing. I rent a flat now near Katelijne.'

'I'm really sorry to hear that…'

'It's all right… Let me tell you a joke. After having steak tartar in a restaurant, a Dutchman asks for the bill. It's nineteen euros. He puts twenty on the table and waits for one euro in change. The Flemish waiter gives him one euro and puts a condom next to it. The Dutchman asks for an explanation and the waiter says, 'We don't want more of you.'

I laugh, ask for the bill and pay it, adding a decent tip. The Flemish waiter seems content.

The rain has stopped, and the evening sun makes the roofs of the buildings shine.

'Let's have one last drink,' suggests Jan. It makes sense – he's free now. No family waiting at home. A flat near St. Katelijne. I imagine that life, that single life again, so foreign, so remote, so alluring. I lied to him without any hesitation. Things at home haven't been good for quite some time now. How long? I don't know. I don't remember how this slow and irreversible distancing between us started. Was it that evening when she told me she felt stuck with three children, the house and me? What did I say? Did I say anything at all? But how to respond to such a statement? To the feeling of being a burden? Stuck with the kids? For me, they've always been only a source of joy and energy, it's enough to look at them and feel immense love and meaning in my life, and hope, and future. And suddenly Jan's single life isn't so alluring anymore. What would life be like if the kids weren't there when I came home? Helping Pauleen with her homework and listening to her school stories, playing with Marisa and Thomas, taking care of them… this is the constitution of my life, its core, its everything. How can Heather and I feel so differently about it?

The outdoor tables of the Thai and Vietnamese restaurants are crowded and so are the four corners of *Sint-Goriks*. People are standing in front of the bars holding their drinks, chatting. We pass in between, suddenly flushed with phrases in different languages, intonations, accents.

Just to the other side of the former covered market, we find ourselves in a completely different ambiance — quiet, deserted, romantic even — with subtle electric lights. Roughly half of the small tables in front of *Booz N' Blues* are taken. We get our drinks and sit outside, next to the open window. It's a great place. The vinyl record sleeves, the jukebox, the musicians' posters on the walls remind me of Chicago. Yet we are in Brussels. A relatively small capital, but then you find all these places which make you feel like you're elsewhere. In one evening, I have crossed parallel universes, each of which is exclusive with its vitality and richness. Fascinating! I take a sip of my bourbon and ask Jan,

‘So how is your new life?’

*

Looking back through the prism of time, I see how circumstances could provide the impetus for actions you would not even have considered if things had been different. If Jan wasn’t away on holiday when I returned to Brussels in August; if the city, outside of the Old Town, wasn’t totally deserted like a stage before a performance; if it wasn’t cool and raining and — and this is certainly the deciding one — if things at home were different.

I remember wandering around the empty streets from the *Métropole* hotel to Sablon and feeling emptiness settling inside me. I didn’t want to go to the places where I usually hang out with Jan, so I picked one of the restaurants at Sablon, checked my notes from the day and had a proper Belgian dinner. Most of the visitors were couples, I think I was the only person dining alone. I called Heather. Her flat, terse answers. Everything’s alright. We’re having dinner so not a great moment to talk to the kids. Yeah, of course, *smakelijk*…

At first, I took it as a relationship crisis. It happens to every couple, right? Not unusual after eighteen years together. But crises are temporary, they have a start and an end. What we had been living in didn’t feel like a crisis anymore. It felt like life. That’s what it was. This is where you’ve got to and it’s not going to change, not going to change, not going to change… Heather and I lived in a spacious house in Frankfurt and apart from the moments when we did activities with the children and acted and probably looked like a normal family, we related to each other like strangers. Even that wasn't right. Strangers are neutral. There was nothing neutral about us. We had a common past, but, perhaps, both of us saw the other as the one depriving them of a chance of love, tenderness, understanding and connection in this life. The thief of all the other possibilities which would have certainly been better. No matter what, for me she was the mother of my children. They would not have been here, nor would they have been the way they were without her. But I feared that she perceived me as the insensitive guy who imprisoned her with three kids in a foreign country. As if the help wasn't there. She got all the help a woman could get. Cleaning, an au pair service, what was there to complain about? Having too much free time, basically. Stuck in life?! How many people on this planet could dream of being stuck in such a way? The couple at the table next to mine talked quietly. He held her hand across the table, she smiled at him and her eyes radiated tenderness.

I went out and walked back to my hotel. It was cool, I was all alone and somewhat lost in this empty city. In my room, I flicked through the channels, but nothing caught my attention. One of the channels was showing "Pretty Woman". I got a glimpse of the scene where they lay in the bathtub, Julia Roberts spreading her endless legs around Richard Gere. I switched it off.

It had been so long since I'd been touched. So long that I'd almost forgotten how it felt to be looked at with tenderness, like that couple in the restaurant, no matter how pathetic it might sound, I felt jealous of this guy.

And then in the spur of the moment, I opened my laptop and searched 'Escort in Brussels'. Multiple entries appeared. I clicked randomly on a website on the first page. It was a website where both girls and agencies advertised their services. Hundreds of photos of nude young women, blond, brunette, red-haired, long hair, short hair, thin, plump, large and small tits, all sorts of poses, supposedly provocative, but actually openly vulgar. A couple of women had put photos of a man's cock half inside them, disgusting! I was just about to close when I noticed a photo of a dressed woman. Not just dressed but elegantly dressed. She was wearing a black skirt to her knees and a white blouse. College style. Her face radiated intelligence and purity. Long, black curly hair, green eyes, tanned skin. Laura. "A classy experience" was her description. Two hundred euros per hour plus taxi costs. What was a woman like that doing on such a website? Was it a joke? Before I knew it, I was dialling her number.

'Bonsoir,' a soft, distant voice.

'Hello... am I speaking with Laura?'

'That's correct.'

'I'm looking for… a classy experience.'

'You are at the right place.'

'Excellent. Will you join me at the *Métropole* hotel then?'

'With pleasure. I'll be there in fifteen minutes. Which room number?'

'I'll meet you in the bar. I'm wearing an orange tie.'

Exactly fifteen minutes later, she entered the bar and fixed her serious look on me, sitting by the bar and boosting my confidence with Irish bourbon. She wore a sleeveless evening dress, wrapping her body, green like her eyes, and medium-high heels. A dark blue scarf covered her shoulders. She approached me, bringing with her an air of calm confidence.

'Hello, I am Laura. And you must be…'

'Herman.'

'Nice to meet you, Herman.'

'Very pleased to meet you, Laura. Would you like a drink?'

'You should know that I am paid per hour and my working time starts now.'

'I saw that on the website… no rush. What can I get you?'

'Still water with ice and lime.'

The waiter brought a bottle of Evian, poured the water over the ice cubes, and went away.

'What service would you like?'

Her green eyes, fixed in mine with an innocent ease, as if we were discussing business. Which we were.

'Where are you from, Laura?'

She paused for a moment, then said, 'Slovenia. And you must be Dutch.'

'Great observation. What made you guess?'

'My sixth sense, I suppose.'

'Hmmmm… and what else is your sixth sense is telling you about me, Laura?'

'That it was loneliness that made you dial my number.'

She said it calmly, her voice staying soft. No challenge, nothing. I sat there caught off guard.

'Very interesting. I'm becoming wary of asking you questions.'

'I've heard that the Dutch can cope with frankness.'

'You've heard right. But your directness is striking, especially coming from a beautiful stranger.'

Her face stayed relaxed as if she had not heard the compliment.

'But no worries, I can handle it, I can handle many things…'

'Can you? So what have you handled so far?' And again, the way she spoke was not challenging, not provoking but neutral, interested without being eager.

'Good question. The overwhelming love of my mother, grandmother and aunt with me being the only child in the family. The joys of a dysfunctional marriage. And the tricky dynamics of the European Central Bank. Not too bad, huh?'

'Overwhelming love – in what way?'

'In its abundance and unconditionality.'

'Isn't that what true love is about?'

'What do you know about true love, Laura?'

'I beg your pardon?' Her eyes turning dark.

'Sorry. A clumsy attempt at a joke.'

'Let's start with the mother.'

'I didn't know I was setting myself up for a psychotherapy session.'

'Shall we go to your room then?'

'The mother... My arrival provided her with the opportunity to experience motherhood. Happy to be a mother and to do all the things a good mother does according to the guidebooks in the seventies, she was focused on applying her perception of a happy family. However, destiny played a bad joke on her with my father's death when I was fourteen. That was the end of the happy family, the end of the idea of happiness. The mother succumbed to her grief and made me the reason for her existence. Being a reason, however, doesn't necessarily mean a happy reason. As a good Catholic, she felt obliged to live for me. Until the birth of my first child achieved a miracle. I saw her face light up after all those years of darkness, but it wasn't for me. Ha ha, I must sound pathetic.'

'Not at all. Your grandmother must have helped during those tough years.'

'Indeed. She stepped in and took over from my mother so that she could be undisturbed in her suffering. A widow herself, she was there to cook for me and check whether I'd done my homework. But other than that, I could be what I wanted. Being her only grandchild, she loved me no matter how I acted or reacted... She would not get angry; she would not criticise me. She would just look at me with her pale eyes and say softly, "My lovely boy." I would try hard to evoke a different reaction. No joy.'

'So the abundance of love can cause as much suffering as its absence.'

'Apparently.'

'How does the aunt fit into the picture?'

'The Aunt is my father's sister. A childless lesbian. I was the missing element. On weekends they would take me out and imitate all the things that 'normal' families do, the cinema, playgrounds, sweet shops, buy me things, ask about school and my friends. But what I remember most was the way my aunt looked at me, her eyes flooded with tenderness. For her, I was a little God. The Child-God. She was close to my father, too, and when, later, he died, I became the living continuation of the missing brother. One more projection to bear.'

'There are worse things in life, Herman, than being loved.'

'Are there? Tell me. Like what?'

'I am afraid my time is over, Herman.'

She got up and stood still.

'I feel a bit awkward. You immediately threw me into deep waters. I haven't said these things to many people, you know. You might consider a career switch.'

'I enjoyed talking to you, Herman.'

I took out my wallet and gave her four fifty-euro notes. She carefully put them in hers. Then she lifted her hand and brushed the tips of her fingers on my cheek. They were soft. She turned and walked towards the exit. A moment later, she was gone. I sat alone with my almost finished bourbon in dismay. Had any of this happened? Or had I hallucinated? But I could still feel the delicate scent of her perfume, the gentle touch of her fingertips on my face.

*

Three weeks later, I walked down *Dansaertstraat*. The new season had started, everyone was back from holiday, apparently, and you could really feel this fresh energy in the air. The diverse crowd in front of the *Beurs*, the crowded bars and restaurants, the cars. Nothing like the deserted city I had left in August. Most tables in *Bonsoir Clara* were reserved but still empty. The waiter, a young woman, showed me to my table. A table for two. I sat and looked at colourful squares on the opposite wall. I always liked the ordered cheerfulness of this place. Eclectic not only in terms of food but also in style. Modern in a cosy way. Classy. I ordered an aperitif.

The first sip went down quite nicely. I needed that drink after a day of meetings. Twenty minutes later, exactly at the agreed time, Laura stood in front of me. I got up and embraced her. Her lips touched my cheek, her perfume again filled my nostrils, and her green eyes looked at me again with that calm and neutral confidence which I had felt the first time. This time I was even less at ease. After opening up so easily and immediately to her and speaking of things which I would not even tell myself, I could not switch to small talk. Ask her how she had been? Too formal. Ask her about her work? A tricky one. Comment on the weather? I didn't want her to find me boring and mediocre. I knew I was paying for a service, but I needed to go beyond the deal, I needed her to enjoy providing it as if it was not work, as if it was life, that normal life in which a woman goes on a date with a man in a cool restaurant for a nice relaxing evening. Furthermore, in which that particular woman goes on a date with me. I was sitting there hypnotised by her green eyes, literally speechless, and speechlessness is something which rarely happens to me, the last thing one would say of me is that I am someone who doesn't have his lines ready to make his case. Assertiveness comes with the job. That's what I am paid for. But now I faced Laura, I didn't know my lines anymore. I didn't know anything.

Fortunately, the waiter saved me by bringing the menu. I opened it and started making my way through the list. Laura just sat and looked at me.

'Aren't you hungry?'

She smiled and continued looking at me.

'Surprise me.'

'You want me to choose for you?'

'Precisely.'

She knew how to challenge.

'There is a book by a Dutch writer. It's called "The Dinner". Throughout the book, two couples have dinner in a posh restaurant and as they move from one course to the other, sinister secrets are revealed,' I say after I have ordered.

'Do you have any sinister secrets, Herman?'

'Ha ha, not really.'

'How are things at home?'

Straight to the point again. Why waste time. Time is money. My money, in fact, so I suppose I should be grateful to her. This shows she cares, doesn't it? At least a tiny bit. She has remembered me. She has remembered what I've shared.

‘What do you think, Laura, would I be here with you, if things at home were great?’

‘Why not? Great marriages don’t prevent some men from looking for a refreshing distraction when away from home. The need for a change is a strong motivator.’

‘I am not “some men.” And I don’t need change when my needs are being met.’

‘Which needs? And is it possible for one person to meet all your needs?’

‘Perhaps not. But at least the core basics, love, connection, care… Why be with someone if there is a deficiency of the key elements that constitute an intimate relationship? What is left then?’

‘But they must have been there if you got married in the first place.’

‘They were. And then they weren’t anymore.’

‘How does that happen?’

‘I don’t know. Should I have known, perhaps, I could have done something. You wake up one morning and a stranger is lying next to you, looking at you with distant eyes and bombarding you with demands and complaints.’

‘It is inside ourselves that people become strangers first.’

‘I’m not sure about that. My wife acted in ways which made her a stranger to me.’

‘You mean she has voluntarily estranged herself?’

‘She has distanced herself, indeed. She has turned cold, unpleasant, negative. Whatever I do is not right.’

‘But then why don’t you do the right thing?’

‘Pardon?’

‘These complaints and demands, as you call them, are often a cry for attention. A manifestation of her needs. How do you expect her to meet your needs if you are not meeting hers?’

‘I’ve been doing my best. I’ve been a faithful husband and a good father.’

‘But is being faithful enough?’

‘Apparently, it isn’t.’

‘Obviously, not. I reckon your wife is also faithful. And I believe she too would say that she’s been doing her best. But you aren’t happy with her. And I am pretty sure she isn’t happy with you either.’

‘The vibes I am getting from her are not exactly happy, indeed.’

‘You see.’

‘I do. She is way too busy being negative rather than trying to reconnect with me and being loving and gentle.’

‘But perhaps she has tried. I believe she has. In her own way. But did you notice?’

‘If her constant complaints can be called trying, she did try a lot. Way too much actually.’

‘You’ve got children, I suppose.’

‘Three.’

‘So there is this woman. Your wife. The mother of your children. Distancing. What do you do to cut this distance? To reach her? To keep her?’

‘It takes two to tango. Why should it be me making the effort?’

‘It’s exactly that way of thinking which creates distance between people. The thinking about the effort. Besides, tango is a dance in which the man leads, and the woman follows. When did you last take your wife out for dinner?’

‘I don’t remember.’

‘You see. Yet you are having dinner in Brussels with a stranger.’

‘Funnily, I don’t see you as a stranger. In an inexplicable and somewhat ridiculous way, I feel safe with you.’

‘So again, whether someone is a stranger has nothing to do with reality but with how we relate to them. Your wife, the mother of your three children, you see as a stranger. And me, a totally unknown woman, you feel safe with. But what of this is real?’

‘Let’s put it this way. I see no pleasure and inspiration in taking a grumpy and constantly negative woman, who criticises me all the time, to dinner. Not least because she expects this. She demands it from me. And I hate being pressured. The fun of it is gone. Whereas me sitting here with you is a voluntary act. It’s exciting, engaging, inspiring. I feel heard and understood.’

Laura’s green eyes were hypnotising me. She took a short breath as if she wanted to say something but then decided not to. She smiled and took a sip from her glass of white wine.

The dinner cost me a fortune, including her fee per hour. But every cent of it was worth it. This stunning woman had an intelligence, tact and finesse I had rarely experiences in my life, certainly not in my love life. But could I really define my encounters with her as "love life"? Well, sadly, that's what my love life had become – having dinner with an escort.

Yet the dinner led to a couple of developments. Laura agreed to speak to me when I was away. She didn't forget to remind me that she was paid per hour, though. What the heck? This was my best ever expenditure. Just before she entered the taxi, she kissed my lips again. I pulled her into my arms and gave her a passionate kiss. It was electric. Shaking. Knee-softening. A real kiss. I was twenty again having my first kiss on an autumn evening on the Scheveningen beach. The wind, the sea, the smell of salt. The kiss. That girl back then was innocent and hot, and I really fancied her. This was our second date, and it all looked very promising. A tongue kiss and briefly cupping one of her breasts. A couple of weeks later, she dumped me for a bastard from a senior grade. He was a real asshole who, a couple of months later, in turn, dropped her like a hot potato. She begged me to give her another chance, but no, thank you. I don't take a bastard's leftovers.

Laura, however, was a completely different story. Classy. I would not have imagined that there might be such women in Slovenia or anywhere else in the ex-Soviet post-communist bloc. A real eye-opener. Laura. I wanted to make love to every letter in her name.

Fantasies gave energy to my days and a thrill to my nights. I would get hard from just hearing her voice, no matter where I was. We regularly talked over the phone after that dinner at *Bonsoir Clara*. I was on a business trip to London, lying in my hotel room, tiny and depressing as hotel rooms in London can be. After a few attempts, I managed to reach her. Her low voice, gentle like a caress, and yet electrifying. I'd never cheated on Heather, and I was determined not to. But there I was, open and helpless, fully in the possession of Laura's voice, as she slowly described all the things she imagined doing to me. It was utterly amazing. The great thing was it wasn't even cheating. Was watching porn cheating? Or masturbation? If not, then certainly a phone call wasn't cheating either.

Fantasies… I played with myself, thinking of Laura. Laura and me. Laura and other men. What she does to them. What they do to her. Only at such moments, these fantasies resulted in pleasure. The rest of the time, they were unbearable. I could ignore the idea of the other men only when I was with her or talked to her (she was busy with me, hence not with anyone else).

In October, I was in Brussels again. After my meetings at the Commission, I checked into the *Métropole* and took a stroll on *Dansaert* towards *St Katelijne*. The days were getting shorter, it was already dark. The liveliness of the early evening held a promise again, which this time I knew would be fulfilled, and the thought was exhilarating.

Jan was waiting for me at *Café Orts* with a beer in front of him. I got a beer myself at the bar and sat opposite him.

'It's been ages!'

'I know!'

'How are things at the ECB?'

'The usual, German hierarchy, French bureaucracy and Italian politics.'

'Still fancy it?'

'Not sure I ever did. You know how it goes, that's a brilliant idea! Let me now explain to you why we cannot implement it.'

'Yeah, sounds familiar.'

'Still, the Commission has more tools for action.'

'True. It's tortuous and slow, but there is progress all the same.'

'Exactly. That cannot be said for the ECB. It's way too slow, people are not willing to take a stand as they don't know what their manager will say, just repeating the exact words of their manager and not showing their cards. The sad thing is that it's full of bright people, but the only ideas taken forward are those coming from a higher level.'

'Tell me about it. It's the same everywhere when it comes to hierarchy. Take the Commission, for example. You might be the expert, but your boss will be the one delivering the contribution you prepared. They will be presenting the topics they know next to nothing about just because they've got to the right level. But I reckon it's the same elsewhere... How're things at home?'

‘The same. Nothing new or special. And you, how’s your single life?’

‘Not so single… I’ve been seeing someone lately.’

‘Wow, that was fast!’

‘Not so fast if you count my miserable married years.’

‘And who’s she? How did you meet?’

‘An Estonian. I went to one of these expat events and voilà. We met. We have been dating for a month now and it’s going pretty well. Fun to be back to the dating scene, takes me back twenty years ago…’

‘Cool. Am happy for you.’

‘Yeah, I’m sorry but I won’t be able to make it for dinner with you tonight. I have a date.’

One part of me really felt like being up front and shouting, ‘Me too!’ but I managed to suppress it. Such a revelation would lead to unwelcome questions which I wasn’t prepared to answer, not quite yet anyway. So I just said that I understood completely. We finished our drinks, and I walked to *Comme Chez Soi* where I had reserved a table.

She arrived exactly on time as usual. Wearing a dark blue dress. Where was she getting her clothes from? Max Mara? Max & Co? I got up, took her in my arms and kissed her on the mouth. Just looking at us, all the strangers around would think that we were a regular couple. This time the conversation kicked off easily. I felt her open up, be less on guard. She was soft, relaxed, laughed and even shared highlights of her days (seeing a hairdresser, going to a bar with a friend), something she had never done before. I was elated. Totally. Perhaps what was going on between us really was different, also for her. After a couple of glasses of wine, I held her hand across the table and told her I felt an amazing flow of energy, which I never felt before. The energy to change my life and rearrange it in a new exciting way. That I was fed up with the bank, that I could easily quit, tomorrow, and move to Brussels. Getting a job here wouldn't be an issue with my experience and connections. I would rent a flat in the centre and perhaps buy a house, after a while. I'd divorce and go to The Hague for the weekends. And, here I paused, hesitated, and then blurted out I wanted her to be part of this life. She wouldn't have to work anymore; I'd be able to meet all her needs, all her whims.

She listened. I saw her blush when I said she wouldn't have to work but she said nothing. Her silence puzzled me. I quickly told her that she didn't have to reply now, she could take as much time as she needed to think about it. She nodded but remained silent.

*

Months passed. I travelled to Brussels every three weeks or so. I always had dinner with Laura, sometimes preceded by drinks with Jan. Once I took her to dinner and a concert in Music Village, one of the jazz haunts in the city. A young Polish singer was on the programme. The concert was really good. She performed one of the greatest interpretations of 'My Funny Valentine' I had ever heard. Incredibly sensual. I gently squeezed Laura's hand across the table. Our eyes met. A wonderful moment of intimacy. I talked to her as often as I could, not being totally oblivious of the cost which came with it. We made love a couple of times more over the phone. Meanwhile, life went on. The bank, the children, Heather and her dissatisfaction. None of this could really reach me. I was professional at work, attentive with the children, cooperative with Heather, but only when in bed with the darkness taking over could I relax and let my thoughts go where my true self belonged – my secret, private world in Brussels.

One night, Heather touched my shoulder and stared into my eyes,

'Do you have a lover?'

'For God's sake Heather! Is jealousy your new thing?'

She looked into my eyes a bit longer, turned off the light and turned her back to me. I know this might sound insensitive and you may judge me. I did pity her, I even felt something like compassion, but it wasn't enough for me to reach out and caress her. Or say something nice. We had crossed that line long ago – the line of loving kindness. She was the mother of my children with whom I shared a bed. And I… I really don't know what I was for her.

A couple of days before Christmas I gave Laura a wrapped box. We were having dinner at *L'Entrée des Artistes*. She opened it slowly. It was a fine piece of jewellery, a gold necklace with sapphire stones. The stones shone and perfectly matched her eyes. She smiled and kissed my hand across the table.

That night I invited her to my room. In my mind, I had already ended my marriage, so I didn't consider this cheating. In my heart, I was already a free man. A man who was now going to make love to the woman in his life for the first time. To avoid the embarrassment, I handed her an envelope containing an amount covering the evening and the night as we took the lift up to my floor. In the room, I cupped her beautiful face, looked into her eyes and kissed her slowly. I will always remember the feeling that this was a dream, that it could not be, was simply impossible for it to be true, the intensity, her loveliness and the sweet weakness I felt running down my body. Still kissing her, I kept my eyes closed as I undressed her and opened them only when I felt the softness of her skin next to mine. Oh, what an exhilarating difference to be able to actually hold her firm breasts and feel the hardening of her nipples in my mouth. Breathless, I looked into her eyes again. We both laughed, a crazy, joyful laughter of disbelief. Then I slowly began to kiss down her body. Until I came to her calla lily and, still slowly, my tongue felt for its spadix. As it sped up its movement, alternating light quick touches with gentle sucking, I was entranced by her trembling, her taste, her wetness, the music of her moans, her arching with a shuddering cry. And then, just then, I slid into her and was lost in fleeting forever.

Even my most passionate years with Heather were nothing compared to the tenderness and wildness of that night. I thought my heart would stop beating from excitement and pleasure. As if each cell of my body were reborn for totally new sensations, the existence of which I could never have imagined. At dawn, Laura fell asleep in my arms, in a fragile Pre-Raphaelite beauty.

I woke up to movement around me. Laura stood by the bed, fully dressed.

'Good morning, my love. What's the time?'

'Almost eight.'

I felt needles in my chest. These were the exact hours I had pre-paid. So very professional.

'Laura, I just want to say, thank you for last night. It was... beyond words. Do you remember what I told you in September? I did mean it. I do want you in my life. With me, you wouldn't need to do this job anymore. Please give it some thought. You could make me the happiest man in the world. And I believe I can make you happy too.'

She smiled, took out her mobile and touched the screen.

'Can you repeat what you've just said, Herman?'

Her sudden playfulness was exciting.

I got out of bed, naked, and fell on my knees in front of her.

'Laura, I love you. I want to share my life with you. You will make me the happiest man in this world if you accept. I would leave the bloody bank and move to Brussels. I would do anything for you. Just say yes.'

She touched the screen again and dropped it in her bag. I got up and took her in my arms.

'Will you think about that?'

She smiled and nodded. Then she was gone.

I had breakfast in the hotel. As usual, there were other people, sitting alone, the businesswomen and men in Brussels for a couple of days, having their last peaceful minutes before rushing into their days of meetings or flights back. There was also an older American couple. They sat close to me, and I could hear their conversation. The woman was telling the man about the phone call she had just had with their son. The man listened and nodded while having his coffee and toast. The woman continued talking about their plans for the day. Where there was to visit. Where there was for Christmas shopping. The man yawned. I had my hearty breakfast, smiling to myself. Endorphins dancing in my brain at the sound of Christmas songs. My life was an exciting, unpredictable adventure. It really was, in the making. But I didn't yet quite realise the dimensions of that.

I checked out and entered the Brussels morning. People, cars, Christmas, snowflakes. The air was fresh, I took a deep breath and walked towards *Nieuwstraat*. Hastily, I got some gifts for the children and Heather. Mango and Naf Naf for the children, a Rituals box for Heather. The snowflakes fell on my face like cold kisses. Reminding me of Laura's kisses the night before. There is a song about that. 'The night before.' Hooverphonic. 'You /are lying on the floor /trying to remember/ what happened the night before…' They happen to be Flemish. Nevertheless, really cool. Her voice. 'I am the prince who wakes youuu…' Am I really? Will you allow me to be that prince, Laura? Do you remember, did any of this night touch you, Laura? Are you already filling your agenda for tonight, Laura, will you be in other beds tonight making… Stop this, I told myself. Stop, stop, stop. I took out my mobile and called her. But hers was switched off. Okay, that was normal, she needed rest after a night like ours. A switched off mobile meant unavailable. For potential clients too. That thought made me happy. I was helpless and happy, so happy in my helplessness, I could have never imagined what would happen.

Her mobile was still switched off when I called her a couple of hours later, just before boarding. And later when I arrived. And an hour later, and an hour later, and a couple of hours later, and in the evening, just before I went to sleep, I spent a quiet moment in the living room when Heather and the children were already in their beds. I left her multiple messages. I talked about the things I had seen throughout the day, the girl playing piano at the airport, the couple kissing on the travelator, the people holding labels with names in the arrival hall in Frankfurt. I remember saying several times, love you, I love you, Laura, I'm thinking of you, I hope you are well, call me, when you can, just call me, call me, call me...

In between, there was Heather and there were the children, and dinner, and the news. Heather was silent. She answered my questions tersely and didn't ask any herself. But I was too overwhelmed with the emotions of the night before to be resentful. And too tired to act as if I were mentally there, to listen, to come up with the expected reaction. The children were excited about the coming holidays. Sweet chatter about school and who did what and said what. I just tried to make sure I was adequate. That I nodded and said the right things.

In the morning, I called Laura. No joy. Nervousness was taking over, no matter how hard I tried to come up with credible excuses and explanations for her silence. She just needs some time to think. If I cannot reach her, no one else can. Which, in her case, should be positive. She will contact me. Today she certainly will. I even considered calling the police. But what would I have told them? What? I had only her number. I didn't even know her surname. Nor her address. Nothing. Suddenly it hit me how little I knew about Laura.

*

The first thing the secretary said was that my boss wanted to see me. This was rather unusual. I left my coat and went to his office. Leila, his secretary, asked me to wait. I sat and looked through the window behind Leila's desk and wondered what Bjorn could be up to. I had been working on my files, there had been no delays nor problems. Perhaps he wanted an update on the meeting in Brussels, but it had also been an ordinary meeting with the Commission. I had arrived at a point where my work in the bank felt like an empty shell. There was a shape to it but nothing inside. To be fair, it wasn't exactly like that. Of course, there was activity going on, people doing their jobs, files being negotiated and further developed but what drove me mad was the slowness of it all. One step forward, two steps back. The politics of it, the intrigue, my colleagues' fear of saying or doing the wrong thing, all of it. The package was too good to just drop it – the salary, the foreign worker benefits, the European school for the children, everything. But in another life, I could see myself living in

Brussels, in, hopefully, a more dynamic environment with more challenges and opportunities for change, and — the sweetest dream of all — with Laura's lovely smile and divine body, lighting up my days and nights. The line between dreams and reality had faded away and they had merged to become one. I wanted this *other life* to replace my life. It seemed possible. Tangible. A separation would be a relief for Heather as well. She was progressively unhappy with our marriage. Apparently, I couldn't meet her expectations and demands. Perhaps someone else could. She could have a better life. Return to The Hague, be close to her family and friends, meet somebody. And the children… I'd do all that it took to be present in their lives, to support them, to see them. When they grew up, they'd understand. They'd see that it had been all for the better. It would be better to have two separated happy parents, than an unhealthy dysfunctional couple. They'd come to Brussels regularly and grow to love it. They'd certainly like Laura too after the initial shock and resentment.

The phone rang. Leila answered, said 'okay' and told me I could enter. Bjorn was sitting behind his desk. His impeccable dark blue jacket and white shirt were what I could see of him. He was looking at the big screen in front of him. My appearance made him turn his head in my direction. His smoothly shaved face stayed expressionless.

'Hello Herman, how are you doing? Please take a seat.' I sat at the table in front of his desk. He stayed where he was. 'I want to show you something, Herman. We got an email to our general account this morning. It contained a link to a *YouTube* video. Take a look, please.'

He turned the screen in my direction and pressed the play button. On his large screen, I saw myself on my knees, naked, my penis hanging between my legs, my face, sleepy and open, and my words, full of sentiment and eagerness, filled the room. I didn't recall feeling embarrassed or blushing in my life till then, but I think I blushed at that moment. Or at least that's what I felt. Instant internal fire. It was difficult to breathe. I wanted to disappear, to dissolve, to erase this moment from the file of my existence.

But I was there. The video was over. Cold silence and Bjorn's light blue eyes on my face.

'It's called, Pretty Woman 3: Dutch banker proposes to escort. Very romantic, Herman. You've managed to impress me. While your private life, even though not so private anymore, is your own business, the way you describe the bank…how did you put it, "bloody"? Coming from a well-respected employee that isn't great for our image. How can we get out of this awkward situation? Any thoughts?'

Half an hour later, I left his office with an agreed resignation package. I avoided looking Leila in the eyes when I wished her a good day. She must have received the video too; her email was on our website.

I had a voice message from Heather. She told me she had seen the video. She was leaving for The Hague with the children immediately and was going to see me in court. She was totally disgusted by me and wanted me out of her life as soon as possible. Freedom had come my way a bit more abruptly than expected. It felt freezing cold.

My resignation was with immediate effect. I took my laptop and went home. The house was empty. The Christmas tree in the corner. It looked as if the family would be back at any moment. Family had turned into a meaningless word. I didn't have a family anymore. I didn't have anything. I was free.

I crashed on the sofa. When I opened my eyes a few hours later it was dark. Only the lights on the tree were still flickering. For a second, I couldn't figure out where Heather and the children were. The realisation came fast. My eyes were still wet. I must have fallen asleep from exhaustion.

*

Three months later, I sat in *Café Orts* with Jan.

'I don't know what to say, my dear friend. You've created a fine mess for yourself. One thing I cannot figure out is why the whore set this shit up for you.'

'Please don't call her a whore. I have no clue why she did it. I treated her like a lady. Ironically, I felt safer with her than with anyone else.'

We finished our beers and left. Jan promised to be in touch soon with some consultancy work. He also said Liisa and he would invite me for dinner. That would be nice. I needed some company and some friends in that city.

I rented a flat nearby. A tiny one – a living area and a bedroom. That was all I needed. The divorce was on its way and it seemed, in the circumstances, I was about to lose the house. I wasn't going to fight. I just wanted it to be over. I spent every weekend in The Hague with my children. Heather proved to be more noble than I expected and had not tried to limit my access to them. She had also spared them the details around our separation. I felt grateful and respected her for that.

I never managed to reach Laura. I suppose that wasn't even her real name. I checked the website where I had first found her, but her profile wasn't there anymore. I checked other websites, going through countless profiles and trying to recognise her face. In vain. She had disappeared as if she never was. But the impact she had left was there, proving her existence.

I didn't feel like going home yet. I had dinner in *Rêve d'Asie*, a Thai restaurant, where I had become a regular visitor. They greeted me with a smile like an insider and that made me feel good. It was a cosy place, always full but not intimidating. I had tried other restaurants in the area, the Chinese and Japanese ones. The food was usually good, and they were inexpensive. Nothing like the restaurants I had been used to, though.

It was around nine, still too early to head home. I crossed *Anspachlaan* and headed for *Bonnefooi*. Another place I liked to spend my evenings in. The concert had already started. I ordered a beer and found myself a table on the mezzanine floor. It was a female singer with a soft, deep voice. I could see her through the balcony railings. Short boyish hair, eyes closed, lost in her singing, fragile. The light of the elegant chandeliers was not strong, it was all intimate, calming. The people around me listened with concentrating faces. They all looked somewhat pale in the light. It was a bit like being in a Madame Tussaud's museum of ordinary life. A nice thought. Being a wax figure. Beautiful and indifferent. The only living creature there was the singer. She hardly moved at all and performed with her eyes shut. I closed mine too and imagined Laura sitting next to me, holding my hand. The touch of her long, pale fingers. By the way, *bonnefooi* means *by chance* in Brussels dialect. The thought made me laugh. I laughed soundlessly, with tears running down my cheeks. Here I was. In Brussels. *Bonnefooi.*

And then she really was there, materialised by the wildness of my desire, gently touching my face.

'Are you okay?' she asked. I opened my eyes in disbelief. A lovely young woman was standing next to my table. She was not Laura.

1080 Molenbeek

2007

Aisha, Belgian

My sister is not a good woman. 'Good women are obedient…' the Quran says. And my sister is anything but obedient. She wants to know the truth behind things. That is what she used to say. But there is one truth only, that of Allah, as our parents have told us hundreds of times. Yet she wouldn't listen. Our mother beat her once, shouting, 'You, silly, stubborn devil of a woman! Stop asking and stop seeking; accept, obey and be a good Muslim!' But no. My sister said being a good Muslim didn't mean being ignorant. Avicenna, Al-Farabi and Ibn Arabi were also Muslims.

'But they were men!' my mother cried out.

'And how about Umm Al-Darda, Fakhr an-Nisa and Amina Wadud?', my sister continued.

My mother didn't know any of them which made her even more angry. Her daughter was not hers, she was possessed by the devil of knowledge. 'You don't need books to take care of your man and children, and that's what a good woman does. Books only distract you from your obligations; they make you want things. And desires are our doom.' Sheila, that's my sister's name, wouldn't listen. She brought books home and read them secretly during the night using a small torch. Whenever my mother found them, she threw them away. But my sister didn't give up and continued reading in bed night after night.

Our parents had registered us at *Maria-Boodschaplyceum*, a Flemish school in the city centre, which was walking distance from where we lived. They had chosen it because it was useful to know both French and Flemish in Belgium but mostly because being educated would get us better husbands. That was what my father said. My mother, however, was of a different opinion and each time she saw me sitting with my books, she would yell at me, 'You lazy thing, throw away these devil books and come and help me!' So I would obey. But my sister wouldn't. She studied, got high marks and once she finished school, instead of preparing to be a good wife, took out a student loan and enrolled at university. Secretly, of course.

One day there was a message on the table, 'I'm going to study. Will live on the students' campus.' My parents were devastated. Mostly my mother. She cried and screamed and cursed, and made my father go and look for her; he found her enrolled in philosophy at *Vrije Universiteit Brussel* and barely recognised her when she came out of her lecture, she wore a short skirt and wasn't veiled. I tried to imagine her reaction when she saw him, did she frown? Or was she happy to see him? He didn't say. One thing was clear, she wasn't coming back but wanted to stay in touch with us.

When my mother heard all that, she screamed at my father, 'It's all your fault, your fault! With your idea of giving them a good education! Education took your daughter away and threw her into the devil's hands!' My mother insisted that she never wanted to see this daughter of the devil again and none of us should ever talk to Sheila, because she was a shame on the family. My father became even more silent and closed himself in like a mussel.

My mother is supposedly a good woman because she cooks and takes care of the household. I'm not sure if good women can also be happy. My mother never smiles nor laughs. There is a deep furrow between her eyebrows which makes her always look angry. Which she is most of the time. From being around her for seventeen years, I thought she was angry with life. I thought she was angry because she had had to marry so young and have children. Then something happened which put things into perspective. After Sheila left, I missed her so much and I wanted a photo of us from when we were children. The thing is that all the photos were in my mother's chest which she always kept locked. I knew where she kept the key; I had seen her when my father wasn't around, putting it in the drawer with her underwear. On a day while she was at the market, I carefully checked among her bras, tops and bikinis and found the key in the very bottom, under the large firm cup of a black bra. Fingers shaking, I managed to unlock the chest. It happened to contain quite a few treasures, but I was in a hurry to find what I was looking for. The photos were there, in a metal biscuit box. Black and white photos of our family from when Sheila and I were little. I looked at them; my eyes filled with tears. Why could things not have stayed the way they were then? I picked out a photo of Sheila and me hugging each other at home and left the box where I found it. And then I noticed the end of a red ribbon. Something — was it the devil? — made me tug at the ribbon only to find out it was attached to a white cotton bundle. I held the bundle, not knowing what to do. My fingers did not wait for me. They were already untying the ribbon. Eight envelopes, all with my mother's maiden name on them, except for one. I sat on the floor, next to the chest, and took out the letters, one by one. My eyes ran through the pages.

Habibi,

I saw you crossing the square last night. The moon was pouring its light over your face, and I felt trapped like an insect, caught in the net of your beauty. You are divine, and I will be your slave forever, should Allah give us His blessing.

Dreaming of you,

Jelab

Habibi,

There is nothing sweeter than your smile, nothing warmer than your eyes when you look at me, nothing more gracious than your walk.

Will you cross the square tonight? I will be near the fountain, waiting to see your beauty, praying to Allah for just one look.

Even if you don't love me, I've got love for two. If you only allow me, I'll spread it over us like an umbrella to protect us from life's storms and scorching sun.

Hold on to it, Habibi, and you will have shelter forever.

Yours,

Jelab

It went on and on. *Habibi, your beauty, goddess…* did he really mean my mother? And then the last letter with her married name on it and our address in Belgium.

Habibi,

The news of your marriage came like a lightning bolt, striking my heart. There is nothing left there now, only the ashes of my dreams of a life with you.

I ask myself again and again, why didn't you tell me? I know that you love me too, I saw it in your eyes, in their sadness that last time when I stopped you by the fountain, in the way you said goodbye and walked away... If only I had known that you would be gone, that you would be taken away from me forever, I would have done anything to prevent it. I would have talked to your parents and touched them with my love and aspiration to make you happy. And if they remained deaf to my words, I would have stolen you away and built a life for us, a splendid life like a castle.

It's over, all my hopes for happiness... dead. I pray to Allah and try to understand the meaning of His will which separates two people who love each other – what for? Who benefits from two broken hearts and destinies? Your husband? My future wife?

Habibi I will always love you. My heart belongs to you.

Jelab

Suddenly, it all made sense, my mother's anger, the furrow between her eyebrows, the desert land of her marriage with my father. But if this was Allah's will, I didn't dare think she was angry with Him as well.

*

Sheila called. She asked how I was, how things were at home. Somehow my mother realised it was her, whether by my tense face or by my brief responses. She grabbed my phone and yelled at her,

'You, sinful woman, shame on our family, don't you dare contaminate your sister!' Then she hung up and shouted at me,

'Didn't I forbid any contact with this daughter of the devil?! If she calls you again, don't pick it up!' She was shaking; there was thunder in her voice, lightning in her eyes.

I did pick up when Sheila called again two days later. Luckily, my mother had gone to the market. Whether or not she was a good or a bad woman, my sister sounded well. She supported her studies by working in a bar! I didn't dare ask her if she drank alcohol. I hoped she still followed at least some of our rules. I asked whether she was still praying and going to the mosque. She said she did. She added that Allah was good to all of us, and she felt she was doing the right thing. She wanted to know how our parents were. I had no news for her, it was all the same at home. I said,

'All good. But I miss you, Sheila, and I am worried about you!'

‘I miss you too, sis, very much. Don’t you worry about me – I’m doing fine.’

On Sunday that same week, I walked to *Masjid Omar Ben Khatab* Mosque. It was only a short walk from where we lived and yet I had never been there. Other than going to school, I rarely leave Molenbeek which is our home. My father’s parents arrived in Brussels many years ago and settled here. Dad was born in Molenbeek and occasionally, when he is in a good mood, he likes to say, ‘In this country there are no Belgians; they are all Walloons or Flemish. I am neither of these, I am just Belgian which makes me more Belgian than they are. I am a true Belgian’. But the truth is he isn’t. He’s Moroccan and that’s it. He’s got a Belgian passport and a Moroccan soul.

For my mother it’s a different story altogether, as she was born in Morocco and moved to Belgium only to marry my father. The only time I saw her happy was in Marrakesh. For those few days she became a different person, somewhat softer and more open. My grandparents, her parents, followed her to Belgium and for a while all of us lived together. As for me, I don’t know. I’m Belgian too, but I don’t really know what it means to be Belgian. We cook Moroccan food, we follow our traditions, we praise Muhammad, go to the mosque and are surrounded by our people, that is, other Moroccans.

On Sundays, mother and I go to the market at *Place Communale* to get our weekly supply of fruits and vegetables, nuts, dry fruit, seasonings, olives, sweets from the bakeries. We meet other women from the neighbourhood and chat with them. We walk in *Chaussée de Gand* with its dozens of shops and I glimpse the beautiful dresses in the windows, decorated with stones and flowers, in red, pink, blue and white. I imagine myself in a dress like that one day. But when would I wear it apart from on my wedding day? The restaurants and cafés are packed with men sipping mint tea, watching Arabic television and conversing. They look at us, but we don't look back. Children cycling or playing with balls and dolls in the pedestrian streets and on the squares remind me of my childhood. It was the only time girls and boys could play together, free and unaware of our norms. Now this ease is gone, even at the mosque we enter from different sides. But as Allah created this order, then it's divine, it's how it should be. And I don't understand why my sister doesn't get it, how she turned out to be so stubborn!

On that Sunday, for the first time in my life, if we don't take into account reading my mother's secret letters, I did something forbidden. I felt both guilty and excited and hoped with all my heart that Allah would forgive me. The mosque was a large modern building, stretching towards the cloudy sky. In the gloomy interior, among the many women kneeling and praying, I spotted Sheila immediately. My heart started racing. I took a deep breath to calm myself, knelt next to her and lost myself in prayers. I prayed for her to be back with us, Sheila and I falling asleep and waking up together, for those shared moments of chatting and giggling, even for the pale light of her torch under her blanket. When we went outside, she embraced and kissed me, wiped away my tears, looked into my eyes and smiled. 'You look beautiful, sis. Let me take you to a nice place.'

We arrived at a large square with the name of a female saint, two rectangular pools and many restaurants. In a bar, over a cup of tea, Sheila told me all about her lectures, exams, friends from different countries, parties, work. At the end of our time together, she mentioned she had met someone in the bar where she was working. He was Dutch, divorced, with three children. I covered my eyes with my hands. There was no salvation for her; she was about to end up in hell and we would be separated even beyond this life.

'Don't cry, Aisha,' she said, 'Please, don't cry. I am happy. Aren't you happy that I'm happy?'

'How can I be happy when you'll end up in hell,' I sobbed.

'Who told you this?'

'My… our mother.'

'Our mother is already in hell, on earth,' she said.

Her words were sharp and knife-cold; they severed any hopes of her returning. I had to admit, she was probably right about our mother. But I didn't want to give up.

'But that's what the Quran says too,' I snivelled, 'A good woman is obedient…'

'That's bullshit, Aisha. Have you read the Quran?'

'I haven't.'

'But that's the problem, there are too few Muslims who have read it. There is nothing like that in it, that women must be obedient;

that knowledge is a bad thing; that we should not enjoy life; that we should not mix with people from other religions. Not a word.'

Back in the square, she stopped to chat with two women. European. The one she knew was Belgian; her friend came from Eastern Europe. We all introduced ourselves. The Belgian said that some years ago the two of them used to live together. But then the Eastern European had to leave and go back to her country. She had just come back to work for some media company and write about European politics. She said she had divorced. Poor woman. Brussels is my new husband, she said, laughing. She must have lost her mind.

'Brigitte organises very interesting city walks. Herman loves history and we have been to a couple of them, really nice. After the walk, she often invites the group to go for a drink and that's how we met and became friends. She is very open-minded and bright, and she's interested in Islam and our culture,' Sheila said when they had gone.

What did she call our culture, I wondered? Was our culture not wearing a hijab, being worldly, leading a life without direction, that is without true service to Allah, being trapped in the mud of knowledge, not respecting your parents' will, escaping your home and being enslaved by the idea of freedom which, in fact, is hell on earth? This wasn't my culture and with pain in my heart I realised that there was no such thing as our culture for Sheila and me anymore.

At home an unusual scene greeted me, my parents sitting at the table and quietly discussing something. My mother's black hair fell over her right shoulder; the uncovered part of her neck shone in the thick darkness of the room. I slipped through the living room into my bedroom, closed the door behind me and crashed onto the bed. Time dissolved like sugar in mint tea, but without the sweetness. My mother's voice pulled me back to the present,

'You, lazy one, get here right now and help me prepare the dinner!'.

After we had eaten in silence, my mother said we needed to talk. My father only nodded slightly without looking at me. I frowned, they knew what I had done! Here comes the punishment.

'We've found a husband for you,' my mother said, 'His name is Salim. He comes from a rich family in Marrakesh, but he will move here for you.'

'How old is he mother?', I managed to ask.

'Twenty-six.'

'May I go to bed now? I don't feel well.'

As I got up to clear my plate away and took the three steps to my bedroom, I could feel my mothers' eyes piercing right through me, dark and distant.

Of course, I knew this was to come one day. But why so soon, so very soon? Kneeling and praying was the only thing I could do to stop my tears.

My days had been like beads in a necklace, simple and round and very similar. A message from my sister was already a big change. A message from Salim broke the pattern altogether. I checked his Facebook profile, he wasn't ugly. My body shivered and so did my mind. Was replying to him a sin? But, but… he was my future husband! We were to marry, so surely it would be better to get to know each other. There was nobody to ask for advice. I thought of Sheila for a moment but pushed the idea away. I knew what she would say. But she was a lost soul.

After more thinking, trembling and praying, a couple of days later, I sent a reply to Salim's message and that was the beginning of it, our chats day and night. The weather in Brussels and the weather in Marrakesh; my school, his business; my parents, his parents; our marriage. He had a trade which he would expand to Belgium. He asked me what Brussels was like. I told him that where my family lives was no different from Morocco. As for the rest, I don't really know. His descriptions of Marrakesh brought back images from our visit there, the markets, the magnificent palaces, the souks and *Jemaa el-Fna* in the Medina, the majestic mosques, the bright colours of the ceramics, my mother's tears when we crossed a small square with a fountain. I wished I could join him there. But I said nothing. A good woman is obedient and I certainly am a good woman. Unlike my sister, who didn't welcome the news of my marriage.

'Are you sure?' she asked when I told her. 'Is this what you really want to do with your life?'

I didn't really know what I wanted to do with my life. It wasn't for me to decide anyway. I'd follow Allah's and my parents' will. That was getting married and having children.

'But are you really sure?' my sister kept asking.

‘It doesn’t matter,’ I said, ‘This is what I should do.’

‘But you shouldn’t!’

‘Sheila, please, I cannot be like you. I’m a good Muslim.’

‘Khadija, the Prophet’s first wife, proposed to him and they married. She was an independent woman, a trader and his boss. And she freely chose her husband. So why should we do differently? The Prophet never said that marriage should be forced. On the contrary, he claimed that marriage is a sacred bond between a man and a woman. And that both sides should agree to it.’

I listened to her in disbelief. Our parents had never told us this. IIow did Shcila know about it?

‘Read the Quran, my dear sister, it’s all there. And do not marry unless your heart tells you so.’

Luckily, my heart was growing less and less against the prospect of me marrying Salim. By that time, we talked regularly, late at night or very early in the morning, when I was in bed. His words were sweet like *chebakia.* He described our life together, how he would take care of me and protect me; how he would buy me beautiful dresses and jewellery; how we would make children, gorgeous like me. This sent impulses through my body which kept me awake long after the end of our conversations.

My sister asked to meet again, but I wasn’t sure how to arrange it. Now, with me getting married, my parents were even more alert when it came to my whereabouts. Luckily, we had a visit to an exhibition, organised by the school, and Sheila joined me there. She came unveiled, her black hair shining loose. She wore light makeup, large earrings and a dark blue dress, outlining her body. After the introduction, they let us look around. We moved from one painting to another, whispering. She wanted to know about my marriage, and it seemed she was determined to talk me out of it. Only after I had repeated three times that I really wanted to get married to Salim, did she give me peace. Still, she didn't miss saying that many people misinterpreted the Quran, that Allah didn't want women to be ignorant and forced into anything.

'Do you know that Muhammad's favourite wife, who had the same name as you, was a scholar, a very smart and strong woman who was among the trusted ones for preserving the true words of the Prophet, and even led the army. Do you know that there have been thousands of female Muslim scholars through the centuries?'

I didn't know any of this.

'Knowledge and education give us power,' she continued, 'They make us free and able to choose the life we want.'

'But a good woman is obedient…'

'Stop this, sis,' she said sharply. 'That is an old version of the Quran and probably untrue. Adapted by men who wanted to overpower and control women.'

Herman waited for her outside. He had auburn hair, blue eyes and looked around forty. He kissed my sister's lips and my cheeks three times. I blushed and stepped back.

'Will you join us for a drink?' Sheila asked.

We had finished earlier than my normal school hours and I didn't want to leave her yet. We went to the Old Town, turned into a narrow street, where staff tried to lure passersby into one of the many fish restaurants, turned again into an alley and entered a bar, which I would have never found by myself. Puppets hung from the walls. Sheila said it was a theatre. She and Herman drank beer, called *Kwak*, in hourglass-shaped glasses, but its two parts were asymmetrical. The beer with its golden-caramel colour replaced the sand; and each sip my sister took, brought her closer to her dreadful end. I understood why our mother was so strongly against education, knowledge messed up one's mind and made it easy prey for the devil. That's what had happened to my sister, she was possessed. She had said that knowledge and education gave us freedom. But what was the meaning of freedom? Being embraced in public by a Westerner, a lot older than her, drinking alcohol, exposing what should only be for the eyes of your husband, staying away from your family and people? If this was the freedom Sheila referred to, I didn't want it. I preferred by far my simple life with its clear rules, the devotion to Allah and the Prophet, the fate of becoming Salim's wife.

*

But then something happened which made me question my own virtues and the meaning of goodness and obedience. Salim wanted to us to talk using a camera. I didn't reply for several hours, not knowing what to do. Then I said yes. I wore my hijab, took out a small mirror and looked at my face. Was I beautiful? Would he like me?

Seeing him was so very different from just talking, his soft eyes, his wide forehead, his thick lips, his dark brown curls. The possibility of happiness, so real and tangible. He smiled and called me *habibi* as he walked around his garden, showing me the flowers, yellow, blue, red and orange.

'Soon they will be all yours, *habibi*. But I have a little request. I want to see you. Please unveil for me!'

I felt cold like the marble in his garden. What to do? He was my future husband and so I should submit. But a good woman should not unveil herself before her wedding. What to do?

'*Habibi*, please, *habibi*, I want to see you in your full beauty.'

I raised my hands, shaking, and slowly untied my hijab; it fell back on my shoulders.

'*Habibi*, *habibi*, you're more beautiful than I imagined! I cannot wait to marry you!'

I didn't dare look him in the eyes. I quickly said I had to go and hung up. My breathing was fast, my mind was racing. What had I done? What had I done? Was I a sinful woman now? Who could tell me? Unveiling is like undressing, it's something you don't do, something a good woman keeps for the eyes of her husband after marriage, but he was to be my husband, but, BUT we weren't married yet. I prayed for hours that night, confessing my sinful deed, asking for forgiveness, asking for answers and fully relying on Allah's mercy.

Two or three days later a date for the wedding was set. My mother informed me at breakfast that it was to take place in ten days.

'Good, mother. But why the hurry?' She didn't find it necessary to reply, kept her lips tight and looked away.

Gifts started arriving. First, my wedding *djellaba* – white, very fine, decorated with lace and accompanied by a matching hijab. I shouted for joy; it was so pretty!

'It's from your future husband. Put it on!' my mother said tersely.

So I did. I thought of Salim seeing me in it, which reminded me of our last call and made me blush. I hadn't been in touch with him since. I had been so embarrassed that I thought it would be best not to have contact anymore before the wedding. Perhaps this would show Allah how deeply I regretted the deed, and He would forgive me and still bless our marriage. My mother watched me silently with narrowed eyes. I walked around a bit and even danced a little.

'Don't be foolish!' she said, 'Marriage is not a party. It is a sacred sacrifice for the woman and a vow to be humble and obedient. Only then can we gain Allah's mercy and find peace in eternity, which follows our short lives.'

Why wasn't it possible to be both happy and have Allah's mercy? I didn't dare ask. Then more presents were delivered, a set of necklaces, earrings and a bracelet in the shape of pink flower petals with green leaves (I had not seen anything more beautiful in my life, but this time I didn't show my joy); dark eyeshadows and a pink lipstick in a golden cylinder; a musk rose perfume. I kept each of them in my palm, thinking of Salim holding them in his, our hands meeting in these precious objects, chosen by him for me.

My only sadness was not having Sheila at the wedding. She was sad too. We were silent for a long time on the phone, then she said,
'In my mind and prayers, I will be with you. Worry not, we will celebrate later, with our men.' If only she knew that Salim wasn't aware of her existence. She said how much she loved me and wished me an unforgettable experience.

Unforgettable it was. My mother, grandmothers, two aunts, three female cousins, four neighbours and two friends from school came to our home. One of my cousins decorated my legs and hands with henna. Another one first spread something white on my face and then, for at least half an hour, painted my eyes and lips with the makeup Salim had sent. The aunts helped me put on my *djellaba*, the jewellery and the veil, and brought over the big mirror, which usually faced the wall, as in my mother's words 'vanity is a sin, leading to even bigger sins.' She was present all the time, overlooking the preparations without uttering a single word. But on that day, I had allowed myself to be vain, to be beautiful and even happy.

More women, wearing their most elegant *djellabas*, joined us in the hall, rented for the wedding. There was traditional music, and we absorbed its rhythm with our bodies. I couldn't help glancing at the door every couple of minutes. Several songs later, someone exclaimed that the men were coming. My knees turned soft. It was happening, it was really happening! In just a moment I would meet

Salim and be his forever. I would find the most gracious movements, which I didn't know I was capable of, to offer to him as a gift.

My father entered first with another man next to him, in a dark blue suit with a yellow tie, so very smart that one would think he was the groom. But he wasn't, for one thing, he wasn't Salim. They walked towards me, the music stopped, the women made half a circle, my mother next to me. The man was sturdy, with a round face and moustache. He smiled at me; I wondered who he was. All the men were in the room now, moving towards us to create the other half of the circle. I looked around for Salim but couldn't see him. My father said,

'Aisha, this is Ali, your future husband.'

The room spun around me, and I stepped back. Someone held me tight from behind. My mother. The man… my husband and I sat together, and everyone brought their gifts and put them on the floor in front of us. It was like a dream, a bad one, from which I couldn't wake up.

Later that night, before Ali and I were to leave for our new home and everyone was saying goodbye, my mother whispered in my ear,

'What did you think – that you'd get a pass? We cannot escape our destiny.'

I raised my eyes and met hers. And in the bottom of their darkness, I saw a spark of something undefined, was it complicity, was it compassion or was it pure evil? Allah forgive me. The rest… I'd rather forget. But I cannot, as this is my life now, as Ali's wife.

When I went online, I found a whole lot of messages from Salim. He said he thought of me day and night. He said I was divine. He said that my parents had broken off the wedding plans and suggested that we run away together. The screen blurred with my tears.

My sister repeated that, in Muhammad's words, a woman shouldn't be forced into anything and added that the Quran allowed divorce. Why was I being forced every night then? My sister wasn't a good woman. But out of all the women I knew, she was the only one who seemed to be happy. Is a good woman entitled to happiness, though? Perhaps my mother is right, we must submit to our destiny and not look for it on earth, so that we can live happily ever after, while my sister was, without doubt, going to hell. But what if Sheila was right? If Allah really allowed divorce, perhaps there was also salvation for me on this earth, while still being a good woman. Perhaps I should, finally, read the Quran.

1050 Ixelles - Matongé

2008

Amadou, Senegalese

In the darkness of the room under the thin light falling through a slit between the heavy curtains, the white duvet looked like a snowdrift. It had taken the shape of a body, the body of a very precious person. My ice queen. Was she already sleeping? I undressed quietly and approached the bed from the other side next to the windows, which looked out onto the back of St. Boniface's church. I couldn't see it now for the curtains were hiding it, but I remembered that first night, a couple of months earlier, when Iris asked me to come over. It was winter then, there was snow. The church, as framed by the window, was like a postcard with an unusual perspective. What had she said then? *God has turned His back on me in this place*. She sat on the bed, nestling the tea mug in her palms as if she wanted to warm her very soul, so fragile, vulnerable. It wasn't cold in the room, the heating was on, but she was entirely covered by the blanket, only her hands exposed, holding the mug. She had called me that morning after many days of silence. I hardly recognised her voice. *I am ill, Amadou. Can you come? I need a strong massage*. We hadn't seen each other for a very long time. I called and sent her messages, but she was either busy or travelling. I hung around *Rue Longue Vie* in the hope of seeing her. And I did see her once. She was walking with a man, his hand around her waist. Her hair had grown longer; she wore heeled boots and a red coat. She didn't notice me; I didn't contact her after. It was many evenings before my phone rang and her name came up on the display.

That night I stayed on the couch in the living room. Now she had requested that we sleep in the same bed. I lay next to her and covered myself with the blanket she had prepared for me. She was so close, two blankets away. I imagined that our breath met and mingled in the air, turned my back to her and, with this image in my mind, must have fallen asleep. How much time had passed I don't know. It could have been a quarter of an hour or an hour. I woke with a start.

'Amadou, Amadou,' Iris whispered.

'Yeah?'

'It's here! I feel it.'

Her whole body was shivering as if she had a fever.

'Shhhh, don't be scared. I'm here.' I reached out to her and caressed her soft hair. Then, for the second time that day, I sang a song that my mother used to sing to me in my childhood.

In the daycare centre where I worked, a girl had become very distressed. She screamed, kicked, cried. Janine, the social worker, couldn't manage. Janine had tried everything to soothe her, but nothing helped. The girl was scratching her hands until they bled, so Janine had to hold her tight to stop her doing it. I stood in the door of the living room and suddenly felt there, in my chest, a song my mother used to sing to me in bed when I was little. I sang it quietly; the girl stopped crying, calmed down, relaxed in Janine's arms and soon fell asleep.

When I mentioned this to Iris, earlier that evening, as we had dinner, she called me a wizard or a healer and asked me to sing it for her. I wasn't either. I was just an African in Brussels. It's not like that with singing, I had told her, it's an impulse born in the soul, you cannot control it. When it comes, it comes and sometimes it might not happen for years. It's true, I hadn't sung for years before that moment when the girl was scratching herself until she bled, it wasn't planned, it just came, I felt it coming up my throat, the song, it was there and needed to come out, to fly, to embrace the girl. So I released it. And then, in the darkness of Iris' room, the same thing happened. I sang and caressed her hair until she gradually stopped shaking and her breathing became even.

I went to Matongé more than usual during that period. My girlfriend Malicia worked in one of the restaurants in the neighbourhood. I always liked it, but I didn't really need to be there, just once in a while to get some African ingredients and fruit, to briefly enter the illusion of home. They say that Matongé was truly Congolese once, but then it became popular among the white people who, because of its proximity to the European institutions, occupied it. Rent went up and the Africans couldn't afford it anymore. Now it had been reduced to two or three streets with barbers and food shops, a few cafés and restaurants, the gallery, and they looked as authentic as they could be. But most Africans only worked or hung out there, living elsewhere, as if they were hired to perform the ordinary life of barbers, cooks, waiters, clients, shop attendants, like a living museum of Africa or the human zoos that Belgium and her neighbours used to organise in the not-so-distant past, so that white people who like exotic stuff could have an authentic African experience in Brussels. Take my friend Mustapha who worked in the gallery in *Chaussée de Wavre* but lived in Molenbeek. These two worlds co-existed without ever meeting. The Africans went to places in *Rue Longue Vie* and the surroundings *Place Saint Boniface* but avoided the square itself, it being such a posh place. You would rarely see a white person in their meeting places, and if there were any, they would mostly walk around and watch, observers of the 'African' reality. The last human zoo took place exactly here, in Brussels, precisely fifty years ago, with the participation of some six hundred 'exhibits' from Congo. Nobody forced us to come to Matongé though, we voluntarily participated in this display. And thanks to that, Iris and I met.

*

In my sleep, I felt a dark heavy energy coming over me and pressing on my chest, so I could hardly breathe. I opened my eyes and felt it. It was there. It's hard to explain what it was exactly. But it was there like a current, a mass of condensed air. A presence. My feet and hands went cold, fear grabbed my throat. I looked around, but there was nothing there, not even a cat.

It had started with the cat. Iris and I sat outside one of the restaurants in *Rue Longue Vie* when she told me about it.

'I was sleeping. I saw a kitten with a tiger pattern, a very cute one, and I followed it to a bush, where it hid. It was at the end of the street, where I spent my childhood. I woke up and saw the cat. In my room. It walked lithely into the middle of the room where it stopped and arched its back. Then the cat went to the chair in the corner, pounced on it and disappeared. But it was as real as the chair and the room and yet it had turned into thin air right before my eyes. I stared at the empty spot where I first saw it, not quite paralysed by fear but by something else, a dense and dark notion that the world of creatures, ghosts and spirits did exist.'

I remember telling Iris a story about Muezza, the favourite cat of Prophet Muhammad. Once, during the call to prayer, Muezza was asleep on one of the sleeves of the Prophet's robe. The Prophet wanted to wear the gown to go to prayer. Rather than disturb Muezza, Muhammad cut off the sleeve to leave Muezza in peace. The Prophet then stroked the cat three times, which, they say, granted Muezza seven lives and the ability to land on its feet at all times.

I liked how Iris listened to me, her eyes wide open, her expression dreamlike as if she had entered the story and only her body was still there with me. Like my first time in *L'Ultime Atome.* I had seen its large windows many times in passing but had never been inside. It was like entering another world and I was a bit nervous, not because of it being alien to me, but because it was her world, Iris' world. She sat by the window, writing on a small laptop, completely insulated from the crowd and the noise, and once again, I had the strange image of her as a lady from a black and white film. And back then, I immediately knew it, this wasn't her world either. Yet, it wasn't foreign territory to her judging by the calm which she radiated, the last light of the day falling on her face. She raised her eyes and smiled. 'Take a seat and let me finish my sentence.'

I ordered a tea and observed her while she was typing, concentrating. Her white skin was almost transparently thin. She had dark curly hair, which she wore short. She closed her laptop and looked at me again.

'Tell me your story, Amadou.'

'My grandmother was into storytelling; she was a griot. Do you know what a griot is?'

'No.'

'A storyteller, like you.'

'How do you know I am a storyteller?'

'You seem like one to me.'

'I don't know. I prefer listening. Collecting stories is my hobby. Will you give me yours?'

'You see, I'm not good at stories. But my grandmother was. She would tell them in a low, slow voice, till I'd fall asleep. The story continued in my dreams and in the morning, I didn't know where one ended and the other one began. When I think about it, it's all an inseparable mixture of memories and dreams.'

'A mixture of memories and dreams… Beautifully said. What were these stories about?'

'The past. My favourite stories were about Sheikh Ahgmadou Bamba. He was born in my village Mbacke Cajoor. A very wise, a holy man he was. A poet. Everyone loved him, his fame spread throughout Senegal and people travelled for days to see him. The Sheikh had a revelation from the Lord in which He told him to look for the city of Touba. So he did. But the French didn't like his popularity and sent him into exile in Gabon for seven years. He spent years in isolation on an island, praying to Allah. When the French decided to have him removed, his pupils wanted to take up arms and fight them. But he ordered them not to, saying violence is prohibited by the Prophet Muhammad. The Sheikh taught his pupils to fight the enemies within themselves, you know, greed, hatred, passion, violence and cheating, all of them standing in their way to salvation. He taught them to work hard and keep faith. After seven years he was able to return to Senegal where he stayed till his death. There is a glorious mosque in the city of Touba now.'

Iris's green eyes shone as she looked at me, and it was so easy to talk, I could hear my grandmother's voice, still vivid and present inside me as if it were yesterday, and the memory of her was a hut I could enter any time to listen.

'You are a storyteller, Amadou. Like your grandmother. Do you ever go back to Senegal?'

'I haven't been there for two years now. Maybe this winter. And you?'

'I came back here last year, after years away. Found a flat just around the corner. My country joined the Union, and that made it possible. Brussels is my greatest lover. I can never get enough of him; he always seduces me, leads me to unexpected places, introduces me to extraordinary people, pampers me with stories, as has just happened with you.'

When she spoke, the green light in her eyes became brighter, I had to almost close mine, but I didn't want to lose sight of her, so I sat there with narrowed eyes and imagined her making love to Brussels.

*

One evening the doorbell interrupted my dinner preparation. Through the spyhole, I saw the stout figure of my second-floor neighbour, Fatima. She's Moroccan, a widow; lives with her two boys, what were their names?

'Good evening, Amadou.'

'Good evening.'

'Can I have a word with you?'

'Sure.'

She stood there, silently looking at me in expectation. I stepped back and let her in. Her eyes ran around the room, she sat on the chair I offered her.

'It's about my boy Youssef, you know him. He's eighteen now and needs to start working. He's a good boy, docile and work doesn't scare him. So I wondered if you could help him.'

'What does he like doing?'

'I don't know. But he'd do anything. He needs to start making money to support us.'

'Okay. I'll check.'

I had seen him a couple of times in the hallway or in the supermarket. He looked like a good boy; a bit shy but he always greeted me respectfully. I knew the guys in the night shop next door to the service where I worked and asked if they needed a hand. They did, so in the morning I collected Youssef, and we went there. He wore trousers and a white shirt as if he were going to college. He started on the following day.

*

I had forgotten about the cat when two or three days later Iris called me.

'Guess what, my landlady used to have a cat. Misty was her name. She died two years ago. I casually asked her whether she had seen the cat since. She looked at me as if there was something wrong with my brain. 'Misty died', she repeated slowly, clearly pronouncing every word, 'How could I possibly have seen her?' Voilà! Isn't it amazing – the cat was called Misty, and it disappeared like mist in the corner of my room as if, even after its death, it expressed its essence; as if our essence goes beyond death; something we bring to the ether to make sense of our existence on this earth and after.'

That's Iris – from a dream to a ghost to essence. But there was something in her words that got me thinking over my lunch break. Our essence is bigger than death. I didn't know about that, but I felt it was bigger than life; the day-to-day activities which create our lives, waking up, getting ready, having breakfast, doing a job amongst people with whom you share nothing but your daily tasks, eating alone, going to bed, your life in a foreign country where you don't belong, day after day, night after night, and that's it, your life on this earth, while you know, you remember, you feel it with your skin, you see it in your dreams, that other place, where the community is bigger than anything; where sharing is the ruling principle; where environment is nature; where you are never alone; that universe of danger, simplicity and unity, called Africa, called home. In searching for a home away from home, we lived with our people, lived in the same neighbourhoods and inhabited the cold inner space of our exile between two continents, two countries, with separated heart and body, and recreating the past as the only way forward.

I couldn't fall asleep after that. I prayed to Allah to give me peace, but with the dark energy around and Iris next to me, peace was impossible. I wanted to protect Iris from any forces which may bring her harm, be they visible or not. And to protect myself from the memory of her skin, that night when she was ill, her burning, soft skin under my hands.

'Would you like some tea?' The sink in the kitchenette was heaped with dirty plates and mugs. 'Sorry for the mess,' she said. Her face was pale, with dark shadows under her eyes. Her lips looked dry, almost colourless, her hair thin and straggly. She wore black leggings and a t-shirt.

'Why don't you go to bed, lady, and let me manage here.'

She didn't protest. I put the kettle on, washed the dishes, made herbal tea for both of us. Later, after she had finished her mug, she removed the blanket, lay on her belly and pulled her top up. My hands were shaking when they first touched her skin and carefully massaged her.

'Harder, please!' she said.

I thought of her body as clay in my hands, which I modelled, recreated, healed.

'That's enough. Now my arms, then the legs.'

She pulled down her top. I obeyed, lost track of time, pressing, kneading, paddling, possessed by tenderness and desire, her slender body, burning in my hands, transmitting its fire. How much time had passed? Half an hour, an hour? I didn't know, and it didn't matter. I could have continued the whole night, the following day, till the end of days.

'Thank you, Amadou,' Iris said.

She covered herself with the blanket, turned over on her side and fell asleep. I switched off her bedside lamp and closed the curtains. In the living room, I made myself another tea, said my prayers and lay on the sofa with ears wide open, trying to register any sound coming from her bedroom. A couple of times during the night I stood in her doorway, watching her sleep, her breathing soft and even.

The light of the day woke me up. Iris was in the kitchenette behind the counter, preparing breakfast.

‘Morning, Amadou,’ she said, ‘I feel a lot better today, thanks to you.’

And indeed, her face had more colour, the black circles were gone, she was freshly showered, her hair still wet. We had toast, cheese and tea, and I left for work. I felt the biting cold under my layers of clothing and shivered; winters were tough. Matongé was waking up, its inhabitants were heading to their offices and Africans were arriving at their workplaces from wherever they lived to perform yet another day of African pseudo-reality.

*

‘Amadou, can I ask you a favour?’ Youssef was standing in the corridor.

I invited him in and offered him a chair, the same one which his mother had sat in three weeks earlier.

‘I was wondering, could you lend me 10 euros?’

‘They don’t pay you enough in the shop?’

‘I give all my wages to my mother, for the housekeeping. There’s nothing left for me. She makes me lunch and gives me some change for coffee, that’s all. But there is this girl, we were at school together. She agreed to see me after work today, it’s a secret from her parents. I want to get her a doner and a coke. I’ll save and pay you back in a week or so.’

‘You like your new work?’

‘Yeah. It’s good.’

*

Iris was my first white friend. I had been in Brussels for eight years by then. The evening we first met, I had dinner with Moustapha at the Congolese restaurant in Matongé, where my girl Malicia worked. Moustapha is also Senegali. Two white women entered. They sat at a table not far from ours, one with her back to us and the other one facing us. The one whose face we could see was beautiful but not like the women from the magazines. There was something old-fashioned about her; she was like a woman from a black and white film. I suppose I kept my eyes on her a bit too long because Malicia became suspicious, tense. She looked at me and then at the woman. She's very jealous, Malicia. A strong character, possessive.

She went to take their order. They said what they wanted and she replied that it wasn't available. I knew it was, so I stopped talking to Moustapha and opened my ears. The women ordered something else, but Malicia again said that they didn't have it. Anything they asked for, it wasn't available. Then they all looked towards our table. The ladies wanted to know what we were having for dinner. Malicia said that whatever we had, that was sold-out too. She also added that I was her boyfriend, so the black and white film woman had better keep her eyes off me. A silly remark, really, because the woman hadn't looked at me at all till that moment. I think she only saw me then. But it didn't make any difference to Malicia, if I was giving my attention to someone else, it was that woman's fault, not mine. The lady looked at me and smiled. I smiled back. She got up, followed by her friend. When they passed by our table, she took out her card and gave it to me. Malicia was furious.

I know this might create a bad impression of Malicia. But she's not a bad girl. Her life hasn't been easy, there was extreme poverty in Congo; there was violence at home. Malicia was five, the youngest, when her mother fled to Belgium with another man, taking only her. She never saw her siblings again. Sometimes she would wake up at night and start crying out all of a sudden, mumbling about being in Congo, with her family, about having to return and see them, having to save for a ticket and go, her weeping stopped the way it had started, she would go back to sleep and say nothing about it in the morning, all that had happened stayed in the no man's land of darkness and dreams. Her stepfather left her mother after some years for another woman. That's why Malicia doesn't trust men. And maybe she's right because on the day after our weird encounter in the restaurant, I called Iris. But would I have called her, if Malicia wasn't so crazy, I don't know. What is certain is that Iris wouldn't have given me her card had Malicia not acted the way she did.

Days after that first time in *L'Ultime Atome* I could still see Iris' face, smile, eyes, fingers, drawing sketches in the air, while she was talking, and as I followed their trajectories, I felt helpless, lost in the streets of the invisible world they constructed. And when her features started becoming blurred in my memory, I called her again and invited her to *Cap Africa* in *Rue Longue Vie.* Maybe I was testing her a bit, she seemed confident in her waters, but how would she be somewhere she didn't belong. Or maybe I simply wanted to welcome her to my world, to see her entering, looking around, noticing me in the corner, sitting next to me, comfortable, warm, relaxed, sipping from her drink, listening, saying things in her interesting way of speaking, her words surprising and real, different from the way anyone else I knew spoke. It was exactly as I imagined it. She belonged there as much or as little as in the trendy bar, she was there, and she wasn't and still she was, I could have touched her pale skin, if only I had dared.

The beginning of our friendship marked the end of my relationship with Malicia. Someone told her that they saw me with a white woman, there was a monumental scene, and it was over. Before meeting Iris, my life had a particular routine to it, I went to work, had dinner at home or at a friend's home, stayed over at Malicia's, went out for drinks with friends but mostly we visited each other's places. We shared our food, difficulties and joys; we were all foreigners in this city, sticking together like rice, and although Matongé was an imitation of home; on the surface at least, it was ours.

If only the weather hadn't been so grey, wet and cold most of the time. In the beginning, I missed my family, the blue sky and the scorching sun of Africa, then I got used to it, to replacing things from home with things which reminded me of home. Life was difficult there, work was scarce, and I came to try my luck in Europe. I already knew other Senegalese in Brussels who came before me and helped me. The beginning wasn't easy but day after day, with prayers and friends, I got used to this foreign city. My first jobs were in bars and shops, then I took some classes, organised by the state, and got a place at the day centre.

I also went to Dutch classes twice a week. All this continued after I met Iris but there was a new element to it, something extraordinary, which I felt even when I wasn't with her, that I knew her, that we could sit together, talk, be silent, share.

That much I knew about her, she loved to write, read, dance tango, go to the pictures. We would have a drink in Matongé and then see a movie in *Vendome*, which she liked better than the modern cinema complexes.

'You see, Amadou,' she said, 'this is real, this cinema, old and authentic like the classical films.'

The films we saw together were both old and new but always slow, without much action and with happy endings. I loved sitting so close to her in the dark hall, observing her face in the faint light coming from the screen, reflecting what was happening – I didn't need to watch to know whether it was good or bad, her face showed it all, a smile, tension, tears. If you asked me, I couldn't tell you much about the plots of these movies, I had hardly seen them. But I could recall her response in the greatest detail, the movie on her face. We would stay till the end of the credits because she wanted us to be the last to leave. 'Did you like it?' she would ask. 'I did,' I would reply, and we would leave it there.

Once after the movie, she asked me to join her in a bar in *Rue de Dublin*, a place where they danced tango. We sat at a table in the corner and watched people dancing. I wasn't familiar with tango then but I liked it. Iris was hypnotised, her lips half-open. The song ended, some fast music started, and couples parted. A new song began, Iris looked at the men, then she nodded slightly, an older guy approached, she got up and stood in front of him. He offered her his hand, she relaxed hers in it, and they danced. Then as before, I saw a different aspect of her – in the dance she was like an angel as if her feet hardly touched the floor, her eyes were closed, her face glowed, she was somewhere else. I felt jealous of how this man could connect to her in a way I wasn't able to. When the sequence of songs was over, he walked her to the table and nodded at me as if to say 'She is yours now.'

'You're an amazing dancer!' I told her.

She looked at me with misty eyes, 'I am just a beginner. But I very much enjoy it.'

In her sleep, she moved, her mouth slightly open, hair falling over her face. If her breathing became jagged, I would caress her hair until she calmed down again.

We walked towards her place one afternoon. A wet and grey day with heavy clouds hanging over the city. At the end of *Rue Longue Vie* police cars surrounded a black middle-aged woman with curly orange hair. She was like a trapped animal. A voice came from a loudspeaker, ordering her to raise her hands. We stopped in the middle of the street and watched. She slowly raised her hands. A policeman got out of one of the cars and approached her with a pair of handcuffs. He was next to her, putting the cuffs on her stretched hands, then just before he locked them, she pushed him and ran in the opposite direction. There was the sound of gun shots, Iris screamed, and we ran into the restaurant next to us. We heard clapping and laughter.

Back on the street there was an unexpected development, the woman was back, the policeman was embracing her, both smiling, the other policemen were out of the cars, watching them and clapping, and so were the African men standing around us.

'They are shooting a film,' someone said.

Iris and I looked into each other's eyes and smiled, we had entered the world of cinema.

*

I was going to have dinner with friends nearby but first I stopped at my place and rang Youssef's door. Fatima opened it, her eyes were swollen.

'Good evening, Fatima. Youssef didn't show up at work today. Mustapha was worried, he came to ask me if he was okay.'

Tears ran down her cheeks, she moved her lips as if trying to produce words, but not knowing how. She took a deep breath and without looking me in the eye, said,

'Youssef… my boy…he's in prison. It's not his fault, it's his friends, I told him so many times not to go with them, but he wouldn't listen.'

'What happened?'

'I don't know. They say theft, jewellery, but I know my boy, he would never do such a thing, he's a good boy, it's his friends, those little devils!'

Her voice choked again.

'I'm sorry, Fatima. Can I help?'

'They won't let him go without paying bail. But I don't have enough money.'

*

As the days got shorter and the darkness took over, the spark in Iris' eyes faded away as well. There was a cloud of sadness surrounding her. An air of something sought and not found. I was happy when, once in a while, something I said would cheer her up. Like when I told her about the lake at Djoudj. She was reading a book at *L'Ultime Atome*.

'What are you reading?'

'A novel. With pelicans flying through it.'

'You know, we have pelicans in Senegal too. There is a lake that is full of all sorts of birds, including pelicans; they stop there during their migration. You can go on a tour among them in a small boat.'

'I can picture it,' she said, 'The lake and all its birds. Thank you for sharing that, it made my day!'

I was amazed how such small things could have an impact on her; that she would give them any importance at all. Take the day when she called me and said excitedly,

'I must show you something. Let's meet tonight.'

I was having dinner with Mustapha and some other friends but said I would pass by her house later. We went to the top of *Rue Longue Vie*.

'*Voilà*,' she said. She pointed at a tree in a big pot in the middle of the street. An olive tree. 'Isn't it amazing?'. The tree of life in *Rue Longue Vie*.

'It's a special day, Amadou,' she told me, as we were having a drink in a nearby bar later, 'The Treaty of Lisbon was signed today.'

'What's the treaty about?'

'The functioning of the Union. Now with twelve more member states, the Union needs new rules to continue to function and be both effective and democratic. There was a constitution, written a few years ago, which was then rejected by France and The Netherlands. So now we have a new treaty, based on the constitution but different.'

'And what's different about it?'

'Some countries were concerned that with a Constitution, the Union would turn into a super-state, that they wouldn't have the same autonomy anymore. Anything which suggests unification has been removed from the treaty, the flag, the anthem, Europe Day, but all the rest is more or less the same.'

'I see... But there is one thing I don't understand, Iris. The countries in the Union, it seems they only want to commit their minds but not their hearts. To come together when they have common interests, but not to *be* one.'

'Well, yes, we're talking about twenty-seven countries, all very different. They want to keep their sovereignty.'

'I don't know. To me what you're saying sounds like a mess. If the head and the heart aren't connected that will create problems.'

She got a message, read it and a shadow fell over her face.

'Your boyfriend?' I asked.

'Sort of.'

'Will it last?'

'I don't know.'

She made an uncertain gesture.

'When are you leaving for Senegal?'

'Won't be this year. Maybe next year.'

*

Youssef sat on the chair silently. He hadn't said a word since he'd walked in, and I didn't pressure him.

'Can I get you anything?' I asked for second time.

'A tea,' he finally said.

When I brought it to him, he looked into my eyes for the first time and said, 'Thank you.' And by the way he said it, I knew he didn't mean the tea.

'I want you to know that I didn't do it. I didn't want to steal; I didn't care at all about the jewellery. Not at all. Jasir and Ahmet made me do it. First, I said 'no' but they persisted. They called me names. *Coward, pussy, fool.* You don't have to do anything, they said, nothing. We'll do the job, you just speak to the lady, ask her questions. That's all you have to do. We'll do the whole thing, but you'll have a share. For just asking a few questions, you'll get two or three times your monthly salary, you must be out of your mind to say no. I listened to them, listened and then thought, why not? I wouldn't do anything. Talking to the seller doesn't make me a thief. And… I needed money. I told you; I give my whole salary to my mother, nothing is left for me. The pocket money I get from her is peanuts. I wanted to ask that girl out again and having a bit on the side would have helped. So I agreed. We went, I spoke to the lady, Jasir and Ahmet did what they did. They said *run*. So I did. A few steps down the street the cops got us and took us to jail. But I didn't…'

He covered his face with his hands, and I felt sorry for him. One wrong move and that was it.

The shop owner had fired him, and no one would give him a proper job now with a criminal record. I didn't know what to tell him, how to reassure him.

'Come on,' I said, 'You have an entire life in front of you to make up for one silly decision.'

*

'Amadou, I have a request for you. I want you to stay over. Something bizarre has been happening ever since I saw the cat. A couple of nights later, I woke up again in the middle of the night. In my dream it felt like the mattress under me had softened and had been moving like water, you know when your body is relaxed in the sea, and it carries and cradles you like a baby. When I opened my eyes, I felt an intense energy running from my head through my body. I couldn't move at all; I just felt this energy like a presence. It only lasted a few seconds, but it was very intense. Something similar happened a few days later. It was early in the morning. The same sensation, as if my body was floating on the mattress, woke me. I heard a monotonous sound and then felt this energy coming through the window. I felt it running through my body, I was paralysed again. It lasted for just seconds, but it was so intense! And ever since, this energy has been here. I feel it almost all the time. Not just when I am asleep. I feel it like a cool breeze moving around me. It's terrifying and I don't want to sleep alone. Can you come tonight?' Iris's voice was tense as if it wasn't hers anymore.

'Okay. I'll come tonight.'

I arrived around 7pm. Iris embraced me and let me in. I couldn't help looking at her legs in her tight jeans as she was climbing the stairs in front of me.

'I was just starting to cook some dinner. Will you help me?'

And without waiting for an answer, she handed me a knife and an onion to cut.

'There is a poem, Amadou, a beautiful poem about love by a British poet. It's called 'Valentine'. It says, '*I give you an onion. / It is a moon, wrapped in brown paper.*' You see, romantic love is an illusion; love holds on to life, to its matter and simplicity, it's not all about roses and stars, but more, indeed, like an onion, it makes you cry at times but also it's life itself, without glamour, and when you truly love you find beauty in ordinary gestures, in gentleness and kindness.'

And as I was cutting the onion, my eyes wet with tears, I couldn't have related more to her words. She cooked, we ate together, some pasta with tomato sauce. She drank red wine; I had water.

In the morning, I didn't tell her anything about the dark energy I had felt as well. I just said,

'You'd better find another place.' She nodded.

Night after night I went to her. Sometimes we cooked and ate together; other times I went later, only to spend the night by her side and scare her fears away.

'And you never tried?' Mustapha asked me in disbelief. I did. One of the first nights, after caressing her hair, my hand went slowly down, down her neck and back, further down, following the contours of her body, but as I went further, her hand held mine and pushed it away, gently, but categorically.

'I love you,' I whispered, but whether she heard me I don't know, as there was no response.

The experience I had the first night wasn't repeated. But there was something disturbing about the place, and I was relieved when two weeks later she found a small flat at *Saint-Josse-ten-Noode*. She spent the last couple of nights before moving alone, saying that she wasn't scared anymore.

On the day of the move, she said she had had another visit. She had woken up in the morning, feeling this energy running through her body, not able to move. And then she had seen a man's face very close to hers, a blond man with blue eyes and a sombre expression. She had felt sorry for him and had told him, silently, don't be sad, it will be alright. Then he disappeared.

She had two cases and three bags; we put them in the car of the same friend she was with when I first saw her. Her name was

Brigitte. Taking Iris' luggage out, I felt immense nostalgia for the evenings we shared, for the nights I spent next to her in Matongé.

1210 Saint-Josse-ten-Noode

2010

Brigitte, Belgian

My mobile display lit up and vibrated.

'Hi, Amadou.'

'Hi, Brigitte. Is it a convenient time to talk?'

'Yes, sure.'

I went out of the office.

'Iris isn't well.'

'What's wrong with her?'

'She has been crying.'

'Crying?'

'Yes. She hasn't been out of bed for a few days now. And she cries a great deal of the time.'

'But why? What's happened?'

'She broke up with Herman. So I thought I would call you…'

On my way home, I stopped at the residential building where she lived. It was a monster of a building – high and ugly, its many floors containing a multitude of boxes. Why on earth did Iris choose this place, I wondered. She seemed to like it, though.

'I feel protected here after that old, haunted house,' she told me when I visited her for the first time after the move.

‘But ghosts know no barriers.’

‘True, but I think they prefer settings with more history.’

‘You seem to know a lot about ghosts’ mentality.’

‘But I like Saint-Josse in its own right. I can sit by the window or outdoors in summer in one of the restaurants on the square with a cup of tea and my laptop for hours, watching life passing by. And the church shaped like a bell or a medieval dress, it’s so pretty and… *dignified.* Whatever I do, somehow, I always end up living around squares and churches in this city. God keeps me close,’ she laughed, ‘And then, those three streets starting at the square, each with their parallel realities. That’s not quite true, of course, *Chaussée de Louvain*, leading from the city centre to the city of Leuven, some twenty kilometres eastbound, crosses the square. It’s like a metaphor for life itself, transient and distinct in its different parts. Dashing down from Madou, becoming balanced and open at the square, closing in on itself and surprising us as it leaves with a sudden curve like a serpent. It’s like in fairy tales, you know. The three paths. Here two of them lead away from the square in a straight line so you can more or less see what they have to offer, but the middle one, the middle one appeals most with the unpredictability of what comes after its meander. Sometimes I want to be like that street. And then the exotic shops, the restaurants, the fruit and veg stores, the vibe of otherness, so potent and alive…’

Iris could be quiet and discreet, and she could also flood you with her thoughts and ideas, which often sounded like excerpts from a book.

I worked in the archive, in the neighbourhood, and I quite liked it, but I didn't relate to it in the same way. What intrigued me was not so much the transience of places in their present but rather the perspective they gave of time; what they used to be, what had been preserved and what lost; what they had become. If you compared this precise part of *Chaussée de Louvain*, which Iris referred to, with a photo taken in the late 19th century, you would see two profoundly different cities. Back then, its architecture and cobble stones reminded me of cities like Prague, Warsaw and Budapest.

The photo we have in the archive, from around the First World War, captures two ladies wearing hats and long dresses, and a boy dressed in the fashion of the day, very neat, with more women in long dresses and men in suits and hats in the background strolling down the street. During the nineteen fifties and sixties, there were several cabarets around and some famous cinemas, including *Marignan*, Century and *Mirano*, which is now a popular night club. Nothing in the photo hints at its current appearance, the pavement, the cars, the Arabic hub it has become.

I passed by Iris' building twice a day, but I hadn't seen her for weeks. Once my workday was over, I was just eager to get home, cook something or get a takeaway, watch a film, chill out. Or go to my salsa classes or a party depending on the day. My job wasn't very demanding, but it was repetitive, bringing about its own kind of fatigue. Iris' work, on the other hand, sounded fascinating, but then she often worked long hours. So even if I wanted to see her after work, she was hardly ever there, whenever I called her, she was at a conference, a reception, a vernissage or just staying with Herman. Besides, we had grown apart after she had stolen Sheila's boyfriend. A rather dangerous place to be, the edge between two friendships. But if you asked Iris, she hadn't done anything. Who had then? Perhaps me, by organising that guided walk where they met. The walk was about the invisible river of Brussels, the Senne. We started at St Catherine, at the water basin next to the church. Iris had met Sheila once, together with her sister, at that same square. The irony of life. Now they recognised each other, and Sheila introduced Iris to Herman. My programme started.

'What is this?' I asked.

'A fountain,' the group replied in one voice.

'No. This is used to be the canal linking Brussels to the Scheldt River. The part of the waterway within the city walls was only filled in in the very early 20th century. The canal was dug in the mid-sixteenth century for economic reasons, as the river Senne, on which banks Brussels was founded, had become too narrow, too shallow and winding. Can you see that banal building to the other side of the church? Let's all go over there.'

In front of Parking 58, I revealed that this is where the Brussels River used to be.

'The Senne. Some called it "the first citizen of the city". Once upon a time, Brussels was constructed along the curves and turns of the Senne, which until 1871 defined the look of the lower parts of the city. Our next stop will be *Place Saint-Géry* with the covered market *Halles de Place Saint-Géry*.'

At *Place Saint-Géry*, I resumed my talk.

'This place used to be an island in the river. The cohabitation of the river and the city was not very straightforward. The river overflowed more and more often and gradually became heavily polluted. It became a source of damage, stench and cholera. It was time to make tough decisions.'

After showing the group a water basin where the river had once flowed, we strolled towards our next stop on *Boulevard Anspach*. Herman walked in the middle, between Iris and Sheila.

'Jules Anspach, the then mayor, was the one to take responsibility. The Sene was made to flow through two underground culverts, situated under the current boulevards in the centre. The city took over. But it was not a popular measure, with Anspach depicted in the media as the one who turned the first sod in the grave of Old Brussels. And yet the local council decided to name a large section of this long street after him, honouring his determination to turn Brussels into a modern city. Our last stop will be at the canal.'

After the walk was over, the four of us went for a drink in a bar by the canal. We chatted a bit and then Iris said something about literature, I don't remember what it was, two years have passed, but whatever it was, Herman swallowed it like a fish taking bait. Transfixed, that's what he was.

'Could you say a little bit more…?' he said, staring at her.

She did. She spoke passionately about the topic and then he would say something, and she would continue, they made a perfect duo. Sheila and I were completely left out of their conversation. Sheila pretended not to notice anything and spoke to me about the unfortunate marriage of her sister and of that man whom she loved, her first fiancée. I nodded and also acted as if the very act of one of my friends seducing the boyfriend of another one wasn't happening right there right then, as if it wasn't all that obvious. At some point, I could hardly breathe, trying to suppress the impulse to get up, grab Iris by the delicate fabric of her dress and scream in her face, 'Go! Go now and don't look back!' I was hoping Sheila would react, but she didn't. She continued talking to me softly and I nodded and pretended that it was all fine and normal. Finally, when Sheila paused, I interrupted the flow between Iris and Herman by saying,

'I will be going, Iris. Will you join me? I need to talk to you about something.' Startled, they looked at us, as if they had just realised we were there as well.

'Sure,' Iris said and got up.

'It was very nice meeting you, Iris,' Herman said and gave her three kisses.

'Have you just spent an hour mesmerizing my friend's boyfriend?' I attacked her.

'Pardon?'

'Don't pretend you don't know what I am talking about!' I was pissed off.

'What are you suggesting? I just talked with the guy. He loves reading, we talked about books…'

'Stop! Not to me, please. I saw you. And him.'

‘This is unfair,’ her eyes were full of tears. ‘So we clicked. So what? People meet and connect all the time.’

‘Are you saying that if Sheila and I weren’t there, you wouldn’t have been in bed with him already? The little that I know of you…’

‘What?! How dare you…’

She didn’t finish her sentence but turned her back to me and walked away fast.

*

A week later, Sheila called me.

‘Herman and I split up,’ she said.

She said he had already been distancing himself for a couple of months. But after that night, he had become strange, edgy, unpleasant. When she had asked him what was wrong, he had replied, ‘Why would anything be wrong with me? Why don’t you ask yourself what’s wrong with you?’

‘I don’t understand,’ she had replied.

‘And that’s the problem,’ he had said. ‘We have been together for two years now and you don’t understand. And that woman, the other day, she understood immediately.’

‘Is it because of her?’

‘Of course not, don’t be so simplistic. She’s no one. How could it be because of her? It’s because of us. I feel we haven’t functioned as an item for quite some time now.’ That’s the word he had used, *item*.

‘So now what?’

'I feel it might be a good idea to give each other a break and see what happens.'

'Are you breaking up with me?'

'No, I didn't say break up, just a break.'

'May I stay with you for a while?' Sheila asked. In the evening, she came to my place with a case. Her eyes were dead. She was a shadow of herself. I hadn't spoken to Iris since that time after my guided tour. I waited two or three more days and called her early in the morning before she got caught up in the day.

'I want to apologise,' I said.

'There is no need.' she said. 'Herman is here. Will call you later.' And she hung up.

Apparently, I had been right. She was a slut. But then the slut was my friend. And so was the victim.

'It's not what you think,' Iris said when she called me back later. 'He called last night and asked to see me. He was pretty lost and depressed, not knowing what to do with himself. I agreed for him to come. We talked until late, then he slept on the sofa. He's a mess.'

'Are you suggesting that he deserves compassion?'

'I'm not suggesting anything, just sharing.'

'But everything that's happened is his choice.'

'Not everything is our choice. We can be lost sometimes. I know that feeling all too well, I've been there myself.'

'Come on. A man in his forties acting like a boy who needs his mummy. Why do you care so much? What's in it for you?'

‘I don’t know. I feel very close to him. It’s hard to explain.’

‘Okay. I hope you know what you are doing. Now it’s Sheila. Tomorrow it might be you.’

‘I love you too. Take care.’

‘Take care.’

Herman became a regular guest on Iris’ sofa for two or three months before he got upgraded to her bedroom. Then they were a couple, an item. Meanwhile, Sheila found a flat in Schaerbeek, not far away from where my mother lived. I helped her move her stuff out of Herman’s flat. During that transition period, it was easier to communicate with her than with Iris. Somehow, I couldn’t get rid of the feeling that she was the victim and couldn’t stop myself judging Iris for her role in Sheila’s suffering. But as time passed, Sheila recovered, with love and prayers, and decided not to look back. She was wise, a true believer.

‘Allah is all good and mighty,’ she said. ‘He would give you anything. You only have to ask for it. But – most importantly – He would give you peace.’

I admired her for her strength and envied her a bit for her faith. If I were in a similar situation, I reckon I would have been in pieces. But not Sheila. Her strength and healing made it possible for me to reconnect to Iris.

Initially, things between Iris and Herman were fairytale material. I had never seen her so happy; she was flourishing. They would go to fancy restaurants, cultural events, weekend trips. My discontent with her gradually melted. At the end of the day, these things happen in life and sometimes it's indeed beyond our control, we should just go with the flow. The unease which I felt when seeing them together sussuring like love birds was replaced by the habit of it. Iris and Herman became a mantra. You could hardly say one of their names without adding the other. This continued for a year or so.

I usually saw her during the weekends when Herman was with his kids. She hadn't moved in with him, but she spent most of the evenings during the week in his flat downtown. When he had the children with him, she would usually stay in Saint-Josse, even though she knew them, and they did things together. She needed her space too 'to connect to herself and write', in her own words. Every so often, we would meet in her neighbourhood after work. We would have dinner in one of the many restaurants in the area and sometimes would go to a concert at Jazz Station.

One evening, unusually, our other friend Alice joined us like in the good old days when Iris and I lived together. Alice had moved back to Leuven where she worked for a law firm and lived with her boyfriend. Those rare occasions when we saw her felt special. That evening, we went to a Lebanese restaurant. Alice was talking about the house they had just bought; Iris was saying the right things, but I could sense that she wasn't fully present. A veil of sadness fell over her face which didn't disappear even when she smiled.

'Is everything alright?' I asked. 'How have you been?'

'I am good,' she said 'The usual – work, Herman, writing…'

'You seem a bit down tonight.'

'It's nothing. Herman and I have been arguing lately… Nothing serious. I guess it's normal after the initial champagne and roses period. We will work it out.'

'I hope so.'

'Do you still tango?' Alice asked. Iris had taken a course in Bulgaria and had continued after her return to Brussels.

'Not really,' she replied. 'Herman doesn't fancy the idea of other men holding me so close.'

She giggled.

'I cannot believe that! It's only dancing! Are you letting a man rule your life now? That's not how I know you.' Alice said.

'It's not like that. Of course he hasn't forbidden me.' Alice raised her eyebrows. 'He doesn't have that power. But I just don't feel comfortable getting so intimate with other men now I have him in my life. And I don't like to hurt his feelings.'

'But you love tango! It's part of you. Why would you sacrifice that?' I said.

'It's not that important, really. And it's not a sacrifice. We all give things up when we're in a relationship. Voluntarily. I haven't seen you for ages, Alice. You also went out a lot more when you were single.'

'It's not about me being in a couple. Roel is very tolerant and respectful. It's just that I live in another city, work long hours and life just keeps you busy…'

'Indeed. I also do a whole lot of things with Herman. Hence, I don't feel the need to tango. But I am excited about dancing with you ladies.'

That was the plan. Dinner and *Mirano Continental*. The three of us hadn't been out dancing for… I don't know how long. We arrived around eleven; the party started soon after. We had cocktails and danced, and the clouds over Iris' face dispersed. Like back in the day at Havana Bar, we were still quite popular with men who came to dance with us and treated us to more cocktails. I remember giving my number to a Latvian guy in the end. When we called it a day, Alice stayed over with Iris, and I took a taxi home. I can picture every single moment of that night as if it happened yesterday. Perhaps because it didn't happen again.

*

It was months before I saw Iris again. We spoke every so often and the music of her voice was different each time, sometimes cheerful and confident, other times melancholic.

'How is it going with Herman?' I would always ask.

'It's not always easy but we will work it through' was her regular answer. And then one day, around two months ago, she called me, and her voice was brittle.

'I lost my job,' she said.

'Oh, no! How come?'

'It's because of the crises. They cannot afford to keep everyone in the agency. I got given a month's notice today.'

‘I’m so sorry! But you will find another job. Have you told Herman?’

‘No. I will tell him tonight.’

‘At least you have got him. It would have been even more difficult if you were alone. Maybe you could move in with him now and save the rent.’

‘Yeah. Let’s see.’

I know I should have called her afterwards, but I didn’t. I had been too entangled in my own crises of not being sure what to do with my life and how to break the circle of the convenient routine, which, I felt, was killing me slowly. And now I was there, in front of her apartment. I pressed the bell with her name and waited. Nothing. Pressed again. Her voice reached me from far away:

‘Hello.’

‘It’s me, Brigitte. Will you let me in?’

She had left the door open for me. Inside, there was devastation. A dirty plate and a fork left on the table; an empty glass with a few drops of red wine and an open bottle, two thirds empty, next to it; clothes strewn on chairs; books everywhere… I walked into the bedroom. Iris lay in bed, her eyes more dead than ever, her face ghostly, her hair a tangled mess. She looked at me, but it felt as if she looked through me.

‘Hi,’ I said.

She smiled faintly.

‘Amadou called you?’

‘It wasn’t you.’

'Right.'

'I could do with a herbal tea. Would you like one too?'

'Yes.'

I went to the kitchen where the mess had spread. A pile of dishes and cups were scattered in and around the sink and empty boxes of takeaway food were abandoned on the counter.

Having washed everything, I returned to her with the warm cups of tea.

'What happened?'

'The usual, I suppose...'

Her voice was weak, she talked with difficulty, her words sounding painful to say.

'He left you?'

'Nobody leaves me.' Her dry lips attempted a smile. 'I left him. But he didn't leave me a choice. Things haven't been good in the past year. There was a lot of tension and struggle from my side to make it work. Love shouldn't be so difficult. When it is love… He was more and more discontent. There was always something… Exhausting. His need for space had increased too. We spent fewer evenings together and if I shared my need for intimacy, he would attack me by saying that he felt pressured and controlled. When I lost my job and shared my worries with him, he would quickly lose interest or say he was tired of hearing me complain and that I could also try other things. Other things meaning babysitting or working in a shop. "It's the crisis," he would say, "We all have to make compromises." Nothing loving nor supportive. And then there was the morning when he was on his phone just before going to the bathroom. I was fast enough to get hold of it before it locked. And what do you think? His history showed multiple searches for "escort" and "Laura." His messenger was full of chats with Russian girls. He came back to the room. "Who is Laura?" I asked. "What are you talking about?" "You know what I am talking about." "Have you been spying on me? You're sick!" "You're right. I am sick. I am sick of you. Get out of here, I don't want to see you again!" He put his clothes on and left. I suppose he was grateful for the easy exit.'

'That's disgusting! I want to kick the bastard in his ass for hurting two of my best friends!'

'Why was I so stupid?'

Tears rolled down her cheeks. I put the cup down, moved closer to her and hugged her as I had done two years ago with Sheila. How I hated that asshole!

'Listen,' I said, 'It's good that it's over, isn't it?! It's over. It hurts, but it will heal, and you will move on with your life. Would staying with him and getting that sort of treatment for years ahead have been better? He's toxic and now he's not poisoning you anymore.'

Iris sighed and wiped away her tears.

'It hurts so badly. So badly.'

'I know. But it will pass. And how is your job search going?'

She looked around and smiled wryly, 'That's how it's going.'

'I see...'

‘I’ve applied for so many jobs. Journalism, communications, civil society and business… anything. I got a few interviews, making it to the top five out of one or two hundred applicants. But I didn’t get any of them. It’s tough at the moment. The competition is wild.’

‘I see. Have you considered going back to Bulgaria?’

‘I have. But I’d rather not. I left everything to come here. I don’t want to give up now just because it’s difficult.’

‘But is being here any good right now, either?’

‘I don’t know what to do. I don’t have the energy or the desire for anything.’

‘How about this, I could help you find someone to sublet your flat to, so that you don’t have to pay. You will still be getting unemployment benefits for a while so you should be able to sustain yourself in Bulgaria. You would only have to go to appointments with the unemployment service and for interviews unless you can do them by Skype. It might do you good to get some distance from here and everything that’s happened. You will recharge your batteries and come back in September, with renewed energy, unless you get a job earlier. Go to your family, get the support and care you need, heal, come back. How does that sound?’

She looked through the big windows, towards the rooftops, the sky, the clouds, all grey, and said,

‘Perhaps you are right.’

‘Why don’t we put an ad out straight away then?’

Without waiting for a reply, I reached for the small laptop next to her bed and opened it.

'Do you know any websites?'

'Expats in Brussels,' she said.

It took just fifteen minutes to activate her ad.

'I am taking you out for dinner,' I said.

'I don't want to... I feel so tired.'

'Have I asked you for your opinion? Get up and put some clothes on. That's an order.'

I went to her living room and started cleaning up. After a short while, I heard her getting up and opening her wardrobe.

Outside it was chilly and wet. As we turned towards *Chaussée de Louvain*, Iris looked at the square.

'It's not that it was always difficult with Herman,' she said. 'We had beautiful days as well, days of seamless happiness. Just a few months ago, we were at the *Saint-Jazz-ten-Noode* festival. They had built a stage on the square, the crowd was diverse and laid back, the music was great, a lot of ethnic jazz, we danced, we had so much fun. In the evening, we continued at the Jazz Station where some contemporary Belgian jazz was on the programme. Herman held my hand during the entire concert. I know it sounds cheesy, but it was very intimate, and I felt so….'

She choked up.

'I know. This place is full of memories. That's why you must leave now. And then… perhaps change flats.'

'Again?'

'Why not? New home, a new beginning.'

'But I like Saint-Josse.'

'But you also liked Matongé.'

She laughed with sad laughter.

'New home, a new beginning. You are right. That's what I need to do. Thank you, Brigitte!'

She stopped and turned towards me, and we hugged under the drizzle. Only then could I sigh with relief and certainty that she would be fine.

Later that evening, Amadou called me.

'She will be fine,' I said. 'Thank you for reaching out.'

'No, thank you… Shall we have dinner soon and you can tell me everything? There is a very nice African restaurant in Matongé.'

'Okay, let's do that.'

The dinner we had was the first of many.

An Italian trainee agreed to sub-rent Iris' flat for five months. One weekend we took Iris' belongings over to Alice's house in Leuven, where she stored it in the attic. She left on Monday.

Brussels, the space of night

2013

Thomas, Australian

Sunday night at *Gare du Midi,* waiting for my Thalys to Paris. From my pocket, I feel the familiar vibration of my phone announcing a new Tinder message.

'Safe travels,' Iris texted.

'I don't want to go.'

'I bet you don't, judging by how busy you've been.'

'I don't want to go without seeing you.'

'You've had your chances. You've missed them all.'

'I have.'

'I hope it was worth it.'

'I'm not sure about that.'

'Tell me about it.'

I'd called from Sydney the previous Friday morning where I was working at the annual book fair. Being in the publishing world also meant following the big international book fairs and scheduling trips according to their agenda. Cairo in January, February – Vilnius and Riga, February or March – Brussels, London and Paris, April – Quebec and so on. What an exciting life, you would think. You can have it. I'd be happy to exchange it for a boring life, a life in which I have a wife, a dog, three children, a nine-to-five job and planned holidays twice a year. Instead, I have to deal with authors, each of whom are convinced of being the yet undiscovered voice of our times, to be proved as such by time and history; who fight over each word with the editors as if it was a lump of gold; who, at the end, of the day, blame you, say that you haven't done enough as a publisher to make their book visible for their millions of potential readers, whose only reason for not having bought and read it yet is the lack of awareness of its existence which is, of course, the publisher's sole responsibility. I'm so bloody tired of it. And maybe that's why I was reluctant to meet Iris. She was a writer. Yet another one. Enough! Moreover, when in a country, try all things local, including women.

Iris wasn't local either, she was an Eastern European and the first woman with whom I had a 'That's a match!' while waiting in line at Brussels airport. Thank God for Tinder, the saviour from loneliness, the key to excitement. Anywhere, any time, there will always be women looking for precisely the same thing, an instant connection, a sheer experience without pre-history and perspective. Just the moment as such in its uniqueness, unpredictability and perfection. Like a novel, consisting of separate, disconnected scenes, each striking and unique in its own way. This time the novel is Brussels. While I am chatting with Iris, I get a couple more matches, followed by a first date for the same evening, with Cecile.

I drop my luggage at Hotel Bloom, next to the *Botanique*, the former botanical gardens, and head for the fair. Richard and Jason have been here since Wednesday night when they set up our stand. I find Richard alone; Jason has taken the morning off to recover from a hangover.

'The Belgian beer, you know…' Richard winks.

The opening had been the previous night; there was a crowd, just like today. We have already had some sales. Our speciality is books about cities, from travel guides to fiction in which the city is a character in its own right.

One of our authors, for example, writes crime stories, each one taking place in a different city. He would go and live there for months, getting to know the milieu before turning it into a crime scene. An excellent read for those visiting that city for the first time, combining an intriguing story with descriptions of restaurants, bars, and the sights. No surprise, his books are all bestselling.

The afternoon is over before we know it, with people passing, stopping, chatting and buying. Tiredness hasn't got a grip on me yet. Luckily, I slept on the plane. I take a quick shower at my hotel and go to the Old Town to have dinner with Richard and Jason before heading for my first date in Brussels.

It takes a while to find *Goupil Le Fol*, hidden in a small street. It's almost invisible from outside, you can easily miss it. The place is dark, lit only by candles. The exuberant decoration makes it look like someone's grandparents' attic, if it weren't for the small tables. I move from one room to another, like in a David Lynch film. No one resembles Celine. I choose a table on the first floor. A moment later, she arrives. A blonde young woman with baby white skin with naturally pink cheeks, light blue eyes, a bit plump, full breasts on display in the plunging neckline of her short satin dress. No more than twenty-three or twenty-four, judging by her looks.

An hour and a half later, I walk her to the underground station and set off on my night wandering. Luckily, it's not very cold. I open Tinder and send a message to Iris,

'Hey!'

'Hey.'

'What are you up to tonight?'

'My bed.'

'Sounds like a great place to be. Do you accept visitors?'

'It depends on the visitor and his motivation.'

'Oh, I can tell you that this visitor is highly motivated.'

'Liar.'

'Why is that?'

'Your date didn't work out?'

'What makes you think I've had a date?'

'What else could it be? It's past eleven, you wouldn't have waited till now to try your chances, would you?'

'Bloody writer!'

'What went wrong?'

'She was too young and too boring.'

'I suppose you weren't looking for a long-term engagement.'

'Boredom is a killer even for short-term ones.'

'True. Why was she boring?'

‘Oh, I don’t know. She wasn’t at all into reading. And she didn’t have enough varied experience from elsewhere to give her any depth.’

‘Depth? For a one-night stand? Don’t make me laugh!’

‘What made you so cynical?’

‘Is giving things their exact names cynicism?’

‘No. Your attitude is.’

‘Please excuse me if my attitude has hurt your feelings.’

‘Ok, you’re pulling my leg now. You’d better tell me where you live.’

‘Sablon.’

‘Let me check… Oh, so close! Shall I come over?’

‘Where are you?’

‘Métropole.’

‘There are a couple of nice bars around there if you want to kill the night.’

‘I don’t want to be killing it. I want to make it memorable.’

‘It already is, isn’t it? I will be your virtual guide tonight. First, stop for a drink at Kafka.’

‘And how about Sablon?’

‘There are a couple of places around here too.’

‘Will you join me at one of them?’

‘I don’t think so.’

Kafka was full. I ordered a bourbon, stood at the bar and opened Tinder again. Like, like and like. Match, match and match. Two more chats commenced immediately. Women in Brussels weren't sleeping. Putting my French into practice with Stephie, English with Maya who is Flemish.

'Hey, did you get lost?' – Iris is back on my screen.

'No, I'm here.'

'Great. How do you like it?'

'It's cool.'

'Describe it to me.'

'It's full. I hear a lot of Flemish. Don't you want to join me?'

'Not tonight.'

'Why aren't you sleeping?'

'I've been reading.'

'What are you reading?'

'Unamuno.'

'Whoever he is.'

'A Spanish philosopher.'

'So you're single?'

'No. My husband is sleeping next to me.'

'Yeah yeah.'

Meanwhile, I've managed to fill the next two evenings. On the following day, I have a date with Stephie, the day after, with Maya.

Unfortunately, neither of them is eager to join me tonight. After a brief exchange, they both disappear.

'Are you still there?' I text Iris.

'Where else could I be. Are *you* still there?'

'Finishing my bourbon.'

'Are you up for more?'

'Always.'

'Your next stop is a former chandelier shop.'

'Interesting. The name?'

'*Bonnafon*.'

I put it on google maps; it's nearby.

With a bourbon in hand, I make my way through the crowd, rocking to the electro-pop rhythm, up the stairs to the second floor where I find a spot by the railing. The splendid chandeliers are the highlight in the otherwise simple decoration, a trace of the past. I scan the crowd beneath. A deep cleavage reveals full bouncing breasts. Their owner looks up and smiles at me. I finish the bourbon in one go, and find myself behind her, our bodies finding a tempo which continues a couple of hours later in my hotel room. In the morning, I message Iris,

'Thanks for the guided tour last night. I had a great time.'

'I don't understand. Why didn't you settle for your date instead of wasting your time only to find more of the same in the end,' says Iris after I have shared my adventures with her, while waiting for Thalys.

'You don't because you aren't a man. Timing and circumstances. Too soon, too straightforward. It's like being served a meal when you aren't hungry yet. No matter how lovely it is, it might not seduce you to taste it. But when you are hungry, even the simplest serving would taste like a real treat, especially if you have to make a bit of an effort to get it.'

‘So you missed your chance to meet me for a simple meal? You disappoint me.’

‘No. It wasn’t a meal that prevented me from seeing you. It was a feast in full swing.’

‘You’ve got me curious. Tell me about it.’

‘What will you give me in return?’

‘What do you want?’

‘A naked photo of you for each story.’

‘You pervert!’

‘I’m not sure who’s the pervert here. The one who fulfils his desires or the one who gets satisfaction from listening to them.’

‘I’m not getting any satisfaction from your sexual adventures. It’s research.’

‘Yeah yeah. And, by the way, you already owe me a photo for the first story.’

‘Too late. It was before you introduced the deal.’

‘But it’s part of the deal if you want me to continue.’

A moment later, a photo. Crossed legs with red toenails.

‘That’s cheating.’

‘You never said that it should be full body.’

‘Okay. You get a pass. Beautiful legs.’

‘Thanks. Your story.’

‘One more photo, Miss.’

The next photo was a close up, dark wavy hair, hiding half of her profile and naked shoulder, the corner of an eyelid, the curve of her lips.

‘I’m starting to hate myself for not meeting you.’

‘Too late Casanova. And the story?’

‘On the following evening, I had a date with Stephie. She picked me up at my hotel and took me for a drive. We did quite a bit of talking.’

‘That was it?’

‘No. She suggested that we get some takeaway and eat in the car. We stopped at a square, I think *Place Jourdan*, where we bought chips and kebabs, then drove to the Palace of Justice, parked there and had dinner enjoying the view. She said it was the best view of Brussels.’

‘Very romantic.’

‘It wasn’t though. She was depressed and only ate about three or four chips. No more! She said she was full. It was weird. She said she didn’t want to put on weight, but she was skinny, her body like a young girl’s, yet she was thirty-four. Tiny and fragile. She told me about her school years when she was bullied about her weight. They called her Winnie the Pooh because she liked eating.’

‘Winnie the Pooh is lovely.’

‘As she was talking, she started crying. I embraced her; her body felt like a piece of paper in my hands. I kissed her and she calmed down.’

‘Your kisses must be magic.’

‘Yeah yeah, that’s what women say all the time. Then we drove some more.’

‘Where?’

'Anywhere. I don't really know. At some point, we saw the ladies of the night on a long street lined with shops, hotels and bars. They stood on the pavement, waiting for clients. "Do you like this one?", she asked and before I was able to answer, she stopped next to one of the girls and got out of the car. She came back in a moment and told me she wanted to offer me a gift, a sexual experience.'

'Now it's getting interesting. Did you accept?'

'No. I said it was weird, but she insisted. She said it would give her a lot of joy and satisfaction. Then I thought, why not? She opened the door and called the girl who sat behind me and started gently massaging my neck. Stephie drove to the end of the street and into a park. We drove on until we reached a large lawn with a lake. She stopped there. I moved to the back seat. The girl was young but very experienced.'

'What did she do?'

'Who is the pervert now?!'

'Don't tease me.'

'She gave me a blow job and when I was close to bursting, she sat on top of me moving up and down quickly. It didn't last long.'

'And Stephie?'

'She looked with eyes wide open, breathing heavily. When it was over, we dropped the girl off where we had picked her up. Stephie drove me to my hotel and kissed me good night. The weirdest experience ever!'

'That is quite a story! And what about Maya?'

'And what about my photo?'

Meanwhile, I had got on the train, and we had arrived in Lille.

A photo message from Iris. This time from the back, dark curls hanging down, a thin waist, the beginning of hips.

'I'm getting off this train and taking the next one back.'

'I'm waiting for you, ha ha. But first tell me the story.'

'Maya. She asked me to take the metro to Simonis and call when I got there. I had to wait for quite some time before she showed up. I was already wondering whether it was a prank. But then a BMW stopped, and a woman got out of it and came towards me. She was in her forties, maybe. Very calm and confident. We drove into a residential area. She parked in front of one of the houses with brightly lit windows. Her living room was huge and almost empty. A red sofa, a thick carpet in front of it and a small table, a large flatscreen TV on the wall, a fireplace with flickering coals. That was more or less it. She said she had moved in recently and had been very busy.'

'What does she do?'

'She runs a consultancy. She took a ready-cooked meal out of the fridge and put it in the microwave. Curry with rice, served on the small table with a bottle of wine. We ate and talked. She was very distant, so distant, that I wondered why she had invited me in the first place. After we had finished the meal, she made popcorn, and we watched a film.'

'Which film?'

'Oh, I don't remember. Some romance. We were just sitting and watching in the darkness; it was bizarre. A good hour passed and then there was a moment when both of us reached out for the popcorn, our hands touched, and then it got wild.'

'Did it?'

'Oh yes. We had sex everywhere.'

'Well done. But this makes half a week.'

'You're right. I saw her two more times.'

'You must have liked her then.'

'She was fun.'

'I'm glad for you. And even more glad for myself that we didn't meet.'

'Why is that?'

'Being one experience among many doesn't appeal to me.'

'But each of them was unique and special.'

'I don't get it…Why couldn't you spend the week with one woman instead of this gross sexual gluttony?'

'I was only in Brussels for the week and I wasn't looking for attachment.'

'Why isn't it possible to have deeper intimacy without attachment? Or see where it takes you?'

'Perhaps, if I had met you, I'd have spent the week just with you.'

'Perhaps. But you didn't.'

'You should have sent me those pics in the first place! I'd have cancelled all my dates.'

'Chance is blind, you know. And if we don't go with it, we might miss it. Enjoy Paris and be careful with your choices! 😉'

We chatted a few more times during my book fair tour, but briefly. Then I was back to Sydney. Ordinary day-to-day life took over and Brussels felt like a distant, weird and very wet dream in which the images of the different women I met blurred into one another under the common denominator of excitement and physical satisfaction. Paradoxically, the only image which stayed distinct and clear in my mind, evoking a mixture of desire and longing, was of the woman I didn't meet.

1030 Schaerbeek

2015

Pauline, Belgian

The girl was around five and had big dark eyes and curly black hair. She wore brown trousers and a green top; she must have been given them in the camp. Her mother was standing next to her; her eyes fixed on my face. She was a bigger version of the girl. Or the other way around. Dark skin, big brown eyes, dark circles under them, long, black straight hair. She wore jeans and a blue pullover. They didn't have any luggage. My daughter and Amadou were on either side of them, like guardian angels.

'Welcome,' I said, 'I am Pauline.'

They didn't say anything.

'This is Layam, and this is her daughter Maryam', my son-in-law said. 'They are exhausted from the journey. They just arrived this morning.'

'Let me show you your room.'

I took them up the stairs, not at all sure what I was getting myself into.

I bought the flat in the early days when it was a nice suburb with a bit of a multicultural twist to it, an oriental and cool air. A bit like Istanbul, which I had visited and had been fully enchanted by its fairytale atmosphere. Why not? I thought. I loved the flat and it was in a predominantly Belgian neighbourhood. The flat was perfect for me and my daughter. A duplex with a large living room, a big terrace, two bedrooms and a spacious second floor with a separate toilet and shower. It was well connected to public transport. There was a supermarket around the corner. I didn't give it a second thought and signed the papers, making myself a resident of the 'city of donkeys.'

Three decades later, it is a totally different place. *Avenue Demolder*, where I live, is still a posh residential street inhabited mainly by white Belgians. In the next street, however, it would feel as if you'd been transported to Turkey were it not for the Art Nouveau architecture. On the tram, I don't see many middle-class people like me. The experience is like being on a trip in a Muslim country, not in my very own capital. Veiled women, men with dark faces and moustaches, teenagers who let everyone know their musical taste by playing music out loud. I look like a stranger in this crowd. A foreigner. That's what really gets me, the feeling of being the odd one out in my own country, in my own city, in my own neighbourhood. I was here before them. They were the newcomers, the ones who settled in my home and took over, making it resemble a Turkish-Arabic colony. And now it feels as if we, the Catholic Belgians, should submit to their ways rather than the other way around. It is we who don't belong here which is so hard to put up with.

In the supermarket and their local shops, they speak a language I don't understand, or at most bad French. I almost feel as if I have to learn their language in order to be integrated into their community which is my commune. How absurd is that!

And this is just a snapshot of what has been happening to my dear capital in the last few decades with the European Union and globalism. Brussels is no longer Belgian, no more ours with the invasion of foreigners who don't understand, respect or try to acknowledge our culture. It's either the so-called multicultural milieu of expats or the segregated communities where one culture is the overwhelming norm, and it happens to be not our culture either! There is no escape.

Maybe I am exaggerating. There are still areas which look and feel Belgian. Like Uccle. But this has changed too since the French started moving there to avoid paying taxes in France. Wine bars sprang up like mushrooms after rain. I like wine and it's not that I mind the French so much. We do speak the same language even though, if you ask them, they will tell you a different story. But this is their arrogance that I most dislike about them.

Uccle is, perhaps, where I feel most at home, it reminds me of the good old days. My friends there organise these dinners. We start with an aperitif — champagne, cava, white port — and some finger food. Then we enjoy a four or five course menu. It's so elegant, exquisite, classy. Often, they hire a chef for the evening, which makes it even more special. And the conversations are easy, relaxed, enriching. We talk about restaurants, hotels, sauna complexes, holiday plans. None of us is much into travelling. We stick to our good old ways – the Ardennes have it all without embarking on exhausting flights. Knokke is as good a resort as any you can find in Italy or Spain. And people are the same as you. The farthest we go is France. Provence is the place to be. We rent a house with a swimming pool and indulge ourselves with wine, cheese, bread, foie gras, *la joie de vivre*. We bring our lovers, partners, children. It's a blast. I dated a Frenchman who lived in Uccle a couple of summers ago. He had a yacht in Zeeland, and we spent weekends there. We would leave on Friday and have dinner with his fellow yacht owners on one of their vessels. A totally different world, on water, always on the move. We sailed during the day, anchored somewhere and made love in the little cabin. What a life. But the summer ended, and our affair faded away. He wasn't the kind of man to settle with one woman, particularly with the whole young international crowd out there. *C'est la vie*. It was what it was, and I enjoyed it while it lasted.

As you can see, I don't have much of a life in Schaerbeek. During the day I am at work. I teach French in Montjoie secondary school in Uccle. And when I am in here, I spend my time at home, in my own artistic oasis. But not anymore. My daughter of all people managed to invade my world with multiculturalism in ways which I could hardly have imagined.

As a child, Brigitte didn't mix much with the kids on the block as we were always with our own kind. Things changed when she went to university. First, she moved out to live in Etterbeek with her then boyfriend, an Italian guy. Later she rented a place in Chaussée d'Ixelles where she gave shelter to a Bulgarian *stagiaire*. Iris. She brought her for lunch once. The first Eastern European I had ever met. She was disappointingly normal. She knew all the writers and other artists I mentioned. She was well dressed. She talked with ease about communism but kept calling it socialism, which I found somewhat annoying. 'We were constantly building communism, but we never saw it happen,' she laughed. I am not sure what I was expecting but certainly something more exotic. Frightening stories from her dark communist past. Traumatic experiences. The insecurity of a wild animal in a civilised environment. Nothing like that. Instead, she talked about her lovely childhood, a hybrid of weeks in a village in a wild mountain and months in a seaside resort where her parents used to work, and she was able to meet and play with foreign kids. I was bored and didn't invite her again. I never imagined that she would be the Trojan horse who would deliver the biggest defeat of my life. Back then she left Belgium, and I didn't hear anything about her for years. But Bulgaria joined the Union, and she returned. My daughter kept me up to date about her life. She was newly divorced now and worked as a journalist. It was via her that Brigitte met Amadou, seven years ago. During Iris' house move.

I look at my daughter and wonder if she really is mine. Where did this come from, her crush on religion and need to save the world, as if the world could be saved. Certainly not by me. Me, I am way too busy with the mission to save my own world, a world of beauty, elegance, art, comfort, all the virtues of good old Brussels. The city of Horta and Van Buuren. Van Buuren was Dutch, but we can forgive him that for the beautiful house he has left behind. I visit it on summer days, contemplating the stylish interior and beautiful paintings, meditating in the garden. Such peace and harmony. Nothing like the insulting mess of Schaerbeek.

Brigitte and I had a big fight when she told me. I couldn't stay still. I walked back and forth and shouted. Brigitte shouted back and slammed the door behind her. We didn't speak for a couple of weeks. Finally, I sent her a message and invited them for lunch.

The next slap in the face was when Brigitte informed me of her decision to become a Muslim. As if living with an African Muslim was not enough! This time I didn't shout. I only covered my face and cried quietly. In turn, she covered both her hair and face with a veil and kept it that way for a while.

'Is he pushing you to do these things?' I asked her in desperation.

'You don't understand, Mum,' she said. 'You never did. Amadou doesn't push me into anything. He loves and respects me. I felt this call from Allah inside me and discovered the beauty of Islam. This is my decision and mine alone. Ever since I became Muslim, I feel peaceful and connected to God. Catholicism didn't do this for me. In the mosque, in my prayers, I become one with the source. As for the burqa, I wanted to experience this; to understand why women do it. And now, I know. You cannot imagine, Mum, how peaceful it is to go beyond vanity, to hide your face and your inner world. It's a feeling of protection, serenity and bliss. And no, I won't do so every day. When I have the need, I will do it. But not every day, not always.'

When you are dying of thirst, even the tiniest drops give some relief.

I went to the wedding but spared my friends the details. Iris was my daughter's maid of honour, and I had to make a big effort to stay civilised and not thank her for the favour. Then I went to Senegal for the African wedding. What an experience that was! His family lived in a brick bungalow, parents and grandmother together in one room and a small kitchen. The kitchen didn't resemble in any way a Western kitchen. They didn't have any electrical appliances and cooked on a gas stove. It was absolute poverty, depressing! But the thing which struck me most was that they didn't seem unhappy, not at all. They radiated joy and something very healthy, vibrant. We stayed in a tourist camp near the village, which also consisted of brick bungalows but thank God, we didn't have to bunk together! It was clean but shabby, worse than a hostel in my part of the world. It was a Muslim village, but women did not cover their hair, not the way they do it in the Arabic countries. Many were wearing turbans, others were not, and their black hair shone in the sun. The wedding was a spectacle. Brigitte went with Amadou's sisters to get ready. He had countless brothers and sisters. We were all waiting outdoors under the scorching sun. I was glad I had a hat with me. Everyone was staring at me, and it seemed that they were openly discussing me. The women touched my MaxMara dress and giggled. I was smiling at them as much as I could, considering they might have called me anything without me understanding. My daughter arrived in a caravan of cars which one would not even see in a breaker's yard in Europe, literally falling apart. She was unrecognisable with the heavy glittering makeup they had put on her eyelids, her braided hair, huge earrings and a long blue dress made of lace and silk. She was not herself anymore. But I must admit she was gorgeous. She looked at me and her eyes were sparkling. She smiled widely, her lips in intense pink lipstick. Amadou, in a traditional robe, and his other male guests started dancing. It was fascinating, like being transported into a documentary on African tribes like they show on National Geographic and the BBC. Brigitte and Amadou were brought together and after saying their vows, whatever they were, they were married. His family was smiling and talking to me in their mess of a language. I tried to smile and nod back. These are my new relatives, *voilà*! *Félicitations*! We cannot understand each other at all, but maybe it's better that way. After all, what could we possibly talk about? Holiday plans? I can't imagine they've ever been on holiday in their lives, nor would they ever have one. And I'm afraid my expertise in cattle is somewhat limited. Anyway, we will probably never meet again. Brigitte and Amadou left with his male friends once the ceremony was over. I was left in the middle of a frenzy of dancing women in long colourful dresses and men in dark trousers and white shirts. I found a chair to sit on in the shadow of a tree and inevitably thought of the day I got married myself. The solemn church of *Abbaye de la Cambre*, my white dress, made especially for me, the tenderness in the eyes of Pierre. That one day, when my being, my young-naïve-and-so-in-love-being, was overwhelmed with hope.

I have lunch with the young family every fortnight. They bought a flat in Schaerbeek too. After all, she is my only daughter. She seems happy, so I suppose I should be happy too. This is not what I had in mind for her, but it's her life, not mine. Amadou isn't bad, after all. He's always very polite and respectful, and regularly brings me flowers. There are worse situations in life. I certainly know that. Besides, they have delivered another mixed-race child into this world, my granddaughter Amaya. Every Wednesday I pick her up from school and we spend some quality time together. She is adorable.

There might be worse things in life, and I might have put up with things, but peace is what I am lacking most these days. Each time I get used to a change, something new pops up.

*

The refugee crisis hit Belgium and, suddenly, Brussels was flooded with Arabs, as if we didn't have enough! Men with dusky faces and veiled women. The area around *Gare de Midi* turned into a camp. Dirty mattresses put straight on the pavement under the bridge, men, women and children lying on them, covered with blankets. The Maximillian Park has become asylum seeker territory too. Reception centres were set up and Amadou got a job in one of them. He speaks Arabic, which, of course, is helpful for communicating with these people, most of whom do not speak any other language.

Brigitte called me early this week and said she wanted to ask me a favour. The reception centre where Amadou works had started a programme to arrange short-term stays for migrants with Belgian families. And here comes the so-called favour (there are better words to describe this: sacrifice, blackmailing), Brigitte asked me to host a Syrian woman and her little daughter as I 'have got space.' It's very easy to see space when it comes to other people. As if it is about the actual space. My mental space is just enough for me, as I am. And there I certainly don't have room for others, particularly strangers. For a couple of weeks, she says. Even a couple of days sounds too much. And weeks will quickly turn into months; it's always like that. I refused at first. But Brigitte wouldn't take 'no' for an answer. That's my girl. Can't blame her. "You have to, Mum, think of these people! They have crossed a cold sea, risking their lives, and then, in Europe, they've moved from one camp to another to get here. And the conditions in the reception centre are terrible, terrible! She's a woman and a mother like you and her little daughter has been exposed to all that. They need somewhere safe and normal. I would have taken them myself, but you know how small our flat is." Yeah. I saw how Amadou's relatives live; he's certainly used to it. But it's easier, of course, to use the mother-in-law who's 'got space.' Damn it! Why don't they migrate to countries nearby? Why didn't they stay in Turkey where they're all Muslims? Why do they have to invade our cities and turn my beloved Brussels into an Arabic enclave? She comes up with a melodramatic story, this woman's husband and her other three children are already in the UK; she and her little daughter only need to stay in Belgium until their documents are arranged so that they can join the rest of the family.

'*D'accord*,' I say after a long silence. 'A couple of weeks, that's it!'

And now they're here.

I showed them the room, explained everything about the bathroom and the kitchen. Amadou translated. The mother nodded and said something in her language. Amadou translated that they were deeply grateful for my mercy. The daughter went to the bed and lay on it with her shoes still on, her little legs hanging over the side.

We left them and went downstairs. Amadou and Brigitte thanked me too as if I had voluntarily offered this arrangement. I just murmured something in return and asked them about my granddaughter. Then they were gone.

My visitors didn't appear all day, nor did I hear any sound coming from upstairs. They must be sleeping, Amadou said, they had just arrived this morning. Towards the evening, I heard faint movement and whispering. But still they didn't come down. Finally, I went upstairs and brought them some of the soup I had prepared. My special pumpkin soup with some bread.

They were lying in bed, the girl cuddling into her mother. She beamed when she saw me and said something in her language.

'*Un peu de soupe*,' I said.

'*Manger*,' I added and made a gesture imitating eating.

The mother got up and took it from me, saying something which I suppose meant 'thank you.'

'*Merci*,' I told her, 'We say *merci* here.'

'*Merci*,' she repeated.

In the morning, I baked an apple pie. I must admit my apple pie is delicious. I have a secret recipe which makes it like no other. I waited to hear some movement upstairs, then cut three pieces, put them on a tray with coffee for the mother and hot chocolate for the girl and took them upstairs. The mother was sitting on a pillow on the wooden floor, with her eyes closed; a sun ray, coming through the roof window, resting on her face. The daughter sat next to her. Both of them wore the same clothes, I noticed. The mother opened her eyes.

'Did you sleep well?' I closed my eyes and put a hand on the side of my face, imitating a pillow.

The mother nodded and said something in return.

I left the tray on the table.

'*Petit déjeuner.*'

'*Merci*,' said the mother.

'*Merciiii*,' repeated the daughter joyfully.

I started preparing my lessons for the afternoon, but I couldn't focus, so I went to my room and opened the wardrobe. Among my multitude of dresses, a blue one seemed suitable. It covered the knees and didn't have cleavage. Should do. I also got out a pair of thick grey tights and a pair of comfortable leather shoes.

The mother was still sitting in the same position, with eyes closed. I gave her the clothes. She smiled for the first time; her smile was a little sad. She got up and took them.

'*Merci.*'

Amadou came to pick them up to go to the authorities for their documents. The mother looked beautiful in my blue dress. I told her,

'*Vous êtes très belle!*'

Amadou interpreted. She glanced at me with her big dark eyes,

'*Merci.*'

On Friday, I have dinner with a friend in Uccle. Samantha is a divorcee; she owns a boutique in Ixelles and cherishes the good things in life. Like exquisite food and wine. We eat in a small Italian restaurant. She does most of the talking, mainly about her business, some issues with the tax authorities and the parties she has been to lately.

'By the way, there is one tonight', she says, 'a special one. It's called Barbarella. And I'm taking you there.'

The party is in an old theatre in Uccle. The dim lighting creates an intimate vibe in the dark hall. We order some cava and remain standing near the bar. Everyone seems to be either French-speaking Belgians or French. Two men come to say 'hello' to Samantha; she introduces me to them. They order a bottle of cava and share it with us. One of them, Gaston, is from Lille, but he lives in Brussels. He is a manager of a high-tech company, divorced, a father of two young men. He has recently been on safari to Namibia with his sons and it was awesome. That's all I get to know about him before the music gets louder, and people start dancing. Gaston grabs my hand and pulls me onto the dance floor. I feel his breath on my face when he gets closer. In the morning, his scent is all over my body. I slip away so as not to wake him up. At home I take a long shower, then go to bed.

I wake up at noon with a terrible headache, get up and go to the kitchen. There is a plate on the table, some bulgur wheat dish with vegetables. First a coffee, then lunch. The meal melts in my mouth, a mixture of flavours. To be waited on in my own house... not bad. I knock on my guests' door, the mother opens.

'*Merci pour le repas*,' I say, showing my mouth, 'It was delicious.'

She shows me some herbs. I have none of them.

'Where did you get them?'

She points in the direction of Chaussée d'Helmet. Schaerbeek is very diverse. There is the Schaerbeek of the eurocrats, mainly around Diamant, Plasky, Meiser with some posh buildings, squares, green areas, trendy restaurants and bars. There is also a part of Schaerbeek which is largely populated by Belgians like me who bought flats or houses here years ago. My beautiful street is like an oasis of Western culture among the prevailing orientalism. *Square Riga* and *Avenue Huart Hamoir* again are predominantly white middle class, as is the area around the *Parc Josaphat*. Between its town hall and the centre, Schaerbeek accommodates many shops and restaurants but it's more derelict and often referred to as 'Little Anatolia' due to the predominant Turkish population. And then there is the neighbourhood around *Chaussée d'Helmet*. It's a long street full of small local shops, fast food places and restaurants. It's all very depressing and sad over there. So I avoid it as much as I can. But my visitors seemed to have liked it.

I had some free time that Saturday afternoon and spent a couple of hours going through my clothes. I found two more dresses to give to the mother. One in a checkered pattern and one in burgundy. I added two pairs of earrings, small ones and hanging ones. She thanked me in her humble way, looked at them and put them aside.

On Sunday, Brigitte, Amadou and my granddaughter came for lunch.

'Mum, shall we ask Layam and Maryam to join us?'

How could I say, no, it's a family lunch without sounding like a sour puss? How could I explain that this wasn't how I imagined my family would be, a mixture of colours, races and religions. Life has its unpredictable trajectories, which we follow like figures in a board game. But who throws the dice? And whose is the hand that moves us on the board?

The mother wore the burgundy dress and the small earrings. She looked so elegant and poised, nothing like the shell of a human being who had stood in my hallway just a couple of days previously. Amadou had brought a bag with clothes for the daughter, hand-me-downs from Amaya. Maryam immediately delved into it, found a yellow dress, ran upstairs and put it on. Mother and daughter, real ladies, who'd have guessed.

I had prepared pumpkin soup, a fish pie with salad and a chocolate cake. Everyone seemed to like the food. Amadou was conversing with the mother in their incomprehensible language, the daughter was playing with Amaya, Brigitte ate some of the food and then asked the mother, Layam, will you tell us how you got here? Amadou interpreted the question. The mother stared straight ahead, through the window, as if she could see it all there, and started talking. Her voice was lilting, followed by Amadou's, translating her words and thus becoming the voice of her story.

'The boat was a walnut shell, crammed with people. It was lurching and shaking, entirely at the mercy of the ever-changing waves; colourful dresses and *jellabas*, toys on the floor, children playing, being noisy, joyful, sad, laughing, crying, tormenting the cat who hissed and ran away; a husband, a dinner, eating together, a flat screen tv, the news, and then a war, just a word like any other word, but then the shooting, the bodies, the fear, the ruins, our parents giving us all their money, telling us, run, run for your life, save your children! That's how from land, a house, a home you end up in a car at night, crossing the Turkish border and then on a boat, among strangers, crammed in the boat, heading to our exile or death. Ruzgar and our three older children had left first.'

'That must have been awful...' Amadou translated my words. 'I'm sorry. I interrupted you.'

'That's ok,' Amadou interpreted. Layam continued.

'The embrace, the tears, the children crying, Ruzgar's kiss on my temple, Allah be with you and see you, see you, on this earth or after. Waiting and praying and more waiting for days before the call comes through. Why are you crying, mommy, Maryam asks. From happiness, my love, from happiness, your father is fine, your sister and brothers, they're all fine. From the camp in Greece, they will continue to England. Maryam and I will join them there when they are settled. But when would this be? Months passed and nothing happened. They had reached England, but it wasn't possible to arrange for us to go. No income, no proper home, no permission. If you want to be with your wife, go back home, he was told. But home didn't exist anymore, home wasn't back there, it was nowhere. Ruzgar had left me money for the journey, so we followed them, ending up on that boat.'

The tension was almost unbearable. Layam's dark eyes still stared out of and beyond the window.

'The sea is mighty and unpredictable. The terror, the thirst, the hunger, the prayer – those are our possessions now. I pray day and night to Allah to save us, for my whole family to be together again, on safe land. Before the trip, we are handed a bit of food and a bottle of water each. I have a couple of bites per day, just to keep me going, the rest is for my girl, my brave little girl, who holds me tight, and doesn't complain, suddenly having to become too wise too soon praying with me or whispering, mommy, the moon, the stars, so many of them, the sun waking up and rising, does it sleep in the sea, mommy. Time stands still, all that we are left with are the waves, the wind, the prayers, the tales from the Quran I tell to Maryam, I whisper them, and this, the boat, the sea, and we in it, is a tale as well, we're now characters, and we'll always remember and share this story, in our new home with your father, brothers and sister and new friends. But I want my old friends, I know, my love, I know, one day we'll return and you'll see them again, but now we're going on a new adventure, to a new life, a new language, new friends, it will be wonderful, you'll see, you'll love it. The other people, so close, pushed against each other, so many of us, men, women, children, connected in our fear, suffering and hopes. Then one morning, there is land at the horizon. Is it a mirage, is it the hunger, I ask myself, or is it true that Allah has saved us and soon we will be on safe land. We're in Greece, they tell us, it could be anywhere, I almost faint when I step on the earth, someone's hands hold me, the warm meal in the camp, the bed in the tent, it's true, we are saved.'

'And then?'

'The first thing is to call Ruzgar. A deep sigh and choked back tears. I'd never heard him crying. The children, asking questions to which I have no answers. When will we see you, mummy? When… A few days in the camp, I want to reach Ruzgar. Go to Belgium, they tell me, it will be easier from there. They organise our travel by bus; we cross cities, ordered, nice cities, without war; it's all very different, distant, unknown, and a couple of days later we arrive in Brussels, go to the reception centre, where Allah meets us with Amadou and you, madam, and your enormous generosity, which we won't ever forget.'

Layam reached out for her phone and showed us a photo of a man with a pleasant face, herself and three children. She held a baby in her hands. That was Maryam, she said. They stood among beautiful gardens with palm trees and flowers.

'Aleppo', she said.

'*C'est jolie, ta famille.*' I pointed to her eyes, then to the photo, you will see them soon.

And then we are all silent. The lunch is over, Brigitte, Amadou and my granddaughter leave, I go to my bedroom and google Aleppo. I find a series of photos, showing places before and after the war. I see richness, cultural heritage, beauty, covered markets, a majestic square, lush gardens with palm trees, as if straight from 'Arabian Nights', lively restaurants and cafés, modern buildings, everything now in ruins. As for the people killed, the numbers are horrific.

I try to take a nap but cannot get Layam's voice out of my head, saying words in a language I don't understand about experiences I cannot imagine.

*

Amadou was helping Layam with her application to join her husband in England, but it was all very slow. She didn't have any documents and getting a residency card in Belgium would take a long time. And even with this card, she wasn't allowed to travel. Her husband, already legal in the UK, was continuing with his attempts to get her there but they were going nowhere. Weeks went by without any change in the situation.

Layam and I got used to understanding each other by using gestures. She and Maryam would come down to my living room, sit on the sofa and we would watch TV or Netflix together. I often invited them to eat with me in the evening and we shared what we had cooked. Sometimes Layam's phone would ring, she would get up, go to the window and talk quietly. At times, I could hear tears in her voice.

Once I joined them as they went shopping in *Chaussée de Helmet*. Just like that, out of curiosity. It felt a bit like an adventure, like being on a trip to a foreign land in your own municipality. The Turkish men who worked there greeted them in a friendly way, apparently they knew them by now. We got fruits, vegetables, nuts and seasonings, which were really '*bon marché*' and walked back home. Chaussée d'Helmet wasn't so depressing, after all.

*

I wanted to take Layam and Maryam to a different place, for a change. Little Maryam especially could certainly do with some fun. Train World had been recently opened in the railway station of Schaerbeek and sounded like good entertainment. But it was more than that. It was like entering a time machine, taking us back to the day when the first passenger train ever on the European continent ran between Brussels and Mechelen, and sending us into the far future with trains resembling spacecraft, crossing ultra-modern landscapes of glass, concrete and water at the speed of light.

An eternal night had fallen in the halls where the oldest steam trains were on display, ready to depart with us onboard, their sole passengers without luggage nor destination. Small screens, attached to the overhead luggage racks, showed people embarking on these same trains in the daylight of a different time. Maryam was in awe; she took a seat in one of the compartments and said 'daddy' in French, looking at her mother and me with anticipation. Layam's eyes glistened.

In another room, time materialised in numerous clocks, took over the space. Wooden clocks, coloured in orange, dark brown, green, standing like guardians of time. A note informed us that all clocks in Belgium were synchronised because of the advent of trains so that they could introduce a national timetable. The thought that once every single village, town and city had its own time was fascinating. Layam was looking at the clocks with a serious face. Was she thinking of the trapped, encapsulated time of her stay in Belgium, while outside its borders the time in which she was away from her husband and children was passing? I didn't dare ask.

There was a hall devoted to the workers in the railway system through the years, built around the authentic house in which the stationmaster used to live with his family, with a bike parked in front, as if its inhabitants were to appear any moment. We entered the house which, indeed, created the illusion of a place still lived in. Through the window of the door in the dark hallway, we saw a staircase leading to the bedroom with a tiny teddy bear, forgotten, on it. Layam held Maryam up and showed her the bear, she smiled and said something. The last hall had large glass windows showing the tracks outside, coming together and then going their separate ways. We sat on a red bench next to the window. Maryam wandered around the trains.

‘*Ma vie maintenant’*, said Layam quietly and nodded in the direction of a train, inside the museum, mounted on rails which continued beyond the glass windows, stretching into the outside world, but ending on a buffer stop. Next to them, other tracks, serving real trains, reached towards the horizon. A fast train flashed by. Layam’s eyes followed it till it disappeared. On the way out, we walked by contemporary locomotives. Layam caressed the muzzle of a Eurostar train as if it were the sculpture of a saint which people touch hoping to get their prayers answered.

*

‘So what’s new with you?’ Samantha asked. We were having dinner with friends in Uccle.

‘I still have my Syrian guests…’

‘I hadn’t realised you had friends in Syria.’ This was Annette, the host.

‘I don’t. My daughter and son-in-law asked me to host a Syrian refugee mother and her little daughter till they are able to make it to the UK where the rest of the family is. You know, I have never been fond of the idea of refugees and expats flooding our country, when we already have entire municipalities which look like the third world… But having Layam and Maryam around made me realise what horror these people live in over there and wonder what their options are...’

‘That’s indeed very sad,’ Samantha replied, ‘But there is nothing we can do about it. We cannot give shelter to all those people who come here, without education, without anything, to contaminate our culture with their habits and religion.'

'So what do you suggest? That we let them die?'

'I'm not suggesting anything. I even sympathise with them but we cannot solve all the problems in the world. Besides, I have enough problems of my own.'

'That's too depressing a topic for a Thursday night,' Annette interrupted us, 'And, I am afraid, we won't find an answer to this grave problem tonight. If there were a solution, they could have come up with it themselves, instead of fighting for years. Anyway, guess where Pierre and I are going this winter!'

I left soon after, saying I was tired. I had a missed call from Brigitte and called her back when I reached home.

'Mum, I want to talk to you about Layam and Maryam.'

'Has anything happened? They seemed fine last night. I didn't see them this morning, as I left early and…'

'No, no, but that's the problem. Nothing has happened, weeks are passing, and they are stuck in Brussels.'

This was a bit offensive. As if they weren't quite comfortably lodged at my place, especially when one looks at those photos on the internet.

'Layam's husband has found someone to take them to England.'

'You mean smuggle them.'

'Whatever you call it, I mean she is joining her husband and children, that's what I mean. This could happen in two weeks. But they haven't got the money. The guy would charge 2,500 euros for her and Maryam. They've only got around one thousand.'

'Aha. And?'

'Iris came up with a brilliant idea.'

And here comes Iris' 'brilliant' idea, to organise a fundraising dinner and invite people who could donate money for Layam's trip, which, and that's the most interesting part, will be hosted by me, as I've got space and friends who are 'well off'. Such a strategist, this Iris, bravo!

'Mum, are you still there?'

'Yeah, I am. Just trying to process the information.'

'It's only one evening. But it could help change the life of a family.'

'You got the wrong job, daughter. Why didn't you become a solicitor or a lawyer?'

'Mum, I'm serious. Will you do it?'

'You mean tell my friends that I am looking for donations to smuggle a refugee woman and her child?'

'No. I mean, let us prepare the dinner at your place and host everyone willing to donate. We can package it nicely. What do you say? We want to offer a ticket of 75 euros per person. Twenty people will get us there.'

'Twenty people? How would I seat them?'

'Don't be silly, mum. It will be a buffet.'

'And what shall we say to these people? What will they be donating for?'

'For helping Layam's family have a decent start in England. They will have all sort of costs you know… Of course, we wouldn't mention anything about… the smuggling.'

'Right. I hope you realise what you're asking me to do and what you're getting yourself into. This is…'

'Mum! Will you do it or not?'

'I will, for God's sake! What else…'

'Thank you! You're a treasure! Talk to you tomorrow.'

And she hung up. I poured myself a whisky. What wouldn't we do for our children…?

The date was set in two weeks. Iris prepared invitations, I must admit they looked very professional. She had put the photo which Layam showed to me on the front, with the following question, *Will you help this family be together again? Enjoy delicious food while making this happen.* On the other side was the menu.

I sent it to my friends, but only Samantha and one other lady said they would come. I got many excuses which I didn't bother to reply to. The children, a long-planned dinner, theatre, trip… I know all that too well. Brigitte, Iris and Amadou shared it in their networks and Layam took a couple of invitations when she went shopping. By the Thursday before, we had managed to get fifteen guests. Two of Iris' colleagues from the news agency couldn't make it but transferred the money nevertheless.

On Saturday, two weeks before Christmas, my living room turned into a cooking workshop. Brigitte and Amadou had done the shopping the previous day. Brigitte, Iris, Alice and another young woman, Sheila, whom I had not met, came in the morning and took over my kitchenette. Layam and I joined them. Brigitte had printed the recipes, and we distributed them among ourselves. I was in charge of the stuffed peppers. Actually, it was fun. We cooked and talked and laughed and the funniest thing of all was that even Layam with whom we didn't have a common language was fully participating. Only Sheila was able to communicate with her in Arabic but all the rest of us managed to interact with gestures and facial expressions, as we had been doing all this time.

We put two tables end to end to make a long one in the middle of the room. The girls had brought red candles which they put everywhere. I had got my regular supply of fresh flowers, displayed in two vases. We were ready well before the planned time. The guests started arriving soon after 7pm. It was a mixed group of people, whom, to be honest, I would not have imagined seeing under the same roof, especially not under my roof. Let me see who was there. Sheila's Walonese boyfriend, Alice's Flemish boyfriend, some friends and colleagues of Iris – a Croatian woman who worked for the Commission, loved art and spoke beautiful French, an English editor who had lived in Eastern Europe, a German reporter who had covered the situation in Syria, my friends Samantha and Jessica, a Turkish family who owned a grocery shop in Chaussée d'Helmet, invited by Layam, Amadou's friend Mustapha. There were nineteen of us and I ended up paying a little extra. One dress less, who cares.

I don't remember when I last had so much fun. Even Samantha and Jessica seemed to enjoy it, and I bet both would file this under the chapter 'exotic experiences,' but whatever it was, I appreciated them being there.

When everyone had left, Layam came to me, her eyes with sparkling. She held my hands and said,

'*Merci, merci, merci, merci*!' We embraced each other.

In the morning, I felt like doing something resembling a normal family Sunday instead of the last Sunday in Brussels for my guests. Yet, I did want it to be special. We had a brunch at home and in the early afternoon I took Layam and Maryam to *Maison Autrique*, the first house built by Horta in Brussels, which happened to be in Schaerbeek. I hadn't been there for years, so it was as much a treat for myself as for them.

We climbed up the wooden stairs and entered its world of simple elegance. In the bedroom, Layam stopped in front of the huge painting depicting white birds flying up from the darkness to the blue strip of sky behind the dark clouds. It was a vertical painting which created an illusion of depth thanks to the play between darkness and light and the layers of clouds, but other than that, nothing spectacular. I don't know what she saw in it and that she would pay attention to a piece of art at all surprised me a bit. Maryam got very excited in the attic where Axel Wappendorf had worked for years on his strange inventions. All sorts of odd objects were grouped together, including a male mannequin with a mask and various maps. It gave a bit of a sinister impression, to be honest, but

Maryam seemed unaffected. We were the only visitors, which made the experience really a bit special. Afterwards, we wandered around. It was a crisp but sunny day. It was a different Schaerbeek again around *Saint Servais* church and *Avenue Louis Bertrand* with its green areas and pretty houses. We strolled down to the playground where Maryam immediately started playing with other kids while Layam and I sat on a bench and watched.

Three days later, Layam had packed their few possessions. At dusk, a man with dark skin came to pick them up. Brigitte, Amadou and I were there like on the first day, in the corridor. I gave Layam a firm hug, took Maryam and kissed her cheeks, she giggled, more hugs and kisses while the guy was standing there with an expressionless face.

'Make sure that they reach their family safely,' I told him, and this wasn't exactly a request. He looked me in the eyes, saying nothing.

Every day I checked with Amadou whether he had heard from Layam. Finally, after three or four days, a photo appeared on my mobile with her family in it. I sent it to everyone who contributed to their journey. Every so often I get a photo from her – of her children, of her with Ruzgar, of their new life.

*

It's spring now. On a Sunday, Samantha and I are having a glass of wine in a brasserie in *Avenue Louis Bertrand*, I take a selfie for Layam and toast to life.

1000 Brussels - Marolles

2015

Bojana, Croatian

She was waiting for me on the landing, leaning over the railing. First, I noticed her expressive eyes and the dark curls framing her face. When I reached her floor, I saw her in full, my height, slim body, a regal posture. The apartment suited her. A long living room with window walls at both ends and balconies. One of the balconies was as big as a room and overlooked *Rue Haute.* I imagined our evenings there, both of us doing our own thing, her child playing, perhaps the huge flat TV screen is on, a family idyll. She offered me tea. Later on, she would only offer me wine.

As we had the tea, I tried to introduce myself briefly. Who I am. What I do. Why I am here. What my hobbies are. She seemed to be listening attentively.

She showed me the room. It was spacious with a king-size bed in the middle. White cupboard with boxes and drawers covered one of the walls. There was a small table, a thick carpet in autumn colours and a big standing mirror in a white frame. Another one hung on the wall facing the bed. The room had a high ceiling with a triangular cone. And windows over my bed. I would have the starry sky and the moon all for myself at night.

'I like you,' she said in her English with a French accent, 'But let me wait until tomorrow. I am like that. I always need to think about things.'

But on the following day, her phone was switched off. I tried a few more times and left her a message. The hope and enthusiasm I had felt after my visit vanished. My search had to continue.

A few days later – a call. She said her phone had not been working. She wanted to rent me the room but first needed to discuss a couple of things. A sequence of messages and calls followed in fruitless attempts to arrange to meet. But, somehow, it never worked out.

I had been seconded to the Commission from the Ministry of Economics in Zagreb. The Ministry was paying for a hotel for a couple of weeks until I found a place. I didn't know anyone in Brussels. I planned to rent a room for two to three months to I give myself a bit more time to look for a proper flat. But finding a place with acceptable conditions turned out to be a challenge. There was a huge demand and not enough availability.

After spending two hours in a rainy evening queueing to visit a tiny studio next to Flagey, whose tiny toilet-bathroom had no door but a curtain, and after hearing the conditions of the owner – a three-year contract and three-month rent deposit – I quickly confirmed another flat, comprising of a kitchen, a salon and a large bedroom with a single bed. Destiny had it that it was situated in *Rue Blaes*, very close to where Diane lived. The room full of light coming through the large windows facing the street did the trick. I left a five-hundred-euro deposit with Hasan, the Moroccan guy who rented it out, and we shook hands.

A week later, I was moving in. When I entered the flat, Hasan was there.

'Listen,' he said, 'My situation has changed. My girlfriend and I've just broken up, so I had to move back in. But don't worry, you can use the room. I will adapt the living room for myself.'

I stared at him, looking for signs that he was joking. He wasn't.

'And what if I don't agree?'

'I'm afraid I will have to keep your deposit. There've been many people calling since you confirmed. I cannot afford to pay all the rent myself at the moment. I'm broke.'

I went into my room and attempted to close the door behind me without much success. I went back to him, 'It's impossible to close the door.'

'I know… I'll fix it.'

'When?'

'As soon as I can.'

I sat on the bed and looked at my unpacked luggage. How had I found myself in this situation?

I took out my pills. Two for emergencies. The doorbell rang, and I heard another male voice, followed by a knock on my door.

'Sorry, but it will be noisy in the next couple of hours. We are building me a hut in the living room. Let me introduce you to my friend, Andrew,' said Hasan.

Andrew, who looked European, stood next to him with some timber in his hands. I nodded and went back to my room only to change, grab a book and leave.

It was Sunday lunchtime, the weather was dry, and the flea market at *Place de Jeu de Balle*, around the corner, was at its peak. People moved slowly, in lines, between the sheets, spread straight on the pavement, with all sorts of objects on them – from porcelain figurines, old jewellery, clothes, accessories and books to furniture. It was a treasure trove of organised chaos. I could lose myself in its richness, observing and holding the objects, imagining that they could take me to other times and places. The cafés around the market were full and a jazz band was performing in the usual corner. I was taken by the bohemian and carefree air. I loved that imaginary oasis of sweet amnesia about the existence of other places, people, times. *The Marolles is full of surprises*, Iris would later say in an article. This I already knew, finding myself trapped in a flat with a Moroccan man.

Her article compared the Marolles to the Underland of the fairy tales to which the hero is taken by a black ram. There he experiences different challenges or finds magical objects, which would then help him go back to the Upperland (again on the back of a ram, but this time, for a change, a white one) to triumph over his enemies and win the princess. In Brussels, the ram has been transformed into a glass lift which takes you from the luxurious upper world of *Avenue Louise* to the magical Underland of the

Marolles. And now I am this hero and the princess who has to be saved is also me.

I went to the *Pin Pon* café, situated in the former fire station, and in the spur of the moment sent a message to Diane,

‘I am still interested in the room and happen to be very close to you now. May I come over?’

‘So nice to hear from you! Of course.’, she replied immediately.

Shortly after, I was sitting again in her beautiful living room.

‘The thing is that since the last time we met a man has rented the room. He is staying for two more weeks. But if you wish to move in sooner, I could clear my daughter’s room for you. She’s staying with her father at the moment. It’s tiny, but it will be fine for sleeping. What do you think?’

I said I'd think about it and let her know the next day. Diane smiled and nodded.

‘I like you. You’re of my kind.’

I didn’t know what her kind was, but it was reassuring to hear that she still liked me and would give me shelter if need be. This calmed me down a bit and I returned to what I couldn’t call home yet.

There was now a hut in the middle of the living room. Andrew was next to it, with a hammer in his hand. Hasan appeared from within the hut.

‘Isn’t it good?’ Hasan looked at the hut.

I said nothing, just entered my room and lay on the bed. The noise in the other room continued until around 9pm. Andrew left. I turned off the light and tried to sleep but I could hear the neighbours speaking and laughing through the wall, which resulted in a restless night with very little sleep. In the morning, I texted Diane asking her whether I could move in on the same day.

'2pm will be fine,' she replied.

Hasan tried to talk me into not moving. He promised to fix the door immediately. Finally, he wished me good luck and kept my 500 euros. This had been my most expensive night's accommodation ever.

Diane and her best friend Julie helped me to clear Lise's room and stow my luggage.

That night, on a mattress in the room, which looked like a doll's house, surrounded by Lise's toys, I felt safe, peaceful and very grateful. I had found a temporary home. And a guardian angel.

The international environment was the first thing that struck me when I started working for the Commission. I expected it, of course, but nevertheless, it was fascinating to have colleagues from so many places. The other striking thing was the clear distinction between permanent staff, the so-called officials, and temporary or seconded experts like me. As if we were from different castes. The officials looked down on us. It wasn't explicit, but it was there. During my second week, one of my colleagues, an official, organised a party at her house to which neither I nor other colleagues with temporary contracts were invited. The officials mingled among themselves. I tried to connect to colleagues from the caste to which I now belonged, but it only went as far as having lunch together once a week or so. A couple of times, I went to after-work gatherings of other expats. But very soon I realised this was not my milieu either. The interactions were repetitive and superficial. I was asked the same questions over and over again, the conversations remained very much on the surface and, most of all, I would never see these people again unless I bumped into them at another after-work gathering.

On Thursdays, everyone headed for *Place Lux* for drinks and some early evening dancing at *Ralph Bar*. All that felt so empty and alienating to me. It was a marketplace with everyone looking around, but what for? Fun, mostly. This was the word I heard most when socialising, 'Come with us, it will be fun; it was such fun last night; he's great fun.' As if it was all about fun in this city. But fun wasn't what I was after. What was I after then? I didn't know. Something more profound and essential than fun. So I stopped going to these gatherings. Perhaps that's why the Marolles appealed to me so much. It was the artist's quarter, full of galleries and antique shops. I wanted to escape the stifling haunts of the EU employees. It was enough that I was working in an institution. I didn't want my whole life to be institutionalised.

I had always enjoyed painting, so I signed up for classes at the academy in *Rue des Tanneurs*, which was very close to my new home. Finally, I felt that it was all coming together; that my decision to move to Brussels wasn't a mistake.

On my second evening at Diane's, I came back from my painting class shortly after 9pm. She sat at the table with a man who had delicate features and an artistic air. It was Laurent, the French musician who lived in my future room. With his light auburn curly hair, long fingers of a piano player and eyes twinkling like the champagne in his glass, he looked like someone taken out of the Renaissance.

They had had dinner. Diane offered me a creamy aromatic soup, which I ate quietly while they continued their conversation. Diane was radiant. Her green eyes flashed tenderness and playfulness when she looked at Laurent. She wore a short skirt, leggings, boots and blouse with a V-shaped cleavage. All in black. She went up to bring something from the second level where her bedroom was. On her way down, two or three stairs before the bottom, she leapt, twirled around the pillar like an acrobat and landed on her feet. She was like a cat, Diane. Full of latent vitality, elastic, purring.

'Will you join me for a cigarette?' she turned towards Laurent and, without waiting for his answer, with two bounds from the sofa in front of the door leading to the big balcony and from the sofa to the balcony she was out. He followed her first with eyes, half-smiling, then joined her. Their dark silhouettes faced each other, the two glowing cigarettes like fireflies. I could hear their voices from a distance, soft, soothing. Drinking champagne and observing them, I felt like a character in an art film. There was poetry in what was happening. In the excited Diane. In her fatalistic beauty. In the enchanted musician. In the flirtation between them. In the long living room with its soft lighting and the champagne I was drinking.

I finished my glass and went to my box-like room. It was freezing, but Diane had left a heater for me. I put it on, and the hot air filled its tiny space. I lay on the mattress among my things and felt blissful.

The following evening the flat was quiet. Diane wasn't there. I saw light coming from Laurent's room, but he didn't appear. I had dined out, so I went to bed early and read. There were sounds of keys and Diane's heels. A moment later, Laurent's door opened, and he went to her. Then I heard their voices in front of my room. I couldn't resist getting up, putting my jeans on and opening the door. Both of them offered me kisses and an explanation that they were checking the radiators. She knelt and looked into a box, her black short skirt revealing her legs in boots. Laurent and I looked into each other's eyes and laughed. She was irresistible. She showed him what he needed to fix. Then she went into the living room. I asked him how he felt about playing the piano.

'Playing is a part of me,' he said, 'It's like talking without using words, yet, and perhaps indeed because of it, expressing your deepest feelings.'

As he was speaking, he was smiling, and his eyes were sparkling. Perhaps he was always like this, a charmed by women charmer. Diane's laughter reached us from the living room; she was talking on Skype.

On another evening, I found them sitting at the table after dinner, drinking wine. Laurent offered me a glass. They were engrossed in their conversation, and I was again like an invisible observer, a spectator of the play of their mutual attraction. Laurent got up and went to Diane's laptop. 'He wants to show me something,' she said with a conspiratorial smile, and approached him from behind. Her pale hand lay on his shoulder. I wished them a good night and went to my room. Their voices reached me for a while, then I drifted away.

I woke up in the middle of the night thinking someone was crying. I got up and quietly opened the door. But it wasn't crying. 'Yes, yes!' Diane's voice, followed by a slow crescendo and diminuendo of moans. I closed my door and returned to the warmth of my bed. Silence was restored again, as if what I had just heard was part of a dream. But in my mind the mingled sounds of their pleasure still echoed for a while before I was able to fall asleep again.

When I returned home from work, Diane sat alone in the living room.

'I have good news for you', she said. 'Laurent has left and when he returns, he will move into his new flat. He said you could move into his room, even though he has paid until the end of the month.'

I finally started feeling more settled in Brussels. Work was what it was. I was completing my tasks and meeting my deadlines, but I didn't get much joy out of it. What inspired me was painting, living in the Marolles, having a proper room of my own.

During the war, when we stayed locked at home for days, we had to turn the lights off in the evening and use candles. It was too dark to read. So my mother would give me some pencils and white paper. As I drew, I forgot about everything, absorbed by the lines and shadows of an imaginary world of harmony and peace. I drew houses, trees, children and cats in the street. I drew peace, which, without realising it then, I now think of as freedom.

At the academy, we painted nude models, both women and men. We would have a model for four classes, who would maintain a pose for a sequence of two classes, so that we would be able to complete the painting. In the other room were the quick poses, lasting for twenty minutes each. Those who worked there were into abstract art – sketches, broad lines, free forms. I started with realistic painting, trying to construct an image, mirroring the model, then gradually shifted to abstraction and experimentation with colours and shapes. The teacher, a Belgian artist, encouraged us to find our own mode of expression. In our room, the models posed for forty-five minutes, then had a twenty-minute break, during which I chatted with the other students. Almost everyone was Belgian or French, but this felt a lot more like home than the Commission. In this artistic environment, I was connected, understood, appreciated. We exchanged information about exhibitions, looked at each other's work and commented. I also found a friend. Perhaps even two. Olivier had both a talent and a passion for painting. There was something romantic about him and the way he looked at me during the breaks, with a faint, thoughtful smile. After a couple of weeks, when we started getting to know one another a bit, he suggested that we meet on a Sunday afternoon and draw sketches in the Marolles. There were four of us, Olivier, Iris, Andrea and me. We met at *Place de Jeu du Balle* and sat in one of the cafés there. It was a sunny and warm October day. The cafés around the square were crowded, but we managed to get a table. We drank beer and drew silently, each of us having picked a different subject. Iris sketched the fish stalls and two people standing with glasses in their hands; Andrea - a couple from the table behind us. Olivier drew Iris and me sitting next to each other. And I sketched Olivier, as he was drawing us, the pencil in his fingers and the little sketchbook in his other hand. Then we changed places and took different perspectives and subjects. The lively music, performed by the jazz band in front of the café where Diane worked, was the perfect background for our activity. Olivier and I were finished. I reached for his sketchbook.

'May I?'

He smiled shyly. '*Bien sûr.*'

The sketchbook was full of scenes, people on the bus, a café, buildings, a bottle of wine and an empty glass on a table. He had added watercolour, and his sketches were alive and shining.

'Making them is like writing a diary to keep memories. Preserving the moment.'

He said this looking into my eyes as if it was just him and me in the swirling, colourful lost and found world of *Place du Jeu du*

Balle. I caressed the pages of his sketch book with the tips of my fingers, as if I wanted to take the colours, lines and memories in, so that they became mine as if talent could be benignly contagious. It only lasted for a moment. A tiny moment during which time, sound and movement came to a halt, like the sketches in his book. Olivier and me. We were a sketch in life's sketchbook.

Iris showed us hers.

'I'm hopeless.'

'You aren't, you just need to be more aware of composition and perspective.'

Olivier took out a tiny piece of soft paper and, pressing his pencil against it, cut a small frame. He raised it and put it in front of his eyes.

'Draw only what you see in the square. That's your composition.'

Iris repeated his gesture and drew the fragment she had captured, his hand and mine on the table and the empty space between them.

He looked at it.

'Very good. Keep on practicing. And better fill the space with objects.'

'Space can be an object. An object of desire. An object of impossibility. Hence the emptiness, manifesting them.'

Iris is a writer. She speaks like she writes her stories.

Olivier blushed, cleared his throat and said,

'Are we done here? Let's move then. I want to show you something.'

We spent the next twenty minutes sketching Bruegel's house in *Rue Haute*. The street was even busier than an average Sunday because of the sunny weather. People passing stopped and peeped over our shoulders in an attempt to see our sketches. We smiled and exchanged a couple of words with them while we continued drawing. We were the artists.

Once we finished, Andrea left. She was as restless and overwhelmed as ever. She put her sketchbook and pencils in her bag, told us hastily that she really had to go now, as if we had insisted that she stayed, and walked briskly towards *Place de la Chapelle*. Iris, Olivier and I stood in the middle of the street and looked at one another.

'It's my turn to show you something,' Iris said.

We stopped in front of the large windows of *L'Atelier dans La Ville*. It was both a furniture store and a café. We crossed its vast space and ended up in a backyard garden. It was not very big but so charming. The brick wall was covered with ivy; there was a big tree in the middle, bushes and potted flowers. All the tables were taken but one. Olivier went to order at the bar inside and soon after the waitress brought us our drinks, Iris and I had a ginger and cinnamon tea, Olivier a beer. His blue eyes moved from her face to mine. It was difficult to decide who he was attracted to. Perhaps to both of us. Iris responded to him in her confident manner while I stayed playful and elusive. Poor Olivier! We finished our drinks and left.

Olivier walked with Iris towards Sablon where she lived. By that time, *Rue Haute* was almost deserted and *Place du Jeu de Balle* must have turned into a carpark. That's the magic of the Marolles, its ever-changing essence. Iris captured it in her article:

The Marolles are full of surprises, hidden treats and obvious charms. Its life has a double dynamic. From Monday to Thursday, it is quiet and feels like almost any other neighbourhood, leading its ordinary, day-to-day existence. Most of the antique shops and galleries and some of the restaurants and bars are closed and there is not much going on. On Thursday, however, Marolles enters its second phase – celebratory and vivid, luring both tourists and les Bruxellois. *Its two main streets* Rue Haute *and* Rue Blaes *fill with people wandering around the shops or enjoying the numerous small restaurants and bars, creating a relaxed holiday atmosphere. But there is more to it. A very particular air of excitement and enchantment, which comes from the possibility of discovery. Of what? A magical object which fulfils all our wishes? One wish for sure – for a colourful, atmospheric Sunday morning.*

The antique shops are exhibitions of the past. From outside they look like ordinary shops, but once inside, you find yourself in an unexpected space, which could be a labyrinth of corridors made up by the shelves stacked with objects, possibly with a second floor, which takes you to the parallel street of Rue Blaes.

*

The space I lived in was changing as well. One evening I came back home and witnessed an idyllic scene. Diane, in a blue house suit, sat on the sofa with a man, her head resting on his shoulder. It was a different Diane. Calm, sweet, tame. The cat that bounced and arched her back around Laurent was gone. A girl was playing with a train on the ground.

She introduced me to Stan, her partner, and Lise, her daughter.

They were watching some television series, laughing. That is how I would always see them together, a happy family. She cooked, they watched a TV programme and commented on it. Or just talked, facing each other. She explained something to him, he listened. I tried to be invisible while preparing my dinner. Then I took the meal quietly to my room.

'Why don't you stay here?' Diane said.

'I'm fine.'

I felt an instant tenderness towards Lise with her blonde curls, peach-colour skin and big grey eyes. She would knock on my door, enter and watch me paint. I did a couple of portraits of her, a mixed technique of dry pastels and watercolour. When Diane saw them, she said,

'They are beautiful. You've got talent!'

I didn't know whether I had talent, but I undoubtedly had passion. Painting was my salvation from the dullness of my work, the emptiness of the expat talks and the loneliness. Like Olivier, I started bringing my sketchbook to work in my bag and over the long lunches at the Commission I would sit in a café in nearby

Berlaymont or, weather permitting, on a bench around *Ambiorix Square*, and sketch.

At the academy, I would show my sketches to Iris, Olivier and whoever was around over the breaks, and we would discuss. Sabine, the teacher, encouraged me,

'This is good. Continue, experiment with bigger formats.'

So I did. I would lose myself in the diversity of techniques and the freedom which I felt while doing this. The abstraction, the vagueness of the shapes, the blur. Hours would pass without me noticing. I would then find text and voice messages from Iris and Olivier. Iris,

'There is a good concert at *Théâtre de la Samaritaine* tonight. Let's go!'

Olivier,

'I am going to an exhibition in Bozar. Would you like to come?'

I would miss concerts, exhibitions, chats in cafés. Painting was what mattered most, it was the only activity which made me feel complete and peaceful.

'Sorry, I can't,' I would reply again and again.

But there was also some of this. Hanging around in the evenings, having a drink, conversing. Sometimes, I would let myself be seduced by Iris' suggestions and, after our classes, we would often end up at *Sol.* The black and white photos from classic films made me feel sentimental and nostalgic. Spontaneously, I bought a photo of Alain Delon and Brigitte Bardot lying on a boat next to each other, their palms crossed, both serious, she is wearing a top with a plunging neckline, he is in a black short sleeve shirt. Both young, beautiful, thoughtful with the sea all around them. I hung it in my room and observed it, while listening to Satie.

'Oh, you are so romantic,' Diane laughed when she saw it.

The jazz, smooth and warm, the black and white photos and a slow drink. I drank wine, Iris whisky. We talked about anything but Olivier. Without saying a word, we never invited him to these outings.

During the *Nuit Blanche*, the wonderland of the Marolles became more prominent than ever. Iris and I walked around with maps in hand and experienced well-known places, transformed into spaces of art. In a fashion shop, we listened to a live jazz concert; the old swimming pool at *Place de Jeu de Balle* was full of big balls, the water glittered in the darkness; there was a shadow show in an antique shop; a cabaret in *Les Brigittines* and a modern ballet performance in the central hall of the Palace of Justice.

But at the academy, we hung around together, Olivier and I, Olivier and Iris, the three of us. We wandered, talked to our colleagues, looked at their work, exchanged looks and gradually, like cats, found our way towards one another. Slowly, unconsciously maybe, innocently almost. And we still got together a couple of times over the weekends to make sketches, see an exhibition, have a drink. But the energy among us was becoming too intense. What were we? A threesome? Tripling wasn't my thing. I was a couple person. That is how I saw myself. In reality, I was just single. That was the catch, I guess. Each of us was single. After an afternoon we spent together, I texted Iris,

'I have had enough of these outings. I cannot do it anymore.' A couple of minutes later, she replied,

'I was just about to tell you the same.'

That is how Olivier dropped out of the picture. Not entirely, though. During our classes, we continued talking, laughing, and exchanging meaningful looks.

One Friday evening, when Iris wasn't there, Olivier ran after me down the stairs.

'Bojana, would you like to go for a drink?'

'Thanks, but I am too tired.'

'May I walk you home then?'

It's a short walk. He spoke about his painting and an exhibition he had recently seen.

'Do you have plans for the weekend?', he asked at my front door. 'Perhaps we could meet and make some sketches, see an exhibition, have dinner, whatever.'

'I've already made plans. I'm sorry.'

'So another time then?'

'Perhaps.'

He looked at me with the eyes of a wounded animal. I saved this look for later, for the hours of my delirium-like solitude.

'I don't love you! Don't you hear me?! I don't. Leave me alone! Let me be!'

Diane was in her bedroom. I crossed the living room as quietly as possible and went to mine. Half an hour later, she knocked on my door,

'I'm going out. Will you be here? If Stan comes, tell him I'll be late. There is no need for him to wait for me. *Bien*?'

'*Bien sûr.*' She was still standing in the doorway.

'I'm in a complicated situation,' she said, 'I don't love Stan anymore. And I don't know what to do. Breaking up would damage Lise. I feel so stuck, so stuck!' Her voice was tearful, her eyes shone. I reached out and she let me embrace her.

'I'm really sorry. But it will be alright, you'll see. Just give it time.'

'I know. I will,' she wiped her tears, smiled at me and left.

I went to bed early and as I was falling asleep, I could see Olivier's eyes, his vulnerable eyes.

*

Iris suggested doing it and this time I said 'yes'. Why this time exactly out of many, I don't know. Maybe I felt that I had said 'no' too many times in a row, so a 'yes' was due. Perhaps I didn't want to lose her as a friend since sooner or later people give up, they stop inviting you, stop reaching out, stop thinking of you. I didn't want that to happen with Iris. So I said yes. And I found myself in a group of some fifteen to twenty people for a full day activity called 'The Other Brussels'. We met at North railway station. The guide, an enthusiastic Flemish man in his thirties, explained what the day would look like. We would have three stops and each of them would be a surprise.

We followed him to a nearby park which had been turned into a campsite. There were hundreds of tents, wet clothes hanging on ropes, stretched between trees, children running after a ball, veiled women, men hanging around and talking loudly. They were all Arab or African. A white woman in her forties approached us, greeted Patrick warmly, and then us. 'This is our first stop today,' Patrick stated the obvious, 'Claudia will be our host here in the Maximilian Park and she will help us experience how it feels to be a migrant.' Claudia smiled widely and said, 'Welcome.' She explained that several hundred migrants, predominantly Syrian and Sudanese, lived in that park, that they had crossed a sea, risking their lives to escape war; had lost relatives and significant others in the war or on the way; that they had travelled through many countries in order to find themselves under the Belgian sky, homeless in a park, facing the risk of deportation. And if we were able to switch from seeing them as strangers who are trying to take over our countries to seeing them as people like us, perhaps we would feel some compassion and reach out to them, try to help them whichever way we could and even invite them to our homes. After this introduction, Claudia opened the small bag she was carrying, took out a bundle of spoons and gave one to each participant. 'I invite you now to get on your knees and dig a hole in the earth with your spoon.'

We looked at one another. It was a chilly November day, and it had been drizzling since dawn. We slowly went down onto our knees and tried to grind the spoons into the earth. It was far from easy. Even though there was a layer of mud, the underlying soil was hardened by the cold. Soon our spoons bent from the pressure.

We were helpless and increasingly irritated by the task.

'That's how it feels to be a migrant. All your efforts bend like your spoons. You're helpless and clueless. You might be irritated and angry with life, but that doesn't help. Could you please do one more thing for me? Smell this earth. Just smell it,' she said.

It stank of urine and shit. I felt an urge to vomit and started coughing. Iris gave me a bottle of water. I washed my hands and nose and drank some of it.

'This is the soil on which these people have been spending their lives for months. They sleep on it and yes, they relieve themselves on it too. Like animals. But they're not animals. They're people like you and me and have the same needs.'

She accompanied us to a nearby building, where migrants could come for advice or clothes, and where volunteers explained to us how we could help. Finally, Claudia came forward again and said,

'I will give you my card and I very much hope that many of you will contact me and offer shelter to the migrants you see here or help in other ways.'

I put her card in my pocket and looked at Iris. I wanted to leave this place as soon as possible.

We walked to the underground in silence.

'We will now be heading for de Brouckère,' Patrick announced.

He took us to hotel *Métropole* where our host was a young woman with dark wavy hair, cut under her ears, and green eyes. She invited us into a luxurious, spacious flat where we sat in a circle. She sat in a big soft chair next to us. Her clothes were simple and stylish, a white shirt, black skirt, pearl earrings, black medium-high heels. She looked at us for a moment, then spoke.

'When Patrick invited me to join this project, at first, I declined. I felt I wouldn't be able to do it. I had never talked about what I am going to share with you today. But he insisted, reminding me how little is known in Europe about what happened just over fifteen years ago, in that same Europe, in my city. He thought it was important to preserve and share this memory, no matter how traumatic it is, as it is our responsibility to make the coming generations aware so that the memory of it is preserved and it is never repeated. As a psychologist, I knew Patrick was right, so I agreed to participate. You are the only people who will hear this story from me, which makes you its guardians.'

Her voice was soft and clear. She took a sip of water. We were all staring at her with great curiosity.

'I am going to talk about Srebrenica,' she said, 'About my very own Srebrenica.'

Cold sweat started running down my body. I took a deep breath and tried to calm down.

'Srebrenica is a green mountain village. We had a small house, three goats, some chicken and rabbits. There was peace but there was always something unsettling in the air. Tensions, teasing, petty crime. It had been bubbling up and escalating even before the war started. War is something which cannot be described. It's like all this unrest suddenly gets a name. Now it's official. Entire villages were destroyed, men killed, women raped. Life became terrifyingly capricious; death could be waiting at your doorstep. My mother kept me and my little brother away from school and started teaching us at home. We would not be let out alone anymore. Three years went by before the UN created its camp in Potocari and declared Srebrenica safe territory. For the first time for three years, I saw a forgotten expression in the eyes of my parents, I saw hope. Three months of relative normality followed. On the morning of the 11th of July, however, this expression was gone again. My father came back home with a different look. He took my mother to one side to talk and then they told us that we were going for a walk. There were thousands of people in the streets. Men, women and children. We walked outside the city. At one point, everyone stopped. There was a large concrete block with two big black letters on it 'UN' and a fence surrounding the territory behind. We crammed ourselves inside like cattle. There wasn't enough space for all of us. Those outside were pressing to get in. Soldiers, Dutchmen with blue helmets, were forcing their way through the crowd, looking at us with their cold foreign eyes, as if we were animals. There was no compassion in those eyes, no humanity. They started pushing the people who were still outside backwards. They spoke loudly in a language which I didn't understand. A thought struck me then, they were scared too, followed by another thought, if those who had to protect us were taken by fear, there wasn't much to hope for. Fear turns us all into animals. Allah, save us! We were pressed into each other, sweating in the heat, thirsty, hungry, but most of all, paralysed by fear. The surrounding hills and the valley were black with people. Our people. Bosnian women, men and children.

Hours passed in unbearable apprehension. Then in the afternoon, the Serbian army arrived and cut through the crowd. The Dutch soldiers started pushing us out of the UN premises. We didn't want to go; we screamed and refused to move, but they opened the fence wide, and, in effect, we were out, in the so-called *safe* territory.

The Serbs, heavily armed, separated the men and the boys from the others. It was all messy and wild. Their faces... Full of lust. Only I didn't know lust then. I saw three of them looking at me and talking out loud, *lepa, lepa.* I looked in the other direction, trying hard to become invisible. Next thing the men were in front of me. One of them grabbed me and started pulling me, laughing. My mother stepped in and pushed him away. They started hitting her and she fell, curling into a ball. They kicked her a few more times and then turned to me. There was a Dutch soldier nearby and I ran towards him screaming. He stepped back and walked in the opposite direction as if I were a ghost. The feeling of total helplessness. The cruel indifference of the soldier. The Serbs grabbed me and held me down. Other soldiers passed but they did nothing. Nothing. They just watched. Two of the men forced my legs open, the other one loosened his belt, took his trousers down, and I saw his erect penis.

Next thing he was between my legs. I felt a sharp pain down there and then pushing. I was going insane. I was crying and screaming. Soon he shuddered and stopped. I thought it was over. But no. He smiled wolfishly at one of the other men who took his place. I couldn't scream anymore as they put my panties in my mouth. A third man followed. When he was done too, they went away. I was lying there, thinking I would die. There was blood between my legs. I don't know how much time passed. I opened my eyes, and my mother was holding me. My body was covered with her scarf. She was crying, she had bruises on her face. Some other Serbs approached us and told us to move.

All the women and girls were pushed into a truck, squeezed together. They drove us to another village where there were other women and children. No men. The men, including my father and brother, never came back. We spent that night in a house with other women. We dared not sleep. We stayed in that village for nearly two years.

My mother never overcame the grief of the loss of my father and brother. She died a year later. I was seventeen by then and my life was over. Everyone knew what had happened to me, I could never get married. An older neighbour approached me and said he would take care of me. I started living with him like his daughter in front of the village, but in the evenings, he came to my bed.

A few months later, a friend of his visited us. He lived in Brussels and had come by car. He was younger than Yassir but radiated solidity. When Yassir was away, he told me he could help me find a job in Belgium. So I escaped with him. He managed to smuggle me across the borders, hidden beneath a blanket, trying not to breathe. It was a long trip. He lived near *Gare du Midi*, in a flat in a large grey building. He let me take a shower, prepared dinner and told me that the promised job consisted of me giving pleasure to men. He started my 'education' that same night and continued it for a week, night after night. Then he took me to a mall and bought me Western clothes and makeup. He also took me to a hairdresser for a manicure and pedicure.

'You're gorgeous,' he said, 'You have a big future.' That night he drove me to my first client. The business kicked off. A few months later, he drove to Bosnia again and came back with two more girls; they were aged fifteen and sixteen. The three of us became very close, like sisters. Roman put us in French classes as this was supposed to boost the business. I also bought some English books and studied alone. I knew by then that this was necessary if I didn't want to end up like the girls in *Avenue Louise*. Education was my gateway to freedom. And freedom was what I was preparing for. Every working hour was a means of setting myself free one day. This vision helped me get through.

As I became fluent in English and French, the business changed as well. I was promoted to an escort. Men started paying not only for sex but also for having me around, at dinners, events, anything. I worked hard for five years to gain my freedom. I became Roman's favourite and trained all the girls he brought to Belgium. When I had enough savings to continue on my own, I asked him to set me free. Although it wasn't easy for him, he agreed. This rarely happens, so I was lucky. He still comes to see me every so often and uses my services when it comes to training and guidance for the new girls. I wouldn't call myself a victim of trafficking. I don't know what would have happened to me had I stayed in Bosnia.

I am my own mistress now. I am studying psychology at ULB. When I graduate and start my practice, I might put an end to my escort activities, even though the money is good. I could work with women who have been in the business and need support, for example.

I have been unprofessional only once. There was a Dutch man who fell for me. The temptation was too strong. I still had flashbacks of the Dutch soldiers witnessing the massacre of my people, of my own family and myself, and doing nothing. I know it wasn't their fault and perhaps it's unfair to blame them for what happened, but they were there to protect us. And their biggest sin was the illusion of safety they created. Impartiality and non-involvement in certain circumstances make you an accomplice. I did the same thing with him; I created an emotional safe territory – so that I could destroy him when he was most vulnerable and open. I'm not proud of what I did. But I enjoyed it, enjoyed the revenge. I did it like a homage to my dead family and to my youth, my brutally lost innocence. Thank you for your attention.'

She got up and left like an actress leaving the stage after her performance. We heard the door close behind her.

I was reeling. The Bosnian insisted we ought to remember what I had been trying to forget ever since this bloody war had ended. The memories flooded back. The hours in the basement. The candles. I haven't been able to stand candlelight since. The family division – Croatian mother, Serbian father.

'What are we going to do, Gorane? What are we going to do?' The end of childhood. No, I had not come to Brussels to be reminded of that. I got up and went to the bathroom. I threw up, washed my face and mouth with cold water and looked in the mirror. It did not lie. A knock on the door. 'Bojana, are you ok?' I breathed in and out. Iris was waiting for me outside the bathroom. 'Are you ok?' I nodded.

'I've never asked you about that… I suppose you have your memories from that time,' she said on the way out.

'I'd rather not talk about it.'

Our next stop was Marolles. At least I was getting close to home. We walked down Rue Haute and stopped in front of a house. Patrick rang the bell and again a woman opened the door. As if women were the guardians of the Other Brussels. She smiled and invited us in. This time the hostess was blonde, wore skinny jeans and a red top. We took the stairs to the second floor and found ourselves in a loft. There were paintings and photos on the walls, many of which were of irises.

There was an antique table in the middle with tiny glass bottles on it, filled with some transparent liquid.

‘*Bonjour à tous. Je m’appelle Hélène.* I represent a female artist cooperative, called ‘Orgasmic’.’

I tried not to look at the faces of my companion-explorers.

‘Orgasmic is a project we started three years ago, and which turned out to be amazingly successful. Our initial idea was to empower women to explore and express their sexuality, but, along the way, the main benefit we have gained, for ourselves and our followers, has been the discovery of the health and beauty effects of… orgasmic juices.’

If it hadn’t been for Iris, I would have left at this point. I had already wanted to give up after the Bosnian escort’s confessions, but I didn’t want to fail Iris once again after so many refused invitations. I was to regret staying.

‘There were five of us at the beginning. But now, only three years later, we are followed by hundreds of women in Belgium and around the world. It’s hardly new that orgasms enhance female power and health. But we went one step further, there is a way this energy can be kept, sustained and reused by collecting our orgasmic juices and benefitting from their divine qualities. I can see bewilderment on your faces. But it’s quite simple. This is how it works. The juices can be used both orally and externally. Drinking your own juices has huge benefits for your health because of the precious elements they contain, but also for your sexual awareness and vibration. All of us who started this experiment have noticed that drinking our juices makes us feel physically better, energized, more sexual inside and more feminine. This has also had a powerful effect on our relationships, sex appeal and sex life. Ever since we have been collecting and drinking our juices, the quality of our lives has increased immensely. *Not a drop is wasted.* This is our motto. If drinking your juices sounds too bold and challenging, you could also sprinkle some drops in your drinks or food. The effect is still the same. Another way of experiencing at least the cosmetic benefits of the juices is by applying them on your skin like a serum or adding a few drops to your moisturiser. It works miracles and makes you look a lot younger. I won't tell you my age, but I believe you would not be able to guess it either,' she smiled with confidence.

'Here is what it looks like. Would anyone dare to try?'

There was silence and an exchange of awkward glances.

'No? Even women? Come on, sisters! Loosen up, let this feminine energy be released. There is nothing scary about it. Look!'

She took one of the tiny bottles on the table, opened it and drank its contents.

'Oh, it's such a divine feeling to take in this mixture of the liberation and pleasure of many sisters.'

Had I not just thrown up, I certainly would have done so at this point. I felt sick.

'Would any brave woman care to experiment? No. Pity! But no worries. I understand that this is too revolutionary to accept straight away. That's why I have prepared some samples for you to take away. In the comfort and privacy of your homes, you may feel more at ease with trying new things and discovering new horizons.' Three women took the bottles.

'And how about the rest? Come on! Don't be shy!'

But no one else took up the offer.

'Let's get out of here,' I whispered and ran out, followed by Iris.

'Sorry, this has been too much.'

'It's over now, anyway, let's have a drink.'

'No, Iris, I am sorry. I need to be alone now. See you on Monday.'

I turned and walked home as fast as I could.

Diane and Julie were drinking wine in the living room.

'Will you join us for a glass?' Diane suggested.

'No, thanks. I am exhausted.'

I went to my room, crashed on the bed and cried. I must have fallen asleep soon after. Something woke me up. Coming back to my senses, I realised what it was, Diane and Julie were singing along to some French pop music. Their voices were as hoarse as old drunks'. Once every so often, they burst into laughter, then continued with the song. It was around midnight. The concert continued till past 1am when it was finally quiet. But I couldn't go back to sleep. The temperature had dropped, and the room was ice cold. I got up, shivering, and put on socks and a sweater.

I only entered the living room after I heard some movement there the following morning. Diane and Julie were sitting around the table with cups of coffee.

'My head hurts so much,' Diane complained, 'We finished two bottles.'

‘Well, I hope you feel better soon,’ I mumbled as I was preparing my tea.

‘We must have disturbed you,’ Julie said, ‘Were you able to sleep?’

‘It was a bit noisy, indeed. But it wasn’t just that. I was freezing as well. Diane, can we adjust the heating so that it doesn’t go off during the night?’

‘But it’s not cold at all! It regulates automatically to a normal temperature. Would you like another blanket?’

‘It was really cold for me. Can we do something about it?’

‘Sorry but it’s central heating. There is no way for it to be adjusted only for your room. Julie and I weren’t cold at all. Lise also sleeps at this temperature, so it’s only you who has an issue. I’m afraid you’ll have to live with it.’

Her cold smile made me shiver as much as the low temperature in my room had. I had never seen her like that, sharp, indifferent, imposing. I said nothing. Just took my tea and went to my room. The heating was on now and the temperature was ok. I took out my brushes and paints and prepared a canvas.

Julie was around in the evenings which followed. It was always the same, the drinking, the laughter, ‘Belgium’s Got Talent’, the singing… And the headaches the morning after. I got the flu as the nights continued to be icy cold. I prepared a quick dinner which I had in my room and went to bed dressed as if I were going hiking at high altitudes. Diane observed me as I was cooking and sneezing, and I could see mockery in her eyes. I must have been a pathetic view, pale, exhausted, a miserable creature.

'Are you ok, Bojana?' she would ask. Smiling. I would nod in return and continue minding my business.

One evening I found Diane alone. She was sitting at the table with a glass of wine. Her eyes were wet. I had eaten outside with a Croatian colleague and was just about to head for my room when she stopped me.

'Come and have a glass with me, Bojana. I need some company tonight.'

I could have done without it. But I felt I had to respond to the desperation in her eyes.

She poured me a glass of wine. I took a tiny sip.

'How's your life going, Bojana? Are you happy?'

'I haven't been well lately. And the weather doesn't help.'

'I think you're not very happy here. You're constantly ill lately and the vibes you radiate are… miserable.'

I was silent.

'Perhaps you could look for another place? You might be happier somewhere else? What do you think?'

'I'll think about it.'

'Brussels is a cold and dangerous city, Bojana. Me and my friends… we have experienced all sorts of things. I was once in a shop when it was robbed. The guy was holding a gun, pointing it at us. We were all lying on the floor. I thought my life was over there and then. But I survived it. A friend of mine who lives nearby was once raped as she passed by the *Midi* station. Another friend of mine was badly beaten at *Gare Centrale* at eleven at night just for his wallet. He was in a hospital for a couple of weeks afterwards. You need to take care.'

Her green eyes watched me closely.

'I suppose these things cannot be predicted. But I am taking care as best I can. These things happen in every big city, don't they?'

'I don't know. I haven't lived in another big city. How is it in Croatia?'

'I think Croatia is relatively safe.'

'Why didn't you stay there?'

'I suppose I needed a change.'

'Did you have a happy childhood there?'

The bombs. The darkness. The candles. The neighbours snubbing us because my father was a Serb. Home becoming a prison. The surrounding world being dangerous.

'I did.'

'You're lucky then.'

'What about you?'

'Mine was interesting.'

She took another sip from her glass.

'My mother was a prostitute, you know. In Amsterdam. She used to be a beautiful woman. Extravagant. Flamboyant. She used to work in the red-light district. I have been there with her. In between her sessions. She would sit in a room with a couple of other girls, smoking, chatting and having a laugh, taking no notice of the clients.

This attitude turns men on; they love it when you don't try to attract their attention. While her colleagues were posing and waving and smiling from behind their windows, men were gathering in front of my mother's.

At some point, she would get up, approach the window and look at them. She would make her choice and point her finger at the one she was about to hook up with.

One of the other girls would take me with her while my mother was working. We would go to her room, and she would let me play with her feathers, lipstick, scarves. I would wear a scarf and some red lipstick. She would laugh and say I was gorgeous.

An hour or so later, my mother would come to pick me up, wearing an elegant dress just like an ordinary mother. She would take me for lunch or dinner or ice cream near the canals. These were my happiest hours. The two of us out of her work cabin. She would look at me gently, caress my hair and tell me,

'Never suffer for men, my dear Diane. None of them deserve it. We are queens and they should be adoring us. And if they don't, then it's better to get rid of them. As I did with your miserable father.'

I never knew my father. Apparently, he was one of my mum's early clients. There was love involved and she even quit the business during her pregnancy. But then he kicked her out just before I was born. He later wanted to see me and fix things, but my mother never allowed it. That's what I gleaned up from the scraps she shared here and there. She never told me his name. It was she and her friends who took care of me initially. When I was of school age, my mother and I took a train to the town where my grandparents lived, and she left me with them. They never mentioned their daughter.

She called me every week. Once a month, she would come to see me. She would wait for me in front of the house, and we would go for a walk, lunch, ice cream. She brought me beautiful clothes. I missed her very much and looked forward to her visits. But as I became a teenager and got a better idea of her job, I became very angry and ashamed of her. I even grew to hate her and cut contact.

Years passed. It was only when I had Lise that she reappeared in my life. Someone had told her. When she came for the first time, I refused to see her. I didn't want to speak to her, didn't want Lise to be influenced by her. But she persisted. I was a single mother then; Stan had not yet appeared in my life.

Finally, I forgave her. She wanted to make up for all the lost time with me by being the best grandmother. She isn't in the business anymore, given her age, and has become a religious and decent old lady. You'd never guess…'

A short sharp laugh. I didn't know what to say.

'And now she's coming to visit us over the weekend,' Diane concluded.

I shifted in my chair.

'I will be heading for bed.'

'Won't you finish your wine? That's a waste.'

'No, it was enough for me. Good night.'

'Good night.'

Under the two blankets, dressed in a sweater, leggings and a hot water bottle, I looked at the distant stars through the roof window, and prayed to a God, of whose existence I wasn't sure.

*

Diane was discussing something with Stan and an older lady in an agitated way over breakfast.

'*Bonjour*,' I said.

'Bojana, meet my mother Josephine,' Diane said.

The lady stretched out her hand towards me, smiling. Her hair was grey, gathered at the nape of her neck. She wore black trousers and a sweater, no makeup. I started preparing my breakfast.

'Have you heard about Paris?' Diane looked at me.

'No.'

'There were terrorist attacks last night at various locations. At a concert. And in a café. At least a hundred victims.'

I bent over the sink.

'Are you ok?'

'Yes, yes… sorry.'

Paris. Attacks. Concert. Cafés. Victims. I had gone to sleep in a familiar world and had woken up at a strange place. A place in which these words put together made an impossible and yet real narrative. I brought breakfast to my room and went online, browsing through the articles and news feeds of the main channels in both French and English. The evil was just around the corner. In Molenbeek. My breakfast remained untouched.

Both Iris and Olivier tried to reach out, Iris by calling, Olivier by sending a message and suggesting that we meet later. I didn't reply to either. Instead, I went back to bed and tried to sleep.

In the following days, I was suspicious of every person with darker skin on public transport, especially men, especially anyone holding a bag or a rucksack. Trust was gone. The world had turned into a jungle where men killed innocent people in public places. It had become a war zone without a clear indication of who was the enemy and who the target. We had all become targets. With the dead people in Paris, a part of me had died as well. We were all victims. All of us.

The business-as-usual mentality at the academy was abnormal. Everything continued as if nothing had happened. The nude models were posing; my colleagues were painting; the teacher walked around and made comments. I arranged my canvas and started painting.

'Interesting. Is this how you see the colours?' Sabine gestured towards my painting.

'I see blood splashing when the wholeness of our bodies is broken. I see Paris everywhere.'

She raised her eyebrows but refrained from commenting. I continued applying red colour on my canvas over a mess of human bodies.

'I called you,' Iris came to me during the break.

'Sorry. I was not in the mood.'

'What's wrong?'

'What's wrong?! The world is wrong. Can't you see?!'

She nodded slowly.

'It's terrible.'

Olivier joined us.

'I saw a fascinating exhibition on Saturday…'

I excused myself, went to the toilet and splashed cold water on my face.

After the class, Iris suggested drinks. I refused.

At home, Diane and Stan were cuddling on the sofa, watching the news about Paris. Lise was drawing men with guns and broken dolls.

I crossed the room, pretending to be a shadow, and collapsed on my bed.

'There is a tank at Sablon. I see it through my windows,' Iris's voice was tense.

'I don't want to know. Haven't been out ever since this madness started.'

'What have you been doing?'

'Working from home. Waiting.'

'Painting?'

'No. I cannot paint anymore, not now.'

'We miss you in the class. It's so close to you. Why don't you come?'

'No. I'm done with it.'

'Are you really?'

'Yes.'

'But why? Art helps in such dire times. Art will save us. Again, and again.'

'Do you really believe that? Perhaps there were artists among the people who died in Paris? Or art lovers. Has art saved them?!'

'Don't take my words literally. You know what I mean.'

'I know. But I disagree. Art, when the world around us is turning upside down, is not salvation but escape. Hiding your head in the sand instead of looking at the reality and feeling what you see.'

'And how is this helping you? What can we do? You and I. What? Nothing other than making an effort not to go mad. When we create, we respond to the destruction with creation.'

'And how will our creating make the world a better place? Will it bring the victims back?'

'Will you being mad bring them back?'

'Sometimes madness is the only healthy and adequate reaction. I would rather go mad than close my eyes and escape the pain of what is happening like a coward.'

'Are you alone?'

'Yes. Diane, Stan and Lise left for the countryside.'

'Should I come over?'

'No. I need to be alone.'

'You know where to find me.'

'I know.'

The Brussels lockdown had been announced five days earlier. Exactly a week after the Paris attacks. In the news, they showed soldiers and armed police everywhere. The *Grand Place* looked like an army training site. I switched off the TV. I didn't need to know any of this. Once in a lifetime was more than enough. Much more than enough.

I went out on the balcony to get some fresh air. The street was empty. Brussels had turned into a desert of fear, desolation and uncertainty. On Twitter, Belgians posted photos of cats. I couldn't tune into that either. The cat I lived with was gone. The only thing I could do was wait. Wait for the time to pass. Wait for something to happen.

*

The bell broke the silence. The ringing was persistent.

'Hello?' It was Laurent. 'Will you let me in?'

I left the door open and put the kettle on.

'Will you have a cup of tea?'

'Yes, thanks. Where is Diane?'

'She left for the countryside with Lise and Stan.'

'Ah... ok... It's just that, all of a sudden, I wasn't getting a reply to my messages anymore. I got worried and came to check... Sorry for disturbing you.'

'You're not disturbing me.'

'Do you know when she will be back?'

'Could be any time. She said she'd return when this madness is over.'

'I'm afraid that could take a lifetime.'

'So am I.'

‘Ok. I don’t want to keep you. Tell Diane that I was here, will you? I will be waiting to hear from her.’

He got up.

‘You’re not keeping me from anything. On the contrary. I’ve been alone for days and I have had my share of solitude.’

He hesitated for a moment and sat down again.

‘Some wine?’

‘Wine would be nice.’

I picked up a bottle of red Bordeaux.

‘What do you think of this one?’

‘Great.’

He opened the bottle.

‘Will you excuse me for a moment?’

I went to my room and looked in the mirror. My face was pale, my lips colourless.

I took out a black dress and changed. Light makeup, perfume.

‘Wow!’ Laurent smiled at me when I came back and handed me a glass.

The sound of chin-chin, followed by the first sips. Beautiful normality. Some wine, some music, a handsome man. Had it all been arranged so that this moment could happen? The Paris attacks, the Brussels lockdown, Diane’s retreat, all so that Laurent and I could finally meet and share our solitude. Stop thinking, stop fantasising, I told myself. Wine helped blur my mind, derail my train of thought. Laurent was changing too. The spark I saw in his eyes when he looked at Diane was back. But this time for me.

‘What is happening is so horrible, Laurent, so horrible! I’m so scared.’

‘I know. It’s a nightmare it’s impossible to wake up from. The saddest thing is that the terrorists are French or Belgian. They were born and grew up here. They got their education here. Their work, friends, everything. And how are they expressing their gratitude? How are they responding to the generosity of our countries? By attacking the peaceful societies of these same countries and killing innocent people. People like you and me who went out on a Friday night to have a drink, food, some music but never returned home. Paris is where I come from, it’s my home and now it has been violated.’

‘I know what you mean. I feel the same. With these people, something in me died too. We are all targets and victims of that act. Our culture and way of living are victimized as well. Nothing can be the same after Paris.’

‘You’re Croatian, right? You must have experienced war.’

I nodded.

He reached across the table and held my hand. Sometime in between glasses and words, we danced. He held me in his artist’s arms. There were no attacks anymore, no fear, no pain. We moved slowly and smoothly as if we had always danced together, as if we were made to perform that dance that evening. Amid the Brussels lockdown.

The bed which had been shelter for each of us individually became our Noah's Ark that night. But we brought nothing with us from the old world. Just ourselves and a lot of tenderness.

Diane blushed when she heard Laurent had been over.

'What did he say?'

'He was hoping to hear from you.'

She smiled wryly to herself and looked through the window.

*

'How are you going to spend the New Year?' I had asked Diane the night before I left.

'Laurent has invited me to join him and a couple of his Parisian friends. They need a female presence to distract them from those terrible events. But I also have other invitations and have not made up my mind yet. I am like this – I go somewhere, stay as long as it's interesting and when I feel like it, I leave and go to another place. My friends know me and take no offense. How about you? Have you got any plans?'

'I don't know yet.'

The only thing I knew for sure was that I wanted to leave this city as soon as possible and never return. During my Christmas break, I regularly checked the real estate websites and found a furnished flat in Woluwé-Saint-Lambert, near the park. Once I was back, I went to see it and decided to take it. It was far away from everything. From the armed men, the guards, the Marolles, my life in Brussels so far.

‘What? You’re moving next week? Why didn’t you tell me earlier that you had such plans?’

Diane’s eyes became dark green.

‘But you suggested that I looked for another place. So I did.’

‘This is so sudden. You should have said something... Will you live alone?’

‘Yes.’

‘It’s hurtful that you’re leaving like that, but I understand.’

On the following day I got a message from her, ‘Can you move out asap? As compensation for those two weeks I gave you shelter. I prefer not to have you around for another week, if possible.’

As I was packing, a couple of pages fell from a book on the floor. I picked them up – it was the story Iris had given me when I was leaving for Croatia. It was called ‘The Grand Sablon’. I had started reading it but had stopped after the first few lines.

Later that night, on her sofa, I took them out. This time I read until the end.

The Grand Sablon

They stood by the large window, looking at the armoured car as it crawled through the square like a huge beetle. She was naked. He was dressed. He took a step forward and embraced her from behind. His hands smelled of turpentine and were covered in blue, red and white paint. The blood of her portrait. He had called her in the morning to check how she was coping with the lockdown.

'I'm doing well,' Julia said. 'I sit and watch the square, that's what I've been doing. The invisible guardian of the square, that's what I've become.'

'I cannot stay shut in any longer,' Serge said. 'When we do that, we let them take away our freedom. And that's exactly what they want. This is my city; my country and they cannot turn me into a voluntary prisoner. Enough. I'm going out. Can I come and see you? Will you pose for me?'

'Yes.' She said it twice.

There is such clichéd romance in the idea of being an artist's model. All these women who made it to eternity by posing for the greats. In reality, there was nothing romantic about it. It was tedious and demanding. The body begins to ache from the effort to keep still. The face stiffens from the attempt to preserve the same expression. The skin prickles as the air starts feeling cooler and cooler.

At the academy, she got annoyed sometimes when a model would slightly change her position after the break. It would sabotage her work. The teacher would come, scrutinise her canvas and say,

'It's not quite correct. Her hand is actually higher.'

Oh well, it was certainly lower twenty minutes ago.

But with every passing minute of posing for Serge, guilty compassion replaces her previous impatience. There are no shortcuts to eternity, it's all lived through, ached through. So that those beautiful portraits can reign over time and kindle admiration through the centuries. For Julia though the destination is uncertain. Serge is in his second year and whether he will really make it as a painter is as questionable as the fame of the greats when they began.

They had met at the academy. September was a month for experimenting, when anyone could try all the courses before settling on their choices. There were two painting classes, and she tried both. Hylke, the Flemish teacher, was serious and ambitious. Even in the first class, she showed her a technique. Elena, the Italian teacher, was more relaxed. She looked at Julia's painting, gave some feedback and let her continue alone.

'You need to find your own style,' she said.

Julia googled them both, compared their work and couldn't quite make up her mind. Hylke's portraits were authentic, vivid, conveying emotion. This was something she wanted to work on and learn herself. Elena's work was abstract and evocative. It blew her mind with merging colours and shapes.

The days passed, and she couldn't make a decision. What helped her set her mind on Elena was not Elena herself, but her absence. One Tuesday, when her classes took place, Serge announced that she was ill and had asked him to replace her. He was the biggest hope of the class, had already been painting before enrolling in the academy and had made remarkable progress during his time there. That evening, he would interrupt his painting every so often and circle the room, stopping next to each of the prospective students and commenting on their work. Julia didn't remember what exactly he had said about hers. Something encouraging about the choice of colours, followed by a suggestion to alter the proportions. He gave her a piece of charcoal, took her hand, raised it and showed her how to get the right measure. The warmth of his hand. That's what had helped her decide.

And now his hands cupped her breasts as he was embracing her from behind. His breathing was the only sound in the silence, in which they watched the armoured car crawling across the square. His lips slid down her neck. She froze. Messing with Serge was a dead-end street. She faced him and looked into his hazel eyes. He tried to kiss her, but she turned her head.

'Did you also call Valentina?'

'Yes… but she didn't answer. Have you heard from her?'

'Did you call her before or after calling me?'

Brief silence.

'I don't remember.'

She walked past him and put on a cotton dress. Then she dialled a number on her mobile. After a short while, Valentina answered.

'There is an armoured car at Sablon,' Julia said.

'It's terrible. Worse than a nightmare.'

'How are you doing?'

'I'm fine.'

'Are you alone?'

'Yes.'

'Shall I come over?'

'No. I need to go through this alone.'

'Have you been painting?'

'No. I cannot.'

They were both silent.

'Thanks for calling, Julia. Take good care.'

'You too.'

Serge's tense expression.

'She's fine. She's alone. You can give it a try. Go there. Play the knight. Kill the monsters. Get the princess.'

'I don't want to.'

He approached her again and put his hands on her shoulders. She felt their warmth through her dress.

'I'm perfectly happy where I am. Here. With you.'

She walked to the canvas and looked at his portrait of her. The woman staring at her was her. And also not her. As always, good art added to reality instead of just reflecting it. The artist's vision.

Looking at her portrait, she saw the woman Serge was seeing in her. That woman seemed to both attract and scare him.

'Let's call it a day,' she said, 'I'm tired.'

'Can I come back tomorrow?'

'I don't know.'

'I'll call you.'

'All right.'

He embraced her at the door and tried to kiss her again. She turned her cheek.

There was a tacit agreement between Julia and Valentina to never talk about Serge. And to never get involved with him. Why had she let him come over then? She didn't know. It must had been the surreal circumstances, the silence, Valentina's sudden distancing. Yet a knot inside her connected messing with Serge with her friendship with Valentina being over. She could sacrifice him. Not her.

It was not a problem to hang around with people in Brussels. On the contrary, it was the easiest thing. The expat network 'The Cosmopolitans' took good care of that. They organised events and meetups almost every day and had a membership-based website which allowed every paid member to track event participants and send them a private message. It was all nice and easy. They met at the lobbies of fancy hotels, in restaurants or bars, made introductions and chatted through the evening. It was a good way to stop being alone. And a definite trigger for loneliness. Superficial conversations about popular places, holiday destinations and men weren't enough of a base for building friendships, not for Julia.

Valentina was a first-year student at the academy like her. She was witty, charming and had a strong drive for art. Finally, someone with whom she shared more than just time. Possibly, a friend?

After the painting classes, they would often go to a nearby bar. Over the weekend, they would indulge themselves in exhibitions, concerts, performances. And then, just like that, Valentina had stopped replying to Julia's messages and calls. The unpredictability of her withdrawal was what made it difficult to bear.

'I am alone in a deserted city. A voluntary prisoner in my own home,' Julia thought.

Her biggest asset had been the square. There was a particular expression that people would wear when they heard where she lived for the first time. They raised their eyebrows and repeated the name of the square with a question mark in their voices. They would see her differently, put her in another category, only because she happened to rent a studio, overlooking one of the poshest places in Brussels. The only other time this happened was when she mentioned the sports club she belonged to. A rather expensive luxurious place with a swimming pool and a sauna in which she spent a great deal of her free time, shaping her body and spirit. That's how two places defined her public value and measured her success in life. Once a wet area covered with muddy, grassy sand, a horse market and an arena of mass execution, the *Grand Sablon* was now home to chocolate shops, galleries, restaurants, an antique market over the weekend, and most recently a local food market on Thursday nights. Julia had been at its opening. There had been live music, it had been raining, the musicians had taken shelter under the tent and had played lively jazz, surrounded by the organisers and a few brave visitors, all holding glasses with desperate determination to drown any sadness. On a sunny day, however, the *Grand Sablon* was a place celebrating Brussels' *dolce vita*, its cramped terraces flaunted prosperity, snobbery and prestige. Julia would fling open the French doors to her small balcony, sit on a soft chair and look out. This made her feel like a queen, overseeing her kingdom. Her studio faced *Notre Dame du Sablon*. God and she were framing the square, looking straight into each other's eyes.

She had turned her back on Him, though, on that memorable Saturday in May, during the annual jazz marathon. She shared a table with an older couple. The first concert was over and there was a twenty-minute break. The square was full of people, drinking, snacking and chatting in anticipation of the next band. The sun poured down its warmth and light, and the world was a peaceful, happy place. She felt gratitude for this moment of serenity. The moment in between two concerts. Being alone but not lonely.

The rhythm changed with the second concert, becoming livelier, more potent. A man came on stage, approached one of the musicians and told him something. The music stopped. All that followed was something she would later define as anti-reality. It couldn't be real that on a lovely May day in the European capital, in the twenty-first century, at a time of peace and unity, such a thing could happen. It couldn't be true that while they were having drinks, snacks, chats and listening to jazz, a mere hundred metres away, three, possibly four people had been killed. It was unimaginable that as they were sitting on the square, those other people, in the museum, were lying in their own blood.

*

Two years later, fear, loneliness and lockdown. Julia was done with all this. She downloaded Tinder on her mobile phone and signed in. The pre-selection began. Swipe to the left for 'sorry, you're not my type', swipe to the right for 'you could do'. Immediately, several 'that's a match'. And messages started to beep in all directions. She chatted with two guys. One was younger than her and too obvious. The other one was a photographer. The latter suggested meeting. OK. Tomorrow? Why not now? Now?! Now. Where? Sablon. Ok. At *Hortense*?

She had never heard of *Hortense*. She googled it, it did exist. To the right of the church. Her usual hang out place was *Chez Richard*, across the street. She used to go there with Jacob every Friday in the late hours after they had made love. Friday was their day. They started with dinner in one of the restaurants on the square, continued in her bed and finished off by going to *Chez Richard* for drinks to prove that they were still young and could have a decent Friday night out. Everything was easy with Jacob. The chitchat, the lovemaking, the laughter. Everything but commitment. They had met at one of the gatherings organised by 'The Cosmopolitans'. He approached her with his boyish smile and a glass of whisky, presented himself and whispered in her ear,

'Don't take offense but you look so disarmingly fuckable.'

His boldness made her laugh. She was used to a gentler treatment and prolonged foreplay. But with Jacob this was a nuisance. What felt real with him was leaving the bar, going somewhere and proving him right. And that's exactly what she did. It was a Friday night. He left her place early on Saturday morning having refused breakfast.

'Let's keep it simple and fresh. No obligations, no breakfasts. Spontaneous and real.'

He contacted her a few days later and suggested Friday again. That's how, without any discussions, their Friday routine began, leaving spontaneity for someone else's wish list. Simple, fresh and clean. No strings attached. No heartaches. That's how she felt until that one time, when after the usual chain of actions, late at night, at *Chez Richard*, he said,

'Julia, I will miss you so much! I've had a bloody good time with you.'

'What do you mean? Are you going back to Poland?'

'No' He paused and sipped his beer. 'I've met somebody.'

'So what? I never thought I was the only one.'

'But this time it's different. I'm in love.'

'I see. To love then,' she raised a toast, trying to keep things simple, easy and fresh. They clinked glasses and he kissed her.

'May I come back with you? One last time.'

She was silent for a moment before she said, 'No.' She finished her drink in one go, got up and left.

'Hey!' he called after her, but she was already on the opposite side of the street. In bed, she embraced the pillow where his head had been an hour ago and wept till she had no tears left. The following week she enrolled in the academy and started a new life. Without 'The Cosmopolitans' and without Jacob.

Blue dress, light makeup. It was 10pm, when she went out. The army car was still there, in the middle of the square. The excitement of doing something risky, forbidden, brave. The excitement of freedom. It's an interesting thing, freedom. No one notices it until it's taken away. They had been as free as one can be. Just over a month before the Paris attacks, she had danced, together with Valentina, in a crowd, late in the evening, on that same square. A group of contemporary dancers showed the choreography, and everyone turned, jumped and moved to the rhythm of a modern song. And now those free-dancing people had locked themselves up or escaped from the city to make room for armed men and an armoured vehicle.

She passed by the gate, leading to a narrow street where lanterns threw a discreet light over the cobble stones, the small windows, the pots with flowers. Julia loved this street. As if it had been taken out of a fairy tale, reminding her of childhood, dreams and magic. The street ended in a circular open space with a tree in the middle, surrounded by buildings – houses, the back of a bar, the windows of an Italian restaurant. It was always quiet, existing in its blissful, contained solitude. Sometimes she would stroll through the gate to the open space, remain there for a moment and walk back. To her, this brief passage was like entering a parallel reality and the sheer proof of its existence gave her hope. A hope that one day, perhaps, she would meet somebody, whom she would show the street to.

Julia crossed the square, slowing down her pace, as she got close to the armoured car, implausible in its threatening ugliness. Its gun was pointed at the church. She had seen the potted candles in passing but had always thought they belonged to a hotel. She walked under the archway, through the short tunnel and saw a heavy red curtain hiding a flight of stairs leading down. Slender white candles, alluring light. In the stony underground bar, candles were the only lighting. *Hortense*, another in her collection of intimate, private places.

There was a whole hidden underground world in the city. Part of it was located around Sablon. Every so often, she went to a performance or a jazz concert at *Theatre de la Samaritaine*. Its entrance was almost invisible in the secluded street and did not reveal what was inside, three stairs leading to a corridor with a bar and a large cellar with a stage. For quite some time, she thought, ignoring its name, that *Caves du Sablon* was a wine bar with one or two tables by the window, which anyone could see in passing. But a day came when she entered and discovered the stairs and the spacious underground restaurant with an intimate atmosphere and candles. Once 'The Cosmopolitans' had a gathering in a night club at

Place de la Chapelle. She had to walk back and forth a few times before she noticed an unobtrusive entrance. She opened the door and — you should know by now what is coming — saw stairs heading down into a long underground club, dark and modern, just the right environment for an extravagant night of drag queen performances and dancing.

He was sitting on a high chair next to the wall. She recognised him from the photos. Dark hair, dark eyes, disarming smile, which he immediately produced for her. *Miguel*. The Portuguese photographer. There was an exquisite glass in front of him, half full of orange liquid.

'They make heavenly cocktails here,' he said. 'Let me choose one for you.'

Her first thought was that he was attractive. Her second thought - that he must have done this many times. The setting, the cocktails, everything that would follow.

'You look a lot more impressive than your profile picture,' he said.

'Is that so?'

'It is. You must post more photos. Photos showing the real you.'

'What for? I'm not selling myself.'

'Sorry to say it, dear, but you are. We all are. And photos help the sale. They get you noticed. Attention gets you dates with attractive individuals. Like myself.' He smiled again widely to show this was a joke, he was not *quite* that arrogant. Or perhaps, with his faux deprecation, exceptionally so.

'Well, with or without photos, we've met.'

'Indeed, we have...'

Her cocktail arrived. It had a gentle pink colour and an exquisite unrecognisable flavour.

'What are you up to in life?'

'I'm a fiction writer making money as a consultant. Or a consultant who writes fiction. Whichever way you prefer. And you?'

'I'm a photographer who makes money by running a café.'

'So we've got something in common.'

'And that's only the beginning.'

'We must both be very brave to be here during lockdown.' Indeed, they were the only people, apart from the staff.

'What lockdown?'

'Which planet are you on?'

'My own. And there are no lockdowns there.'

'Sure. Paris was a joke.'

'No. It's all very real. But I'm not letting anyone lock me down. I've been out every day, documenting everything. That's what a photographer does.'

He took out his camera and showed her some of his photos. Deserted streets, closed shops and armed men. And then a young couple, sitting in the middle of the empty *Grand Place*. A contemporary Adam and Eve, preparing to recreate humankind.

'How about you? Don't tell me you've allowed them to keep you in.'

'I've got large windows. And a square. And, obviously, I'm here now.'

'Yes, you are. This makes me very happy.'

He raised his hand and touched her face. A brief gesture.

'Sorry, I couldn't resist. You've got very soft skin.'

She pretended she hadn't heard this, her eyes fixed on the flame of the candle, her mind on the quality of its light, subtly revealing the essence of everything it fell upon.

'What are you after?' he asked.

'I don't really know. But when I find it, I will recognise it.'

Of course, she was lying. But telling the truth to this stranger would have been embarrassing and, potentially, hurtful. He didn't need to know about the vast empty space inside her. He should have known that very well himself. If he didn't, then he wouldn't be the one, they would be on a different quest. And even when he said, 'I'm tired of searching.', she didn't feel reassured. 'I'm tired of searching' could mean anything. We all get a little bit more tired with every day passing but does this make us stop?

They returned from the cellar into altered surroundings. It had been snowing. It made the armoured car seem playground innocent, as only snow can do. The tree branches glittered with this sudden and premature Christmas decoration. The falling snowflakes created a mist. If only it could erase memories, Julia thought and glanced in the direction of the gate, imagining the street, which must have been exceptionally beautiful.

'Do you need company? Shall I come up for a drink?'

The flame in his eyes, the close distance, the corners of his lips, poised in smug expectation.

'No, I'm fine.'

The ends of his lips twisted slightly down, a tiny movement. He kissed her cheeks.

'Stay safe and free. Sweet dreams.'

But how to sleep on a night like this. She pulled her desk over to the French windows, opened her laptop and started writing. Writing was an escape from life. Yet writing gave life and perspective to everything. Made it reachable.

1060 Saint Gilles / Sint Gillis

2015

Alberto, Portuguese

'You've got the best *pastéis de nata* in town. As I eat them, I close my eyes and see myself back in Lisbon. Sitting on the stairs, descending to the delta.'

She closed her eyes while saying this, her face turned slightly upward, and her neck stretched as if expecting to be kissed. I wished I had my camera with me. Her eyes opened slightly, and she gave me a misty look as if she were emerging from a beautiful dream.

'You've been there many times?' I asked.

'I did my Masters there. Long ago, now. Then I kept returning. Part of my soul is there and keeps calling me back.'

Her Portuguese flowed easily, with its own charming melody, tinged by her Italian accent.

'Perhaps we could have a Portuguese dinner sometime and share our memories.'

'Perhaps we could.'

Did I see a flirtatious gleam in her dark eyes? She walked away with a paper bag full of *pastéis de nata*, leaving her business card in my hand and me swirling with excitement from the encounter and its possible continuation. That's the beauty of working at a place like this. You meet all sorts of people. Mostly friendly people, Portuguese or with some connection to Portugal, like this woman. Our *pastéis* are the taste of home far away from home.

Fifteen years ago, when my cousin Pedro suggested I join him in this venture, I didn't hesitate. I was stuck in a troubled marriage and had already realised that photography would not make me rich. It took a couple of days of thinking about the 'how', the 'whether' already answered.

A visit to my mother, who shed a couple of tears. Fresh flowers for my dad, who blessed me from his grave. An evening out with Jose and Luis, who kept topping up my glass with wine under the sounds of fado. And *adieus*.

My wife Luisa said nothing as I was leaving that morning, but I know she was angry, not sad. Mad that it was me who was managing to escape from our dysfunctional existence, not her. I left Portugal only to find another Portugal here. From Saint Gilles, through Ixelles to Etterbeek, reminders of my country surround me. Portuguese shops, cafés, restaurants, each one a small island offering shelter to my compatriots' longing for what we have left behind. And even if this was an illusion, a pale imitation, Pedro and I seized the opportunity and joined the others keeping the pretence alive. *Pastéis de nata*; a taste of home.

Even Fernando Pessoa has found a home here, at Flagey. I visit him every so often for a silent conversation while having a smoke, facing the stone scrutiny of his eyes.

Fernando, 'The feelings that hurt most, the emotions that sting are those that are absurd; the longing for impossible things, precisely because they are impossible…'

Me, 'Tell me about it, man. That's the story of my life…'

'...nostalgia for what never was; the desire for what could have been; regret over not being someone else; dissatisfaction with the world's existence.'

'Indeed. The tireless hope that perhaps this time…'

'All these half-tones of the soul's consciousness create in us a painful landscape, an eternal sunset of what we are.'

That's the problem with communicating through the ether, the greats don't listen, do they? They just pour their wisdom over you whether you get it or not, you've got to move on with your little life, get lost in your own painful landscape, kill the monster, hold the thread which will take you out of it so that you most probably commit your next betrayal and find yourself in a landscape which looks different but is even more painful than the last, till you realise that there is no exit. Just standing in front of Pessoa's statue makes me a philosopher. The one book I took with me when leaving Portugal was his 'Book of Disquiet'.

As the eternal sunset colours the sky over Brussels, I finish a beer in *Maison du Peuple* and recall Elisa's eyes. I send her a message,

'How about having that dinner tomorrow?'

Two minutes later, my phone beeps.

'With pleasure,' but the message is not from Elisa. It's from Iris.

'Damn it,' I'd already written her off; she'd taken too long to reply. We'd met three days ago on Tinder and ventured out on an immediate date in *Hortense*, the bar I prefer for setting the scene. She was attractive and smart, and, perhaps, a bit lonely. It was an interesting rendezvous and warranted a follow-up. I invited her for dinner at my place. She had been silent ever since. I laughed at myself. What are the odds? If Elisa accepts, I could cook for both; a special Portuguese dinner with dessert served in my king-size bed... But Elisa quickly extinguishes my boyish fantasies,

'Tomorrow, not possible. How about Friday?'

The following evening, I welcome Iris to my flat, just around the corner from *Parvis de Saint Gilles*. She wears a blue dress. Dark, with short sleeves and a hint of glitter. It suits her. Her wavy hair falls freely across her back in a way that makes me want to caress it. I don't. Impatience is the biggest enemy of being strategic. And, without sounding cynical, that's what I have learnt to be with women. Not like a lobbyist, only following my own interests. No. Romance is about allowing the woman to take her time, to relax, to breathe, to feel the space around her and the space between you while you plant the seeds of desire and begin cultivating them. That's the beauty of it. That's what makes each date unique and exciting. The different sense of space around every woman; her own timing. It's like in photography. You will never get a good portrait by telling the model what to do, how to turn, where to look. This results in cold images of living statues. Soulless. Give your model the freedom to explore, move and search, connect to you and to the camera. That's when amazing things can happen. Art can happen. And in relationships, it's the connection that happens. The art of seduction is slow dancing in one rhythm.

Iris eats the fish I have cooked and drinks the white wine I have chosen for her, then looks at me with anticipation. A mixture of suspicion and curiosity; her writer's gaze.

'Fernando Pessoa said that to write is to forget and that literature is the most agreeable way of ignoring life. Literature retreats from life by turning into slumber, but then, it also simulates life.'

I throw the subject of literature on the table like dice, hoping to get the lucky number.

'He must be right. Interestingly, I came up with a similar thought in a short story after our date.'

'I'd love to read your story.'

'Perhaps one day.'

She eats slowly, with measured sips after every bite. The fork and the knife rest on her plate as she chews.

'Cheers to our freedom. The end of the lockdown!' I mock.

'As if that changes anything... cheers.' She smiles, then drinks.

'Of course, it doesn't. Today is no different from yesterday, and yesterday no different from all the preceding days.'

‘I am not entirely sure about that. People being killed in cafés, museums and concert halls in Europe isn’t something that happens every day. But you’re right that the lockdown was exaggerated, and that the security presence means nothing. I don’t feel any safer today because I know this could still happen at any time, despite the troops and their tanks.’

By the time we have dessert, I know as little about her as when she entered my apartment. I wonder whether being mysterious is her fashion or her true self? I imagined her talking about the books she has written and the books she has read, drowning me in an ocean of intellectualism, spiritualism and many other isms. But she’s not trying to impress me. She’s just sitting here, eating the food, sipping the wine and listening to me. And as she is so silent, I feel obliged to do all the talking. Lisbon, Brussels, Pessoa, photography… I talk, she listens. Only when she tastes my *pastéis de nata*, does her expression change.

‘You made these?’

I think I’ve finally managed to impress her. Afterwards she goes to my photo wall. Some of my best shots, along with favourite photographs by others, hang there. I join her.

‘My wall of fame.’

She smiles and looks at me. Suddenly it’s easy to raise my hand and caress her hair. I take a short step forward and kiss her. She responds in the same knowing manner. There is a special quality to it, which I’m trying to name. Sophisticated purity. That’s what it is.

Somehow, the way she kisses is both experienced and tantalizingly chaste. She says,

'It's getting late. I'll call a taxi.'

It's only eleven. I walk her downstairs and kiss her again. As her taxi departs, I head to *Bar du Matin*. People are standing in front of the bar, talking and smoking. Inside, it's busy. An Afro-American band is playing something full of rhythm and sun. I order a beer at the bar and look around. A mixed crowd, as usual, laid back. Artists, students, NGO workers, the jobless, newly single. The beer goes down nicely.

Two women come up next to me and order drinks.

'Bourbon,' says the one closest.

'Cheers,' I say, once she's holding the glass of golden liquid.

'Cheers,' she smiles and then follows her friend to a table. Blond hair, not very long, slender body. She sits opposite me and our eyes meet. I could get up, go to them and ask to join, then sit close to her, discover the scent of her hair and perfume, talk in her ear, give myself over to the night and its unpredictability. I could. And that's what matters. The potential of it. I finish my beer, throw her one last look, nod in her direction and walk to the door.

In bed, I send a message to Iris,

'It was lovely. Let's do it again soon. Sweet dreams.'

*

There are two types of light that make for good street pictures, the earliest morning light, and the very nearly evening light. The silver of the awakening, and the gold of the fading day. I never get tired of trying to capture the light as it hits the features of the city. Cities are living beings, organisms, each one a micro-universe functioning with perfect simplicity. Their features change every day, reflecting time and events.

In the days, weeks and months following the so-called lockdown, armed men in public spaces become a permanent feature. My camera avoids them as much as possible. There have been enough of these photos. However, in an early morning, as I pass by the Haitian embassy, something unusual happens; the features change. A young woman with an angelic face approaches one of the soldiers in front of the Embassy and gives him a box of chocolates. She looks into his eyes, says something, and then leaves. There is grace in how she walks away without looking back.

The soldier holds the box with an astonished expression. Then a smile brightens his face, making it look completely different – gentle, human. Miraculously, I've captured the moment when she gives him the box and they look into each other's eyes. It is easily my best and most acclaimed photo.

Equipped with my camera, I'm not a lone walker. I'm an observer. A moment catcher. An unconventional beauty discoverer. The *Parvis de Saint Gilles* is a great spot for portraits and street shots. The crowded cafés, the drinks and food trucks with people standing around, the passersby, the market on Thursday nights and at the weekend. This is where I make my 'Unlock, Free Brussels' series. I include a photo of the prison building as a reminder that everyone on the outside is free to live their life. What fascinates me is that at social gatherings, nobody talks about what has happened, as if ignoring it makes it non-existent. Freedom means forgetting the past and not fearing the future.

On Friday evening, I am having a *caipirinha* in Coimbra, waiting for Elisa. The tables around me are occupied. It's mostly my compatriots. Luisa and I spent a weekend in Coimbra once upon a time, in another life, when we were still in love. We walked around the river one late summer evening holding hands, marvelling at the golden reflections of light in the indigo water. We stopped and kissed under a tree, and that kiss, that night, the tenderness and excitement it contained felt like a silent promise for eternity.

'*Olá*!'

Elisa has arrived with her wild, dark hair, disarming smile and misty eyes. I get up and give her a hug, one peck on each cheek. The strong, heady smell of her perfume. She's wearing black skinny jeans, high heeled boots and an orange top revealing a tiny bit of her lacy black bra. Just looking at her creates that familiar tension that needs to be released as a matter of urgency. Self-control man. Breathe in, breathe out. Going through all the pleasantries and savouring every course, each with its matching drink. And as we laugh and talk, the only thing I can think of is making love to her.

Later that night, all the unspoken promises are fulfilled. In the darkness of my bedroom, with Elisa, I experience the most exhilarating state of freedom.

*

Friday, the week after, I walk through a dark open space at the bottom of *Rue de la Cellule*, not far from *Bar du Matin*. I haven't seen Iris since our dinner. I send her a message,

'When can I see you?' to which she replies,

'I'll be at a milonga in Saint Gilles after 10pm tonight. Come and join me.'

I take the stairs up and find myself in a corridor with a clothes hanger and a pile of shoes all around it. I pay the entrance fee to the young woman sitting at a small table just beyond the entrance. Couples move on the dance floor in a coordinated manner, as if this is a choreographed scene from a film. There are chairs and small tables next to the wall; the light is muted. People hang around the bar, chatting and throwing looks at the dancing couples. I go to the bar and order a small whisky, stealing glances at the dancers. Iris is there, dancing with a taller man, in a very close embrace. Their cheeks touch, her eyes are closed. Her hair is gathered at the nape of her neck. She's wearing a black dress with thin straps and red shoes with very high heels. Her movements are smooth, sensual; she seems to be enjoying every single stretch. Nothing is rushed. Then, one fast kick in the air and she's back to her serene flow.

The harmony between her and the man is striking, their movements completing each other. I reach for my camera, bump up the ISO, and take a few close shots. I capture the expressions on their faces. Their legs. Their hands.

'It's the heart that matters in tango. All the rest only enhances that connection. That's why the leading comes from the chest,' Iris tells me later as we sit at a small table, slightly off the dance floor.

I gently massage her fingers; her hands are cool. We look at the other couples and don't talk much. It's peaceful. So different from the experience I had with Elisa. The thing is, I need both. The mysterious and tranquil air of Iris; the voluptuous presence of Elisa. The problem is, I cannot have both. And making a choice…!

A slow kiss in the street before the cab takes Iris away. As I walk back to my home, I think of the words of my famous compatriot. 'The longing for impossible things, precisely because they are impossible; nostalgia for what never was.'

That's saudade. The quintessence of my love life.

1040 Etterbeek

2016

Claire, British

It was an early evening, just after 6pm. The 13 Degrees wine bar at *Place Jourdan* was still empty. Two women entered and took a seat at a table. The waitress came and t their order. She returned with a glass of water for one of them and a bottle of red wine. She poured a little of the wine and handed the glass to the other woman. The woman closed her eyes, breathed in its aroma, took a sip, ran it around her mouth and swallowed. She stood still for a second, then looked at the girl who was patiently standing and waiting for the verdict. A year or so ago, she had been to an introduction to wine tasting session in a stylish loft near Montgomery. There were nine of them – two couples, two women and three French men, including the sommelier who worked for NATO and did this as a side job. The other two men were the hosts. One of them sat between the two women and the three of them talked about travelling. Both women appeared to be interested in him. One of them, an American, always found a way to touch him, nonchalantly, as a friendly gesture. The other one, a Bulgarian, was more closed in her body language. It was her eyes that said most. Claire watched them, amused. The American seemed to stand a better chance, as he responded positively to her effusive friendliness, which made her eyes sparkle even more, until the moment when he mentioned his *boyfriend*, pointing at the other guy. The tasting started and in the next hour they had to rank five wines by temperature, body, flavour, acidity, sweetness and tannin… Ever since, she hasn't missed a chance to practise the ceremony of tasting. She nodded, the girl filled the glass and walked away.

'Thanks for taking the time, Claire. You must be very busy with the exams coming up,' said the woman who had ordered water and curled her fingers into her wild dark hair.

'It's fine, Elisa, we all deserve a little break once in a while. Life isn't only about EPSO.'

'No, it isn't. My head is spinning from all these logical tasks, abstract reasoning… But that's not what I wanted to talk to you about. I'm in a complete mess and don't know what to do. But, please, keep what I'm going to share for yourself. You'll be surprised to hear but I've been having an affair with Luigi for two years now. He's been very sweet and full of promises but always gets cold feet when it comes to separating from his wife. A couple of months ago I met a very lovely man and have had something going on with him too. Please, don't judge me for this. I got tired of Luigi's indecisiveness. Alberto has been really good to me, and I quite like him. When I told Luigi, it was a big drama. He asked me to stay with him and said he was going to tell his wife. Which he did. But meanwhile, I found out I was pregnant. I don't know who the father is. Such a mess! I don't know what to do.'

‘This is a simultaneous congratulations and *oh* situation. Look at it from the positive side, though, some women cannot even get one man, and you have a choice. And a baby on its way.’

‘Oh, please. Having a choice is sometimes a shortcut to madness.’

‘I understand, especially when not knowing who the father is. But this will be clear when the baby is born. It will show, or a DNA test will tell. But then you will have to throw light on the situation for everyone involved.’

‘Yeah…’

‘Listen, I’d suggest that you don’t think about the baby right now. Instead, follow your heart. Who do you want to be with? He will be the father of your child. Full stop.’

‘I agree, but even following my heart isn’t straightforward right now and I have to decide sooner rather than later, as in a few weeks it will show. But still, thank you, it does help to put this into words.’

‘An answer will come to you.’

Outside the spring evening went on as usual. The full tables of the nearby restaurants and cafés; the line in front of Antoine’s kiosk, because of their reputation for making the best chips in town.

The two women exchanged a few more words and took different directions. Elisa headed for the bus stop, Claire towards *Park du Cinquantenaire*. As she walked, she took out her mobile. A short signal, then the familiar smiling voice of Iris.

‘I have just been to a wine bar with a colleague and remembered how we met at that wine tasting last year. So I thought I would give you a call. You cannot imagine what a mess my colleague is in! Getting pregnant while having an affair with two men and not knowing who the father is. And so naïve to think, that her affair with the Head of Unit was secret when it’s been on everybody’s lips! A married man with two children! I wouldn’t be surprised if he had set his mind on her during the interview and gave her the job to have her close at hand. Looking like a man’s wet dream certainly helps you get a career in the Commission…’

‘I suppose it helps anywhere, not just in the Commission. Where are you?’

‘Walking home through the park. You wouldn’t believe how busy it is. I can see the yogis on their quest for nirvana, which, most probably, will never happen. Everyone’s becoming a yoga teacher these days. A colleague next door went to India for two weeks and came back a teacher. She runs a small group twice a week in her living room now. Could be a career for me as well, if things get desperate, hahaha.’

‘You never know. It’s very noisy there, what’s that music?’

‘I don’t know. A big group of people running in a circle, then jumping and doing some funny movements like aerobics from the 80s. Must be out of their minds… But well, a good body does help in life. That Russian prostitute Oksana got another exciting project, which should have come my way if tasks were assigned according to experience and skills, and not to the depth of the cleavage and the promise of possible pleasures. This is her set of tools, and it works well, at least in our unit...'

'Ah, Oksana again… Wasn't she married?'

'Second time. First to a British official, a lot older than her, who got her out of her troubled motherland and helped her land at the Commission. After he completed his mission and was, clearly, not getting any younger, she quickly got divorced and almost as quickly arrived at marriage number two with a Flemish businessman. They live in a palace on the outskirts of Brussels.'

'Yes, you said before…'

'But judging by her interactions with other men, I bet her extramarital adventures aren't over yet. What is most annoying is that with just a twitch of her long artificial eyelashes she snaps all the interesting projects from under my nose. What can I do when I am no longer twenty-six, nor even thirty-six, don't have fake boobs or a slim waist and my biggest asset is my brain, which happens to be a rather devalued item at the Commission… Or at least in our unit which has turned into a meat market of Oksanas.'

'You make me laugh being your usual cynical, hilarious self. But that sounds too extreme. Sorry but I can't imagine that what you describe is the norm. And you can find exceptions anywhere…'

'Perhaps I should join the traditional dancing group over there. Or the martial arts class to learn some defence techniques, much needed in my environment. Believe me, it's not just Oksana. If you look around my unit, you'd think you were in a beauty agency not in the EU executive body. Many of these young models are contracted agents, which is the easiest way to get in without passing through the EPSO hell machine. But still, six years at the Commission with a very comfortable package isn't a bad start in life. The senior civil servants hang around those divas, horny like rabbits. Married men get involved with female colleagues and married women are no different. Sodom and Gomorrah, that's what our unit should be called. SG, as we love acronyms here. A bottle of wine and two glasses, how romantic! He might well have a wife at home, expecting him for the weekend, of whose existence the long-legged lady in a white dress might be completely clueless. But a picnic would be nice; I could do with a picnic. Or a cocktail at the pop-up bar on one of those sunbeds. Or with a novel like that lady over there, lying on the grass. Oh, I wish!'

'Don't be so hard on yourself, Claire. EPSO will still be there. You will have opportunities. And a treat every so often might help you manage the situation in a more balanced way.'

'Ah yes, the postponing of pleasure, that's my mantra. So that later I can have more of it, once the work is done. Thinking about all the goodness to come helps me stay focused. My results improve every day, the promised land of a lifelong status in the Commission is getting closer and closer... Then I will indulge myself in pleasure. If others have managed, so can I. One of my colleagues runs sessions of EPSO training, organised by private companies. Another one chose to mask her desperation by enrolling on courses to become a healer. A healer! She's been spending a fortune on her training, including regular trips to the States. Now she claims that she can help anyone fix their life while she can burst into tears in the middle of a conversation. And guess what, she's got clients! She offers online sessions in the evenings, over the weekends and even over lunch breaks. If you were living this day after day, you'd be cynical too.'

'But then why do you want to stay? Why all this effort?'

'I wouldn't get that package anywhere else without working crazy hours and being overwhelmed with tasks. So I'm trapped, I have to stay and use the system instead of being used by it… I might start my own business on the side to give me joy and meaning.'

'But don't you realise, that's exactly the sort of attitude that's grist to the mill for your Brexiters?'

'No, Iris! The only fuel they need is their own stupidity. As for the Commission, it's just as ineffective, clumsy and corrupt as any other system. You can't expect anything else when you have too many human beings gathered in a huge machine. It's in our very nature to be imaginative and find ways of abusing it. The Brexiters know nothing about EU politics nor about the way the Union functions, they need a scapegoat for domestic political problems, somewhere to project.'

'I know… But still. In my work, I see a lot of good projects realised with EU funding and lives changed for the better. That helps me keep the faith.'

'Sure. But enough of this. How are you doing?'

'Pretty good, actually. Just moved to a new flat.'

'Again?'

‘It’s not ‘again’. I stayed in Sablon for two years.’

‘Where did you move to?’

‘Uccle.’

‘Uccle? Well done!’

‘Yeah. I love it there. When will I see you?’

‘Let me get these exams finished and we can get some quality time together.’

‘Deal! Good luck, Claire!’

Claire walked under the arch and out of the park. She took the wide boulevard, passed by the *Carpe Diem* bistro, and entered one of the residential buildings further up.

A girl of around five ran towards her ‘*Mummyy.*’ An embrace, a kiss, one on each cheek. A man stood in the door of the living room. He stepped towards her and kissed her lips. ‘How was your day, my love?’ he asked. ‘The usual,’ Claire replied. There had been a time when they brought home their frustrations, but at some point, they had realised that it was doing them no good and the no-work-topics rule had been introduced.

Rafael had prepared a seafood paella.

‘How was your day, sweetie?’ Claire asked the girl.

‘Angela grabbed my toy, and we had a fight. The teacher took the toy away. But it wasn’t fair. That’s my toy!’ Sophia’s tiny voice went up.

Ah, be prepared for life, my little girl.

‘It’s not fair, sweetie, I agree. Go to your teacher tomorrow and explain that it’s your toy, and you want it back.’

'But she took it!'

'Yes, but she will give it back to you. It's yours.'

Sophia kept babbling in a mixture of English, Spanish and French. Claire just nodded and agreed.

The dinner was over, it was homework time. Claire kissed Rafael and locked herself in the study, spending the rest of the evening over the EPSO tests. She had been doing this for half a year now, determined to fix life's injustices and attain the golden status of an official. Once this happened, she wouldn't be bothered by anything. She wouldn't fight for projects anymore but would spend her time on other things – her business, nice holidays, social activities. They wouldn't be able to touch her anymore and she could go seamlessly through her work life and retire early with a pension in Spain, Italy or some other lovely place with a pleasant climate. That was the vision she kept in her mind, while she was going through those bloody tests.

Meanwhile, Rafael and Sophia were in the park, but later the girl would knock on the study door, crying, '*Mummyyy*!' Rafael would take her away, talking quietly, 'Mummy is busy. Let's leave her to work', would put her to bed and would read her a story. Claire's heart was bleeding, but her mind stayed focused, telling herself that she was doing it for the good of the family.

It is a late Sunday morning. Claire and Rafael are walking through the park; Sophia running around them. A flock of green parakeets flash from one part of the park to another, before settling and half vanishing in the crown of a tree, blending with its leaves.

'Mummyyy, look at the parakeeets!', Sophia screams as if it is the first time she has seen them. 'Come here, lady,' Claire stretches her hand towards her and holds Sophia's tight, as they leave the park. Schuman Square lies in front of them, deserted. The officials, the cars, the lobbyists, gone. Tomorrow the spectacle of European politics will be back on stage, but now it is only an empty theatre of glass buildings.

They arrive at *Place Jourdan*, crammed with stalls. The Sunday market. Fruit, veg, cheese, olives, meat, sausages, the abundance of it, the freshness, the colours. Claire and Rafael fill two bags with produce and have a glass of cava sitting at a table on the sun-drenched terrace of the corner café. When they have finished their bubbles, Rafael goes to get some chips from Antoine's kiosk, while Claire and Sophia make their way to Leopold Park. Sophia runs, screaming with excitement, towards a goose, waddling beside the pond, followed by a dozen goslings. The goose honks and quickens its steps; the small yellow balls hurry behind her and all of them slip into the water.

Claire sits on a bench and reads the news on her phone, while Sophia plays on the grass. The UK referendum for exit from the Union is happening in two months. Millions of pounds being wasted to satisfy the ignorance of a handful of lunatics! They will never succeed anyway. The tragicomedy of British politics. There are moments when she misses London. The hustle and bustle, the theatres, the pubs, the beast that London is. But she has done all that, she has had it. All. Her life in Brussels, albeit framed be a routine or precisely because of that, is a lot more settled and peaceful. When she was younger, she would never have imagined getting any joy or satisfaction from such things. Not for a second. She would have laughed and forgotten about it on her way to the next performance, vernissage, night club. And now her whole life is taking place in a district of a small city. That is her real life.

Rafael arrives with a big cone of hot chips. Sophia abandons her activity and joins them.

'You've got muddy hands, little lady. Let me clean them. Can you give me the wet wipes, my love?'

'The Brexiters are gaining more and more support.'

'That's insane. But it's not going to happen.'

'I know. Still, it's disturbing.'

'It is. But try not to think about it. Those empty heads won't have enough of a majority.'

'I don't know… I hope so.'

*

In a restaurant near Mérode, Claire and Rafael raised their slender glasses of cava for a toast.

'To your success, my love! Congratulations!'

'Well, half the job done. Passing the exams doesn't secure me a job. And if next week those lunatics win in the referendum, all will have been in vain.'

'Don't worry. With your experience and skills, you will definitely get a position. Brexit won't happen, the whole referendum thing is a folly. Let's focus on something nice. I've got a surprise for you.'

'A surprise? What is it?'

'Next month, you and I are going to New York for a long weekend.'

'And Sophia?'

'My parents will babysit.'

'I have to see whether I can get away... We are swamped around the conference.'

'They can do without you for two days, no matter how irreplaceable you are. Aren't you happy?'

'I am. Thank you! That would be...great!'

'It will be.'

They hold hands over the table and continue talking about their forthcoming trip, Sophia, Claire's ideas about how to get a permanent contract, as the waiter brings the starter, the main, the dessert, followed by coffee and tea, all beautiful and fine, and for the first time in a year Claire can almost fully relax and think that the panna cotta tastes of freedom, the freedom of a life without tests and EPSO. She even allows herself the luxury of having a bit of faith that, perhaps, one day in the near future she will finally get the golden *official* status.

1180 Uccle

2018

Iris, Bulgarian

The white screen insults me with its whiteness. *You are infertile*, it says. I know, I am. The white of my dress that morning accentuates the aesthetic. The aesthetic is important. Especially here in Brussels, where we all aim to be elegant, chic, trendy, stylish, branded, amazing, unforgettable… We wear thin dresses in all seasons and high heels despite the cobble-stoned streets. Guys wear trousers and shirts all the time. Going to an after-work party feels like a very special occasion, everyone dressed up, the atmosphere festive. That's Brussels. Brussels which you so unfairly consider boring, grey and dull. I want to see you at *Aperitivo Milano* on Thursday evening where they serve a free buffet with salads and pasta, the DJ, a guy like us, in his forties, starts at 9pm and all these dressed-up people aged from their mid-thirties to sixty, even seventy, look around, meet, dance and later on fuck, having the time of their lives. Is this what you call boring? Or at *Place Lux*, on Thursdays again. The square full of people, standing and chatting, holding glasses, wine, cava, beer, whatever, suits, dresses, skirts, shirts, jeans, eyes, hands, body language, all the possible languages, but mostly English, French, German, Flemish, Spanish, Italian, we all speak at least a couple of these. Ralf's Bar is the place where my kind goes;

people with jobs that need qualifications, the so-called *professionals*. We are the lucky ones to live here in our endless youth, eternal students in spirit, while having all the attributes of successful adults. This is us. The only grey here is men's hair, and it only adds to their attractiveness anyway. Everyone is beautiful, sexy, successful and single. But isn't this the ultimate freedom? We are the beloved children of all the Gods. The prodigal sons and daughters of our times. With a significant difference, we have all made it. Our concerns and choices are about whether to have dinner in this or that restaurant, which after-work *apéro* should we go to tonight and what would be more satisfying for our spoiled senses, either the vernissages, the wine tastings, the concerts in trendy jazz clubs or a private initiative we have heard about recently. That is Brussels. That is how we are here. And anyone who claims it is boring, dull and grey is nothing but ignorant. In front of the while screen, I am alone, empty, naked. Abandoned by my words. By any words.

It's time to go to the conference on the future of the EU, organised by the Bulgarian Presidency. I close my laptop, put on my coat and leave. Spring is in the air. Blue sky, curly white clouds and glimpses of sun. We do have such days here. In a city where sunlight and clear skies are not routine, they do make a difference. They really do. The presence of light changes everything. It makes you notice it. It makes you appreciative and grateful. Especially after a dark, dull day in which the idea of the sun coming out is dismissed as wishful thinking. And then, shortly before sunset, the miracle happens. The clouds part and the sun appears. It caresses the tops of the buildings, showing the colours in a warm, soft light. Only the tops. The rest of the buildings remain in shadow. It is a sight full of hope and promise. It is an unexpected gift before the day is done, which helps us get through the darkness. I recall that this pre-sunset light was one of the first things which captivated me in Brussels.

The tram is full at this hour. All seats are taken. I stand next to a woman who is reading on her Kindle. The tram takes off, the driver jams on the brakes and we all stumble forwards. Me into the girl with the Kindle, she into the man in front of her. *Excuses, pardonnes…* The tram continues. *Avenue Louise* is getting ready for another day. A moving line of cars, weaving cyclists, people walking or crossing, a homeless man waking up on his mattress in front of a posh furniture shop, cafés and bakeries ready to offer breakfast, the shops enticing with elegant clothes in their windows. It's one of the marks of Brussels eccentricity, this street. It is the poshest street accommodating several embassies, luxurious hotels, bistros, cafés, bars, shops, supermarkets. It's classy and prosperous during the day. In the evening, however, once dusk falls, the young ladies of the night stand two metres apart from each other, swaying on their high heels and waiting for the next client. 'Our first priority is to stop demand,' all the officials say at a high-level anti-trafficking conference. Yet these girls blatantly offer their services in front of everybody. Have all of them chosen this fate? How many of them have been trafficked? Is anyone at all interested in finding out? And what do parents say to their children when they ask what these girls are doing there? All around are residential neighbourhoods.

On a Friday night the previous summer, I joined, for once, the Friday night cycling and skating through Brussels. The route crossed the red-light district in the vicinity of *Gare du Nord*. It was a few hundred of us, cycling and skating, and trucks with DJs at the front and the back of the long line. An impressive and very noisy sight. The working girls were out on the street, in front of their cabins, taking pictures of us with their mobiles. This was so very different from the usual swaying of hips and throwing come hither looks at potential clients that it struck me, we had traded places – from being an attraction they had turned into observers; we had become the attraction now. This switch of roles, triggered by the casual normality and innocence of the act of taking a photo, was fascinating. Obviously, I have also taken a mental picture of them, which I am scrutinising at this very moment, as I am recalling this.

The tram stops at *Place Stephanie* and the driver asks all passengers to alight due to a technical problem. I walk to the nearby underground station. There was a long period of time when I avoided using the underground. It started on that March morning two years ago when the tram halted few stops earlier and two policemen got on and asked that we all get out. We were clueless, puzzled, checking our phones. Then someone said, 'attacks.' The word which had been hovering around our minds ever since Paris like a wasp. I walked back home feeling disoriented, trying to grasp the unthinkable connection between 'victims', another word with a sting, and the sheer ordinariness of life. I was at once both shocked and unsurprised. We all had known it was coming. After Paris, after the lockdown and despite the armed men in the streets, the raids, the arrests, the heavy police presence, that it was inevitable, had always been there. The day after, I went to Maelbeek underground station and made my contribution to the growing heap of dead flowers, ten white roses.

Two days later, at the academy. Olivier arrived late. He was always there on time but not that night. His cheeks were red, his eyes wild. People wouldn't, normally, pay any attention to latecomers. But something made us all stop painting the plump model and look at him. He took a deep breath and blurted out, Bojana… Bojana has died… at Maelbeek. We froze. Cold silence. No complex thoughts. Nothing. Icy emptiness.

There was a time when Olivier, Bojana and I hung around together. Exhibitions, outdoor sketching, films. But it didn't last. Olivier's unclear intentions confused us both and our friendship continued with him out of the picture. Not for long, though, Bojana left me out of her picture and stopped coming to the academy altogether. In the broadest of terms, I had accepted that loss is part of life and the only thing that remains is gratitude for the time shared. But there are different types of loss, and I hadn't imagined, nor had I been prepared for this. You might think that common grief would have brought Olivier and me together. In fact, exactly the opposite happened. We grew further apart and hardly ever spoke. The two of us together would have inevitably summoned the thought of her, the illusion, that she might appear from the other room with her angelic face and mischievous smile.

At this hour the underground is crowded. We are as crammed in as tinned herrings. I recall my mornings in Sofia, a few lives ago, when I had a life, which, seen through the lens of my present, seems predictable, mundane. All that followed has been a roller coaster, never knowing when the next deep drop or steep rise will appear, where it would end and indeed whether it would have an ending at all.

The ending came as abruptly as all that had preceded it. One rainy evening I was hit by a car on a zebra crossing. For the brief moment when my body was in the air a thought flashed, 'So that's how it ends.' The wetness of the asphalt was the last sensation I felt. Next came the whiteness. The lightness.

This must be heaven. I was alone. And alive. The door opened and a woman entered. She smiled at me and said in French,

'Hello. My name is Ellen. You have been hit by a car. But you are lucky, everything is fine, no broken bones, nothing... The man who brought you here left you this. He asked for all the invoices to be sent to him.' She gave me a business card. His name was Mattias, he was a Director General at the Commission.

'How long have I been here?'

'Two hours. You had lost consciousness.'

'May I go home now?'

'No, you have hit your head. Not badly, but still, we will have to observe your condition for the next 24 hours. All being well, you will be discharged the day after tomorrow, after the doctor's morning visit.'

I messaged Mattias to tell him I was fine. He called me back, all nervous and apologetic.

'I am so very sorry. I was out of my mind that day. My wife had been diagnosed with… something serious. I had just heard a few hours earlier, as I was working on a complex report with a tight deadline. I finished later than I had planned and was in a hurry to reach home and be with her. With the darkness and the wet weather, I didn't see you.'

The following day he came to see me, bringing me Neuhaus chocolates. In literature, Mattias would have been a Prince Charming. That is in a certain type of literature. In reality, he was average, medium height, unsettled blue eyes and a reserved expression.

'I want to thank you,' I said.

'Pardon?'

'I want to thank you. I know it was an accident, but, still, you were the one through whom reality gave me a wakeup call, you know. I needed this… to see things in my life… more clearly.'

Mattias was completely puzzled. I could hear him wondering about my mental health and whether it had been affected by the accident or if I had always been a weirdo. He stayed a few more minutes, repeated that he would cover all the costs, asked me to call him if anything was needed and then left.

I did mean what I said to Mattias, the car accident had been a wakeup call; the only way life has found to shake me and shout in my face, 'Look what you are doing to yourself and to me!' Nothing.

That's what I had been doing. I had grown so used to doing my work without any creativity nor enthusiasm. In other words, I had professionalised. I had been partying with other single women. I had gone back to 'The Cosmopolitans' just to get a lover and the crumbs of tenderness he was offering to me once a week were feeding the self-deception that I had a sort-of -significant-other. But on the wet asphalt, I was alone. And so I was in the hospital.

There was no significant other to call so that he would immediately come, be with me, soothe me. I was forced to stop pretending. To face reality and accept it, I was alone. Full stop. A permanent lover didn't alter that, nor was the shared dissatisfaction with other women in a similar situation.

When my lover contacted me to confirm our weekly rendezvous, I replied I was busy. This repeated the following week. And the week after. Until he stopped asking.

*

The flood of people takes me out of the train at *Arts-Loi* towards the platform where we embark on the next train to Schuman. It is more or less a homogenous crowd in terms of looks. Suits, shirts, dresses, skirts, heels or sneakers which will be later, in the office, replaced by heels. The uniforms of the builders of the bright future.

Later, at the conference, I think of all of us who left our home countries years ago chasing the ghost of the bright future, only to find out that we have arrived not to a place but to a time, the time of the bright future's mortality. Speaker after speaker addresses the challenges of aging populations, political instability, terrorism and the prospect of our children ending up less well off than us, the vultures circling the feeble future. Yet there are blue paper birds on the pages of the EC White Paper on the Future of Europe, included in our conference packs. In nature, vultures would have these small blue birds for breakfast.

I take out my laptop and start taking notes, which will later become a neat report for my client. The fact that I am still using this laptop is a sheer miracle. Soon after the attacks, I left it on the 38 bus. I only realised that at home.

'It will take Lost and Found one month to respond to your enquiry,' the STIB employee informed me.

'One month? I need my laptop now. I cannot work without it!'

'Yes, everything has slowed down after the attacks. I would advise you to go to a bus stop and ask every 38 bus driver about your laptop. Within one hour, hour and fifteen minutes, all the buses should have passed, so you will know whether your laptop has been found or not.'

I thanked him for the great tip, hung up and started laughing hysterically. Then I pulled myself together and went back to the bus stop. One after another, the buses arrived.

'*Est-que vous avez trouvé mon ordinateur?*'

'*Désolé, madame.*'

Forty-five minutes and five *désolés* later, a driver took out my laptop bag with the smile of St Nicolas. I thanked him profusely, grab the bag and set foot again on *Avenue Molière*. I was still trying to absorb what had just happened, the absurdity of the situation transcending into the beauty of its resolution.

Speaking of beauty, *Avenue Molière* with its avenues of trees, and magnificent houses with small gardens at the front, many of them embassies, is undoubtedly the most beautiful street in Brussels. At night you can get a glimpse of the rooms with their high ceilings and walls lined with books and paintings. The street stretches from Ixelles, through Uccle to Forest and radiates the stability of wealth. I had moved to the neighbourhood shortly before the attacks. The lower part of Uccle, Upper Ixelles and Saint Gilles mark the map of my existence, my new Brussels geography. The marvellous and completely self-sufficient neighbourhood of Bascule, a hub of small galleries, cosy wine bars and international restaurants. *Place du Chatelain* with its handsome buildings, Wednesday market, restaurants and bars attracts an international crowd in the evenings. In good weather, I wander around, without purpose, and connect to my very private Brussels. Crossing *Guy d'Arezzo Square*, I hear an unmistakable noise coming from above. It's not the Gods quarrelling but the green parakeets, a hundred of them at least, hanging from their huge oval nests. This must be their version of a residential building.

The presentations continue. There are…how many…seven speakers in this panel. Way too many to keep one's attention. I google 'green parakeets' and 'Brussels'. An article from 2nd October, 2014,

'The Brussels-Capital Region has not yet found a solution to the rising number of parakeets in the city, currently estimated at around 12,000. The city has tried different measures without effect and has now moved on to destroying nesting sites and employing scare tactics, reports Brusselnieuws.be.

The rapidly growing number of parakeets in the region is alarming. The feral population of nearly 12,000 rose-ringed and monk parakeets started out as a small group released from the Melipret Park *in the 1970s and continues to reproduce at an alarming rate. The problem with the parakeets is that they take over the nesting and perching places of indigenous birds, and sometimes damage parked cars.*

The region has in the past made attempts at euthanasia and sterilisation, but the parakeets proved too difficult to capture. A spokesperson for the region admits that the city is helpless against the growing population. 'The key is to find a solution that doesn't harm the indigenous birds.'

Indigenous birds vs foreign birds like locals vs expats, like Europeans vs refugees and so on and so forth.

The morning sessions are over; everyone is getting up and heading for a hearty lunch. It's a walking lunch so that people can network. Any communication around events is not just socialising or catching up with colleagues from other organisations or structures. It's networking. As I am walking around with a full plate in my hand, giving nods and half-smiles in different directions, a woman smiles at me widely.

'Hi!' she says.

'Hi!'

'I'm Elisa, Antonio's girlfriend. We met at his exhibition some time ago. I was pregnant then.'

Now I remember. Antonio was a Portuguese photographer. We had dated briefly. Our story had ended before it had really started; it was like a scene without a prelude and without a conclusion. His withdrawal hadn't been hurtful and that's why I hadn't hesitated much when I had noticed on Instagram an announcement of his forthcoming vernissage. It was called 'Unlock, Free Brussels.' I remembered him talking about this series during our dates. But I wasn't prepared for what I saw when I entered the exhibition hall. Moving around with a glass of wine in hand, I reached the highlight of the exhibition, an enormous black and white portrait, depicting a woman with angelic beauty giving a box of chocolates to a soldier. They were looking into each other's eyes; her face shining. My knees buckled; I almost dropped the glass. But then I pulled myself together, leaned against the nearby wall and looked again. The woman in the photo was Bojana. I saw the two of us in *Sol*, after the lockdown, her telling me of a soldier 'so masculine and strong, giving me a feeling of protection which I'd never experienced so far… except with my father, a real man, not a cheesy artist.' And her wanting to bring him a box of chocolates as 'a gesture of humanity, of reaching out, of showing appreciation.' I would have never imagined aristocratic Bojana with her aristocratic tastes being attracted to a soldier. She must have read the astonishment in my face,

‘I’m scared in this city. I need someone to protect me.’

So she had done it. My tears blur the photo.

‘It’s my favourite too,’ says the woman standing next to me, with a strong Italian accent.

She’s heavily pregnant. I nod, unable to utter a word. A man approaches and kisses her while I am still concentrating on Bojana holding the box with her long artist's fingers.

‘Hi, Iris.’

It’s Antonio, the man who a moment ago was embracing the pregnant woman. He steps towards me and gives me a polite kiss, his lips devoid of the passion they were transmitting the last time they were so close to mine. Then he introduces me to Elisa, his girlfriend, as he puts it.

Elisa has a disarming smile. Her whole being, even the proudly protruded belly, radiates sensuality.

It all makes sense.

After a couple of pleasantries, I excuse myself and leave.

And here she is now, without her belly, just as radiant.

‘Sorry, Elisa, I didn’t recognise you. Last time we met, you were pregnant. How are you doing?’

‘I’m good, thanks. We have a boy.’

‘Congratulations!’

‘In the beginning, it was pretty tough with those sleepless nights… But it’s getting better now. You’ve got children?’

'No.'

'Ah, wait and see!'

'You work in the Commission?'

'Yeah. I changed DGs last year and I'm now working on migration.'

'That's a hot topic. I have an interesting story, showing what happens in practice.'

'Listen, let's have lunch one day. Here is my card.'

We separate with the agreement to meet soon, and I join a group of colleagues from the civil society, standing around a high table. That's Brussels; inevitably, you meet people again; we are all in the same bubble.

By the end of the conference, my report is ready. I have also replied to a dozen emails, tweeted some quotes, further and ritualistically networked during the coffee breaks. In other words, I have earned my consultant's fee and can go home, content with the day.

As I approach my street, I hear the calming sound of falling water. But there is no fountain. A tiny cascade, flowing from between the legs of a man standing in the corner, in full daylight, blissfully releasing the tension. Anywhere, at any time of the day or night, I could see a peeing man. A *clochard* in the middle of the *Avenue de la Toison d'Or*; in *Avenue Louise* around midnight, a young guy watering one of its elegant buildings, the golden stream flowing across the pavement, me crossing over it in my high heels, his friends bursting into laughter; in an early spring morning at

Sablon, I am looking at the sky from my open windows and hear the familiar sound, coming from below me – the peeing man is there, next to my neighbour's door; I am sitting on a bench by *Étangs d'Ixelles* talking to a friend with a man watering a bush five metres away... So many images of peeing men that they evoke the ridiculous philosophical question, who was first – *Manneken Pis* or *Man Pis*? Did the peeing men of Brussels inspire the creation of the statue or was it the other way around – the statue of the peeing boy empowered them to follow its example and spray their golden showers all over the city? Through the years, I've seen public urinals at the most unexpected places, such as next to St Catherine's church. Passing by this holy place, you have to pinch your nose to survive the stench. The advent of public urinals didn't bring a change in *Man Pis'* ways.

I enter my rented flat. I have furnished and decorated it; it's a home. A brief stopover, just enough for me to change and refresh my makeup. Brigitte and Amadou are waiting for me at *Chez Franz*. They get up and we hug each other. It has been two years since we last met. Brigitte got a job in Philadelphia, and they moved there.

The terrace is full – the usual middle-class and mainly white crowd. It's a show of false ordinariness, the simplicity of the clothing silently screams of brands, quality, wealth.

'How have you been, Iris?' Brigitte asks.

'I'm good. Still enjoying Brussels.'

'Are you?'

'Oh, you know, like in any relationship, we have our moments. Things change with time. It's not an affair anymore but more of a marriage. I live in Uccle now, very close to here.'

'So you made it to Uccle?! Amazing!'

'Isn't it? It's still on the border with Ixelles so I can have the best of both worlds – the peace, green and quiet of Uccle; the art, restaurants and bars of Ixelles.'

'How is your writing going?' Amadou asks.

I see myself that same morning sitting with a cup of green tea and toast on the desk in the study. And my open laptop. One hour for writing. One hour of staring at the white screen. This has been my writing lately. But they say it's essential to maintain the routine. It helps, keeps the rhythm going. And when there is nothing to be kept going, what then? Keep the silence going. There is no louder silence than the one between a writer and the white sheet.

'Iris?'

'It's going.'

A man in a torn and worn t-shirt and jeans approaches with a slightly uncertain walk, stops next to the first line of tables and looks at the diners. His eyes are raw and faded. He could be fifty or sixty.

'Where are you from, mister? And you, lovely lady? I reckon you are all Europeans, working in the institutions, to give… long… longevity to the European project.'

The people sitting in the first line of tables pretend he isn't there and try to continue their chatting. But he won't let us ignore him. His voice gets louder.

'I'm using the right terminology, right? A project, that's what you call everything there. And me, ah, let me introduce myself, I'm a dignified citizen of the kingdom of stupidity which has proudly, and I repeat, p-r-o-u-d-l-y decided to leave that project of yours. As mediocracy often happens to be… proud. Am I proud to be British, you may ask. And rightly so. Am I? Let me tell you something. We now have five countries in the kingdom. You'd know four of them.'
He started raising the fingers of his right hand and naming the countries. 'We've got England. And we've got Scotland, Wales and Northern Ireland. And now, now, ladies and gentlemen, I am announcing here, in front of this distinguished audience, the fifth country, recently founded, the Country of Lunatics. The representatives of all the other ones are its citizens. This new country is the child of a bitch. It's called democracy, its mother, a real whore, I'm telling you. And now this new country has made a decision for all the others, a grand decision, for their future and the lives of all their citizens, including my humble self. But you should know, ladies and gentlemen…'
The barman comes out and politely asks the man to stop disturbing his customers and leave.

'Have I disturbed you, ladies and gentlemen? Please accept my mooost sinceeere apologies. And come and see us one day… you may need a visa, though…'
The barman steps towards him, pointing him to the direction of the street. The man takes a few steps, stops for a moment, raises his hand to his forehead as if he were trying to recall something, then

continues and disappears around the corner. The crowd, silenced during his performance, finds its voice again.

'Sad man. He must have been drinking. But there's truth in there. We're also having the time of our lives with Trump in the States.' Brigitte says.

'Yes. The fifth country. I like that. As for Trump, his one-man show has the whole world as an audience with all of us as its subjects,'

'We haven't been very lucky with moving to the States. Being a foreigner there isn't fun right now. So we'll see how long we'll last.'

'You could always come back.'

'Or go to Senegal.' This is Amadou.

'Seriously?'

'Why not? Things seem stable there and we are tired of Western civilisation,' says Brigitte.

'How about Amaya?'

'We'll wait until she turns eighteen and goes to college and then see.'

'So that's the big plan?'

'Let's see what happens.'

'How is your mother, Brigitte?'

'Ah, you won't believe it! She finally met someone. A Turkish man.'

'Did she?'

'She did. She's happy with him. They keep separate places but spend most of the time either at his or at hers. She comes to visit us once a year. Last time he joined her, and we had a good time.'

'That's fantastic! And what happened to the migrant mother and child who lived with her for a while? Do you have any news?'

'They're doing well, considering the circumstances…' Amadou says. 'Layam emails us every so often, usually around Ramadan. Maryam is a big girl now. She is fluent in English and has been studying French as well, in school. All their children are in school. Layam cleans houses, her husband works on building sites… They manage. They do miss Syria, but they don't really have a choice.'

'Yes, choice, that game we play. It still makes me shiver when I think of how we organised that dinner and got the cash for them to be smuggled. *That* was a choice.'

We smile silently.

'Haven't you met anyone, Iris?' Brigitte asks when Amadou goes to pay the bill at the bar.

'I've met quite a few… And that's the problem.'

'That only means you haven't met the one. So he is still to come.'

'Or maybe I have met him. You know, I met a girl the other day at a milonga, a tango party, you know. She asked me,

'What brought you to Belgium? A man or work?

'Love,' I said. Her eyes sparkled. 'I fell in love with Brussels.'

Brigitte bursts out laughing and looks at me tenderly.

'I miss the time we lived together. One of the happiest periods of my life.'

'So do I.'

Amadou has returned and we prepare to leave.

'Listen, I want to throw a party for you,' I say, as we are about to part in front of the bar.

'That would be awesome!'

The restaurants on *Chaussée de Waterloo* are full of other *dolce vita* practitioners, as I walk home in the darkening dusk. Cars flash by, rushing their passengers to the next stage of their Friday night project. That's the Brussels I fell for. The city which will suddenly offer you an unexpected party with a nonchalant gesture. Then I think again of the drunk and Brexit. Had the hundred wise men and women who were drafting and crafting the European Constitution fifteen years earlier seen that one coming?

Later that night, words finally found me. Whether it was prompted by seeing my good friends after a long time or the drunkard's Brexit speech, I don't know, but as I walked home, an idea had already started to form inside me. As soon as I got home, I made myself a cup of herbal tea and sat at my desk in the study. What I wrote was a monologue of an English temporary agent at the Commission, studying for exams to gain *official* status, while sharing all the disgusting things she saw in her work environment and hatching plans to also start cheating the system once her dream was fulfilled. She managed to pass the exams and make it to the waiting list, but meanwhile Britain voted in favour of Brexit.

In fact, the story was inspired by my friend Claire and what I had put in it very much reflected her thinking and experiences at the Commission. Her contract had expired the previous year, and she had been unemployed ever since, still getting her salary as compensation. She had spent long holidays with her husband and daughter in different places – France, Spain, Italy. But each time I spoke to her she sounded bitter, angry, unable to get to grips with life's injustices. Our unusual friendship had ended as it had started – out of the blue, as often happens in Brussels. We met at a wine tasting event in Etterbeek, where she was with her husband. I found her sense of humour bordering sarcasm refreshing and went to chat with her after the session was over. She happened to work in a unit in charge of an area in which I was writing an article. She agreed to help me get an interview with her Head of Unit. She accompanied him during the interview and the two of us had lunch in the Commission canteen after.

Then we had a couple of more lunches, followed by an after-work drink. But seeing her after work proved to be difficult, as she was very determined and disciplined about her EPSO preparation. Nevertheless, she had granted me her trust and expressed her views on the internal doings of the Commission and her own role in them rather freely, with her typical mocking smile and narrowed eyes. I could visualise her face during our phone conversations which had become more regular with her reduced time for meeting up. She would call me every fortnight, as she was walking home after work, and give me an account of the relationships in her work environment, interrupted by funny remarks about her surroundings. But ever since her contract had finished, she had been brimming with resentment regarding her situation and British politics, and all my efforts to offer her a positive perspective hit a wall and bounced back over me with a flow of accusations that, of course, it was easy to preach when it wasn't me trapped in an ugly reality. This resulted in me quickly ending the conversation and feeling drained afterwards. After two or three exchanges like that, I stopped contacting her. I had enough on my plate without accommodating large portions of someone else's negativity. She called me a couple of times, and, probably sensing I wasn't providing the understanding and support she needed, stopped reaching out as well. And now she had turned out to be a character in a short story. No. Not *a* short story, but the first one I had written after months of continuous writer's block. Thus, our friendship had led to something.

*

'How have you been, Iris?' Alice looked at me in that serious attentive way which is so typical of her. We were standing on my balcony, overlooking enclosed gardens. Opposite us, in the middle of this small, secluded world, was a tree which attracted all sorts of birds throughout the changing seasons. I observed it through my study windows when I was writing.

'I've had my ups and downs.'

'It's been ages since we last saw each other. It's my fault, I know.'

Indeed, a year had passed since our last get together. Two children and her own law company hadn't left her much space for keeping in touch.

'It's not. It's life. It's good to see you.'

Brigitte appeared at the door holding a bottle of cava.

'We need some bubbles, ladies.'

I brought out flute glasses and she opened the bottle. The cava fizzed and we raised a toast,

'To us!'

'Isn't it amazing? Fifteen years!' Brigitte said.

'Look at you, Iris. I'm so proud of you! It wasn't easy, I know, but you've got where you wanted to be,' Alice said, 'And now you are hosting international parties in your lovely flat in Uccle.'

Words failed me again. Or was it my thoughts that were failing me? Had I made it? Looking back at the starting point and at where I had arrived, objectively, it seemed so. Now what?

'Thank you, Alice,' I said.

It was almost eleven, the night was gradually taking shape. We had started at 4pm; the other guests were already gone. Amadou and Alice's boyfriend, Jan, were chatting inside. I felt a bit tired and nicely overwhelmed. I had invited thirty people, some twenty had made it, including Brigitte's mother and her Turkish boyfriend, Sheila, Herman's ex-girlfriend, and her French-speaking Belgian husband. She was a good friend of Brigitte, so I had suggested she extended the invitation to her despite the sensitivities which Herman leaving her in order to land in my life and stay in it for the following two years brought back on the day. But this had been ages ago and seeing how happy she appeared to be with her husband; I thought she might, after all, be grateful to me.

'How is your sister doing?' I had asked her, recalling that the sister was trapped in an arranged marriage.

'She's good. You know that she divorced?'

'Did she?'

'She did! It took a while, but she was so miserable. Finally, she left her husband and stayed with us. We have a house in Laeken. And you know what happened? Ah, that's a beautiful story, maybe you can write about it one day! Initially, she was supposed to marry another guy, also arranged by our mother. That guy found her online and they liked each other. Then, something happened, and my sister cut off contact with him a couple of weeks before the wedding. She's so religious that I think she just wanted to have some time for cleansing her thoughts and emotions before becoming his wife. And then, on the wedding day, surprise-surprise! The groom wasn't him but another guy. Someone from the neighbourhood. Apparently, our mother had found out about Aisha being in touch with her future husband and had broken off the engagement, after securing a replacement. But as my sister wasn't in touch with the guy in that period, she didn't know! Anyhow, I convinced her to contact him and tell him about her divorce. He responded immediately and came to visit. She left with him for Marrakesh and lives there now.'

'That sounds like a story from 'One Thousand and One Nights'.'

'Doesn't it? I am very happy for her.'

'And how about your parents?'

'Both Aisha and I stay in touch with our father, secretly from our mother. She's evil!'

Sheila and her husband were among the first ones to leave in order to 'release the babysitter', as she had put it.

'This is where the party has moved to,' Amadou stood in the door with a beer in his hand. Jan was behind him. They finished their drinks and helped me carry everything to the kitchen.

'I cannot wait to go to bed,' Brigitte said. 'I am so tired! Amaya is an early riser, it's a nightmare!'

'We're free tonight. The kids are with my parents. We'll check out a bar or two before going to bed,' said Jan. Alice looked at him with wide eyes.

'Kidding, darling, don't kill me!'

Brigitte and Amadou were leaving in a couple of days. Each of them kept me a bit longer in their embrace.

'Come to visit us!' Brigitte said.

'I will.'

'Let's meet soon!' Alice said.

And then everyone was gone. I sat on my balcony and looked at the dark tree. The birds were quiet. Or they had gone as well. I thought again of Alice's remark that I had made it. I looked at my life and asked myself, is this how I imagined it, my life so far? It wasn't. Not that it was worse or better. It was different. I had achieved more than I could ever imagine. I loved my life. My international life, the diversity of people, languages, cultures. Tonight, for example, how many nationalities had been here? Eight, nine? Eating and drinking together, united in diversity. I now spoke both French and Flemish, had travelled the world, had friends everywhere, had contemplated art, tasted local gastronomy, got lost and found. A couple of years earlier, I had seen an art installation of a huge cylinder full of water. In it, a woman in a coat holding a case in her hand, frantically swimming up and down, as if running to catch yet another bus, train, plane, but, in fact, being locked in that cylinder and only able to observe the world through its glass. Am I this woman? I asked myself. And, perhaps, once, I was. Not anymore. I had arrived on my own island of relative peace and safety. In Brussels, my one and only Brussels… Yet the human soul is greedy, is a slave to change, never to be fully satisfied. Or should I say, MY soul and stop projecting onto all humanity? Whatever.

The thing was, I had a new dream.

To spend a weekend in Sofia. Without contacting anyone. Just me and the city of my youth.

And shall I tell you my secret?

There is one word which I can whisper only in Bulgarian.

Господи.[2]

[2] God

"Cities, like dreams, are made of desires and fears..."

Italo Calvino, "Invisible Cities"

I've had a few lives in this city and at least a couple of deaths. Each of them feels entire and complete like a written page. From the safe distance of the present moment, I can access any of them and read it through. Then rewrite it. Or mix them all. This is the kind of freedom that writing gives us.

Would any of this have happened in any other place? Would I have acted the way I did, related to everything in a similar manner, been the person I was if it were not for this city? I never chose it in the first place. It chose me. And perhaps this is always the case. Perhaps places desperately need us, beings, for the sole objective of filling them with content, giving them life and creating their history.

In which case, all my lives and deaths in this city are not mine but belong to it. They shape the contours of its soul, intertwined with the paths of all its inhabitants, current, past and future. The life of any place manifests in the stories we tell about it. The stories of our lives. And deaths. They feed its existence. For the city will be here and we will be gone. Becoming a tiny part of its history is our chance for anonymous eternity.

Acknowledgements

'Brussels, Naked' is the first novel I have written in English. I am deeply grateful to my editors, the Welsh poet Phil Madden who allowed me to include his poem at the beginning of my novel gave me some invaluable ideas which have been reflected in the novel and edited the style, Rachel Robson who did a thorough final line edit and proofread, and to Hristo Dimitrov-Hindo, who edited the Bulgarian edition and was instrumental with his guidance and insights. My beta readers, the filmmaker Zlatina Rousseva and the authors Ali Bader and Luis Quimper offered critical and stimulating feedback to the first draft, which inspired edits in the following drafts. So did Jan Dorpmans who also proofread an earlier version of the novel and Athanase Popov helped with some final touches. My French teacher, translator and friend, the Belgian artist Viviane Defosset gave me a lot of materials about Brussels which served as sources of some of the historical facts included in the book but, most importantly, a new sense of belonging to the city. It was a privilege to work again with the illustrator Nevena Angelova. When I first saw the cover project, I had tears in my eyes – she could have not captured better the essence of my novel. I am grateful also to Zuzana Miyahara Kratka for her trust and support in the past year. I am very lucky to have been backed by such amazing professionals and individuals. Heartfelt thanks to all of them and to you, my reader, for giving my book's existence a meaning.

By the same author

SHE, THE ISLAND

A novel

'She, the island'

A novel

"On the bare island we were all naked. And each ostensibly voluntary next step of ours would lead to the inevitable denouement. We were all characters in a novel. The novel being written by the island."

The paths of two couples - Marina and Gerard and younger surfers, Carla and Gerd - cross on Fuerteventura. They meet a writer who is working on a novel about the exile of the real-life philosopher Miguel de Unamuno in 1924. The writer soon finds herself lost in the labyrinth of their complex relationship. She escapes by returning to her book and by travelling the island, absorbing its landscapes, history and culture. Her name appears only at the end of the novel, and it is not by chance that it is the name of the main character in 'Brussels, Naked'.

"I haven't read for a long time such an exquisite, contemplative work, both very human and wise. With an intriguing love plot spread through Fuerteventura's history. Irina Papancheva has described the island so well as a scenery, sensation, magic and mythology that the reader, inevitably, will feel impelled to visit."

Emil Andreev, Author

"An intellectual and emotional feast, 'She, The Island' could satisfy any taste. It has it all, an engaging plot with many story lines, memorable characters, dramatic turns, and authentic philosophical and psychological interpretations coming from Miguel de Unamuno himself. All of this captured in the mystical landscape of Fuerteventura."

Luis Quimper, Author

"The book is a unique and valuable addition to the Bulgarian literary tradition. It vaguely reminds me of the research approach of Umberto Eco... All the characters have come to the island with a specific goal – sometimes almost criminal. But they don't find what they are looking for, instead they find... themselves."

Georgi Yanev, Literary critic

PELICAN FEATHER

A novel

The novel tells the story of Martin, a ten-year-old boy who spends a summer with his mother and grandmother in the seaside city of Burgas after his father has left his mother for her best friend. Martin is the main narrator. His narrative is interwoven with monologues of the seven adult characters showing their deepest feelings and life experiences which have influenced them and their views. The novel also gives a fascinating glimpse of the world around Burgas's salt and mud pools and the lake with its rich birdlife. The city itself becomes a main character.

I want to write a tale about the pelicans. A tale so enchanting that it would replace all the tales about swans. I want to write it with the pelican feather. I want it to tell it to me.

"'Pelican Feather' is a story of romantic love told by the ten-year old Martin after the separation of his parents, it depicts the experiences of his mother at the end of her marriage, her wry and brave path to recovery, contrasted with Martin's first experience of romantic love-gauche, idealistic but still very real and intense.

Set during a summer by the sea, the novel is spiced with vivid accounts of contemporary Bulgaria and just the right sprinkling of magical realism."

Phil Madden, Author and editor of the English translation

“‘Pelican Feather’ is a panorama of contemporary Bulgarian society. It covers political protests, ecology, confusion in moral values, poverty, but also goodness, friendship, and hands reaching out. Life in the book is colourful, authentic, true, full of sounds, and above all alive. The story is so real that at times you have the feeling it is happening in front of your eyes. You are a witness but not from a distance. An involved witness; a witness who somehow actively feels for the characters as they are close to you, as you are close to them… Proximity of feeling – perhaps this would be the best short definition of the novel ‘Pelican Feather’.”

Mitko Novkov, Literary critic and editor

About the author

Irina Papancheva was born in the Bulgarian city of Burgas. She holds an MA in Czech language and literature from Sofia University, St. Kliment Ohridski and an MA in European Politics and Social Integration from Vrije Universitet Brussel (VUB). She is the author of the illustrated children's book 'I Stutter' (Ciela, 2005), the short novel 'Almost Intimately' (Kronos, 2007), the novels 'Annabel' (Janet 45, 2010), 'Pelican Feather' (Janet 45, 2013), 'She, The Island' (Trud, 2017) and 'Brussels, Naked' (Znatsi, 2022), the novella 'Welcome Nathan!' (Fast Print Books, 2019) and of short stories.

'Almost Intimately' received the audience nomination in the 2008 Bulgarian national literary competition South Spring (Yuzhna prolet). 'Annabel' was shortlisted in the 2014 January Contemporary Bulgarian Novel Contest of the Elizabeth Kostova Foundation and Open Letter Books at the University of Rochester. 'Brussels, Naked' ranked second in the same competition (2022). The manuscript of 'Brussels Naked' was also shortlisted for the first Prize Orpheus in 2022.

Irina Papancheva's work has been published in English, French, Spanish, Arabic and Persian.

Website: ipapancheva.com

Printed in Poland
by Amazon Fulfillment
Poland Sp. z o.o., Wrocław

43372218R00184